LADY EVE'S LAST CON

Also by Rebecca Fraimow

The Iron Children

LADY EVE'S LAST CON

REBECCA FRAIMOW

SOLARIS

First published 2024 by Solaris
an imprint of Rebellion Publishing Ltd,
Riverside House, Osney Mead,
Oxford, OX2 0ES, UK

www.solarisbooks.com

ISBN: 978-1-83786-159-0

10 9 8 7 6 5 4 3 2 1

A CIP catalogue record for this book is available from the
British Library.
Designed & typeset by Rebellion Publishing

Printed in Denmark

MIX
Paper | Supporting
responsible forestry
FSC® C104608

This one, of course, is for Beth.

CHAPTER 1

IT WASN'T ONLY the Mendez-Yuki money I was there for. We could have made it with the cash we had on hand. Ever since we got in on the luxury-liner gambit, money had been dropping into our hands like coolant from a leaky ceiling: a drip here, a trickle there, and the bucket filled up before you knew it.

I hadn't figured then that I'd be spending it all so soon. This debutante's wardrobe hadn't come cheap; the people whose party I was crashing could spot imitation Io-spider silk a mile off. There couldn't be any little sniff of imitation about me, not for this job. I had to look the real deal. The shopping would've been more fun if my sister Jules had come out to give me a hand with it. But Jules was still a galaxy away on Bellavu, suffering from nausea and a viral case of embarrassment, with complications induced by a broken heart.

So I was here alone at the front door of the Mendez-Yuki manor on New Monte, dressed to the nineteens. The bell had already rung, and at a party like this, you didn't ring twice. When the door opened, I was ready.

You could tell the Mendez-Yuki were real money because the butler was a real butler. Most people these days went for steel-tech instead. Shiny, easy to design to spec, and they don't eat, so you save money in the long run. I'd heard rumors they were starting to make them more realistic these days, but if this fellow was a robot then the Turing test was toast. He took one look at me in my six months' income of fancy dress and ushered me graciously into the hallway. "If I may have your name," he said, "to check you off the list."

"Evelyn Ojukwu," I answered, in my manufactured accent. I wasn't worried about keeping it up; I could do over-educated provincial in my sleep.

The real Evelyn Ojukwu was from Kepler— one of the more distant colonies settled in the first panicked wave of the Expansion, when the waters started rising back on Earth. The most impacted often went the farthest and fastest, then, skipping past the first proto-settlements on Centauri straight to the K2 and HD systems in a bid to claim their fair share of galactic real estate before the rest caught up. As a strategy, that had its pros and its cons: once it started getting too hot for the big fish, they suddenly decided it was worth their while to clean up their home planet after all, and pretty soon it became clear that Earth wasn't going to be giving up its position at the metaphorical center of the galaxy any time soon. Still, while Kepler might be a bit of a backwater, a planet was a planet, and resources were resources, and people like the Ojukwu had more than enough simoleons for their scions to go party in the Sol system.

I'd never been to Kepler myself; I was a satellite brat through and through. Still, my father had been from there—at least, so I'd been told—so it had seemed as good a place as any to start looking for lookalikes. Miss Ojukwu's skin tone was more or less the same brown as mine, and her nose had undergone so many refinements over the years that I wasn't too worried about someone calling me out over an old glossy-pic. More importantly, she had crashed her shuttle on a joyride recently and would be in the hospital recovering for months, so there would be no new news to show me up. The Ojukwu were keeping the accident on the down-low, as little Evelyn might have been a little tipsy at the time. There's no blessing like other people's bad luck.

The butler trotted ahead of me to announce the entrance of Miss Evelyn Ojukwu into the party. I made sure not to bat an eye at all the shine decorating the anteroom as we walked through it. It didn't impress me much anyway. You got twice that level of sparkle and gold on the luxe-liners we'd been riding. Of course, none of the cruise deco was any more the real deal than I was. This stuff was probably the genuine article, but I couldn't make out much difference without looking like I was looking. To my eye, the fakes had seemed a little brighter.

There was a coatroom, where I left my coat, and a hatroom, where I left my hat—you didn't need either in the manufactured climate of New Monte, any more than you needed two-thirds of the other junk it was de rigueur to wear, but I had them anyway—and then a mask-room, where you could leave your breather if you wanted, though almost nobody did. The satellite-side fashion these days was for little gemmed breathers on sticks, and you brought them into the ballroom with you and flirted over the tops of them. You could barely get any kind of decent vacuum seal on them, and one of these days there would probably be a tragedy and we'd all go back to carting around big old diving helmets, but in the meantime they were all the rage.

I'd picked a breather trimmed in a delicate silver filigree, studded all through with the tiniest of discreet diamonds. The dress had silver trimming, too, and swooped out extravagantly from waist to mid-calf before folding under itself to bubble demurely above the knees. The shine was meant to hint at the fact that the Ojukwu had bagfuls of money from the Kepler diamond mines. The fullness of the fabric was just fashion, if you wanted to be nice about it, or conspicuous consumption if you didn't. I stepped out into the low-grav of the ballroom, and waited to see the reaction I would get.

The room was chock full of debs in every shape, size, and color. Some high-rolling hotspots in the Sol system still skewed pale enough to make problems for me, but New Monte could be called a regular melting pot, so long as all the ingredients came from the same income bracket. I'd never seen so many baby billionaires together in one place. On the luxe-liners, they'd wallflower up, keeping a careful three feet between themselves and the rest of the world in case they breathed in some middle class by accident. Here you could barely move without tripping over them. They shrieked with laughter and somersaulted over each other in the ballroom half-grav, and most of them had even learned the trick of doing it without dropping their champagne.

Of course you'd never find the fellow I was looking for in any of the knots of people having actual fun. It only took me a few seconds to pick him out: standing stiffly by the drink table, back to the wall, clutching a cocktail-box (half-grav was hell on liquids in glasses) and squinting through his spectacles as if he'd rather be anywhere else on the satellite.

As far as I could remember, the Honorable Esteban Mendez-Yuki had looked more or less the same way the first time Jules and I had run into him on that luxe-liner. I hadn't paid too much attention at the time. The glossies we read to ID our marks all said he was a real egghead—and not the kind that came hard-boiled, either. No matter how deep his pockets were, it wasn't worth the effort to drag him to the gaming tables if he didn't want to go. There were plenty of other moneybags on that ship who were happy to show a pair of pretty little airheads like us the rules of grav-dominos and wild-hand dreidel. Anyway, it always looked a little obvious if you made a dive straight for the biggest wallet.

It was better to keep it low stakes, on the luxe-liner gambit. As long as we didn't bet too high, the fat cats practically fleeced themselves.

But that was before Jules had gotten a good look at the Honorable Esteban's aristocratic nose, with a pair of old-fashioned glasses balanced awkwardly on top of it. My sister always did get weak for a whiz kid, and Esteban Mendez-Yuki seemed like the whole package: looks, brains, and cash coming out his ears. What really sealed the deal for her, though, was that fatal dose of awkwardness. Jules was too smart to fall for smooth, but anyone that bad at interacting with other humans just had to be on the level, right?

She'd spent that whole first night trying to tease him into a game. Instead, he'd pulled her into a different one—and boy, had she ever bet reckless.

Well, this time around, it was going to be Esteban's turn to bet high. A trust-fund tommy like Esteban could play around however he liked on a luxe-liner, but here on New Monte they had things like engagement agreements, and breach-of-contract suits. Any promises he made to proper Evelyn Ojukwu, he'd have to pay through the nose to get out of. I wasn't asking much: just a reasonable return on my sister's stakes, plus a nice cash bonus in the way of interest. You might call it vindictive, but given all the cards he held, I'd certainly say it wasn't more than he could afford to lose.

Of course, first I had to coax him back into playing the game—and just like luring a mark to the card table, the surest way was to let him think it was all his own idea.

I snagged a cocktail-box from the nearest wait-bot and took a few elegant sips while I surveyed the landscape. On a luxe-liner, where the comestibles were always questionable, I'd have popped an anti-rad pill before ingesting anything, but that wasn't something I'd have to worry about in the halls of the rich and well-regulated. Then I set off in the direction of the libations and tripped over the first deb I could find along the way, making sure to tighten my grip around my drink as I fell.

Bright red hooch blasted all over the back of the unlucky deb's gilt-encrusted bodice. She screamed. The two girls next to her shrieked. Heads turned my way from all directions. I stammered out my apology—"I'm so sorry! I can't think what I was doing!"—and made it a point to wither under their glares.

"Oh, it's not so bad," said the fourth person in the cluster. She was the only girl in the group wearing a slim-cut suit instead of a bubble-hem skirt or billowing breeches. The look was a little retro, but clearly on purpose, and no less obviously expensive; that kind of tailoring costs about an arm and a leg per limb. "It's just over the back. Here, Gaea, mop up with this—" And she pulled off her jacket and held it out towards the unlucky lady.

Gaea stopped screaming at once. "Your jacket! I couldn't!"

"Well, wear it then," said the other woman, carelessly.

"It'll hide the stain."

She draped the cream-colored silk jacket over Gaea's shoulders, then took a step back and lowered her breather, making a whole business of surveying her handiwork. "It suits you," she said. Her lips curved in a smile. "Of course, just about anything would."

All three of the other debs giggled. I had to bite back a laugh myself. Miss New Monte Chivalry over there knew her lines. I almost hated to step on her scene, but she could vamp the debs any day of the week, and a girl only gets one first impression.

"I'm so very sorry," I said again, and all four sets of eyes swung back to me. "I can't think how I came to be so careless."

Gaea scowled. "Careless is right. Maybe you'd better break in your heels a little before—"

"Never mind," said the woman in the suit. "Some of us don't mind pretty girls tripping over us."

The line came packaged up with the same exact smile she'd been aiming at the other debs—not a bad-looking smile, on the whole, and why change things up when it clearly got results? I pulled out the big baby eyes and said, apologetically, "Kepler's planetary. We don't do so much grav-shifting."

"If the problem is lack of practice on the dance floor," said my new friend, "people will be lining up to help with that." She held out a hand. "I'd be honored to get in before the rush."

I looked down modestly, and took a second to run my odds. She'd made it a point to stand out, there was no doubt of that—taller than most of the other girls, with heeled boots that bumped her up even higher, and flashier by far in that cream-colored suit than the gentlemanly eligibles in their respectable black. If Esteban had somehow managed to miss the shrieking debs, it couldn't hurt to cut a rug with one of the most noticeable people in the ballroom.

I lifted my eyes back up and gave her a smile of the blushing-flower variety. I was good at what I did; I'd have given fifteen to one against anybody catching onto the fact that mine was just as practiced as hers.

I was about to take her offered hand, but before I could, Esteban Mendez-Yuki grabbed my wrist, which was a better reaction than I could have possibly hoped for.

Esteban Mendez-Yuki doesn't have the gift for making crowds part naturally. His father might have been hosting this shindig, and Esteban might have as good as owned the whole ballroom, but those little facts don't make up for a certain personal presence that Esteban has not got. In order to make his way over to me, he'd had to shove through a whole lot of people who didn't want to be shoved—which accounted for the delay, and also for how red and flushed he was now that he'd finally gotten here. The whole time we'd been on that luxe-liner, I'd never seen him this worked up. I honestly hadn't thought he had it in him.

"What are you *doing* here?" he demanded, breathing hard. Then I turned to look at him, and his face turned an entirely different shade of red.

I look a lot like my sister, especially from a distance, but up close you'd never mistake us. My skin's a little darker than hers and hair a little thicker, face a little rounder, lips a little thinner—small things, some from Ba's people on Kepler North Central and some from Mame's back in Brooklyn. Had Esteban Mendez-Yuki met me? Sure he had, a dozen times on that liner, though my hair had been relaxed then, and the makeup palette different. Had he ever really taken a good look at me? Well, why would he have? We'd been playing our usual demure angle, and he and Jules had only had eyes for each other that whole ride. At least until he decided she wasn't worth looking at anymore.

Anyway, Esteban Mendez-Yuki wasn't exactly noted for his keen attention to detail. Even a pretty girl had to go to an effort to make herself noticed—just ask Jules, who had pulled out every stop she had. Most people couldn't afford to be that oblivious, but the Mendez-Yuki weren't most people. If you asked Esteban Mendez-Yuki, he'd probably deny that he expected everything around him to sort itself to suit his convenience, but that didn't usually stop it from happening.

It wasn't happening now, but not even a Mendez-Yuki bats a hundred every day. "I think there's some kind of mistake," I said, and lifted my breather to half-hide my face, which indicated in a ladylike fashion such sentiments as *what are you, some kind of creeper?* "I don't think we've been introduced." Evelyn Ojukwu wasn't the kind of girl who knew a whole lot about the world, and she certainly wasn't the kind of girl to make a fuss, but she was rock-solid on the notion that strange men probably shouldn't be grabbing her at high-class parties. I glanced down at his hand, and waited politely for him to remove it.

"Hey, Esteban," said my dapper new friend. That was all, words-wise. Face-wise, she was indicating pretty loudly that he was making a fool of himself, and she wished he would quit it already.

Esteban dropped my wrist like a hot rocket. "I'm so very sorry—I thought you were—" He coughed, stepped back, and did his best to pull together a credible bow. "It seems I've made a terrible mistake, Miss—"

"Ojukwu," I said, and let my mask drop a little, to indicate a thaw. Four months ago, Jules would probably have said his bow was adorably clumsy. I might even have agreed then, but I was wise to that now. Evelyn Ojukwu wasn't, though. "Evelyn Ojukwu. I'm just arrived in New Monte."

"Hell of a welcome," said the woman in the suit. She surveyed Esteban with an ironical eye before glancing back at me and sliding me another half a grin, inviting me in on a joke. "If it helps, Miss Ojukwu, you don't remind me of anyone *I* know."

Under other circumstances, I might have grinned back. It was clearer than ever to me now that she was the kind of girl who was used to having sweet little ingenues eating out of her hand before they knew what was what. If I'd been the kind of girl I was pretending to be, I might have been one of them. As for the kind of girl I really was—well, I'd been around the block a few more times than Evelyn Ojukwu, and the Don Juan special didn't really do it for me anymore; I liked them with some more scratch to their polish. Still, there might have been some profit in letting her spin out her script for a little. She clearly had money to burn, and it was always more fun to play someone who thought they were playing you.

But none of that mattered today; today I was here for bigger stakes. I looked at Esteban, who said, with dignity, "It wasn't anyone on New Monte I was thinking of."

"Then who?" I asked.

"Someone else." Esteban gave the middle distance what he probably thought was a wounded look. "It doesn't matter."

Gaea rolled her eyes.

"Miss Ojukwu," said the woman in the suit, "will you let me apologize for my brother?"

I had to work hard not to show my surprise. Esteban had spent a fair amount of time complaining to Jules about his sister. Jules had said she sounded like a terror. To be fair, I wouldn't be surprised if Jules had managed to give Esteban the same impression of me. "There's no need," I said, turning to look at her through limpid eyes. I could see the resemblance, now I knew what I was looking for: a certain set of the eyebrows and nose. "I'm sure Mr. Mendez-Yuki didn't mean anything by it."

That was a mistake. Her eyes narrowed; I'd missed a beat. I reviewed what I'd said, and could've kicked myself. Of course the Mendez-Yuki were hosting the party, and it might have been expected that a guest would be able to recognize them. Still, to be safe, I should've waited until we were introduced. It was a rookie mistake.

The only thing to do at this point was to brazen it out. Anyway, Esteban didn't notice a thing. "I really am sorry," he said, earnestly. "You could take it as a compliment. The person I mistook you for is—she's one of the most beautiful people I've ever met, but now I come to look at you closely, your eyes are much kinder than hers."

"Oh!" I lifted my mask again to cover the twist in my mouth, and told myself that this all looked awfully promising. I'd wondered how long it would take Esteban to forget his vacation fling, now that he was back in his native environs. Instead, it seemed he was getting his kicks out of wallowing, with Jules cast as a wicked girl what did him wrong. It was going to be a pleasure to show him what a real liar looked like.

"To make it up to you," said Esteban, gallantly, "would

you let me have a dance?"

I did my best to look like a girl who wasn't so sure about a fellow, who was being won over in spite of herself. My best has always been pretty good. "Oh, well, I suppose," I said, and cheerfully blew off Esteban's sister to follow him onto the dance floor.

The band was just striking up a love ballad from Luna. Some of the dancing debs, bored with the slower pace, stopped somersaulting and took themselves off to get some food. There was plenty of space on the floor for Esteban and me.

Jules and Esteban had done their fair share of dancing on board the *Simoleon*. They'd looked good, I'll give them that. Well, she'd looked good—Jules can cut up a dance floor better than almost anyone—and he'd looked mostly stunned, as well he should have.

We wouldn't dance like that here. Nice girls didn't, at least not at parties where their parents might see. We swayed decorously around the room at the stiff-armed distance that a Mendez-Yuki grandma would've considered appropriate. I asked Esteban about himself, like you're supposed to, and got the same spiel he'd given Jules on the *Simoleon* that first night and that Jules had repeated back to me—he was twenty-two, he was working on a doctorate, his research focused on the integration of Earth vegetation into other planetary ecosystems, he really didn't enjoy the whole New Monte socialite scene, he wanted to do something *real* with his life. Then it was back to planetary ecosystems. Jules had teased him for it, and he'd blustered a bit, and then laughed along with her. Evelyn Ojukwu couldn't follow the Jules playbook too closely, so I asked, naively, why he thought New Monte wasn't real, and got rewarded with a long, rambling metaphor about artificial environments and stifling social illusions for my sins. I could hardly get a word in edgewise.

Not that I was really trying to, either. I was starting to get a good sense of my angle. Having bounced hard off Jules, Esteban was clearly ripe for the rebound, and this wide-eyed look of mine was working wonders on his ego. It wasn't so hard to get someone like Esteban to think that you were their romantic ideal; all you had to do was present an attractive outline and leave plenty of space, and they'd fill in the rest all by themselves.

Speaking of attractive outlines, Esteban's sister had found herself a spot where she could keep an eye on us and look debonair doing it. She was leaning her million miles of leg along the wall, sipping something from a cocktail-box, and tracking our progress round the room. As luck had it, the end of the slow dance deposited us back in front of her, and she didn't hesitate to seize her moment. "Miss Ojukwu—" She handed the cocktail-box to Esteban and swept me a bow that was about ten times more elegant than her brother's. "Mind if I claim that dance now?"

I murmured my delight, and left a flummoxed-looking Esteban standing on the floor behind us. I wasn't here for her, but I didn't exactly need to make that obvious yet.

I didn't know the song that had just started playing. It seemed almost as slow as the last one; the band didn't have much of a sense of pacing, I thought. "I don't think I got your name," I said to Esteban's sister, as we moved around the floor in a stately fashion.

She raised an eyebrow. "You already knew my brother's."

I laughed, letting her see I was a little embarrassed, but willing to make a joke out of it. "To be honest, I recognized him from a glossy. We get all the *Most Eligibles*, even out on Kepler."

"Sure," said Esteban's sister. "Known and cataloged. No mystery about it at all." The pace of the music was picking up after all, but her feet didn't miss a beat. "While you have the advantage of entering our orbit as a beautiful enigma."

She tipped me into a backbend, and I tilted my head to look up at her. "Do you know, I think I should maybe be insulted? It's not like the Ojukwu aren't anybody."

She laughed. "Turnabout's fair play, Miss Ojukwu. You don't know my name, either."

"I guess I must've skipped your page," I said. "You come on a little stronger in person."

"Oh, I'm not eligible in the least." She sent me into a spin, the bubble of my skirt lifting around me as I kicked out, then caught me in a dip and smiled down at me. "But I try to make up for it as I can."

It was that same charming smile as before, but this time it wasn't anywhere near her eyes. She thought she had me pegged—matrimony-market warrior, just off the shuttle and going straight for gold—and it wasn't like she was wrong, either.

"And me?" I said—playing with fire, a little, because I only halfway resembled the real Evelyn Ojukwu, but nobody on New Monte was reading up on glossies from all the way out on Kepler, and only a Kepler heiress would think that they possibly could be. "I am pretty eligible. What's your excuse?"

"You caught me," said Esteban's sister. "I don't read the glossies at all." She spun me deftly out of the way of another couple. The corner of her mouth curled upwards. "I'd rather look at what's right in front of me."

Boy, was she ever laying it on thick!

The music was still getting faster, and debs and their dates were tapping out left and right around us. I had to give my partner credit. The pace we were going, most people wouldn't have been able to hold a conversation, but her voice was barely ragged at all. "One thing's for sure, Miss Ojukwu," she said, "you're quite a dancer."

"I could always use more practice," I said sweetly, and slipped a little extra shimmy into my swing-out somersault to show as much leg as the bubble-skirt would allow. She didn't miss a step, but I could tell that she was looking. Well, I hoped Esteban was, too.

As it turned out, my efforts weren't wasted. By the end of the dance we'd collected a circle of onlookers—including Esteban, who was looking more miffed than moony. I brushed down my skirt, just as demure as if I hadn't been six feet in the air six seconds ago, and gave a polite curtsy. Thank God for manners; they gave you a chance to catch your breath, which was probably why they'd been invented. "Thanks for the dance," I said, as I rose up again, and fluttered my lashes like a person who'd never heard of a leg in her life. "I hope I kept up all right."

"Oh," said Esteban's sister, "you more than hold your own. If this is what you're like when you're not used to dancing in half-grav, there'll be no keeping up with you after a few weeks." She swept a bow, then gave me a smile of her own, slightly sharp. "I'll look forward to following your career."

She stepped away before I could answer, which was probably just as well. "Boy, you Mendez-Yuki sure know how to sweep a girl off her feet," I said to Esteban instead, and fanned myself with my mask. A real New Monte girl would never do that, but a girl fresh off the

liner from Kepler ought to make one or two mistakes—
as Miss Mendez-Yuki had pointed out.

"Well," said Esteban, stiffly, "I can't dance like my
sister can."

"Your sister seems awfully nice," I said, "but I couldn't
go two dances with her." That was one of the less true
things I'd said that night. I glanced at him out of the
corner of my eye, and added, "I like a pace that's a little
slower—a partner who doesn't make you feel all used up
at the end of the set."

Esteban smiled at that. Jules had always said he had a
nice smile, but all I could tell you was his teeth were the
kind of white that made you figure someone had been
flossing them for him since the day he was born, and I
could have happily punched every one of them out of
his mouth. "Well, there I think I can oblige you, if you'd
allow me another dance."

"I suppose I ought to give you a *little* more of a chance
to make up for that first bad impression," I said, and
smiled back, to make it clear I was making a joke—
mostly. I didn't want to make anything too easy on him.
I might be on the hunt, but I wanted him to work harder
to be caught than any prey ever had before. I didn't want
him to have anyone to blame but himself.

We danced together plenty that night. A couple other
people came up to ask me, most of them rich boys, and
almost every one with 'cad' written plain to see right on
his face. I danced with all of them, of course. Esteban,
so far as I could see, didn't dance with anyone else when
I was off twirling around the floor with some Tom or
Devere or Hikaru. That fit with what I knew of him.
Esteban wasn't the type to play the field. He thought of
himself as a romantic.

His sister was another thing. Plenty of people, boys and girls alike, came up to ask her to dance with them. The boys, she turned down flat. I wondered that they still bothered—but she was still a Mendez-Yuki no matter what she'd said about not being eligible, so maybe they were just optimistic. She did dance with the girls. Not just the pretty ones, either; she saved her fanciest footwork for the plainest of Gaea's cohort, a stumpy girl with a face like an etrog. They danced like they were daring each other into more complicated steps, with bursts of laughter in between whenever one of them tripped up. It was a lot less polished than the way she'd moved with me, but it looked like a good time.

That was about the only time she really let loose. The rest of the flirtations seemed almost perfunctory, and I could tell she was keeping her eyes on me and Esteban as consistently as the shifts of the dance floor would allow. She played a good game for an amateur—if I hadn't been a professional, I probably wouldn't have noticed. It was flattering, in a way. I've never minded being the center of attention.

Midnight hit. The dance floor was starting to open up a little—old folks going home, younger ones sneaking off into corners and back rooms to see what sorts of less respectable fun they could get going for the next couple hours. There was probably a mean game of drunken double-stakes bridge going on somewhere. I could've probably won back everything I'd spent on all these glad rags, if I wasn't stuck being Evelyn Ojukwu.

But I was a good girl, temporarily, so instead I curtsied to Esteban and said that it had been a lovely party, lovely to meet him, and I was going home.

"So early?" said Esteban's sister, wandering up.

"Party's just getting started, Miss Ojukwu. This is your first entree to the New Monte social scene—don't you want to get the bang for your buck?"

Her refined upper-class accent slid into a drawl as she drew out the slang. She was testing me, but Esteban just thought it was good old-fashioned innuendo. He scowled at his sister, though of course he couldn't say anything without making it worse. I blinked, like the ingenue I wasn't, and covered my grin with my breather-mask. "*I* think," Esteban said, "Miss Ojukwu is very wise to leave now. If I wasn't obliged to stay for Father's sake, I'd be slipping out about now myself. I understand that these entertainments serve a business function, but—"

"You hate them," completed his sister. "No need to pretend, we all know it."

Esteban was unperturbed. "Hate is a strong word. Events like this have their compensations. It's rare, of course, but every so often you meet a person who's really worth spending time with." He looked at me warmly, and I batted the old eyelashes back at him.

"You remember the way out, Miss Ojukwu?" said Esteban's sister.

"Oh," said Esteban, "I'll walk her."

He did walk me all the way down the corridor, then grandly demanded that the butler summon my driver before I could explain that I'd taken a rental. A girl like Evelyn Ojukwu would probably have bought her own new one she got to New Monte, but I didn't want the responsibility of training up a transport bot, and it seemed mean to let one start shaping itself around my personality when I knew I couldn't keep it.

Once the misunderstanding was cleared up, Esteban promptly called me a cab and bade me a very correct goodnight. I hadn't figured on anything else—for all his flaws, Esteban never seemed the grabby type—but it was a relief to know I'd calculated right.

I let him hear me give the AI my address before we drove off. I was staying at the Detroit, which was right square in the middle of the top tier of deluxe hotels on New Monte. You'd have to do some real digging to find out I was paying for my classy suite with a pile of voucher coupons I'd won off a down-on-his-luck former hotel manager in a bar three systems away. You could win all kinds of things off of fellows down to their last roll of the dice. Some gamblers scorned to take anything other than hard cash, but I always figured it paid to hang onto the little odds and ends. You never knew when they were going to come in lucky. Jules said I was a pack rat and I should learn to stop picking up so much junk, but that never stopped her from taking advantage of my collection when it turned out something or other she needed for a job had been sitting there on my portable shelves the whole time.

I'd always thought I'd cash in those Detroit vouchers someday. If I'd been a swoonier kind of person, I might've fantasized about honeymooning it here with Mr or Miss Right, taking a nice long vacation and appreciating the romance. As it was, I'd pretty much just figured I'd come with Jules.

If this all fell out the way I planned it, maybe we'd come back together. Have just one more laugh on the man who made it all possible. Money aside, that was the point of all this: get Jules to where she could laugh again.

CHAPTER 2

I SPENT THE next two days well away from the Mendez-Yuki stomping grounds. I didn't want anyone getting the idea that I was getting myself any ideas. Instead, I kicked back, caught up on my favorite trashy earial, and did a little extra research.

Miss Mendez-Yuki's full name, it turned out, was Solada Alvaria Mendez-Yuki—or Mendez-Yuki Solada Alvaria; the metadata was mixed on which moniker went where, but the glossies mostly just called her Sol anyway. It wasn't a subtle choice. If the gossip writers could be believed, she had half the girls on the satellite orbiting around her at any given moment—and as for the other half, it was only a matter of time.

Still, she never rated much more than two sentences in the who's-who and the what's-what, and that was usually on account of whichever glamour girl had been snapped on her arm that day. Sol was only an honorary Mendez-Yuki, the daughter of Esteban's ma by some former marriage that didn't work out. Dear old step-dad had set her up with a MYCorps trophy job and a courtesy option on the corporate-family name, but as far as long-term prospects went, the glossies said, she didn't rate. Anyway, she didn't go for the boys, and there weren't all that many girls in her social set looking to latch themselves long-term onto persons of a non-opposite gender. Not that it never happened, but it limited their options on where to build summer homes; some settlements still had real old-fashioned ideas about what exactly counted as 'spousal contract' and 'legal control of shared assets.'

In other words, Sol didn't have too much to worry about when it came to fortune hunters on her own account. Maybe if she did, she'd be a little less focused on who might come in to make eyes at her baby brother.

All the same, I didn't think I needed to be too concerned about Esteban's glamorous older sib making things hot for me in New Monte. In all the years I'd been looking out for Jules, my opinion on her romantic prospects had never counted to any more than squat. I was pretty sure that if Sol tried to warn Esteban off me, he'd just get his back up and chase me all the more to spite her. I folded up the glossy, leaned back in my sunbed at the Detroit, and closed my eyes with a certain sense of smugness: bring it on, sunshine! Whatever she did, it'd all end up playing straight back into my hands in the end.

RUNNING INTO ESTEBAN Mendez-Yuki by convincing accident wasn't anywhere near as hard as you'd think. New Monte's not exactly full of hustle and bustle—at least, it isn't anymore. The satellite was built last century, right next to the first ERB transit station, the Einstein-Rosen Bridge that opened the way up for settlement in the Centauri system. There was a while there when nearly all trade going out of the solar system passed through New Monte before wending its way through the wormholes to the far reaches of the galaxy. Then those first Expansion-era traders became trillionaires and quadrillionaires, and had children and grandchildren whose jobs involved managing fortunes rather than making them. The junky trade ships coming through the ERB didn't generally make their first stops on New Monte anymore, but wealthy outer-settlement visitors often did, hoping to get some face time with their corporate collaborators. The social scene became a hot spot for mergers and acquisitions made the old-fashioned way, and the hotter it all got, the more exclusive it became.

Well, it's an old story: the rich get richer, and the poor get priced out.

Not that everyone's rich on New Monte, of course. Somebody's got to keep the life support running and the AIs bug-free. But if you don't count the cube farmers— and the topside folks of New Monte never do count them—you can squeeze most of the satellite's full-time population into one oversize room. They go to each other's parties, they go to the anti-grav opera, they go to the space races until they fall over; then every few weeks it's the dark of the moon and they catch up on all the sleep they missed while they were staying up all night playing Debs in Toyland. Visitors stay for months, and write off their costs as networking expenses. If you want in with the elite, it's pay to play. And worth it, to land a contract that ties you to any of the corporations that control what comes in and out of Earth's solar system, the glue that sticks the whole galaxy together.

Esteban had ranted about the whole nonstop schedule to Jules in great detail, and she'd passed it all onto me— well, so that was how the other half lived! Pretty soon Esteban would start wiggling on his father's hook, but he'd been away long enough that for right now I didn't think he could escape the regular parade.

The night after the Mendez-Yuki party there'd been a wine-tasting event at the Krasilevski palace. The night after that, a sphere concert. I'd skipped out on both of them, although not, I'll admit, completely sans qualm. I'd only ever heard the low-grade sphere music you get on the big luxe-liners, and I'd always wanted to compare it against the so-called superior art form. Still, Miss Evelyn Ojukwu wasn't the kind of girl who partied every night. And there was plenty of wine on Kepler, and plenty of sphere musicians.

But there was no way a girl just in from Kepler was going to miss the season opener of the anti-grav opera, the pride of New Monte. If Esteban Mendez-Yuki was looking for me—and I was pretty sure I'd left it long enough that he'd be looking for me—he could reasonably expect to find me there. I wasn't about to disappoint him.

The show that night was some postmodern production about Icarus and Amelia Earhart. They sang at each other poignantly in Broadcast English (subtitles in Espero Trade) and zoomed around the stage like a couple of swallows. The story was nonsense, but the dancing was awfully good. I didn't have to fake Evelyn Ojukwu's provincial delight.

Then intermission hit, and all the muckety-mucks immediately bobbled their floating boxes on over to chew the fat with the rest of their set. Half the audience looked ready to fall straight into the orchestra pit as they leaned over each other's balconies to bestow air-kisses. Me, I didn't have a social set yet, so I just took advantage of all the shuffling to steer a course that would give me a little bit of a better view of the stage, as anybody would do. It also happened to bring me into the general vicinity of where Esteban sat solo and sullen in the Mendez-Yuki box, but who could have predicted that? Certainly not little Evelyn Ojukwu, who never even looked in her new friend's direction; she was too busy studying the grav-contained stage set, the likes of which you'd never get out in the far systems.

A vendor stopped by me and lifted a tray to show off the popcorn, chocolate, and booze he had for sale. I waved him off, though I felt like a drag doing it. It was up to the vendors to navigate around the swells playing at high-class bumper cars, like rats among the elephants. The little air-scooters the vendors used were manually piloted—like the opera boxes themselves, though the controls on the boxes were simplified to hell and gone, and their nav-paths equally limited. Buying a bag of popcorn seemed about the least I could do, but I had a big scene coming up, and I couldn't afford to have anything stuck in my teeth.

The runaway opera box is one of the oldest plays in the book, if you read that kind of book, but Esteban wasn't the genre-savvy type. When my box started bumping against the wall of the opera house behind him, with me clinging bravely onto the balcony for dear life, he raced his own box straight over just as if he'd read the role I'd written for him in the script.

"Miss Ojukwu!"

"Mr. Mendez-Yuki!" I half-turned, eyes wide. "My goodness, I—"

"You've got to come away from there," said Esteban, earnestly. "It's not safe to have the box so close to the wall. You could damage the propulsors."

All right, so he still had a few lines to learn. Esteban hadn't picked up on my perils; he just thought I couldn't drive. "I'm trying, Mr. Mendez-Yuki," I said, patiently.

"I think the steering mechanism's stuck."

"Oh," said Esteban, "I'm sure you've just not worked out the mechanism yet. If you just grip it firmly—"

I unclenched my jaw, with an effort. "I'm doing my best, Mr. Mendez-Yuki, but it just doesn't seem to want to—"

The box dropped down a good six feet in the air, and I let out a small scream. That wasn't even feigned; I'd only meant the box to drop two feet. Well, I never went to engineering school, and my sabotage hadn't been subtle.

Esteban stared down at me, his mouth a round circle. He looked a perfect match for the gilded cherubs that clustered round the edges of the box. "Miss Ojukwu," he said, "maybe you'd better get out of there."

I gave a helpless little sway back against the plush velvet of the seat. "If I had a way to get out—oh!" I gasped, as the box dropped another five feet.

By this point, we'd gotten the attention of the rest of the opera-goers. People were starting to hover in close, plaster cupids knocking heads as the boxes jostled against each other. Nobody wanted to be the unlucky fellow who'd been too far back in the stalls to miss the real-life disaster at the opera.

There wasn't going to be a disaster to me personally, of course. I'd dropped a fair chunk of change on the hover-belt I was wearing under my gown to make sure my landing stayed smooth. However, I'd already decided that the Ojukwu opera box was an acceptable casualty.

I clung nobly to the balcony of my box and took deep breaths. A few smirking young spectators started calling out suggestions: "Try climbing out and jumping over to the wall!" "Maybe you could use your curtain to anchor the box to the chandelier?"

"Where on Earth is the manager?" fussed a middle-aged woman with a hat like an entire florist's window. "Someone ought to call the *manager!*" I was willing to bet that someone already had; I could see an official-looking person in a plain wooden box attempting to break in through the thicket of gilded banisters. He didn't look like he was having much luck.

Esteban, meanwhile, had finally gotten the right idea in his head, and was slowly piloting his box to come down alongside mine. "Hold on, Miss Ojukwu—"

The box plummeted another ten feet. The floor of the opera house was about thirty feet down from me now, and approaching fast. "Oh, *please* hurry!" I said, faintly, and slid my hand towards the hover-belt at my waist.

Before I could do much, though, I heard the sound of another motor roaring behind me, followed by the screech of a brake. I don't know why it is that little motors are always louder. The one that powered my behemoth of a box was practically a kitten purr next to this.

I spun around and saw—well, of course it would be Sol Mendez-Yuki. She'd somehow managed to commandeer one of the little air-scooters that the vendors used, and was hovering just an inch or two above the floor of my box. It must have taken some pretty fancy driving on her part; I hadn't even felt a jostle. Most people I knew couldn't manage a manual, and certainly not most debs. I wondered where she'd picked up the skill.

She looked every inch the hero of the hour, and didn't she know it! Today's fancy suit even had a cape to it, which is the sort of thing even the swellest of swells can only get away with at the opera.

"You'd better hop on board," she said, cool as a cucumber.

I cast one last wistful look at poor flailing Esteban, and heaved an internal sigh. I didn't have any kind of an excuse to say no. "I guess I'd better," I agreed, and hopped on up behind her. She cast me a slightly sidelong look—I think she'd been expecting me to get on in front of her, where there was a pretty secure spot between the seat and the concessions tray—but it was a strategic decision. If I was in front, there was a good shot she'd be holding onto my waist, and I didn't want any chance she might notice the telltale bulk of the hover-belt under the back of my gown.

Of course, that meant that in order not to fall off the air-scooter seat—which was really only designed for one person at a time—I had to not just grab onto *her* waist, but practically glue myself to her back. If she'd been my target, I'd have taken my cue straightaway to commence with the bodice-heaving and remind her what kind of assets I was working with. As it was, I was just glad her cape provided not only a decent level of cushioning between us, but a relatively safe array of fabric to grab onto.

Just as the air-scooter kicked off again, the opera box that I'd been in gave a shuddering jolt and dropped the rest of the way to the mosaic floor. I craned my neck to watch it fall. I won't lie, it gave me a case of the heebie-jeebies. I would've been fine with the hover-belt—probably—but it wouldn't have been pleasant, and the worst part would've been knowing it was my own damn fault. Too cocky by half, my sister would say, and she would've been right.

"You're all right," said Sol Mendez-Yuki, in front of me. She didn't turn around, but she must have felt me shiver, even through all the layers of that nonsense cape.

"You were lucky, though."

"Unlucky, you mean," I said.

"Lucky," said Sol, "that I was there."

I stifled a snort. What a peacock she was! Still, under the circumstances, I guess I couldn't say that she was wrong.

We pulled up onto the side of a walk-along balcony. She dismounted in one smooth motion that gave the concessions air-scooter the borrowed panache of a classical motorbike, and then held out a hand to help me do the same.

"I'd bet that no one ever accused you of false modesty, Sol Mendez-Yuki," I said, and smiled at her. I meant that smile to be devastating; it always helps if it's genuine. "But I'll admit, I'm grateful for the rescue."

I saw her blink, once, before bowing over my hand so I couldn't see her eyes anymore.

Then Esteban came pelting up to us, having parked his own box right alongside. "Miss Ojukwu! Are you all right?"

"I'm fine," I said, and gave him a brave smile, which—in my professional opinion—wasn't anything like half as good as the one I'd sent towards Sol Mendez-Yuki. But he'd missed his cue so badly, it was hard for me to muster up much enthusiasm. "At least I got the whole first act in, though I suppose I won't be coming back to the anti-grav opera any time soon, without a box—"

"If you ask me the whole thing's an awful waste of time anyway," said Esteban, which wasn't what I was hoping for. But then he added, "But of course, if you don't want to miss the end, you're welcome to join us in our box—there's plenty of room, and we'd be glad to have you."

"Don't feel you have to say yes to avoid giving offense," said Sol. She was still holding my hand, all solicitousness. "Nobody would blame you for not wanting to get right back in an opera box."

"My mother always said, the only thing to do after falling off a horse was to get right back on," I said, bravely.

Sol cocked an eyebrow. "Horse?"

"An herbivorous quadruped," said Esteban. "Terra native. People used to use them for transit. A quaint expression, but a noble sentiment."

"Very noble," murmured Sol. "Still, martyring yourself to discomfort seems excessive, under the circumstances."

I made a mental note that if anyone ever asked, I should tell them that Evelyn Ojukwu's mother had grown up on Earth, like mine. Out loud, I said, "It'd be a shame to spend the rest of my life afraid of opera boxes. And I'm sure I'd be much less frightened to get back into one if I was with the two of you, rather than on my own or with strangers." I looked up at Sol innocently through my lashes. "I've got proof the Mendez-Yuki won't let anyone fall on their watch."

There wasn't much Sol could say to that, short of telling me she didn't want me in the box—which would make her look a real boor, and it seemed the Don Juan of New Monte wasn't ready to look boorish. So when the curtain went up on the second act, there I was, exactly where I wanted to be, sandwiched between the Mendez-Yuki siblings and having a grand old time. Esteban even bought me chocolate, which I felt at this point I had earned.

Sol waited until the middle of the first aria to lean down and murmur, "Still, it's a little peculiar, isn't it?

The box failing like that, so suddenly, and so close to us."

"Pardon?" I said.

"*Sol*," hissed Esteban. "Miss Ojukwu has expressed an interest in seeing the end of the *show*."

"My apologies," said Sol, but the glance she shot my way told me that she didn't buy for a moment that I hadn't heard.

The opera ended with a standard hot-Earth metaphor, with Icarus flying Amelia Earhart right into the star at the center of the Sol system, and everything going up in flames (real flames, kept in check by the boundaries of the performance area's grav-field). The plot might have been hackneyed, but the fireball was a stunt and a half. I was glad Evelyn Ojukwu was supposed to be a rube who'd never seen a thing like this before, so I didn't have to worry about letting my mouth hang open a little.

When I finally dragged my attention away from the stage, I found Sol Mendez-Yuki watching me. I blinked at her, and she smiled. "Seems like you liked the show all right, Miss Ojukwu."

"That obvious?" I blushed, and glanced from one Mendez-Yuki to the other. "I guess it's old news to the two of you, huh? It's probably not fashionable, to look so impressed—"

Sol laughed. "Fashionable's not fashionable. If everyone does the done thing, that just makes the done thing dull as ditchwater."

"I'd much rather spend time with a person who's *genuine*," said Esteban, with emphasis.

For a moment, the two of them looked awfully alike. The corner of my mouth twitched downward.

I knew what Esteban really meant when he said 'genuine'; I knew who he was talking about. I could hear the stiff-necked hurt lurking at the back of his voice. He'd told me the other night he wanted something outside his own gilded world, something real, but when he'd had it, he'd tossed it straight in the trash. For all his sister's grandstanding chivalry, she probably would have done just the same in his place. She was a deb, after all, born and raised on New Monte, and people like that didn't think people like me were really people at all.

I ducked my head. Let them think I was embarrassed at the compliments. Let them think I was shy.

Sol laughed, and took the controls to navigate the opera box into the line for the lobby. Esteban said, "Miss Ojukwu, I'll be the first to tell you the opera doesn't mean much to me—it's just one of the things we're expected to do—but it means a little more, watching you get so much out of it. It'll take a while for them to fix your box, won't it? Why don't you just use ours for the rest of the season?"

"Oh, I couldn't possibly impose like that," said I, of course.

"Oh, it wouldn't be an imposition," said Esteban, of course. "It would be my pleasure—my genuine pleasure."

I worked up another blush. "Well, if you're certain—but I won't just pop in at any time, I promise! I wouldn't want to get in the way of a family party, or if you were bringing a special friend, anything like that—"

"There's nobody like that," said Esteban, with emphasis. "Nobody at all—not just yet, anyway, though I hope—" He took my hand. I let him do it, raising my eyes up to his face. I didn't have to fake the way they widened with surprise; I hadn't expected him to be moving this fast. "Well, if you'll pardon me, Miss Ojukwu, I might be so bold as to say that I hope that might be changing soon."

Evelyn Ojukwu might be naive about the opera, but

she'd grown up in the elite circles of Kepler. She knew how to handle herself in a situation like this. I took my hand back, holding his gaze. "That *is* a little bold, Mr. Mendez-Yuki."

Esteban swallowed. "I hope I've not offended you in saying—only that I'd like to spend more time with you, Miss Ojukwu, and—"

"You haven't offended me," I said, slowly. I waited just long enough to let him squirm for a bit, and then I smiled. "I suppose I wouldn't mind spending a little more time with you, either, Mr. Mendez-Yuki. You've been making up for first impressions in spades."

Esteban's face went a pleased fire-hose red—and, I noticed, he shot a small, triumphant glance in the general direction of his sister.

Sol, as far as I could tell out of my peripherals, was just looking ironical. "If you lovebirds are done," she said, "we're holding up the docking line."

It was slow going back through the lobby towards the exit. Nearly every person we brushed against had to stop and tell me how frightened they'd been for my welfare, and how glad they were that I'd come to no harm. Gaea St. Clair, the girl I'd spilled the wine on yesterday, gave me a smile of dislike and said, "You *do* come to mishaps, don't you?" A no-nonsense-looking woman started explaining to me and Esteban about the propulsion mechanism that kept the boxes hovering, while the manager I'd noticed in his plain box earlier seemed to be trying to make sure I wasn't planning to sue.

In all the hustle and bustle, I almost didn't notice when Sol stopped short. Her gaze was locked on someone across the lobby—someone who, from her face, she didn't expect to see, and didn't want to see either.

The person bowed his head and politely doffed his breather to Sol. When he straightened again, and I got a look at his face, I found myself feeling pretty much the same way she looked.

Albert Alonso is the right-hand man of a certain individual whose name it's not good safety practice to bandy around too much. Actually, the individual in question's got so many right-hand men out doing his dirty work for him that you could easily mistake him for an octopus. Still, Albert takes a certain pride in his job description, and I've got no call to quibble, though if you ask me, he's less of a hand than an elbow—kind of a blunt instrument.

Albert turning up usually means bad news for somebody. His gang might call themselves the Terran Original Undertakers, but these days they're involved in just about every shady scheme between here and the Betazed asteroid belt. However, before Jules and I went into business for ourselves, we didn't have the chance to be particularly choosy about our company, so I knew old Albert reasonably well. He was a decent enough fellow in his own way—polite to widows and orphans, when it wasn't in his job description to be otherwise—but I couldn't say this was the time or place I would have chosen to run into an old friend.

I only had to hope that if he recognized me, he'd have the sense not to show it here. I turned my eyes away just in time to encounter Sol Mendez-Yuki's gaze, narrowed and suspicious and set on me.

I gave her a faint smile, and fanned myself with my breather. "My goodness, I'm afraid the crush is affecting me more than I'd realized. Do you think we could get to the door?"

Esteban didn't exactly swing into action to sweep the crowds manfully aside, but we did up the pace of our shuffle, and before too long we were safely out of the theater—minus Sol, who'd somehow got left behind in the crush. As my rental car pulled up to take me home, Esteban eyed me like he wasn't sure exactly how to play the wrap-up.

I kept my hands behind my back, in case he was thinking about grabbing for them again. I didn't want to put up all the green lights too soon; I was A-OK with him going well below the speed limit. "Thank you for a lovely evening, Mr. Mendez-Yuki."

"Thank you for joining us, Miss Ojukwu," answered Esteban, and then, all in a rush, "and—and I hope that you'll consider joining me for a firework demonstration. It's not the sort of thing I usually attend, but—but if you've never been out to Lorelei Beach, it's really a sight to see, and—"

"Joining you," said I, yellow lights flashing, "or joining a party, Mr. Mendez-Yuki?"

"Oh—a party, of course! It's a planned expedition. My sister and our cousins—I wouldn't, I mean, we wouldn't—"

"Well, in that case." I unbent enough to give him a smile. "That sounds lovely, actually. I'd love to."

"Wonderful!" Esteban beamed. "I'll send you the date and time. And—will I see you again before then?"

"Oh, I expect so," I said, airily, and got into the car without telling him when or where.

Sol came out to join Esteban just as the rental was pulling away. Her face still had that set look on it. I called a cheerful farewell to her out the window, and then leaned back against the car seat and wondered when, exactly,

New Monte's golden girl had made the acquaintance of
Albert Alonso of the T.O.U.

It wasn't any of my business, of course. And I wasn't
planning on making it my business, either—at least, just
so long as Sol Mendez-Yuki didn't decide to make my
business hers.

If she did, that was her lookout. Nobody was getting
in my way on this job. I had plenty of reasons to make
sure of that.

HEY KIDDO, I dictated back in my fancy hotel room,
surrounded by all the first-class swag that a person could
land on a couple of gift vouchers.

> *How are you doing? Doc appointments go OK? The
> gig's going fine, nothing to write home about. But
> anyway it's never a swell time unless you're with me,
> you know that?*
>
> *Are you eating? Getting out? Counting down
> the days until you get to kick the sprog out into an
> incubation tank? Hang in there—by the time you see
> this you'll have less than a month to go.*
>
> *Wish you could be here. More than that, wish I
> could be there.*
>
> *Hope you're keeping your head up.*
> *Buckets of love,*
> *BSIDV*

Beste shvester in di velt, world's best sister—that's how
I'd always signed off on messages to Jules, with a heart
and a wave all wrapped up in a one-click custom image.
Maybe a person couldn't claim to be the best sister in the

universe, but any single given world couldn't offer all that much competition. Of course, right now, for the first time in as far back as I could remember—for the first time in our lives, probably—I couldn't use that little image. Any data bloat could cause big delays on messages going between worlds. The trouble is, once you start talking about two different worlds, you double the odds of someone being a little bit better of a sister than you are.

Maybe that's why I felt so strange signing off that letter. If you're entering the best-sister sweepstakes, it probably helps not to be telling any lies. As far as Jules knew, I was off on the luxe-liner gig without her, laying up a little more of a nest egg for her and the littlest Mendez-Yuki while she rested up on the resort moon of Bellavu and waited for the prenatal surgery that would drop the kid in an incubator for the most dangerous months of pregnancy—standard on places like Bellavu, standard for people like my new friends on New Monte, though well out of range of most of the folks we'd grown up with.

If my plan went right, I'd get a bigger payout on this operation than if I'd spent decades riding the liners. Jules and I could retire on Esteban's dime, live safe and easy until whatever tadpole she popped out got to be a full-size frog prince. I thought it was only fair for Esteban to shell out that much for his sprog—even if he didn't believe it existed, or didn't believe it was his.

Actually, I wasn't even sure that he knew it existed. The only thing I'd ever gotten, when I wrote him about it, was a stiff-necked letter from a lawyer saying that any further contact would result in legal action for extortion.

Jules would never have let me go through with all this if she'd known about it. Leaving her behind was my least favorite part of the plan, but I hadn't seen much of another choice. Even if she'd been on board with the whole thing from the beginning, she needed to stay on Bellavu, with the free healthcare and five-star doctors that made sure no one ever took lasting damage from the resorts' variously experimental and consistently expensive spa treatments. I wouldn't be back by the time she had her operation—they did that at four months, usually, and it had taken me a month just to get out here—but I'd promised I'd make it before the nine-months-along date when they pulled my new niece or nephew out of the incubator. That kid was going to be born lucky. None of the bouncing around that we'd had as kids. None of the uncertainty, the loneliness, the dangerous days and hungry nights.

Still, writing that letter got me pretty broken up. Maybe the best sister in two worlds could've figured out a way to finagle the payout without leaving Jules on her own.

On the other hand, I'd been with her practically every minute for the whole first two months after Esteban smashed her heart, and so far as I could tell it hadn't done a single lick of good.

"Send," I said, and didn't stay to watch the message flicker off the screen and disappear. Bellavu was all the way off in the Eridani system, two ERB-hops away. It would take at least three weeks for the message to reach her, even without factoring in the routing processes I'd set up so the mail would look like it came from where she thought I was. I couldn't expect an update from her any time soon either, for all the same reasons, and never mind any others.

In the meantime, the New Monte social sphere wasn't going to start eating out of my hand all by itself.

CHAPTER 3

THERE WERE ABOUT a dozen events over the next week at which it'd be appropriate for Evelyn Ojukwu to show her high-class face. There wasn't a chance in hell I was going to go to all of them—even New Monte's year-rounders didn't have that much stamina—so I wrote the details of each one down into a random-card program and set it on shuffle. I figured they were all likely to be more or less the same. It didn't really matter much who I met at any of them, so long as I kept in character while doing it.

The first event I ended up at was an afternoon networking affair thrown by some old stiff, where I charmed the pants off a whole posse of sweet little old ladies who cheated at grav-dominos like their living depended on it. They were the last of New Monte's first wave—hustlers turned heiresses, wheeler-dealers from every continent on humanity's home-world, back when there was barely anywhere else to be from. They'd bet on the idea that the Sol system was still a going concern, and made their fortunes fleecing everyone who passed them on the way out. Now that time had proven them right, they took their leisure as seriously as they once had taken their business. There's a certain kind of idiot who thinks they can make an easy living by conning the grand-dame grannies, and eight times out of ten that idiot ends up losing their lunch money if they're lucky, and getting thrown straight off the luxe-liner if they're not. Personally, I always angle to lose just enough that they can feel a little smug about beating me. The goodwill of the grannies is worth much more than their cash. They never catch me fixing the games, either, so long as I puff up their egos enough. They've all been rich a long time now; I've got more in common with them than I do with any of their descendants, but that's a pretty low bar to clear.

I don't think I talked to anyone less than forty years older than me at that first party—though as I left I did pass by Sol Mendez-Yuki and a few of her friends playing at doubles freecell, badly. None of those cutthroat old ladies would've wasted their time on them.

After that, I dropped in on a lecture that the heir to the Heinz fortune was hosting—some pseudo-scientist from out of system prating on about the disintegrating effect of wormhole travel on the psyche, using quote-unquote evidence from black-market memory-scans. I thought it was possible I'd catch Esteban at this one, but he didn't show his face. I caught sight of Sol in a back corner there too, murmuring in the ear of the prettiest deb in the room. She had to be cracking wise about the lecture, I figured, because the deb just about collapsed into laughter every other minute, and had to hold onto Sol's arm just to haul herself straight. Neither of them seemed to mind that too much—not that I was paying too much attention, or at least I certainly tried not to. Still, there were one or two times I thought I saw Sol's eyes cutting over to me when there wasn't any particular reason that she should be looking anywhere but at her own date.

I wondered if she'd come over to speak to me after the

lecture, but as it happened, the speaker ran over; by the time he'd finished droning, Sol and her lady-friend had vanished off elsewhere.

I got lucky at the next party, two days later. That one was probably what passes among the upper crust as real hot stuff, with the system's best skizz band hired for the occasion and everything. Of course, the New Monte crowd in its current iteration has no idea of the kind of dancing that good skizz deserves, and Evelyn Ojukwu wasn't going to be the one to show them. Also, it's just about to be expected that the band the upper crust think is the system's best is nothing like as good as your average set of spaceport swingers. Still, I guess I put enough sizzle in my step that I caught somebody's eye, because pretty soon I was dancing with Yusuf Medina himself, Most Eligible of the Eligibles, heir to an ERB shipping company that raked in about three times the profits that even Esteban Mendez-Yuki could ever hope to claim. Moreover, the glossies had been putting it about recently that Yusuf Medina considered himself on the market. His ma thought it was time he settled down and made a corporate alliance, and apparently he wasn't opposed to the notion.

I'm sure Yusuf Medina is as fine a fellow as any other trillionaire playboy, but I've got just about as much interest in him personally as I do in the steel-tech server who made daiquiris on the *Simoleon*—or less, since I happen to be partial to daiquiris, and Yusuf Medina probably doesn't know a blender from a banana-gram. However, as it happened, Sol Mendez-Yuki was also on the dance floor that night. She had a different girl on her arm today, just as pretty as the last, and just about as weak-kneed too, apparently. Well, I don't know what else I'd expected.

The point is, I did my best to make sure Sol had a front-row seat to see me demonstrate just about as much polite disinterest in Yusuf Medina as I could manage without getting a rep for rudeness all over New Monte. By the end of our dance, I was all but yawning in his face.

I'll say one thing: the fellow can take a hint. When he bowed at the end of our set, I knew I wasn't going to be dancing with him again any time soon. That was A-OK by me. I reckoned there wasn't a gold digger on New Monte who'd turn down a chance to hook Yusuf Medina for a smaller, duller fish like Esteban Mendez-Yuki. Whether or not Sol had been paying attention when we were dancing, there was no way the gossip wouldn't get back to her in the end.

The last shindig I went to was a little more like the Mendez-Yuki affair at which I had made my first grand entrance. There was music, champagne, and debs bouncing everywhere you looked, but at first glance I didn't see either Mendez-Yuki sib. My randomized party selection trick was apparently doing a real swell job of making sure I didn't overlap too obviously with the quarry.

Most of the debs scattered out to the dance floor after one or two songs, but I wasn't feeling like dancing just yet. I held onto the champagne and made small talk with Louanne Hachi, one of the new pals I'd made over the course of all my industrious networking. She was the plain girl I'd noticed the first night—the one who'd been busting a lung with Sol Mendez-Yuki on the dance floor.

Given which, maybe it wasn't a surprise that we both caught each other looking when Sol Mendez-Yuki herself made her grand entrance into the party hall in the fanciest suit I'd seen her wear yet and a breather that flared out about two inches on either side. She didn't have a girl on her arm today, but within half a minute she was the center of a whirl of activity.

Louanne had already seen me watching; it couldn't hurt to get some info while I was at it. "The Mendez-Yuki have been very kind to me," I said, as artlessly as I could. "I'm sure you heard—"

"Your big day at the opera! I guess it must have been awful for you, but I hope you know how many girls were biting their breathers in envy when they saw that picture of the rescue in the glossies. It looked like something straight out of a serial."

I gave Louanne a sharp glance around the edge of my breather, but I couldn't tell that she was anything but sincere. "Well, I felt silly," I said, and lowered my breather again to show my sheepish expression. "It looks exciting in the serials, but you certainly feel like a ninny when it happens to you! Still, if Mr and Miss Mendez-Yuki hadn't been there—"

Louanne laughed. "I ought to congratulate you, Miss Ojukwu. You can't really say you're part of the New Monte scene until you've had a Moment with Sol Mendez-Yuki."

"Can that be so?" said I—seeing as I'd been a good girl, and done my research, and I knew that Kepler tended a little more towards the stiff-necked. "Surely not every girl—well, you know—"

Louanne's eyebrows arched high.

"Meaning no offense," I said, quickly.

"Oh, none taken," said Louanne, easily. "I know how it is." Her gaze went from me to Sol, and her mouth quirked—a little dry, not entirely kind. She thought she had provincial little Evelyn Ojukwu pegged. "Anyway, there's girls, and there's Sol."

"She does seem popular," I admitted.

"If you think this is something," said Gaea St. Clair, sweeping up to us in a cloud of feather boa, "you should've been here two years ago. She was a real catch then."

I widened my eyes, all naiveté, as I felt Louanne stiffen beside me. "What do you mean, when she *was* a catch? She's a Mendez-Yuki, isn't she? How could she be anything but?"

"Oh, well—" Gaea gave a studiously casual shrug. "Sol's not really a Mendez-Yuki, only a stepdaughter, and old Mateo somehow never did manage to get around to adopting her properly. Of course for a long time nobody thought it mattered, when his contract-candy—"

"Gaea!" said Louanne, sharply.

Gaea didn't miss a beat, just went on, airily. "—Sol and Esteban's mother, you know, seemed so sure to outlive him and inherit all his assets direct. Once she was a MYCorps shareholder in her own right, her own two children would naturally have been her heirs, and Sol would have gotten into the lineage properly. Most likely Esteban would have taken the property and some cash, and Sol would've gotten the bulk of the business. It's really too bad. Sol's got the head for it, you know, and Esteban doesn't want it either."

"Couldn't Mr. Mendez-Yuki just leave the business to her anyway?" I said. Both of them looked at me as blankly as if I'd been speaking my mother's Yiddish, and I belatedly remembered my research into corporate engagement contracts, and their endless clauses meant to ensure that assets didn't slip through the fingers of the marriage-merged. I amended my question, hastily—"I mean, couldn't he still adopt her, even if her mother's passed on? That would be in the spirit of the marriage contract, surely."

Gaea laughed. "You'd better let go of any pipe dreams in that direction, Miss Ojukwu. Now I realize Sol's *personal* charms are considerable, and we all just adore her, but you must understand—simply *everyone* understands—that it's only her absolute lack of current prospects that allows her to be quite so outrageous." She arched an elegant eyebrow. "Isn't that right, Louanne?"

Louanne gave a one-shoulder shrug in response. "I don't know why you're asking me. You all know I wouldn't catch a flirt if it hit me on the head."

"That is *terribly* noble of you," said Gaea, with warm cruelty, "and you *know* I think it's too bad. Of course there's a dozen reasons to be sad about Sol's mother's early passing, but let me assure you, Louanne, that I for one would have been delighted to celebrate a Hachi-Mendez-Yuki merger—oh! Mr. Medina!" She flitted off in pursuit of Yusuf, leaving me and Louanne behind.

Fending off awkwardness was a thing I was more than prepared to do as myself, but I didn't know that Evelyn Ojukwu had the skills. I lifted up my mask and said, inanely, "So you and Miss Mendez-Yuki—"

"Are friends," said Louanne, calmly. "And have been, for a long time now."

"You certainly seem like you admire her."

Louanne turned away, to look out over the crowd. "Maybe a genuine heiress like yourself won't appreciate this, Miss Ojukwu," she said, "but you'd be hard-pressed to find a girl here who could afford not to marry rich."

I tried my best to look only surprised, and not at all sarcastic. "Here?" Of course I knew that the debs were as mercenary as anyone, and maybe more than most, though I didn't expect most of them to admit it as bluntly as Louanne Hachi just had. Still, in a room packed full of spider-silk coats and sapphire-studded breathers, I thought 'couldn't afford' was likely to be a little bit of an overstatement. Miss Hachi herself, in her layered charmeuse gown with its stiff gold-wire overlay, didn't exactly seem to be suffering.

"New Monte's got all kinds of costs, Miss Ojukwu," Louanne Hachi answered. "Money's only the half of it."

"Well—" I glanced out at the dance floor, where a deb all draped in diamonds was giggling herself into a fit over something Sol had just whispered in her ear, and then looked back at Louanne, wide-eyed. "It doesn't seem like her popularity's dropped much. Aren't you the one who said that every girl in New Monte's had a flirt with her?"

Louanne Hachi might not have been anything like pretty, but she had a hell of a face for making faces. "It's true, Sol has a flirt for every day of the week these days. But Gaea's right about one thing—nobody's playing for stakes, you understand? I've told her a hundred times—"

But before I could find out what Louanne had told her, Sol Mendez-Yuki herself swept up and draped an arm around Louanne's shoulders. "Hachi! What are you doing holding up the wall over here?"

Louanne's skin was fair, and her gown showed a lot of it, so I got a pretty good view of the flush that went through her, but she answered cool enough. "Talking about you, of course. Were your ears burning?"

"They always are," said Sol, "so I suppose someone always is." Her arm still comfortably settled around Louanne, she turned to me and sketched a bow with her head and free arm. "Miss Ojukwu."

"Miss Mendez-Yuki." I dipped a curtsy, and then glanced around the room. "Is your brother with you tonight?"

"I'm afraid not. But I'm sure Esteban's told you all about how dull he finds these parties."

"Oh, of course. I should've known that somebody as clever as him would have more important things to do than come to something like this." It was lucky, in this role, that I had blushing down to an art. "I'd just hoped, is all."

Louanne's eyebrows had gone up again, and she was inspecting me thoroughly over the top of her breather. Behind Sol's grandiose mask, I could hardly see her face at all.

The chords of the next song were striking up. It seemed likely that Sol was about to ask Louanne to dance. Well, I'd had a lot of fun dancing with Sol myself, but it seemed a little unwise to repeat the experience at this point. "Pardon me," I said, "but I think I'm off to find the ladies' room."

Sol tilted her head. "You know where it is?"

"Well—" I smiled, a little sheepish. "As a matter of fact, I don't."

"If you go through the third door, then cross the terrarium," Louanne offered, "then down the hall to—"

"I'll show her," said Sol. "After all, it'd be an awful shame if New Monte's newest ornament never made it back to the party." She flicked Louanne in the shoulder. "Next dance after I get back?"

"What if I'm dancing with someone else when you get back?"

"You'll drop them for me," said Sol, with confidence. Louanne pulled another one of those faces, but didn't argue a bit of it. Sol un-draped her arm from Louanne, and offered it to me, her cape spilling off her elbow like she was the Phantom of Kaladan Nine. "Shall we, Miss Ojukwu?"

I glanced back, as we swept off, and met Louanne's gaze. As soon as I did, she rolled her eyes upwards towards the hovering chandeliers. She might have meant it to be a shared joke, but if so, I didn't know which of us—Sol, me, or herself—she was mocking.

I let her arm go as soon as we'd gone through the third door. "It's a grand show you put on, Miss Mendez-Yuki," I said, "for something as prosaic as showing a girl the way to the bathroom."

"You're one to talk about putting on a show, Miss Ojukwu," said Sol, and we crossed into the terrarium.

"What do you mean?" I said, and then: "Where's the other door? Seems this place goes on forever."

It was more an arboretum than a terrarium, darker and bigger than I'd imagined, stretching out as far as I could see with no light but the transparent dome of the ceiling that let the starlight through. There had to be hundreds of trees in there, in every shape and size—no more than two or three of each, because people as rich as the ones that owned this place didn't have to worry about little things like efficiency and discount by volume.

If you looked among some of the nearer trees, you could see the silhouettes of other figures, usually paired up, that didn't look much like any kind of plant. There were all kinds of rules on New Monte, and for all the upper crust's outward propriety, everyone knew exactly when and where you could get around them. It would've been the same for Evelyn Ojukwu, even back on Kepler. You had to keep up your company's credit—didn't want to start any rumors that would shake up the stock exchange—but anything went where the glossy-reps couldn't see.

I snuck a glance over at Sol. In the dim light, in her cloak and fanciful mask, she might have been a figure out of an old story, whisking an ingenue away to some kind of other world.

Lucky me for me, I guess, that I wasn't an ingenue.

"The door's right behind the mulberry over here," Sol said, and strode forward, me following along after. Her matter-of-fact tone halfway shattered the spell, but only half. "The terrarium's not half the size it looks. Most of it's mirrors—speaking of putting on a show."

And, sure enough, when Sol pushed some kind of button behind the mulberry, a door opened up to a hallway. Light spilled into the terrarium through the open door. The stars above dimmed, and a couple someones under a tree a few feet away lifted their arms to cover their eyes, or maybe to cover their faces. "Shut that door!" one of them shouted.

"Sorry!" Sol shouted back, and we stepped through into the hallway, the door sliding shut behind us.

The hall was relatively plain by New Monte standards, and had a backstage air to it. After all those days party-hopping, it felt like forever since I'd been to a place that didn't have shine everywhere plastered an inch thick. It was kind of a relief. But Sol was still wearing that mask and cape of hers, and that sense of something—danger, maybe—that I was feeling in the terrarium hadn't quite gone away.

"I guess it really was gallant of you to come show me," I said, as I trotted after Sol down the hallway. "I would've gotten lost in there for sure. I can't believe these people haven't got a bathroom closer to the ballroom!" I hadn't thought to research how bathrooms tended to be placed on Kepler, but I had to believe, out of faith in the human condition, that it made more sense than this.

I saw Sol's face crease in a grin around the edges of her breather. "You'd be surprised what people don't think of, when they're designing a space to show off in. Anyway, depending on the fashion that's in, half the people here have just got in the habit of holding it until they get home and their personal bots can cut them loose."

"You can't tell me people never get sick drunk at a party like this."

"Oh, if it starts to look very bad, someone else or one of the staff-bots will show them where to come. But it's early enough in the party that there's not much worry about that yet." Sol opened the door ahead of me with a grand air. "Here you are."

"So you're saying I just marked myself as more provincial than ever, just for wanting to use the stalls?" I walked in ahead of her, trusting as a little lamb, and then turned to thank her again for showing me how to find it—but before I could do so, Sol had stepped in with me, and pulled the door shut behind her. "Hey!"

The bathroom had an enormous sink, an unbelievably fancy john, and correspondingly little floor space. I had a choice of stepping back against the opposite wall, or staying where I was, with barely an inch between us.

I decided to step back, for all the good it did. Sol let me take the space, but kept herself firmly between me and the door. "Actually," she said, "I'm not sure provincial is the word for you at all, Miss—well, what should I call you? Because I'd say it's only even odds at best that your name's Evelyn Ojukwu."

So this wasn't part of some kind of seduction game— or if it was, there were some layers to it. I looked up at her, but of course I couldn't see her face, on account of that ridiculous breather she was wearing. She looked like she was playing a role in the anti-grav opera herself, and maybe that's how she did think of it. She'd certainly staged the scene with enough drama. I lifted my hand and flicked the edge of her mask. "If you're going to accuse me," I said, "you might as well look me in the eye when you do it."

There was a pause, and then she shrugged, and pulled the mask over her head. It dropped on the floor behind her, clattered, and bounced a little. For all its fanciful shape and the shine that covered it, it was made of synthetic rubber like any other breather. "Better?"

"More polite, anyway," I said. I lifted my chin and locked eyes with her. "Now you want to try this scene again, Miss Mendez-Yuki? What exactly do you think you're calling me out for?"

"Well," said Sol. She had a good few inches on me, and was using it to loom for all she was worth. "We had the pleasure of your company at the opera the other night."

My heart was bumping a little faster now, in spite of all my efforts to keep it cool. "Sure," I said. "I'm not likely to forget it."

"There was a man at the opera that night. You remember him, too?"

"If I remember right, there were more than a few of them," I said. "People on New Monte do seem to love their opera."

"I wish I thought you didn't know who I was talking about." She did lean in closer, then, her breath stirring the curls of my hair when she spoke. "But I'm certain you recognized him when you saw him. And I'm equally certain he recognized you. Which really makes me wonder, Miss Mystery, exactly what your business might be here on New Monte—and what it's got to do with me and my brother."

I gave a disdainful shrug, and saw the reflected light-patterns from the shine on my gown's strap flit across Sol's face. "Could be he's been to Kepler, I guess."

"Could be," Sol agreed. Her straight-set gray eyes were locked on mine. "We'll find out soon enough, I suppose. I spent a good chunk of change to send a high-priority message off to Kepler this morning, asking for some solid info on the Ojukwu family."

Then I understood why she'd leaned in so close: she wanted to be sure she got a real good look at my face when she told me that little piece of information. Whatever she saw in my eyes made her smile a sideways smile. "Sorry, Miss Ojukwu," she whispered. "Please believe me when I say I do hate to spoil your fun."

I looked up at her, our faces not six inches apart.

"I think you're having a little too much fun yourself, Miss Mendez-Yuki," I said, and smiled back up at her with all the insouciance I had in me. "You must be awfully bored up here, to make up such a drama about me."

So she'd sent off to Kepler? What did that matter to me? Kepler was even further away than Bellavu. It would take at least three months for word to get there and back, and if the game took me that long to play, I deserved what I got.

"You seem so pleased with yourself," I went on, "I almost hate to disappoint you. You ever think it's possible that gentleman to whom you were paying so much attention mistook me for someone else?"

"Oh?" said Sol, pleasantly. "Just like my brother did?"

I kept my eyes locked on hers. "I suppose I just have one of those faces," I answered, softly. "You're certainly looking at it closely enough to tell."

Her eyes flicked open wider. She pulled back a little, like she hadn't realized just how close she'd got to me, and then let out a short laugh. "You're charming, Miss Mystery. You can brazen it out all you want, but when the mail comes in from Kepler—"

"Uh-huh," said I. "So how did you see this playing out, exactly, Miss Mendez-Yuki? Did you think you'd march in waving empty accusations, and I'd keel over with beans spilling out? Cry, beg?" I suddenly straightened up against the wall. Now I was the one in her space, and I saw her tense up, but she refused to give ground. "Try to bribe you? One way or another?"

I saw Sol's short black brows draw down sharply over those nice gray eyes. She didn't like that implication, not at all—which was cute of her, I thought, given her rep. She opened her mouth and then shut it again.

"Well, one way or another—" I let my voice go soft again, looked up at her through my lashes.

I lifted one hand and put my palm flat on her chest, where the silky shirt under her cape hung low; felt her give a quick startled breath in response. It really was a little bit funny. Did Sol Mendez-Yuki think she could intimidate me? Maybe she lorded it over the debs of New Monte, with her long legs and her low voice and her lofty ways, but she'd have to work a lot harder if she wanted to bowl *this* girl over.

"Whatever you've convinced yourself about me," I whispered, feeling her heart beating away under my hand, and then raised my voice back to its normal tone—"I've got a bladder like anyone else. And I don't know if you've noticed, Miss Mendez-Yuki, but you've kind of been interfering with the purpose of this little expedition?"

I pushed her—not too hard, but hard enough.

She stepped back, staring at me.

Then her eyebrow slanted up again, and she shot me a

dry look. "Would you like me to wait for you, or do you think you can find your own way back to the party?"

"It seems a little late for you to 'come chivalrous again now," said I, and closed the bathroom door in her face.

I listened for a minute to hear that she was really going. Then I sat myself down onto the seat of the john—of course it was about the comfiest toilet seat I'd ever been on—and let the adrenaline slip its way out of my system. I'd let the high run away with me a little there.

I had a deadline now. Well, I'd had a deadline anyway; I'd promised Jules I'd be back in time to meet the sprog, and in any case my money was only going to take me so far. So what if my window was narrowing? I knew how fast Esteban could move when his head went over his heels; I'd seen it firsthand, and he didn't show any signs of having caught a case of shyness from his last near brush with matrimony.

His sister didn't have anything solid to hang over me yet, and she'd as much as said she wouldn't move without proof. I could certainly do what I'd come for, just so long as I didn't let her threats throw me off my game.

And it would be downright embarrassing if they did; after all, I was a professional. I smiled a little, thinking of the look on her face when I flipped the script on her, and the feel of her heartbeat picking up under my fingers.

If my own heart was still going a little fast to match— well, that happened all the time, in this kind of a job. High risk, high reward.

CHAPTER 4

THE NEXT DAY, I got the swankiest invite you could possibly imagine, delivered straight to my hotel suite through pneumatic tube: Mr. Esteban Mendez-Yuki requested the pleasure of my company for a small supper party that evening, in honor of his cousin's return to New Monte. Apparently I'd done a good job playing hard-to-get. The invite was printed on real paper, with the MYCorp logo on it picked out in gold and embedded with a microchip to ensure validity. I couldn't remember the last time I'd seen something printed on real paper, and I made a mental note to put it away into my scrapbox after I'd used it. You never knew when a real certified version of the Mendez-Yuki logo would come in useful.

However, the Mendez-Yuki dinner invite wasn't the only piece of interesting mail waiting for me that morning. The other one didn't come on any fancy paper with any fancy seal; it got sent straight electric to my dummy account from the hotel front desk, just like anybody else's mail.

The message was short enough, though I don't know that anyone would call it sweet.

Miss Ojukwu—seems like we've got some things to discuss. Mind paying me a call this afternoon? 4071 Tacet Street, second floor. Don't be ostentatious.

I had a fair idea who this might be from, and this wasn't the kind of date I could decline. Within the half-hour, I messaged back:

Dear sir,
Thanks for the kind invitation. A girl alone on New Monte has certainly got reasons to appreciate all the friends she can find.
That said, I'm sure you can see how in my position, it wouldn't exactly be appropriate for me to pay you a call at your house. There's a karaoke cafe on Rio Street that's supposed to serve a mean ice-cream sundae. If you'd care to join me there at about four in the afternoon, I'd be happy to chat about anything that falls within the realm of polite conversation.
Respectfully,
Evelyn Ojukwu

I'd picked the karaoke cafe for a few reasons. First, it had a rep for discretion; pseudo-celebs could hyuk it up safely in their song-booths without fear of compromising photos ending up in the glossies. Second, it was near enough to the Mendez-Yuki house that I didn't have to worry about turning up tardy to dinner—and third, I really did have a craving for ice cream. At least this way the afternoon wouldn't be a total loss, even if my old pal didn't show.

I was halfway through my sweetmaize-and-meteor-salt ice-cream soda by the time the karaoke girl ushered him into the private room I'd reserved.

"Well," I said, gesturing to the wall remote, "what'll it be? They've got a dandy selection of Jezebel jive. But you're more for the classics, if I remember right."

"No jam like Pearl Jam," agreed Alonso, amiably. He took a seat across from me and gave me a thorough going-over. On the luxe-liners, the silk of my skirted trousers would definitely mark them as formalwear. On New Monte, the outfit was just about good enough for a casual chow. "Well! Looks like someone's come up in the world. Where's little sis?"

He always had thought it was cute, the way I looked after Jules. "Nowhere near here," said I. "It's a solo operation, this time." I brought up the ice-cream menu. "You having anything? Sundae's on me today, Mr. Alonso, to show how much I appreciate you coming all the way down here to chat."

"No, thanks. I'm off sugar these days." Albert Alonso leaned back in his seat, crossed his arms, and smiled at me. "No, I get why you're playing your cards close. Can't fault you for that, Miss Evelyn—how d'you pronounce that name you're going by?"

"Ojukwu," said I, neutrally. The T.O.U. were all old Earth boys at heart and didn't worry themselves too much about gaining a broad cultural fluency. They could afford to offend. "I appreciate that, too. Mr. Alonso, I'm not here to get in your way—"

"Of course not." Alonso waved a hand. "Once I'd started thinking about it, didn't take me long to put two and two together. I heard that Mendez-Yuki kid knocked your sister up."

I lowered the menu to stare at him over the top of it. He couldn't have gotten that info in the couple of days since I'd seen him at the Mendez-Yuki house; it would've taken weeks to send the query out and back. "You been keeping tabs on us, Mr. Alonso?"

I couldn't think of any good reason why the person

Alonso worked for would have a particular interest in me or Jules. We did all right at what we did, sure, but we were small fish in a big, big pond, and that was how we liked it. There were plenty as good or better running the numbers rackets along the Golden Belt who could draw the eyes of the sharks, if they wanted.

Seeing my face, Albert cracked out a belly laugh. "Don't look so heebie-jeebified! You girls ain't in anyone's bad books so far as I know. We've been making it our business lately to know anything that's going on with the Mendez-Yuki, and you sent that letter—that's the only way you come into it."

I couldn't say I much liked the sound of that either. The last thing I wanted was for my own operation to get tangled up in some business affair run by the Funeral Director of the T.O.U. Still, I kept my voice light. "Is that so? Guess it's too much to hope it got them in any kind of a tizzy."

"The lawyers who passed it round didn't even consider it worth double-encrypting. If they had, we might not have gotten hold of it. But you know that type. You can't have expected much."

He looked sympathetic, and he probably was. I'd heard him mention a daughter or two stowed away somewhere back on Earth. A man who appreciated family values, Albert Alonso. "Can't say I did," I agreed. My hand had gotten tight on my menu; I relaxed it. "An off-chance, that's all."

Alonso eyed me tolerantly. "You're planning to run the old Lady Eve on him, ain't you?"

I put down the menu and gave him my most charmingly sheepish smile, holding my hands out in a shrug. "You got me." I picked up my spoon and took another bite from my ice cream. It was delicious, of course, though the meteor salt didn't taste any different from regular salt to me. "That won't be a problem, will it?" I gave Alonso a big-eyed look.

I knew I had some goodwill to trade with him. We'd met back in Biraldi City, when Jules and I were still in the South Twenty-five gang, handing off nine-tenths of anything we scammed to the big cheeses who ran us. Alonso's boss was in good with the South Twenty-five, and he liked to frequent their casinos. We'd played more than a few rounds of poker while I was waiting around for someone to take my earnings away from me.

Some folks get mean when they win card games. Others just get pleasantly superior and take a certain paternalistic joy in giving inferior little you a helping hand after they've trounced you. Alonso was the latter kind, which was why I'd made it a point to let him win so much. "Well, lucky for you," he said, expansively, "your plans don't interfere with ours any. In fact, there's ways you could help us out, if you'd a mind to."

I tried not to sound as wary as I felt. Gift horses, and all. "Sure, I'm listening."

"Now, I know you're acquainted with Miss Sol Mendez-Yuki. Quite a hubbub you caused at the playhouse, didn't you?"

"Best-laid plans," I admitted.

"Hooked the wrong fish," agreed Alonso. These things happened in the business. "For your job, at least, but it might be good for ours. See, Miss Mendez-Yuki owes the boss a sizable sum of money."

"She *does*?" My jaw dropped, and I quickly shoveled another spoonful of ice cream into it. Of course I'd been running reasons in my head why a fellow like

Albert Alonso would turn up at the anti-grav opera to put the shakes into Sol Mendez-Yuki. A question of money owed was one of the most common reasons for a fellow like Albert Alonso to turn up anywhere. Still, I'd have thought that anyone who could throw around the Mendez-Yuki name would have had plenty of ways to resolve a simple cash-flow emergency. "How's a girl like that get mixed up with your boss?"

"The boss has more of those upmarket clients than you'd think." Alonso looked a little wistfully at the dregs of my ice-cream soda. "Sometimes people need a stake for something they don't want all their friends at the high-class bank to know about. You know how it is."

"I guess," I said, trying to imagine what an heiress—well, an almost-heiress—could have wanted bad enough to borrow from one of the toughest syndicates in the Sol system.

"The why of it don't much signify to the likes of you and me." Alonso liked to think of himself as an everyman; it could be endearing, when the big stick was out of sight. "We're mostly concerned with making sure that our friend Miss Mendez-Yuki don't find herself in any kind of financial position to pay him back."

To a person who knew less about this kind of operation, this might've sounded like something of a rum deal. What kind of financial institution doesn't want to recoup its investments? However, I'd been in the game long enough to have a tolerable kind of notion why a savvy fellow such as the Funeral Director might have an interest in seizing some of Miss Mendez-Yuki's assets against her original stake. "What'd she put up as collateral?"

"Oh—the boss don't require collateral. When her debt comes due in a few months, he'll take what the law lets him take. And New Monte's laws are very interesting on that score."

Alonso looked at me expectantly. I shrugged. "I haven't made a study of it." I'd made it a point to be well versed in New Monte's legal strictures around prenups and alimony, but debt and bankruptcy were outside my expertise.

"Well, it don't matter. Suffice to say the boss has got an interested buyer already, and looks to make a tidy profit, so long as he can grab what he means to grab. That's where I might be able to bring you in, if you were interested."

Alonso made it sound like a favor to me he was doing, and probably he thought he was. I raised my eyebrows, and attempted to slurp up some of the dregs of my soda—unsuccessfully, as there was a piece of sweetmaize stuck in my straw. Alonso said, "I know you've got the personal grudge against the Mendez-Yuki boy, but how would you feel about switching targets?"

I practically spat the straw back out of my mouth. "To *Sol*?"

"It'd be an easier job," said Alonso. "You sure wouldn't have to get her all the way to the altar! Just a little bit of a flirtation. Keep her distracted until the bill comes due, and keep us posted in a few topical areas—where she plans her jaunts to, and so on. You've already got the in with the family. And from what we've been able to tell, the dame has a type."

He leaned forwards, placing his hands palm-up on the table between us. "Now, seeing as we're pals, I'll be straight with you. You'd get your cut, and it wouldn't be small, but if you play every card right on this Esteban racket you might walk away with more. But the route you're on is risky, and this is pretty near a sure thing. Surer, if we have an inside man—" he tipped his hat, politely, "—or woman. And I can promise you that when we pull this off, Esteban Mendez-Yuki will end up near as sorry as if you'd tore his heart out personal after all."

"Golly," I said, slowly.

I couldn't deny that the idea of ditching Esteban to spend more time with his sister had a certain appeal. Batting my eyelashes at the boy who hurt my sister was a chore: had to be done, but I couldn't say I enjoyed doing it. Sparring with Sol last night, on the other hand—well, it couldn't be denied I'd gotten a little bit of a kick out of it. With her, the game might actually be fun.

On the other hand, I'd never been one for mixing my business with pleasure. I didn't like the idea of the scene that followed, once the business was all wrapped up. I didn't like the way Albert Alonso had talked about the particularly interesting nature of New Monte's laws, either. And I sure as hell didn't like the notion of depending on the T.O.U. for any of the things I was in this for: Jules' future, and Jules' revenge.

Still, when it came to talking about risks, I couldn't deny that Alonso had a point. I thought I could do it— was *almost* sure I could do it—but didn't I owe Jules the surest bet I could find?

"I'll need some time to think about it," I said, finally. "Can you get me a little more info? Some hard numbers?"

"Hard numbers might take a little while." I'd figured that would be the case. The boss was back on Earth, and Alonso would have to send a proposal out to him and get it approved before he could hundred-percent guarantee me anything. Data moved faster within a solar system than over the ERBs, but a three-billion-mile transfer still took a little bit more than the blink of an eye. "And the longer you wait to confirm, the less value we'll get from your participation, the less of a cut you'll get. If you're aiming for a bigger payout, you might want to jump on board sooner rather than later. Could be as much as ten percent, if you play your cards right."

"Percentage is nice, but I'll need the ballpark figure. You can send it through this address—" I pulled out my PD and flashed the address of one of my dummy mails on the screen. Instead of pulling out his own to tap, he grinned at me, then got out a data-pen and wrote it down. A fellow like Albert Alonso was not going to trust just anybody with anything as personal as his personal device, not even an old pal like me. "Once we've got that to talk through, we can raise this topic again."

"Fair enough." Alonso finished writing down my address. I saw it hang in the air for a minute, then fade away to be called back from the pen next time he wanted it. "I'll have something for you in a day or two."

"Dandy." I tried to take another sip of my soda and didn't get anything but dregs, which probably meant it was time for me to kick off. Besides, I didn't want to be late for my next date. "Well," I said, reaching up for the call button to bring the waitress, "I sure appreciate—"

"Hold on, Miss Ojukwu." Alonso tucked his pen back into a pocket somewhere and leaned back again in his seat. "Before I let you go about your day, how about you drop me any facts you might happen to have about Sol Mendez-Yuki's social plans over the next few days?"

"I told you," I said, "I need some time to think it over before—"

"Before you sign on with us on the project, sure, I got you. If you decide to chase the bigger payout, no hard feelings; you stay out of our way and we'll stay out of yours. This would just be in the way of a professional courtesy. A lot like my professional courtesy in keeping under wraps the little fact that you're no more a deb from Kepler than I'm the Premier of Europa."

I felt myself stiffen. "I won't be much use to you if you blow my cover."

"Now, see," said Albert Alonso, comfortably, "I ain't so sure about that. I figure, a resourceful gal like you could probably manage to distract Miss Mendez-Yuki to one degree or another, even starting out a little behind the gate. It'd certainly scupper your Plan A, though. Not much chance of dragging Esteban Mendez-Yuki to the altar when he learns he's been fooled the second time around." He folded his arms behind his head and smiled at me, friendly-like. "But as I've said, I'm plenty willing to keep your identity under wraps. As a professional courtesy."

"I certainly appreciate that." I smiled back at him, and didn't let any of my teeth show. I didn't like being bullied, and I didn't like being blackmailed, but he had me between the airlock and the spacewalk. Anyway, sometimes you have to let someone think they're winning in the short term. "Well, as a professional courtesy then, I guess I can tell you that Miss Mendez-Yuki has plans to accompany a small party—her brother and myself included—on an expedition to Lorelei Beach a week from today, but that's about as much as I know myself."

"Lorelei, huh?" Alonso tapped his fingers together thoughtfully. "Next week? We might be able to do something with that. I'll be in touch to get the details."

He tipped his hat to me and slid his breather down over his face. "Have a good afternoon, Miss Ojukwu. A pleasure, as always."

And then he was gone, leaving me with only the dregs of an ice-cream soda to console me in my time of trouble.

BEFORE LEAVING THE karaoke bar, I took a minute to throw on my evening jewelry and my Evelyn Ojukwu game face. Wing-shaped ear-cuffs, wispy choker, wide-eyed expression: check, check, and check. I gave myself a winsome smile in my PD's reflector, then snapped it off and slid out of the booth. In an ideal world, I'd have had some time to think through the implications of Alonso's offer before my next venture into high society. But I'd never lived on an ideal world yet, nor even an ideal satellite, and if you sat on your cards for too long, you might never get a chance to use them.

A few minutes later, I was showing my gilded invite card to the Mendez-Yuki butler, who scanned it blandly and then bowed me into an anteroom where Esteban was waiting to greet guests. His face lit up when he saw me. "You did come! I was afraid you'd be busy."

I smiled, and lowered my breather. "How could I say no to an invitation from my rescuer?"

Esteban frowned. "Really it was my sister who—"

"You're the one who rescued my opera season," I said, smoothly, "by offering up your box. And now you've rescued my evening as well, by giving me an excuse not to go to the Vasilii-Henson ball. I'd much rather a dinner among friends than a grand party among strangers."

"Truthfully," Esteban said, "I'd much rather have the chance to really *talk* to you than be obliged to have the same conversations I've had a dozen times with a whole lot of dull people I've known all my life."

It was Esteban's luck, of course, that the butler ushered Louanne Hachi into the anteroom just as he was saying this. At his look of consternation, I had to work to keep my face straight. Louanne didn't bother to try. "A classic Stevie bon mot," she said cheerfully, as she handed the butler her hat. "How many times has he managed to accidentally insult you today, Miss Ojukwu?"

I glanced at Esteban over the top of my mask, and thought about what Alonso had said about the Mendez-Yuki lawyers. "Well," I said, flirtatiously, "I guess the night's young."

Red-faced, Esteban said, "Let me show you both to the supper room."

It was further to get to the supper room than it had been to get to the ballroom that first night. I tried looking out for landmarks, but the décor in the different hallways didn't have much to distinguish it—just the swoopy calligraphy of the MYCorps logo, picked out over and over again in crystal and black and gold. You'd think the Mendez-Yuki could remember what it looked like without the help.

Jules might have lived in this house, if things had worked out differently. I tried to picture her heading through these halls every morning to go to the bathroom—no, she wouldn't have, her room would have a bathroom in it. Every person in a house like this had a bathroom to themselves. She would've liked that. She might've liked the glitz, too, or at least liked laughing at it. She had an easier time laughing at money than I did, maybe because she never worried as much as I did about making it. I squinted at Esteban and tried to imagine Jules in his place, making the lefts and rights as easy as he did, the way a person does in their own home. To be honest, I had a rough time making the mental image come out. But then, I didn't have a pattern to work from. It wasn't like the two of us had ever had much of a home before.

Fortunately, we hit the supper room before I could get too maudlin. Looking round the table, I clocked plenty of familiar faces from the last week of balls and social events. Gaea St. Clair gave me an insincere smile, Yusuf Medina frowned, and Sol Mendez-Yuki, lounging in her favorite pose against the wall, lifted her wine glass and took a slow, deliberate drink.

I beamed indiscriminately at all of them. Esteban pulled out a chair for me next to Gaea, and then made to grab the next one for himself.

"Hey, Esteban," said Sol, "are we waiting on anyone else?"

"Only Jay and Sumitra," said Esteban, "and I think they're perfectly able to find their way through—"

Louanne Hachi laughed. "Nice way to treat your guests of honor!"

Sol arched an eyebrow, and Esteban heaved a sigh. "I'll go greet them," he muttered, and released his grip on the chair.

As soon as he'd gone back out into the hallway, Sol dropped into the seat that he'd been about to claim, and gave me a smile that didn't reach her eyes.

It's easy to knock knees or brush elbows with someone when you sit down next to them at a crowded table. Sol Mendez-Yuki, sitting down, had taken care not to touch me one bit. After that confrontation in the bathroom the other night, I felt like the taking care might be a mistake on her part. Alonso had said that the dame had a type.

Alonso had said a lot of things, and I hadn't made up my mind about any of them yet. I turned my eyes from

Sol's long fingers, wrapped around the wine glass in a way that wasn't quite casual, and aimed a smile at Gaea. "I'm awfully glad you're here. I was hoping to apologize again for my clumsiness the other day, and you ran off last night before I got the chance."

"Oh, you mustn't worry about it, it wasn't anything," said Gaea—there wasn't much else she could have said.

Louanne chimed in, "Miss Ojukwu, I understand some people find clumsiness charming, but you'll have no luck if you want to claim *my* title. You stained one little dress? I've destroyed more couture than everyone here combined."

While I considered the cost of all that couture Louanne talked about so casually, Sol said, "Will you stop embellishing your reputation, and let Miss Ojukwu tell us about herself for a change?" She turned her attention back to me, her eyes bright and dangerous. "My brother's too polite to pry into other people's circumstances—" I was glad, once again, for the practice at keeping my face straight; that was a pretty generous way to characterize Esteban's tendency towards monologue, if you asked me. "But now we've got you captive, Miss Ojukwu of Kepler, and we plan to make you talk."

"Oh, well," I said, lightly, "I don't know that there's anything mysterious about me, but of course I'd be happy to tell you all about Kepler, if you'd like. Have any of you ever been?"

"Once," drawled Gaea, and lifted her breather. She was making a point of looking uninterested in the fascinating topic of Miss Ojukwu of Kepler. It might have had something to do with the fact that demographics in the K2 system skewed darker on average than Sol or Centauri; the closer to Earth you got, the more certain attitudes asserted themselves, and Gaea St. Clair was the palest person in this room. Then again, she might just have been the kind of person who tuned out of anyone else's show. "On business."

"Perhaps we met then!" I chirped. "Though I'm sure I'd remember someone so glamorous. Unless you were there before I came out? I'm afraid I must seem a child to all of you." (Evelyn Ojukwu was, in fact, a youthful eighteen. Me, on the other hand—well, what's a fudged decade here or there? I've always had the kind of face that wears innocence well.) "Did you ever attend any of the Gutman-Okoro soirees? Or of course I've always loved the Nkume Club—"

Gaea yawned, and said, languidly, "I honestly can't say I found much about the social life worth recalling one way or the other."

Of course she didn't, and of course she hadn't. Feeling a great surge of warmth for good old Gaea and her predictable prejudices, I aimed a triple-watt smile in her direction. You had to love the third-generation rich—the easy livers, the always-hads. They were always looking for a reason to think they were better than you, and it barely took any effort at all to get them to pick the wrong one.

Gaea looked somewhat taken back by my enthusiasm. Out of the corner of my eye, I saw Sol's mouth twitch very slightly. "I know you must think of it as a backwater," I said, earnestly, "but if you'd just let me tell you about the *real* Kepler I'm sure you'd want to give it a second chance."

If Sol wanted me to talk, I was more than happy to oblige. I'd prepped enough facts and figures about the Kepler social scene that I was pretty sure I could send the whole party to sleep.

But before I could get into my groove, Esteban came charging back into the dining room with two more bright young things trailing behind him. "Jay and Sumitra are here," he announced.

Yusuf Medina looked up from his cocktail. "Finally, food!"

"Good to see you all, too," laughed one of the bright young things. The whole room fell into a babble of greetings, while Esteban scowled at Sol, and Sol pretended not to notice. Eventually Esteban gave up on trying to loom her out of her seat, and took one on the other side of her in a visible huff.

The whole thing felt familiar. I'd deadpanned Jules the same way plenty of times, when she tried to signal to me that she thought it was time to wrap up some scene or other, and I wasn't yet done. Jules, on the other hand, had never quite learned the trick of ignoring me without looking either smug or sulky—at least, not until these past few months. Heartbreak seemed to have done wonders for her ability to tune me out.

But it was a bad idea to think too much about Jules here, with both Mendez-Yuki lined up and locked on. My chat with Alonso had already set me dangerously on edge. The points might bounce right off Esteban, but I felt sure Sol could catch the barbs in the repartee. As long as Esteban was my target, that was something I couldn't afford.

Now, if I switched my sights to Sol, as Alonso had suggested, that might change things some.

"Miss Ojukwu," said Sol, and I blinked and turned to her, a little too fast. She held out a serving dish. While I'd been distracted, the first course had followed Esteban into the dining room. "Would you like some fruit with your raindrop cakes?"

"Oh," I said, "raindrop cakes, how lovely!" and absently fished in my purse for an anti-rad pill to take with the food. I swallowed, made a face at the taste, and looked up to find nearly everyone around the table staring at me. Louanne just looked puzzled, and Yusuf Medina's eyebrows were furrowed, but Gaea had the beginning of a sneer lurking around the edges of her mouth.

The pill seemed to free-fall in my stomach as I realized what I'd just done.

Debs popped anti-rads before every meal on the luxe-liners, just like everyone else who was human enough to have to eat in deep space. Of course they did. You couldn't trust the food on a liner for beans, no matter how many certifications the company stuck on their promos. Transport and hydroponics ships cut corners on their cargo shielding all the time. If you didn't have a portable Geiger counter to run over your dinner, you took your pills and you liked it.

But a commercial cruise was one thing, and a high-class household something else altogether. Pulling out my anti-rads at a Mendez-Yuki dinner party was as good as implying that I didn't trust my hosts to have purchased quality ingredients. It was either a calculated insult, or an incredibly gauche mistake. The kind of mistake that could easily get a girl laughed straight off the social ladder.

I rifled frantically through my deck of excuses, worst-case scenarios spinning out in front of me. I'd waltzed my way into the heart of New Monte's social scene mostly on chutzpah. A few false steps would get me removed from guest lists, cold-shouldered out of clubs—once I lost my position, there wouldn't be anything left to do besides use the last of my savings to slink home, while the Mendez-

Yuki muttered a good-riddance behind me. I'd be out all the money I'd invested in this job, the money Jules and I had earned together, with nothing to show for it.

Gaea's sneer was broadening now, impossible to ignore. I had to say something. "I—"

"Esteban!" Sol smacked her forehead with the heel of her hand and turned to her brother. "Louts that we are, did we ever think to ask Miss Ojukwu whether she had any allergies?"

"Allergies?" Esteban looked appalled. "No, I didn't think—"

It was a lifeline, and I couldn't afford not to grab it. "Oh, it's my fault!" I cried. "I didn't think to ask for the menu in advance, either." I held my pill case up, not at all embarrassed or ashamed, and gave it a merry shake before sliding it back in my purse. I had no idea what kind of allergy I was supposed to have, but there had to be at least something in raindrop cakes that would serve the purpose. "That's why I always come prepared."

"It's too bad," said Gaea, whose sneer had subsided into a kind of careless pity. "If you'd been born here, or on Earth, or a really modern satellite—but then Kepler's so backwards about scientific advancements."

"Backwards isn't fair," protested Esteban, rising nobly to the defense of my ancestral lands. "Say cautious, rather. There's certainly an ethical argument to be made about prenatal biological modifications."

"Kepler goes a little far, though, you must admit. They've banned everything from gene-plans to memory-scans."

"Memory-scans are barely legal on Earth," Yusuf Medina pointed out, "let alone out in the far systems. Even here, it's R&D only. The implications—"

"Can we save the ethical arguments until at least the main course?" said one of the bright young things plaintively; everyone laughed, and the conversation moved on. The moment of danger, it seemed, was past. I stuck a fork into my raindrop cake, and mechanically levered a lump of gelatinous blob into my mouth. It was almost completely tasteless, but then, I gathered that it was supposed to be.

Out of the corner of my eye, I saw Sol laughing with the others. She wasn't looking at me anymore, but I knew I'd felt the weight of her gaze in that moment that could so easily have gone from mistake to catastrophe. She was at the center of this little soiree. The others followed her lead. All she'd have had to do was lean in, and instead, she'd given me a way out. There was no denying it: Miss New Monte Chivalry had come to my rescue again.

I didn't know why, and I didn't trust it.

I did the wallpaper fade all through the rest of that dinner. I didn't break any rules of etiquette, and I didn't talk out of turn, and I didn't let my arm or knee brush Sol's no matter how crowded we got. You might think that would be restful, if you didn't know how much care and focus it took to play it safe when you're playing someone else. By the time the second dessert course came wheeling around the table, I was more than ready to get home and kick my shoes off.

But I was Esteban Mendez-Yuki's special guest, so I couldn't exactly be the first person to bail. Anyway, as the party started breaking up, it turned out Esteban wanted to talk Lorelei logistics. My feelings about that whole expedition were pretty mixed by this point, but I wasn't about to broadcast the fact that I'd more or less invited a major crime syndicate along on the outing, so I did my best to look enthused as Esteban fussed over shuttle schedules and carpool plans. "Now, if we all meet here at one, we'll have plenty of time to make the two o'clock—"

"Actually," Sol said, "would it inconvenience anyone wildly if we shifted the date by a day or two? My schedule's gotten a little bit tricky, and I'd hate to miss the fun."

Esteban scowled. "Some meeting or another, I suppose."

Sol shrugged. "It's been busy."

"The number of times I've heard that from you lately—"

"Never mind, Stevie," said Sumitra. Both the bright young things looked nearly as ready to crash as I felt. "The day before's fine by us. Our schedule's hardly had time to fill up yet."

"It's the *principle*," sniffed Esteban, "but *never mind*." He turned to me. "Well? Miss Ojukwu?"

While they'd been talking, I'd been doing some calculations. "Oh," I said, slowly. "I'm so sorry—I'm afraid you'll have to go without me. I was keeping the date you specified free, but I seem to have booked myself up for the rest of that week." I lowered my gaze, and pushed the last bite of star-bean pudding apologetically around my plate. It was supposed to be a Kepler delicacy, or so the guidebooks said. Esteban had probably done all the same research on Kepler cuisine that I had in his attempts to impress. "It's too bad. I was so looking forward to seeing the ocean."

"Of course you'll see the ocean, Miss Ojukwu," cried Esteban. "If you can't make another date, we'll keep the one we've set." He aimed a pointed look at Sol. "As *would* have been polite to begin with. If Sol can't make it, she'll just have to go another time."

I fluttered my eyes upwards. "Are you sure?"

"Sol's been to Lorelei a hundred times. She won't mind missing this one. And *you're* the visitor, Miss Ojukwu.

You ought to see all the sights."

"It's really too bad about Miss Mendez-Yuki, though," I murmured, and ignored the sharp glance from the next seat over. Sol didn't know the solid I was doing her. Whatever Albert Alonso was planning for her on Lorelei, it couldn't be anything good. If Sol's schedule changed last-minute—well, he might not be thrilled, but he couldn't exactly blame me for the fact that my tip had turned out to be a bust.

Besides, Sol was turning out to be trouble for my focus. If she did come along on my outing with Esteban, she'd surely be trying to throw a wrench in the works, and I'd just as surely be distracted by it. It was better for everyone, really, if Sol stayed safely home and gave me a clear chance at the target—because somewhere along the course of this dinner, I'd more or less decided that my target was going to be Esteban. Whatever her motives, Sol had saved my skin tonight. It wouldn't sit right with me to backstab her on the rebound.

While I was congratulating myself on my ethics, I felt Sol stretch up her arms next to me. "Putting words in my mouth, aren't you?" she said, lazily. "Who says I won't mind? If Miss Ojukwu can't make another day, of course we'll go the day we already set. I may miss the fireworks, but I'll still get some time to sunbathe."

"Well!" Esteban huffed. "Honestly, then why even bring it up?"

"Apologies!" Sol held up her hands, laughing. "It was tremendously selfish of me, and I atone from the bottom of my heart." She pressed her palms together. "Esteban, brother mine, would you, could you, find it in your heart to forgive me?"

Esteban flushed red and snapped an embarrassed retort.

The other guests exchanged smiles or eye-rolls, and I focused down on my pudding. Under all that teasing affection, there had been an edge of triumph in Sol's voice. She thought she'd won a skirmish, and in a way, she was right.

I'd tried, I told myself. I'd wanted to help, but there was only so far I could go.

Scratch that: there was only so far I was willing to go.

CHAPTER 5

I FOUND A message in my dummy account when I woke up the next day, asking for details about the who, where, and how of the Lorelei jaunt. It was unsigned, but I didn't have to work too hard to guess where it came from. Alfred Alonso wasn't the kind of fellow who slept on an angle.

Given that I wasn't on payroll yet, it seemed a little rich for him to be asking me to play social secretary, but I wasn't exactly in a position to give him the cold shoulder. I sent him back a summary of the guest list and the shuttles we planned to catch, and added a note that since Sol had another appointment later, I had no way of knowing exactly how long she planned on staying. I'd given him all I knew; it wasn't my fault if the info wasn't actionable.

The answer I got showed I'd played him plenty sweet, but all the same it left a sour taste in my mouth.

Thanks for letting an old man hear about what the kids are up to. It means more than you'd think. I wouldn't worry too much about your friend skipping out early. Have yourself a grand old time on Lorelei, and my apologies if you end up missing the fireworks for one thing or another. I hope it'll make up for it a little if I tell you to go ahead and grab a drink on me—you've earned it.

The digital check that came with the letter was more than enough to buy the whole Lorelei party a round, even at New Monte markups.

Cash is cash, but that bonus got my hackles up for all kinds of reasons. It felt like working the casino, getting tossed a tip at the roulette wheel from today's big winner. I wasn't in his league, and I didn't want to be, but he still ought to give me the professional courtesy of treating me like a colleague rather than a customer service girl. If he thought he could string me along with dribs and drabs without ever making me a real deal, he had another thing coming.

But I'd never been able to afford too much pride around people like Alfred Alonso, and there didn't seem any reason that should change now. What worried me more was the size of the tip. I didn't think I'd given him so much that he should feel like he'd gotten a lucky break, but clearly there was something I was missing. What was he planning on doing out there on Lorelei?

I wanted to hop on a secure voice chat and ask him to give me the lowdown straight-up, but of course I didn't have a way to do it—another consequence of being a second-stringer—and I didn't want to ask him for another meeting through mail; that would make me seem nervier than I wanted to play things. It wouldn't be a bad idea to put some preparations in place beforehand, though. A little due diligence never hurt anybody.

Alonso had hinted at some interesting provisions in New Monte's Satellite Code. I tracked down Articles 51, 52, and 53, then chased them up with a slew of guides of varying levels of helpfulness meant to explain said articles to the laypeople who were liable to get screwed by them. Legalese is not my best language, but so far as I could make out, New Monte's laws on debt allowed a relative maximum of penalty with a relative minimum of hoops. After the payment came due, an entity holding a contract could repossess just about anything 'up to the value' of the stake that they held. All they needed to make it legal was a letter of valuation from an accredited appraiser proving that the thing they were trying to take wasn't worth more than the amount of debt in question, and any organization that dabbled in financials had dozens of appraisers in their back pocket up and down the galaxy.

All well and good for Alonso's boss, but I couldn't think of anything Sol might have in her possession that would raise enough money on the black market to be worth all this trouble. None of the tawdry options I'd seen with other predatory contracts made a whole lot of sense here. Debt-slavery wasn't legal most places in the Sol system, and this would be an awful lot of effort to obtain one well-known and well-connected woman when there were easier targets available just about anywhere you might care to look. If she'd been a Mendez-Yuki by blood, I could see how someone might pay for DNA—there was always the good old clone-heir scam, which people kept on running even though it never worked—but the cells of a Mendez-Yuki stepdaughter wouldn't be of any use to anybody, not unless her birth father was somebody a whole lot more important than I'd gotten the impression that he was.

BY THE TIME the Lorelei trip came around, all I'd gotten out of my research was more questions than I'd had when I started. Still, Lorelei should offer some opportunities. If I kept my wits about me, maybe I could pick up a clue about what Alonso wanted from whatever curveball he decided to throw us. All the while fascinating Esteban, fending off Sol, and maintaining the mask of the perfect Kepler debutante. Piece of cake.

In his invitation, Esteban had emphasized the importance of punctuality. I showed up right on schedule and found Esteban sulking in the entrance hallway like a teetotaler waiting for his friends to leave the bar.

He sprang to his feet when he saw me. "Miss Ojukwu, I've got to apologize. It seems we'll be delayed—there's a board meeting running over. My sister won't be ready to leave for at least another half hour, by which time we'll have missed the shuttle, and the next doesn't leave for an hour after that."

I thought about suggesting that we just leave without her, but it felt like too much of a risk. Whatever plans Alonso had set in motion, I didn't know if he could call them off on short notice. He wouldn't be happy if I put a wrench in things, and anyway, at this point I was kind of curious to find out what exactly he was playing at. If our trip to Lorelei went perfectly smooth, I thought—like an absolute fool—it would almost feel like a little bit of a letdown.

"She always seems so busy, your sister," I said instead. "I don't mind waiting. It's awfully sweet of her to frivol away the day with us."

"She was already planning to leave early for another one of her endless meetings," complained Esteban. "I hardly know why she bothers coming at all."

"What's this board meeting about?"

"Oh, I don't know—something dull about data encryption," said Esteban, with utter disinterest. "There are new standards coming through or something. I don't know why they're so fussed about it. I hope she doesn't spend the whole trip talking with the Yuki-Chattiar about insurance."

By rights, Esteban should have been the one sitting on that board meeting rather than Sol; he was due to inherit, but it seemed like it wasn't news to anybody that he had no interest. Sol, on the other hand—I'd figured her title was just a way to dress a pity allowance up in a suit and tie, but it looked like she might have more fingers in the Mendez-Yuki pies than I thought.

I didn't know much about insurance, but sooner or later most everything that originated in the Sol system went out of it, and everything that went through an ERB got insured. Maybe this whole thing was just part of a T.O.U. plan to pull MYCorp into bed with them. If so, it was no skin off my nose—except that they'd tapped me as go-between, and between a megacorp and a megamob a person could easily get crushed.

"ARE YOU COLD?" Esteban said.

"What?" I looked down at myself. Sure, I was wearing a swimsuit, but the white wrap I'd slipped on over top of it was classy enough for ballroom wear, and over top of that I had the biggest silk shawl I could find, which draped me from neck to knee. Anyone with sense knew to layer up for space-shuttle travel. "No, I'm all right. Sweet of you to ask."

"I thought I saw you shiver," said Esteban. "They always put the air up too high in this building. Honestly, I can't think what's keeping my sister—"

"If you ever sat in on a meeting," said Sol, "maybe you'd find out." She came swanning out in a sharp-cut maroon jumpsuit, cut low enough in front to slip in and out of easy. When she tugged off her elegant scarf, it showed off the black bathing suit underneath. "Sorry to keep you waiting, Esteban. Miss Ojukwu." She gave me a half-bow that kept her eyes hidden, then turned back to Esteban. "Did you let Jay and Sumitra know we'd be late?"

"Yes, they'll meet us for the next shuttle. Are you ready, Miss Ojukwu?" Esteban offered me his arm, and I took it.

It takes about an hour to get from New Monte up to Lorelei by the official shuttle service, and there aren't too many other ways to do it. Lorelei is a whole lot smaller than New Monte, and much more strictly controlled. You need a fair amount of futzing with pressure and false gravity to create the illusion of a beach, complete with waves, in what's basically just a bubble full of water and sand. The equilibrium of the whole system could easily be overset by some careless space jockey getting a little too enthusiastic about parking his hog.

That's the reason they give for the lockdown, anyway, and maybe it's about half true. The other half of the truth is that the people who built Lorelei as a playground for classy New Monte clientele don't want too much space riffraff getting in to spoil the atmosphere. Anyway, the marketers know what they're doing. The more effort it takes to get somewhere, the more festive it feels when you finally arrive. Even Esteban finally stopped sulking once we all piled out of the shuttle-port onto Lorelei's diamond-white sands.

Jules and I fall squarely into the category of space riffraff, so of course I'd never been to Lorelei before. I didn't bother to hide my wide eyes, any more than I had at the anti-grav opera. Kepler's primarily a water world, with a few artificial landmasses used mostly for docking spaceships. It's got plenty of bio-bubbles, but no beaches. Wonder was perfectly in character for sweet little Evelyn Ojukwu.

As for me—well, I'd thought that I had a pretty solid impression of what Earth beaches used to be like from the old flicks Mame used to watch when she got homesick, and the snaps of her and her sisters laughing on the last remnants of the Long Island sands. Still, old flicks didn't quite get at how it made you feel, looking at water shimmying back and forth over itself all the way back to a horizon (a low horizon, admittedly, Lorelei being as I've said a small satellite, but horizon nonetheless). Waves danced, lacy-like, over the edge of the beach, and I started down towards them.

"Look at her go!" laughed Sumitra. "Honey, you'd better let us put down a marker first or you'll never find us again!" By this point I'd picked up that Jay and Sumitra were sibs, and some sort of cousins to Esteban a few times removed. They'd both been about as friendly as could be, but I'd caught them sharing smirks back and forth a few times—though if I had to make a guess, their smiles were more at Esteban's expense than mine. Either way, I liked them fine. I would've picked them out at a gaming table as my favorite kind of targets: the kind who laughed off their losses, because they knew their stakes didn't matter.

I smiled sheepishly back at Sumitra and came back over the sand. Another thing the old flicks don't get for you is how much harder it is to walk—let alone walk gracefully—when the ground underneath you is only half-solid. I could feel bits of sand shaking themselves into my shoes.

The bot we'd brought along with us to carry the

gear laid out a couple of blankets and enormous plush waterproof pillows on the sand, and everyone got down to the business of ditching their clothes. I turned my head away from Sol so as not to be caught looking. That sleek black bathing suit was all function, but even I had to admit that she had a hell of a form.

But as Esteban removed his casual outer wraps to reveal what was underneath, I had to turn my head away from there too, or the wobble of my lips would've given me away. You couldn't say Esteban was a bad-looking kid. He had his sister's tall, lean lines, and the smug good health of someone whose genetics had always cooperated with the doctor's guidelines. Still, there wasn't a human frame in the world that would've been flattered by the mustard-yellow plastex wetsuit clinging all the way up from his ankles to his collarbone.

In concession to the artificial heat, he'd left off the sleeves. Small blessings.

"You planning on winning any races today?" Sol teased him.

"It's the most efficient swimming gear available," said Esteban, with dignity. "Tried and tested."

"And if you *can* have the most efficient," agreed Jay, straight-faced, "why settle for anything less?" Jay was wearing a loose pair of trunks and a sleeveless shirt with about thirty little twists and tassels tacked all over it, about the least efficient outfit for swimming you could possibly imagine, and didn't seem to have any notion of stripping further.

"Well, exactly," said Esteban, unaware of any irony. The sibs slid another set of grins at each other. Esteban didn't see it, but Sol did, and she didn't look best pleased. It seemed it was all right for Sol to make fun of her brother, but she didn't like it when anyone else got in on the action.

Well, I wasn't here for the comedy show either. Ignoring all the others for the moment, I settled down to the business of unpacking my gear. With no experience to guide me, I'd brought along more or less everything the travel pages recommended: snack bars, giant fluffy towel, shea butter and spritz water for my hair, and a waterproof case for my PD. It made for a lot to haul, but in a new situation I always figure it's better to be a little over-prepared.

I also had a full-face breather that incorporated goggles with UV light protection, but that stayed in the beach bag for now. Not even the trendiest debs wore their breathers out and about at the beach, and anyway, it served to cover up a couple other little security precautions I'd stowed in the bottom of my bag. It might be a little hard to explain why a girl out for a harmless day of fun had brought along a taser and a personal-grav-field hover-belt.

Meanwhile, the bot that'd brought our blankets hunkered down in the middle of them and mushroomed itself out into a black-and-cream umbrella that tilted jauntily over our heads. The brilliant yellow of the emblazoned MYCorp logo clashed with Esteban's suit (though to be honest there wasn't much at the beach that didn't clash with Esteban's suit).

"All right, kid," said Sumitra kindly, now stripped down to a sarong bikini with some kind of holographic print flitting over it, "now if you want to go paddling, you shouldn't have any trouble finding us again."

I'd have guessed that Sumitra was a little older than Jules—twenty-three, twenty-four maybe—which made her nearly half a decade younger than me. I finished sealing up my bun with shea butter, then gave her a shy smile. "Anyone else want to go down to the water? I know it's all old hat for all of you." I looked at everyone in turn, but I let my gaze linger a little longer on Esteban, who jumped obligingly to his feet.

"Why come to the beach, if not to go swimming?" He started off towards the ocean, then belatedly remembered the others and looked back. "Ah—"

"Not yet for me," said Sumitra. She settled herself back onto the blankets and pillows and tilted her sunglasses down over her eyes. "I have some serious UV time scheduled. Anyway, someone's got to make sure our bot doesn't get blown away."

"I need to get the taste of shuttle air out of my mouth," said Jay. "I'm going for a caipifruita. Anyone else?"

Sumitra raised her hand, without opening her eyes.

"I could stand to get my toes wet," said Sol. "That is, unless I'll be a third wheel?" She glanced at me and Esteban. "I could always stay with Jay and have that caipifruita."

"Well—" said Esteban.

"Of course not!" said I, all politeness. "Why come to the beach, if not to go swimming?"

Kepler is supposed to turn out some stellar swimmers. I didn't have a chance to learn that from Ba any more than I did anything else, but I'd started teaching myself the basics on the luxe-liners, and now I can just about make a lap round the swimming pool. While Esteban and Sol got competitive, racing each other out into the ocean, I stuck to the shallows and let myself get enchanted by the little ripply waves and currents that tugged at the frills of my swimsuit, and the feel of the sand between my toes.

Swimming in a luxe-liner pool wasn't anything like this. I knew the whole thing was designed according to some grav-engineer's elaborate calculations, but the water did a real good impression of having a mind of its own. For a minute there, I even forgot to be cynical about the amount of time and money that went into it. People like me didn't stumble into wonder on the daily. I wasn't braced for it.

So it took a couple moments for me to notice that Esteban had come freestyling his way back and was watching me.

That was a good thing, I reminded myself. I wasn't like the rest of the folks here to romp around in the artificial waves, who didn't care what it cost to make or get to this place. I was here on a job. "Esteban!" I turned to him, and switched on the smile. "Hey, this is some date!"

Esteban smiled, a little fond, a little patronizing. "You only think that because you've never seen a *real* beach." He crouched down and dipped his hand into the soft white sand, then pulled up a handful and watched it run through his fingers, a disdainful twist on his mouth. "You can tell that nothing ever lived in this ocean. There's no fossils here, no seaweed, nothing to *discover*—nothing genuine about it at all."

Trust Esteban Mendez-Yuki to make a person feel stupid for enjoying herself.

I looked down through the clear, clean water at my brown feet buried in the sand below. I was angry, but Evelyn wouldn't be. "Oh," I said, and kicked up the sand a little so the water clouded. "Well, if you're bored—I mean, I'm sorry if you wasted time coming somewhere you don't like, just for my sake. It's sweet of you."

"Oh, no—no, I didn't mean—" Esteban floundered, foot-in-mouth again. "Of course I'm glad to be here. I just meant that if you knew what it could be like, in the preserves on Earth, or—"

Before he could finish explaining to me how I ought to've felt about the beach, Sol popped up behind him, grabbed him around the shoulders, and dunked him into the water.

Esteban rose up, sputtering. "Sol! What was that for?"

"I'm teaching you about romance," said Sol. "Rule number one: if a lady's having a good time with you, you don't tell her she ought to be having a bad one." She shoved Esteban in the shoulder and then looked at me. "Lorelei's a marvel of modern engineering, Miss Ojukwu. There's no shame in enjoying it." She pushed herself up and waded off in the general direction of our umbrella, leaving me and Esteban looking at each other, both flushed—though for different reasons.

"My sister likes sticking her nose in," said Esteban awkwardly, "but she's right. I get—frustrated, by the artificiality of places like this, but that doesn't mean I'm not happy to be here with you. I—I'm glad you're having a good time. Please don't think that—"

"It's all right," I said, and it was, though not because of anything he'd said.

Which meant I did feel just a little bit guilty when I grinned at him and said, "You know, I bet if I distracted her for you, you could dunk her."

"You know," said Esteban, thoughtfully, "I bet I could."

We hopped through the water, moving stealthily, and then I slid off to one side and shouted, "Hey! Miss Mendez-Yuki! Miss Mendez-Yuki!"

Sol turned towards me, startled, and then fell into the water with a shriek as Esteban tackled her around the knees. It was the least smooth I'd ever seen her, and I didn't bother to hold back my shout of laughter.

It was fun. It *was* fun, splashing around in the water, watching the Mendez-Yuki sibs shove each other and laugh like they were kids again. They were easier together here than I'd ever seen them before. I could see why Esteban had wanted Sol to come along; whatever he said about fake beaches, it was clear they both got a certain nostalgic kick out of the place. I could imagine them when they were little, playing together on the sands: Esteban building sandcastles, and Sol scaring off their cousins from stomping on the things he made.

For a minute there, I really liked them. I liked both of them.

Then Esteban dunked Sol again and shouted with triumph, and looked over at me to see me applaud him, and I thought—couldn't help but think—how Jules would've done the same, if she'd been here with me; how gleeful she would've been to get me underwater and ruin my hair. As I smiled sweetly back at Esteban, I felt all my enjoyment sour in the pit of my stomach. What right did he have, to be happy, and easy, and cute with his sister, when mine was back home with her eyes still red from the thought of him? What right did either of them have, did any of us have, to frolic in this million-dollar manufactured marvel like it was normal to spend more money on a day trip than someone else would need to eat for a month? On most satellite systems, water wasn't something you played around with. While little Esteban and Sol splashed around on Lorelei's sands, Jules and I had been rationing our drinkables and pissing into filters. It wasn't until I was twelve, working for the South Twenty-five, that I saw water just sitting around on its own. The Biraldi City casinos had fountains as part of the décor. Back then, I'd thought that was the most amazing thing.

Jules would've loved Lorelei. I knew that. Maybe I could've loved it, too, if she was here. But she was out there, an ERB away, and I wasn't here to love anything.

I fixed my fake smile more firmly on my face.

By the time we got back to where we'd left Jay and Sumitra, they were both on their second caipifruita. "You two want to go out in the water?" Sol asked them.

Jay glowered down at the puzzle. "Don't suppose you know a seven-letter word for 'interplanetary lounge lizard'?"

"What language?" said Esteban, interested.

"Broadcast English, Espero Trade, or RJ."

"Romanized Japanese?" Esteban made a face.

"Gonna take that as a no. Miss Ojukwu?"

I laughed and shook my head. I knew a word in Espero Trade that could suit, but I didn't think that the refined Evelyn Ojukwu would volunteer it.

Sol glanced up from her PD. "Here, let me take a look."

"Oh, no! You're not stealing our puzzle, no, ma'am—"

"Didn't you ask for help?"

"Didn't anyone ever tell you that you can help someone out without taking over their whole project?"

"Miss Ojukwu," said Esteban, "would you like a drink?"

I smiled at him. "I'd love a Martian Sangria."

"Martian Sangria," repeated Esteban, and wrote it down on his PD for good measure.

"You could get me another caipifruita too, while you're up there," said Sumitra. "Sol, you want anything?"

Sol shook her head. "I've got to catch the shuttle down in twenty minutes—I won't have time to drink it."

"Boo!" said Sumitra.

"Just make sure to be back for the fireworks," Jay said

to Esteban. "Lines were long when I went, and sunset's in less than an hour."

"Don't worry," said Esteban, "I'll hurry back." He gave me a smile, and then set off across the sand towards the bar, about a hundred meters down the beach from where we'd set up shop.

Jay, Sumitra, and Sol bent their heads back over the jumble. All around us, people in designer swimsuits were splashing through the water, or building sandcastles, or showing off for a date. I pulled my sunglasses over my eyes and lay back on the fluffy pillows, pretending I wasn't on high alert. If Sol was leaving on the next shuttle out, then whatever Alonso's gambit was, he'd have to make it soon.

After a couple minutes, Sol checked her watch again and said, "Well, kids, I hate to say goodbye, but—"

It was right then that the gravity flickered.

Shouts came from all round the beach. Jay and Sumitra grabbed onto each other, I grabbed onto my bag, and Sol grabbed as many of the blankets and pillows as she could hold onto with just two hands. Then I couldn't see what was happening anymore; I had to shut my eyes to shield them against the millions of tiny grains of sand that rose gently up with us.

The whole thing only lasted a second or two before the grav came back in full force. I tucked myself instinctively into a crouch, letting my hands and knees absorb the shock as we plummeted down. Another chorus of shouts rose up all around us, accompanied by the rain-patter of a beach's worth of sand falling back into place. I felt something bonk me on the head. Lucky for me, it was a cushion.

After a moment, I opened my eyes again to find Jay, Sumitra, and Sol all so covered with sand that for a minute I couldn't tell who was who. The bot had landed hard on its side, tipped over by the weight of the jauntily tilted umbrella, and lit itself up like a holiday party with malfunction lights.

"What was—" Sumitra began, when an automated loudspeaker-voice began echoing out from the sky.

"WE ARE EXPERIENCING TECHNICAL DIFFICULTIES. PLEASE PROCEED IN AN ORDERLY FASHION TO THE SHUTTLE EVACUATION POINT. WE ARE EXPERIENCING TECHNICAL DIFFICULTIES. PLEASE PROCEED IN AN ORDERLY FASHION TO THE SHUTTLE EVACUATION POINT."

We all looked at each other. My heart was hammering with adrenaline. I had an advantage over most of the people here; I was more or less sure that the malfunction had been staged, and that Alfred Alonso didn't *really* intend on scuttling the satellite with all of us on it. All well and good, and hopefully sometime soon all the nerves that were screaming at me in a panic about life-support system failures in artificial environments would catch up.

"Well," said Jay—who did not have that advantage, and looked it—"so much for fireworks, I guess."

Sumitra was already grabbing up blankets.

"Leave them," said Jay. "Do you want to still be here when that happens again? Hey—Sol!" Sol had pushed herself to her feet and was facing off in the direction of the bar. "Where do you think you're going?" Jay demanded, voice cracking into the upper registers. "The evac point's in the opposite direction!"

"Yes, but Esteban isn't, and you know he gets nervous. I'll meet you at the evac, all right?" She looked at me. "You'll be fine if you stay with them, Miss Ojukwu," she said, and then she headed off down the beach, at the shuffling run that was the fastest pace the sand would allow.

"Stevie is a *grown adult*!" Jay yelled after her, and then turned to me and Sumitra. "Well, come on—"

"I think perhaps I'd better stay with Miss Mendez-Yuki," I said, snatched up my bag, and set off after Sol.

There were reasons, all kinds of reasons, that this was a good idea. I counted them out in my head as my feet slid and sank in the shifting sands. As far as the Yuki-Chattiar sibs knew, I was a sheltered girl from a planet with an atmosphere; I was out here for a social outing, so why would I stick with strangers and ditch my date? Evelyn Ojukwu didn't have satellite safety protocol drilled into her bones. This was all a charming adventure to her. She wasn't scared, so I couldn't be, either—and if Jay and Sumitra thought she was an idiot, so much the better.

If Jules was here, if she'd asked me, I'd have told her it was all part of the mission. The romantic peril playbook was a classic for a reason. Esteban had fumbled the scene at the opera house, but maybe he'd come off a little better when the danger was halfway real. At any rate, it would be negligent not to let him try. The satellite malfunction wasn't anything to panic about (I told my pounding heart). It was just another opportunity, and I wasn't about to miss it.

(Though if Jules had really been here, I would have gone with Jay and Sumitra to begin with. She'd have insisted on coming with me, and I don't take this kind of risk with her.)

And then there was Alonso—who hopefully never would ask me, and even if he did, I'd never tell him. If anything, this whole incident was proof of how little I could afford to offend him. A man who could disrupt a whole satellite on a whim could squash me without thinking twice. Still, I had my pride. I wasn't his tame little tip operator, to get sent off into something like this with barely a word of warning. Whatever he was planning with the intel he'd winkled out of me, I wanted to know about it. He'd taken control away from me; I wanted it back.

Setting off after Sol was the only way to send that message—to myself, not to Alonso. It should never get to Alonso. But I needed to have sent it all the same.

So I kept Sol in sight as best I could, straggling after the solid black of her bathing suit as I shoved my way reverse-wise through the crowd. Jay and Sumitra's voices had long since faded behind me, drowned out by the noise of people shouting instructions to each other and the loudspeaker shouting instructions to all of us. Then the gravity wobbled again—just a half-grav flux this time, but it was enough to unbalance a good portion of the people heading in the opposite direction from me. I heard another set of screams as a wall of water splashed over a group of folks who'd thought to get there faster by running across the packed-down wet sand of the lower beach.

I took a moment to shove my breather over my head after that, and I saw most others around me doing the same. It didn't seem like the oxygen was going anywhere just yet, but on a malfunctioning satellite you never knew what other systems were going to take it into their heads to fail on you. Anyway, the goggles kept the sand out of people's eyes. This being a New Monte crowd, all the masks were studded with as much sparkle as a designer could cram onto them.

The evacuation was getting itself in some kind of order now, a long line stretching from the bar ahead of me to the evac point well behind. A lane had been cleared for bubble-cars, which rolled through one by one carrying party-goers from the further reaches of the beach. I was one of only a very few now going in the wrong direction, and a few heads turned to watch me as I passed, but I didn't pay them any heed. Under our masks, we were all invisible. And the black patch that was Sol ahead of me never turned to look back.

My heart wasn't pounding so fast anymore. I'd hit a kind of glassy, hallucinatory state. The disco shuffle of faceless evacuees, artificial sunlight bouncing rainbows off their breathers, looked like something out of a dream or a drug trip. It was hard to remember I was a real person, in a real place; that when I caught up to Sol, the whole thing wouldn't just dissolve around me before she had a chance to see me there.

If I ever caught up to Sol. No matter how fast I scrambled over the sand, her long legs carried her faster. The only reason I could keep up at all was that she slowed whenever a bubble-car passed her, squinting inside to see if Esteban was there.

She'd just gotten within a few steps of the bar when the gravity shook again—not just off and on this time, but half-grav, no grav, full-grav, and then a sudden stomach-shaking shift where down was sideways for a millisecond or two and we were all falling off into a ground that didn't exist.

It was only a millisecond, and then everything was normal again. A millisecond's not long enough to do much damage to anything except your stomach and your panic reflex, but it was more than enough to bring me back to earth with a vengeance, all that glassy calm shattered. Everything around me was suddenly extremely real again. "Shit," I whispered into my breather, clutching my legs until they would hold me again, and then, again, as I straightened: "*Shit!*"

She hadn't been more than twenty paces ahead of me. Now I couldn't see her anywhere.

I flailed my way up to the bar, kicking sand in all directions behind me. Outside, a line of people filed their way into a bar-branded bubble-bus. Some of them still clutched their martini glasses.

None of them were wearing black, but I thought I caught a flash of mustard-yellow through a window at the back of the bubble-bus. I hesitated a moment, then headed for the open doors of the bar, preparing to call out for Sol and tell her Esteban was all set.

Her name caught in my throat.

She was there in the empty bar, all right. She was there, crumpled up by a table, in front of a man wearing a Lorelei Libations uniform. The light was too dim for me to see what he was holding, but I could just make out the salt-pepper of his hair and the relaxed set of his shoulders. As I watched, I saw his hand hover over the cluster of abandoned drinks on the table. He picked up a toothpick studded with olives, and brought it, meditatively, towards his mouth.

He hadn't seen me yet. Hadn't heard me either, I was fairly sure; the loudspeaker overhead was still screaming out for everyone to get to the evac point, and the door had been open, and my feet were bare. All I had to do was slide carefully back out again the way I came in, join the line to get on the bubble-bus, and fall gratefully into Esteban's arms. Sol Mendez-Yuki wasn't part of my plan.

I'd already decided that. She'd been nice to me at dinner when she could've been cruel, and my thanks to her was that I'd stay out of her way.

I hadn't heard a shot, and whatever he'd been holding, it hadn't looked like a gun. Probably his orders had just been to knock her out and make it look like an anti-grav accident. Probably he didn't even want her damaged, not really.

Probably. *Probably.*

I thought about the idea of getting on the bubble-bus, and then on the evac shuttle—of waiting down-planet for hours, or even days, to find out what had happened up here while I was gone—and decided I didn't like it much.

The gravity shuffled sideways again, and for another heart attack of a moment I was falling down the rabbit hole, clutching the door lintel to keep myself anchored. From inside, I heard clattering and curses. The bar's furniture was anchored, but the table settings weren't, and Alonso's henchman wasn't having a fun time with all those floating pints.

My stomach was roiling, but I wouldn't get better cover than this.

Before the system could stabilize again, I pushed myself off from the door lintel and swung behind the counter of the bar.

CHAPTER 6

I'D JUST BARELY made it to cover when the gravity switched back on full, and everything came thudding back to the ground. I flinched and bit my tongue as something came raining down on my head; it turned out to be a shower of orange slices. What a foolish place to be in a gravity flux! What the hell had I been thinking?

Out past the bar, I could hear Alonso's man, still cursing with quiet dedication. I wanted to see what was happening—had he been hit by anything bad? Had Sol?—but I didn't dare look out. It felt like forever before his voice finally trailed off, replaced by the sound of footsteps crunching over debris. I held my breath as they got louder—but they didn't slow, and soon the sound of the loudspeaker overhead drowned them out completely. He'd missed me, and passed me.

Something moved in the corner of my field of vision.

After a moment in which I nearly jumped out of my skin, I realized it was a grainy security cam, set down below the bar for the tender to keep an eye on what was happening in the outside seating area. The flash of movement I'd seen was the man in the Lorelei Libations uniform emerging from the building. Features registered before I could look away—broken nose, groomed goatee, well-tended eyebrows—and I swallowed, my mouth suddenly dry. It was never a great idea to get a good look at someone doing a bad deed, not in the circles I ran in. Now I couldn't say honestly that I hadn't seen his face.

Good thing I was a professional liar.

I took another breath, and kept my eyes on the screen. I wasn't a kid on Biraldi City anymore, making desperately sure that me and Jules never knew more than was good for us. The goal was to stay clued in, wasn't it? I'd followed Sol because I wanted to remind myself I was a player, not a patsy. In a game this high-stakes, I needed whatever edge I could get. If I caught a glimpse of Alonso's cards, that was all well and good—so long as he didn't catch me looking.

As I watched, the man on the security cam spat out his toothpick and climbed onto the bubble-bus. It was a little hard to tell, but I thought he got into the driver's seat. A moment after that, the doors of the bubble-bus closed, and the vehicle started moving. It wasn't long before it disappeared from the camera's field of vision; a little longer, and the sound of its engine faded away too.

Alonso's man was gone. He hadn't seen me, hadn't noticed me. I was safe.

As safe as anyone could be, stuck behind a bar on a malfunctioning satellite.

I listened for a moment more. It was hard to hear anything under the yammering of the loudspeaker, but I didn't want to make the same mistake Alonso's man had, and find someone waiting to surprise me. Once I was moderately sure we were alone, I pushed myself to my feet and scrambled across the scattered plates and sticky patches of spilled beer, over to Sol.

Either she hadn't put her breather on yet, or Alonso's man had taken it off. Either way, it was lying on the floor next to her. I bent down, pushed her fine flyaway hair out of the way, and checked her pulse with two fingers on the side of her neck.

Beating. Steady, and beating.

I hadn't even wanted to think the worst of my fears. I'd been fairly sure Alonso wanted her alive, but I already knew that I didn't know everything, and sometimes an independent contractor took it into their head to exceed their mandate. It had happened before.

I looked up towards the ceiling and took a couple deep breaths to get my own heart rate back under control before turning back to Sol. The beach must be more or less empty now. I could use my hover-belt without worrying that people would see it and ask questions. Down at the evac point, they'd be running through their roll calls now, checking off everybody listed as currently on-satellite. If we went fast, we could still make it.

No point trying to wake her up; she'd just want explanations I couldn't give. I put her breather on her, then grabbed the hover-belt out of my backpack and strapped it around her waist, setting it to lift her a few inches above the ground. As she started to lift, I stabilized her shoulders with my arm so she didn't go flopping over at the waist. It wasn't exactly a graceful maneuver, but it was a hell of a lot more likely to succeed than if I tried to sling her over my shoulder, or pull some kind of princess carry. She had a good six inches on me at least.

As I started maneuvering her through the abandoned bar, the loudspeaker message changed. I'd gotten so used to tuning the overhead out that for a few moments I only registered it as atmosphere. We were just about at the door when the actual meaning of the words finally got through to me.

"PREPARE FOR LOCKDOWN," the ceiling above me

declared. "PREPARE FOR LOCKDOWN."

So the bubble-car had reached the evac point and unloaded its cargo. Nobody had taken a roll call after all—or they had, but whoever was doing it was just as much under Alonso's thumb as Mr. Lorelei Libations back there, and they'd accidentally on purpose skipped a name. Maybe Esteban and the Yuki-Chattiar had already noticed we were missing, or maybe they wouldn't figure it out until halfway back to New Monte. The shuttle would be packed with people; it would be easy for them to assume they just hadn't seen us yet in the crowd. Either way, I was certain and sure that there wasn't anything any of them could do about it now. Lockdown meant lockdown. We were both stuck here.

For a moment I just stood there, Sol's weight heavy on my arm. The noble impulse that had propelled me into the bar a few minutes ago was already slinking its way shamefaced out the back, leaving nothing behind it but a sinking feeling in the pit of my stomach.

Then I felt the gravity start to go again, and I hastily hauled her the rest of the way through the door before either of us could get beaned on the head by another floating pitcher.

I got us outside just as the shake hit. All I could see through the glass of my goggles was whirling sand and water. My hands clutched Sol's shoulders. I couldn't seem to shake the mental image of her getting swept away into the false sky.

A beat later, everything clunked back into place. My stomach unclenched, and so did my fingers. I spared a moment to be glad Sol hadn't been awake to see me clinging onto her like a lost kid in a shopping center. Then I felt a different kind of shaking, and looked up to see the shuttle shooting away. It would take an hour to get back to New Monte, then probably some time to round up the proper technicians, and another hour to return. Two and a half hours until rescue, at minimum, and even then I didn't know if they'd release the lockdown straightaway, or wait until the techs had a chance to confirm that the satellite wasn't going to shake itself apart.

In the meantime, we'd have to wait somewhere. Tempting to just set up shop here and not have to move anymore, but with all that glass and furniture, the bar was probably about the worst place we could be. We'd be better off right next to the shuttle-port. The lockdown meant that we couldn't get into the building, but we'd be in place for whenever rescue turned up, and they wouldn't have to waste time looking for us.

The way things had played out, I couldn't say I'd achieved anything particularly heroic in staying behind, but at least I could do that much.

I'm stronger than I look, which isn't very. Sol wasn't any featherweight, either; she might look lean, but she'd spent enough hours at the gym to build up plenty of muscle. The hover-belt helped, but I couldn't risk setting it as high as I wanted, in case I lost hold of her in the next grav-flux and she went sailing off somewhere I couldn't grab. Fortunately, the shifts didn't seem to be coming so fast anymore. There was one just after the shuttle took off that flipped the orientation of everything upside-down, coating me all over with sand like a piece of fried chicken in breadcrumbs. After that everything kind of hunkered down at three-quarters grav, and, for the most part, stayed there.

The paradise of Lorelei Beach looked a hell of a lot less idyllic now. A couple good shakes of the snow globe had tossed all the expensive party paraphernalia into piles of flotsam and jetsam. At one point I spotted the MYCorps' umbrella we'd brought, half-buried in the sand. Out past the beach, the waves whipped after each other like somebody was chasing them.

Sol didn't stir all the while I was getting her there. Once we made it, I took the hover-belt off her, propped her up against the back of the shuttle-port, and went digging for the silk shawl I'd been wearing on the shuttle. The artificial heat must've malfunctioned, or maybe they'd turned it off to avoid the risk of a blowout, because it sure wasn't that beach-perfect twenty-five degrees anymore. The white wrap I'd had for the beach was long gone, along with everything else we hadn't quite remembered to grab, but I'd been keeping the shawl in my waterproof bag, and it was about the only thing left on the whole beach that was still dry.

I tucked it around her shoulders, then hunkered down next to her to wait—which was really a joke and a half, seeing as the only reason I was out here was because I couldn't stand the notion of waiting to begin with.

The effort of dragging her over here had warmed me up for a little while, but now we were settled I was cooling down fast, and covered in sand to boot. At least I had my PD and the glossies I'd put on it for beach reading. I wrapped my arms around my knees and settled in for an attempt at distracting myself from the chill. I didn't want to think too hard about the fact that I didn't know a damn thing about head injuries—if that was even what she had. I could see the purple edges of a bruise on her forehead, but that could be verisimilitude only. If I was the one planning this operation, I'd have stuck her with an injector of something first, then given her just enough of a cosh afterwards that anyone who found her would assume that was what had knocked her out. For all I knew, she could be asleep for the next twelve to twenty-four. That was a real fun prospect.

No way for me to tell; no way for me to know, either, what Alfred Alonso got out of trapping Sol here on Lorelei while the rest of us ran home with tails between our legs. Was it just a scare tactic? It seemed awfully elaborate for that, and anyway, if he really wanted to scare Sol, he'd have stuck her baby brother up here to fret over instead; there'd certainly been the opportunity. (Though, now I wondered if that might have been what was behind Sol's ill-advised dash back to the bar.) No, there was a reason he wanted her pinned down here, something that was supposed to happen on New Monte and now couldn't. The grav-problems had only kicked in when Sol was about to leave for her appointment. When I got back, I told myself, I'd do a little research. Speculating now was just a waste of time.

I was mostly failing to read an article on Earth's most exclusive ocean-platform resorts when I heard the noise of someone shifting next to me, and turned my head to see that Sol had her eyes open.

"Sleeping Beauty's awake!" I said, and then caught myself: Evelyn Ojukwu didn't have to cover her relief with a wisecrack. "Are you all right? How's your head?"

Sol shoved herself a little more upright against the side of the shuttle-port, then put her hand up to her head. "To be honest, it's been better." Her voice came hollow through the breather. "What's going on? Where's everyone else?"

"Safe on their way back to New Monte by now. The shuttle took off about an hour and a half ago, and I certainly hope your brother and cousins were on it—"

"Why weren't you?"

That was a question I didn't particularly want to answer. "Bad luck," I hedged. "Like you, I guess."

"I guess," echoed Sol, with a twist of sarcasm.

I pretended I didn't notice. "They had to put the place on lockdown, but they must know we're missing. I can't believe they left without us!" The indignation in my voice was more than a little bit real. This was exactly the kind of thing that satellite safety protocols were meant to avoid. I'd *never* been part of a drill where they didn't do a roll call, and at least make a token effort to round up the missing. "The oxygen's been behaving itself, at least," I added. "Grav, too, for the last little bit."

Hearing that, Sol promptly pulled off her breather. That gave me a better look at the nasty shiner on her head. I leaned forward, frowning. "Do you know how you got that?" If the attack had come from the front, that might tell me something.

Sol's fingers brushed her bruise again, and she shrugged, her eyes sharp on me. "I had maybe an idea you might tell me."

There wasn't any good reason that the accusation should sting. "I found you that way," I said, a little stiff, and sat back on my haunches in the sand, arms wrapped again around my knees.

Sol raised her eyebrows. "You came looking for me?"

"I'd *been* looking for Esteban." I didn't try to hide the irritation in my voice. It wasn't like I was happy to be trapped on a malfunctioning satellite. She didn't have to know it was my own damn fool choice that got me here. "I was following you—I wanted to find Esteban, too. I kept calling after you, but you never heard me, just kept going, and I couldn't keep up. You really don't wait around for anybody, do you? Anyway, when I finally got to the bar, you were like this. And then they took off without us and left us here."

Sol opened her mouth—likely to snap off another question—and then stopped, her forehead drawing right down as she gave me another look. "You're shivering, Miss Ojukwu."

"I could have sworn I saw somewhere that bathing suits were good beachwear. Serves me right for believing everything I read."

"You ought to—"

"I'm not your little sib, Miss Mendez-Yuki," I said, and hunkered down further into myself. "I'm all right."

I'd always known she was the noticing kind, and it didn't seem like the knock on her head had damaged that any. She put her hand up and tugged on the edge of the wrap I'd put around her, then lifted up one of the arms to look at it. "This is yours, isn't it, Miss Ojukwu?"

I raised an eyebrow at her. "Not your style?"

"Well, why don't you wear it, then?" she said, and started to pull it off.

"Hey!" I said, more forceful than I meant, and grabbed her arm to stop her. "I'm not the one who got herself knocked out, am I? I'm all right. I'm dandy."

"I'm a little more dressed than you are—"

"An extra little bit of fabric down the middle doesn't exactly count as 'more dressed,'" I snapped back. "Look, I know you've got a reputation to manage with that whole Miss New Monte Chivalry of '32 thing you got going on, but there's no one here but you and me—can't you let yourself get taken care of for a change?"

I stared her down and she stared right back, two cats

ready to go at it and neither one planning to back down.

It lasted a few seconds, just up until Sol's mouth started twitching. I rolled my eyes and sat back. "Just because it's a silly thing to fight over doesn't mean I'm wrong."

"You're as stubborn as a bot with bad orders." Sol scootched further back against the plastic padding and stretched out an arm. "Why don't you just come over here? This monstrosity of yours is practically big enough for ten."

"That's some smart talk," said I, "from a person who goes around wearing capes." She was right, though. There was no reason for one or the other of us to shiver when the shawl was plenty big enough to wrap up two. I set my breather aside, to where it would be in easy reach if the oxygen went out all of a sudden, and hitched myself over next to her so she could fold me in.

Even given the whole mess of the situation, it wasn't all that bad, sitting there snuggled up to Sol. It really wasn't bad at all. I'd been alone and cold and worried, and now I was warm.

If I thought about it for a minute, I couldn't remember the last time someone had tucked their arm around me like that when I hadn't more or less planned it out beforehand that they should. I'd forgotten, a little, how comforting it could be, that simple human contact. How safe it could make a person feel.

But that was a dangerous thing to think about, and so I didn't, much. It was an illusion anyway; not one single thing about this situation was safe.

I don't know how long we sat there before I noticed her breathing was coming in and out real even. I looked over, and her eyes were closed. That got my alarm spiking again. "Hey," I said, and shoved her with my elbow. "Hey,

Sol!" Then, catching myself: "Miss Mendez-Yuki!"

Her eyes flipped open. "What?"

"I'm no doctor, but I've got a kind of a notion you're not supposed to let a person with a concussion go nodding off."

"Who says I've got a concussion?"

"Nobody," said I, "but who says you don't?"

Sol looked down at me, her face enigmatic. "It didn't seem much like you wanted to talk," she said, politely enough.

I almost laughed at that. Stuck together like we were, it was the perfect opportunity for her to ask all the questions she wanted to, but it seemed her chivalrous impulses had kicked in to hamstring her again. She was like a person on a crowded shuttle-car—the closer someone else had to press into you, the harder you worked at pretending that they weren't there, just to give them a little dignity about the situation.

Not that I figured Sol Mendez-Yuki had ever spent much time on crowded shuttle-cars. "I don't mind talking," I said. That was good as giving her carte blanche to pry, but it was better than letting her drift off again, and worrying she might not wake up. "What else have we got to do?"

Which maybe wasn't the smartest thing I could have said, as I realized in the short pause that followed. She didn't blink an eye, but all of a sudden I was about ten times as aware as before of her arm along my shoulders, my bare leg pressed against her bare leg. I realized suddenly how careful she must have been not to shift all this time I'd been sitting against her, not to touch me, accidentally or otherwise, in any way I hadn't invited. That very stillness was doing something awfully inconvenient to me now. I could feel the potential energy of all the movements she hadn't been making, sparking between our skin.

As I met her measuring gaze, I was glad my skin didn't show flush easy. Still, there was no way she'd missed what I'd not been able to help but think.

What she said, however, in even tones, was, "All right, Miss Ojukwu. If your sparkling conversation's going to keep me awake, why don't we talk about something interesting?"

I didn't like the sound of that, but what was I going to do, let her go back to sleep? "All right," I said, warily. "Like what?"

"Like the fact," Sol said, "that Jay and Sumitra should have shown you exactly how to get to the evac point, if you'd just stuck with them. Coming after me was foolish, Miss Ojukwu, and you've never struck me as a fool."

I did my best to keep my breathing even. She'd be able to pick up on any tension in my shoulders or back. "They say it takes one to know one, doesn't it? I went after Esteban, just like you did. In case you forgot, he was supposed to be my date on this ill-starred little jaunt. Why would I go chasing after you?"

"What a good question that is," said Sol, quietly. "Here's something else rather mysterious—the folks who run the Lorelei shuttle keep track of every single person who gets on and off, just to make sure something like this never happens. There should have been lifeguards checking all along the beach to make sure nobody got left behind in the evacuation, no matter what injuries they might have sustained."

I met her gaze direct. "It sounds like shady business to me."

REBECCA FRAIMOW

"Doesn't it just." Sol rested her head back against the plastic of the buffer and closed her eyes again. "That still doesn't answer your very good question, though, does it? You've got two perfectly good guides to get you off-satellite, and you come after me instead—why?"

When I didn't answer, she opened one eye again and surveyed me through it. "I thought you said you didn't mind talking, Miss Ojukwu."

"Didn't ask me a question, did you? You just repeated the one I asked you."

I felt a puff of air on my cheek as Sol gave a half-amused snort. "All right—I'll try my best to come up with an answer, or at least talk through the possibilities. Option A is that you're telling the truth. You didn't fully understand the seriousness of the situation, and you didn't want to make a bad impression on Esteban by leaving without him." She paused, to give me room to say something; if I wanted; since I certainly didn't, she went on, "Please don't be offended if I tell you that I don't put much stock in Option A. You're just a little too competent, Miss Ojukwu. You brought me all the way here, which couldn't have been easy. You even put my breather on for me. Nothing you've said or done is consistent with someone who doesn't understand evacuation protocol. You must have been perfectly aware of the risks. So let's move on to Option B—that you're here to protect Mr. Alonso's investment. You followed me here to ensure I didn't make it onto the shuttle. You did—whatever you did, and then stayed here with me to make sure I took no permanent damage from the adventure." Another small pause, before she went on, "Option B seems most plausible, to be honest. But there's facts that don't fit."

I took a breath in, and then out again. I didn't know why I suddenly felt so mad. It wasn't true, but it wasn't like it couldn't have been. "I don't care about anyone's damn investment."

There was another small pause. When Sol finally spoke, it was so quiet I almost couldn't hear her, and her voice was almost sad. "I wanted to hear that."

In spite of myself, I could feel the anger sliding out of me. It sounded like an admission of weakness. It sounded like vulnerability.

There was even a chance it might have been the truth. After all, she'd only said that she wanted to hear it, not that she believed it.

"Two," I said, "isn't multiple. You got an Option C in there?"

"Possibly," said Sol. She opened up both eyes to look at me, with an expression I couldn't read.

Then she leaned over, slow enough to give me room to back away if I wanted, and kissed me right on the mouth.

I'm a little embarrassed to say that in spite of everything, it caught me by surprise. It took me a moment or two to collect myself enough to sit up on my knees and take her by the shoulders. She let me push her back a little, let her hand politely drop to her lap, but the steady way she was looking at me flustered me nearly as bad.

"Look here, my girl—you've had a knock on the head! It seems somehow it's not ethical to go making time with a person who for all I know might have their brains loose—"

"Are you saying that because you don't want me to kiss you again?" Sol interrupted, politely.

I was still too startled to be anything but honest, which I shouldn't have been. "Well, no—"

116

She kissed me again.

When it came to kissing a girl, Sol Mendez-Yuki knew what she was about, and I was only human. My knees practically melted away under me, and my bottom came to rest on the sand with a thump. As her hand started sliding its way along my collarbone, I had just about enough wits left to me to figure I'd done my due diligence. I wrapped my fingers round the back of her head, and pulled her in closer.

Before too long her mouth started making its way down my neck, slow and intent. "Is this all right?" she whispered, as her fingers slid across the edge of my bathing suit. I turned my head to capture her mouth again, in response; she picked up the cue immediately, and kissed my breath away while her hands moved further down.

I'd told myself I was armored up against charmers. What a lie that was turning out to be! I'd forgotten how long it had been since anyone had touched me with this much attention, since anyone had touched me at all. There hadn't been anyone for me on that luxe-liner, and since then I'd had other things on my mind—and now, everywhere she trailed her touch over my skin, it felt like I was catching fire.

Her methodical care was driving me half-wild, and she'd not even touched me anywhere below the waist yet. One of her hands slid down my side and came to rest on my thigh, her fingernails tickling at the soft skin of it. Again, she asked me softly, "Is this all right?"

I caught my breath, and the corner of her lip quirked up.

She'd probably smiled just that way at a half-dozen of the debs who circled her at all the fancy New Monte parties. I could picture it clear as a serial: each bright little rich girl, leaning back and letting Sol do all the work of showing her a good time, and congratulating herself on how adventurous she was.

It was too much care, too much practiced gentleness. Here I was falling apart, and Sol—oh, it wasn't like she was getting nothing out of this. But she had a narrative in mind, and she didn't expect any shake-ups from my end. This wasn't a girl carried away by the moment. I was being favored with a page from some kind of standard Sol Mendez-Yuki playbook: her as Don Juan, and me the weak-kneed, wide-eyed ingenue, putty in her hands.

Humans are hardwired for some kinds of stupid. She must have practice at recognizing that by now. The irony was that this was probably the role Alfred Alonso would have wanted me to play for her, too.

I fisted my hand in her fine black hair—not too hard, but hard enough to get her attention—and tugged her up to look at me. Her fingers paused in what they were doing, and though part of me was shouting that I was a fool to stop her, I pulled back a little instead, pushing myself to a seat, and scowled at her.

She pulled her hand back immediately. "If this isn't what—"

It was my turn to cut her off with a kiss this time, harder than before. Then I put my hands on her shoulders and pushed her back down to the ground.

I caught her lip in my teeth, then moved my head down. Her skin tasted like coconut oil; she probably used it for body butter, just like me and Jules did. I would have thought she'd use something more expensive, but I liked it just fine that she didn't.

My ear was in a dandy position by then to hear the way

her heart was picking up speed. She arched up a little, hands reached round to pull me closer against her, and I could tell her breath was going ragged. Seemed to me like Miss Mendez-Yuki was a little less in control now than she had been, and to be honest, I was feeling a little pleased with myself about that—at least, until I heard a hiss that didn't seem to match up to anything I was doing.

I lifted my head up just in time to catch her grimacing. She caught me looking, and said, quickly, "It's not you. Just—"

I made an educated guess. "Little bit more concussed than you thought?"

"Headache coming back," she admitted; then, as I made to pull back, grabbed my shoulder to keep me where I was. "Don't—"

I did my best to ignore all the parts of me that were shouting to know why I'd stopped what I was doing. "Sol, even if I was willing to risk knocking your brains out, I'm not buying that the horizontal spacewalk on a head injury is anyone's idea of a good time."

"I can still give you—"

"Oh, no. I've got fingers of my own if I need 'em, but *we're* not doing this until the ravishing can be a little more mutual—hell!" I broke off, hearing the broadness of my own vowels, the spacer slang in my speech, and the total absence of the crisp Kepler twang I'd been cultivating all this while.

I rolled off Sol—she let me go this time—and collapsed flat on the sand, pressing the palms of my hands into my eyes. Now that the mood was well and truly killed, all the reasons why this had been a bad idea to begin with were rolling back over me. "What the hell am I saying?

We're not doing this at all!"

I wasn't looking at Sol, but I could hear her breathing coming a little ragged still. I couldn't tell if that was a score for me, or for the head injury. It settled down eventually, and after a while I turned, worried that maybe she'd fallen asleep again.

But when I turned to look at her she was just looking at me. The halter of my bathing suit was untied, the sarong skirt disheveled, and I could see her re-cataloging all the things she'd probably first seen a few minutes ago, when our hands were all over each other: the splatter-burn marks running up my hip. The scarred-over graze on my upper ribs. The cheap blurry tattoo on the small of my back—put there when I was much smaller, and never renewed.

Finally, she said, quietly: "Who are you?"

Now that the flush of adrenaline was fading, I was starting to feel the chill again. I don't know what I was thinking—or maybe I wasn't thinking at all—but either way, I guess that spell of ill-advised honesty was still on me. I pulled my knees back up to my chest, wrapped my arms round them, and looked up at the dome of the sky.

"Ruth," I said.

"What?"

"My name. It's Ruthi Johnson."

CHAPTER 7

"DOESN'T SOUND QUITE so high-class as Evelyn Ojukwu, does it?" I couldn't tell what she was thinking, and I didn't know if I wanted to know. I kept on talking instead, letting my native spacer accent settle in, my vowels stretching wide and getting comfy. It felt good. Telling the truth felt good too, in an ill-advised, zit-picking kind of way. "I think I like the other better, to be honest. It's got kind of a ring to it. Johnsons are a dime a dozen anywhere you look. There's a real Evelyn Ojukwu out there, you know, I'm just not her. I'm what your type of folks might call galactic flotsam."

Out of the corner of my eye, I saw Sol sit up, pushing the straps of her bathing suit back up her shoulders as she did. "You're kind of putting words in my mouth, aren't you?" she said, in careful tones. The wrap we'd been rolled up in was crumpled on the ground next to her. She had to be as cold as I was, but she didn't make a move to pick it up. "Why don't you start from square one, Miss Johnson?"

She looked at me steady and said my name perfectly naturally, and it struck me as stranger than if she'd stumbled. There weren't too many people who ever 'Miss'-ed the Johnson girls.

"There's nothing complicated or mysterious about me, Miss Mendez-Yuki," I said, finally. "Alonso didn't send me here, if that's what you're thinking. I wasn't lying about that. We've crossed paths a time or two, and he happened to recognize me when we bumped into each other." I looked up to meet her gaze direct. "I'm just what you thought I was to start with—a small-time crook turned good old-fashioned gold digger. I'm aiming to marry your brother for his money, and I'm going to do it, too. You ready to call me space trash now?"

Sol picked up the shawl, thoughtfully, and then held it out to me. "You must be cold."

My face must have been a picture. "Really? We're going round this circle again? There's no reason you should—"

"Miss Johnson," Sol interrupted, "you can't possibly think you've landed some terrible revelation on me. Must I remind you that I've known you were lying for the past two weeks?" She didn't say that she'd kissed me in spite of that—or maybe because of that—but of course she didn't have to; it wasn't like either of us was going to forget. "It doesn't make you any less cold," she added, and held out the shawl to me again.

I said, "I've been plenty colder than this before."

"I'm sure you have been," agreed Sol. "I've got a general impression that small-time crime isn't exactly a bed of roses."

I shifted a little, uneasy. I hadn't particularly planned for this conversation, but even if I had, this wouldn't have been how I'd have expected it to go. "You asking for a sob story? I could spin you one, if you really want, but I didn't figure you for such an easy mark as that."

Sol raised her eyebrows. "Didn't you? I thought it was fairly obvious that I've got a soft spot for hard-luck cases. There but for the grace of, and all—there's plenty of people that would say that my own mother was a good old-fashioned gold digger herself, and they're not so far wrong either." The fact of it didn't surprise me, after all the gossip Gaea St. Clair had dropped the other day, but I hadn't expected anyone like Sol to say it outright. She knew she'd offset me, too. She was watching me as close as I was watching her. "If she hadn't seen her chance to marry into the Mendez-Yuki money, it could easily be me in your shoes right now. I was young at the time, but not so young I don't remember."

"So that's why you came charging to my rescue the other day," I said, as two and two came together. I was willing to bet Sol's mother had made some mistakes that were more embarrassing than popping an anti-rad pill in public. "I couldn't work out what your angle was, but you're just a sentimental girl at heart, huh? Didn't want to see a poor little girl made a laughingstock of?"

"I don't particularly like public mockery," said Sol, "no."

"Well, they weren't lying when they said you had a way with the ladies. 'You remind me of my ma'—who wouldn't fall for a line like that?"

"You don't remind me of her, Miss Johnson," said Sol. "To be honest, I hope you never do. She didn't have many choices, and I don't blame her for those she made, but they didn't make for a happy life, in the end."

"Oh," I said. "Well, I'm sorry to hear it." I was trying not to sound as annoyed as I was starting to get. This conversation might have caught me off-balance, but Sol sure thought she knew what she was about. Talk about sob stories! "That's the reward of the wicked, I suppose."

"That's not what I meant." Sol looked at me seriously. I might've lost the narrative for a little bit, but I had her pegged now. Oh, she was all ready to be generous, Sol Mendez-Yuki—all ready to lend a helping hand to this poor lost lamb she'd found, the good-time girl with a heart of gold, and seduce her back onto the straight and narrow. She really was having a hard time shaking that ingenue idea. "It's not a question of just deserts. But tying yourself to a person you don't care for as much as you might want to—it takes a toll on a person."

"Well!" I tugged at a clump of my hair, and watched the sand shake down out of it. "I never thought of it that way before. It's just my good fortune that someone happened to come along to tell me so."

Sol frowned. "Miss Johnson—"

"Now, I hope you'll take no offense," I interrupted her, sliding back into my nose-powdered Kepler accent, "if I agree with you that the day I see the last of your charming little brother can't possibly come too soon." I let the affectation drop. "I appreciate your concern, Miss Mendez-Yuki, but I'm afraid it doesn't apply in this case. When it comes to tying knots, I'm thinking a little more slipknot than a constrictor."

Now it was me who'd gotten Sol off-script. She stared at me, as I added, "You're right when you say I'm not much like your ma. I've got no intention of sticking out the high society life for the sake of Esteban or anybody. There's another girl who meant to do that, and she meant to mean it. Now that you mention it, I bet she reminded your brother of his ma, too. I thought the way he took fright seemed a little over the top, even for a stick in the mud like Esteban."

"Who," said Sol, "is 'she'?"

"Did your brother tell you much about his last long trip?" I grinned, mirthless, at the look on her face. "Yeah, I thought not. But you knew something was up, didn't you? I'd bet you anything he came back sulking and ready to fling himself on the fainting couch without ever explaining himself one way or another. Lucky for you I'm here to fill in the backstory."

"It's only lucky if you're actually planning on explaining," said Sol, "rather than going around in circles like the villain from an earial."

"Sure," I agreed. "It's not complicated. My sister fell hard for your brother. She thought the falling was mutual. Turned out it wasn't quite mutual enough to make up for the checkered Johnson past. I'm a little bit curious here, now you mention it—your brother have some issues maybe tied up in that whole backstory you just gave me?"

Sol was doing her best not to look shook up, but I could tell she hadn't expected this. I lifted my chin and smiled at her; she returned me a look that was flat-out incredulous. "You're trying to marry my brother for revenge. You *are* the villain from an earial."

"And for the money," I said. What did it matter to me if she thought it was ridiculous? "Let's not forget the money. My niece or nephew's gotta have something to live on."

"Niece or—" Sol sat straight up. "Your sister's *pregnant?* Where is she?"

"Set up with a good gyn on Bellavu."

"She's on—and you left her there, to come *here?* What the hell are you doing, Ruthi Johnson?" Sol was mad now, I realized—really mad, all that smooth polish peeling off her as her low voice rose in volume. "Fooling around with plots and schemes while—what do you think this is, the Spaceless Age? You don't think if he knew he wouldn't help? That *we* wouldn't help? What do you think we are?"

"You don't think I tried?" I snapped back. Well, I was mad too. Who did Sol Mendez-Yuki think she was to judge me? What kind of a younger brother had she turned out, anyway? "You Mendez-Yuki are neck-deep in lawyers. I wrote and got back nothing but dead letters. He doesn't want to know, or if he does know, he thinks it's some kind of scheme. A scheme! She didn't even want to tell him. Well, I guess I can't blame her for that. She's been stomped on enough in this whole thing, why should she want to go into the courts to get stomped on some more? And it's not like people like her and me could ever win in the courts against people like you and him regardless."

"Esteban doesn't know," said Sol. "If he knew, he'd have told me."

"Oh, *would* he?"

Sol opened her mouth, and then shut it again. I'd taken a little bit of the air out of her, I could see that, but it wasn't like she was ready to crumple. "All right," she said, more calmly. "Whatever might have gone down between my brother and your sister—and I hope you won't be offended if I say I don't feel quite comfortable taking your word on all that as gospel, Miss Johnson—"

"No reason to be offended. It's exactly what I'd expect."

Sol pressed her lips together. "*Given* that in a situation like that, there's always two sides to a story—I can see how Esteban, being hurt, as you say, having seen our mother's unhappiness, and knowing perfectly well that most people would rather spend time with him for his money than for himself—"

I pressed my left hand to my heart to show how woebegone I was at Esteban's fate.

"—I can *see,*" Sol continued, brows drawing down, "that he might not be in a mind to listen just yet, especially with the family lawyers talking in his ear about what he is and isn't obliged to do. But once your sister has her child, it should be easy to prove paternity. However he felt about the mother, Esteban would never let his own child want for anything. The rest of the family wouldn't, either."

"That's nice for the kid and all," I said. "But 'the mother' doesn't exactly deserve to be tossed out like a dishrag either." Sol opened her mouth to protest; I held up a hand to stop her. "My sister doesn't want to have to deal with Esteban. This way, she won't have to. He won't have to deal with her, either—isn't that what he wants? Sure, his feelings might get stepped on a little. You'll pardon me if I'm not exactly crying about that. I expect he'll get over having his heart broke by me a whole lot faster than my sister's getting over having her heart broke by him."

Sol was quiet for a long time, looking at me as if she'd never quite seen me proper before—which of course she hadn't, though it was even odds as to whether she was seeing me any better now.

"That's fine for you to say," she said, finally. She was doing her best to control the anger in her voice, but I could hear it loud and clear. "I can see how being gratuitously cruel to my brother would be quite satisfying for you. But you can't really imagine I'm going to sit back and let you take him for a ride, can you?"

"Can't I?" said I. "Do you have a choice about it? I do like you, Miss Mendez-Yuki. You've got style, there's no denying it." It was easy to say to her at this point, since I knew that she was going to think the worst of me no matter what. "If the stakes on this weren't so high, maybe I really would have let you have a go at looking for that heart of gold I've got lying around somewhere. But that won't pay the bills. And if we're talking strictly mercenary—and we maybe could be talking strictly mercenary, revenge isn't everything—you don't have the dough to buy me off yourself, either, not with Alonso breathing down your back. So how are you gonna get me to stop?"

"As charming as you are, Miss Johnson," Sol said, "if you

think I won't tell my brother what you've told me—"

"You won't," I said, and played my winning card. "You won't, because there's too much I could say about you."

Sol blinked. She looked more taken aback than anything else. "Are you... blackmailing me?"

"Call it mutually assured destruction," I suggested. "You torpedo my plans, and I'll blow up yours. I told you I'd met with Alonso, didn't I? I might not be on his payroll, but that doesn't mean we didn't trade some professional gossip. Now, I wish you all luck in getting out from under the boot of the T.O.U. I understand it's not a pleasant place to be. But in the meantime, it strikes me that if MYCorps' investors heard about all these shady goings-on, you might be looking at a pretty nasty stock crash. Not to mention the damage to the Mendez-Yuki reputation, if it comes out that Sol Mendez-Yuki herself has her name down in a certain person's little black book."

Sol tipped her head to consider me, and then, surprising me utterly, let out a dry laugh. "Miss Johnson—if I didn't believe you before when you said you weren't working for the T.O.U., I certainly do now. If you spilled those particular beans, don't you think the destruction really would be mutual? Alfred Alonso has as much invested in secrecy right now as I do."

"What's that to me?" I said, recklessly. Bluffing, of course—I couldn't afford to make an enemy of Alonso now any more than I could've ten minutes ago—but Sol didn't know that. An earial villain obsessed with revenge wouldn't stop at anything. She'd no way of knowing exactly how big a fool I might be. "You've got much more to lose than I do, Miss Mendez-Yuki. What do you think your brother cares about more: the Mendez-Yuki name and fortune, or some short-term problems with a girl he hardly knows?"

I saw Sol wince. At first I figured I'd hit a nerve with that justified dig on Esteban, and prepared to go on with my monologue about how much I'd enjoy causing those short-term problems—but then she raised her hand to her head, and I revised my assessment. I'd nearly forgotten about that concussion headache of hers.

Under the circumstances, it seemed a little cruel to go on chewing the scenery. I closed my mouth again and resisted the urge to tell her to stop being stubborn and put on the damn wrap.

IT WAS DEAD quiet on Lorelei. Not even the waves were splashing. Whatever artificial gravity equation had kept that pile of water acting like an ocean had settled down with the rest of the fluctuations. The beach wasn't anything more now than a pile of mostly anchored sand next to a pile of mostly anchored water. Of course the hum of the life support that generated oxygen and gravity and heat and all the rest of it (however half-heartedly it was doing all that at the moment) ran steadily underneath everything, but to a person like me, who spent their life hopping from one artificial system to another, that hardly counted as any kind of sound at all.

I was pretty much figuring we were going to sit there in silence until Doomsday—or at least until the rescuers finally turned up, though they were taking their own sweet time about it—when Sol finally opened her eyes and looked at me again.

"So," she said. "Mutually assured destruction. To be honest, I don't love it for either of us." She startled me with a smile then, cool and polite as the satellite's classiest cucumber. "I suppose I'll just have to figure something else out."

The polish was back on, but I'd seen a little of what lay underneath it now, which, unfortunately, made it more interesting. "Sorry if I don't wish you good luck with that," I said.

"In the meantime, I suppose we both have an idea of where we stand," Sol went on, and flabbergasted me even more by holding out a hand, like the opponent at the beginning of a skateboxing match.

Well, what was there to do? The woman had panache, that was for damn sure. I leaned forward to shake her hand.

Her fingers curled around mine, long and strong. While I was trying not to think too much about what those fingers had been doing not half an hour ago, she took advantage of the opportunity to reach out with her other hand and drape the shawl over my shoulders.

I snatched my hand back. I don't know when I've ever been more exasperated in my life. "Goddammit, Sol—"

She was laughing at me outright.

I pulled off the wrap, bundled it up, and tossed it in her lap. "All right, look—can we just call a truce long enough to share the damn thing again?"

"If you can, then I can," said Sol, so promptly that I immediately began to suspect that that's what she'd been aiming for to begin with. Still, it seemed like it was either both of us use the wrap, or neither of us, and the waste of it would've driven me up a wall.

She didn't put her arm around me this time, and I did my best not to lean into her. Still, we sat, arm to arm, wrapped in the same shawl, until we heard the whir of the shuttle coming back into the sky.

CHAPTER 8

THERE WERE ONLY three people on the rescue shuttle, and none of them wore a goatee. Whatever Alonso had wanted from this little interlude, it seemed like he'd already got it. Still, I didn't feel myself relax until the shuttle landed on New Monte and the door opened to reveal Esteban waiting for us, flanked by glossy-cams and looking wobbly as melting gel. It was maybe the first time I'd ever been genuinely glad to see him. Esteban on New Monte carried a bubble of privilege around with him, and right now, privilege meant safety. If Alonso was going to pull anything else, he wouldn't do it with the whole Mendez-Yuki entourage around.

When I stepped down the ladder, Esteban practically threw himself towards me. "Miss Ojukwu! Are you hurt?"

"No, but—"

But before I could say anything he saw Sol clomping down the gangway, bandage on her head, and turned to her at once. "Sol! What happened to you?"

"Nothing to make a fuss over," said Sol, irritably. "Just a bruise, that's all." The medic on the shuttle had been hovering over her for nearly the whole hour, and while she'd borne it with her usual courtesy at first, her tolerance had been decreasing by the minute. That might have had something to do with the way I'd spent the whole ride thanking them for the care they were taking with her every chance I got.

Well, winding her up had been a good distraction from thinking of all the other things that could go wrong before we hit the ground. Now I just had to stay in character. I leaned up to Esteban, my eyes wide, and told him, "Your sister's had a concussion!"

"A concussion!" echoed Esteban, aghast. "Sol—"

Sol interrupted him before he could go into a full-blown flutter. "It seems Miss Ojukwu came looking for me, and found me unconscious on the beach." She glanced back at me; her voice was melting, but her eyes were cool. "I'd no idea before this that you were so concerned for me, Evelyn."

Esteban's brow started, very slightly, to furrow.

I ducked my head, quickly, and let myself blush. "I couldn't bear to think of what you'd say," I murmured, in Esteban's general direction, "if we'd come back without your sister."

The faint furrow disappeared. Behind him, the glossy-bots flashed excitedly to each other. "I'm just so glad you're both all right," said Esteban, his voice wobbling, and then swallowed. "And I *can't* think what took them so long. Nearly three hours to get the rescue shuttle back up there! Anything might have happened to you! Father says there's grounds for a lawsuit—criminal negligence—"

"I suppose they'll say it would have been more negligent to risk a shuttle and pilot until they knew the system was stable. Still, the whole thing's bad enough publicity for the company that there's a chance they might settle just to get it out of the glossies." Sol rocked back on her heels, eyes set on nothing in particular, and I recognized the look of someone running numbers in their head. Then her eyes came sharply into focus again, and she blinked. "I guess we can talk about that later."

I wondered, uneasily, whether Sol suing Lorelei Enterprises was all part of Alonso's plan. Odds seemed against it somehow. I still didn't know why he'd done what he did—or how the hell I was going to explain to him why I'd done what I did, come to that. Next time we talked, I was going to have to spin him a hell of a convincing yarn. I hoped he'd give me enough time to think one up. After everything that had happened on Lorelei, I was so tired I didn't think I could lie my way into a third-rate klez club, let alone the good graces of the solar system's most powerful syndicate.

Which meant it was probably about time to make my exit. "You must get poor Miss Mendez-Yuki off her feet and home to rest up as soon as you possibly can," I chirped. Esteban's eyes came back to me just in time to witness my tactical totter. Then I hauled myself back upright, as brave a little soldier as anyone ever saw.

Sol looked like she was tempted to roll her eyes, but if it was possible to lay it on too thick for Esteban, I hadn't yet seen the proof of it. "Miss Ojukwu, you've had an ordeal, too—you mustn't forget to take care of yourself! One of our transports is here to take you back to your hotel so you can rest. If it weren't for Sol, I'd take you myself, but—"

Sol drawled, "Terribly sorry to be such an inconvenience."

"Don't talk nonsense! I didn't mean it like that, only—" He bit his lip, sounding very young. Well, it's not like it ever was hard to forget that he was my sister's age, not mine. "Well, it's difficult when two people you care about are in trouble at once, isn't it? You don't know which way to turn."

"To your sister, of course," I said, and I didn't look at Sol when I said it. "Of course your family comes first, Mr. Mendez-Yuki. I understand that—it would be the same for me, and I'm sure you'd think less of me if it didn't."

"It would take a great deal to make me think less of you, Miss Ojukwu," said Esteban. "Especially after the help you've given my sister today." He swallowed, and then bowed, politely. "Won't you let me show you to the car?"

He opened the door for me, and then closed it after me as I clambered into the backseat. The AI controlling the car solicitously arranged the seat around me for maximum comfort, and didn't give me the least bit of sass when I asked for the klezmer-swing channel from Brukhim-Haboim.

I sort of wished it had. I'd rather have been trading barbs with a bot than thinking too hard about the gratitude I'd seen in Esteban's face after the insecurity got chased out of it. It wasn't like it was a surprise. Only a monster wouldn't be grateful to the person who'd rescued their sister, and I'd never thought Esteban was a monster—just a stuck-up idiot with his head shoved so far up his ass he couldn't see anything but horseshit. It didn't mean he deserved what I was going to give him any less.

I just didn't want to think about it too much.

I'D BEEN DREAMING of keeling over for hours, but once I finally did get back to my hotel room, I found I'd gone all the way through tired and hit that awful point where you can't sleep for anything.

I tried listening to music, then switched to a soothing meditation; neither of them got me anywhere. Finally, I shut the sound off my PD altogether. I stared at the screen for a moment, then clicked over into dictate mode.

> *Hey kiddo,*
> *It's not the same without you here to talk things through with. I'm talking to myself all the time here*

instead, and I don't know if I give myself such good advice.

You rag me sometimes about getting a kick out of cutting it close, but I never thought that was a fair cop. I'll take a risk if it's got to be taken, but I keep my wits about me. I don't go too far. Chasing the thrill, it's a kind of disease. A person can make a living off the poor folks that got it, but people like you and me can't afford to go catching it ourselves.

But to be honest, kiddo, I'm starting to wonder if maybe you didn't understand me better than I understand you these days.

I want to give you all the choices I can. Have the kid, or don't—well, you made that one already. If I still don't know why you picked what you did, that's on me. Still, having a kid to take care of makes your options after that a little narrower. I guess I know that better than you do. You were the kid, so I wasn't. Not your fault, never your fault, but that's the way the dice rolled.

Some choices that I wish I could give you, I can't. Sometimes when I think about all the choices that you should have had, it gets me so mad that I can hardly think. Maybe that's why I've let this girl—did I mention there's a girl?—make things more complicated than I mean them to be. It's not like being a couple systems away means I worry about you any less, you know. If I didn't have a whole lot of plates to keep spinning, if I couldn't keep my mind off things that way, I might just find myself looking up shuttle schedules back to Bellavu.

And I can't come back yet. Not without having done something to make all of this better for you. I lied to you, kiddo. If I come back now, I lied to you for nothing.

Anyway, I already spent all this money to get here, and you know how I hate waste.

You know me. I don't change my plans once I've invested something in them. I sure as hell don't let a good-looking piece pull me off course. You're always going to be more important, so why bother? I've lost track of the number of might-have-beens that I've watched walk away and never thought twice about it.

But I can't necessarily promise I'm not going to let myself get just a little bit thrill-sick. Just enough to keep that fight-or-flight adrenaline up, keep my head where it should be—that's here, in the moment, on the job— and not where it wants to be, out there, with you.

And that's I guess what I mean about giving myself bad advice.

I didn't know how to end the letter—the letter I shouldn't have talked up, and couldn't send—so I just lay there for a while, staring at the words on the tiny glowing screen.

I do hate waste, just about more than anything. I'd spent an hour at least sitting here talking to my PD and making all those words, and there wasn't a single thing I could do with them. It went against the grain, but I deleted the whole thing.

THE NEXT TWO days spanned that period of the regular cycle poetically known as dark of the moon, when Pluto got itself in between New Monte and the sun. You wouldn't think that would mean much, on a fully powered top-of-the-line satellite—who needed anything as chintzy as real sunlight to keep the streets shining?—but the couple of hours in Pluto's shadow when the megacorps couldn't send or receive memos from off-system was enough to justify a kind of commercial Shabbat. Nobody who was anybody on New Monte would have dreamed of throwing a networking event during dark of the moon. It would have been gauche as all get-out to intrude upon the one chance those poor rich folks had to stay home and collapse on a couch without Seeing or Being Seen by anybody except their own dear mothers.

After everything that had gone down on Lorelei, I was more than looking forward to a few days of peace and quiet to get my head clear and figure out what my next play was going to be. One thing I was sure of: I needed to step up my timeline. Things were already entirely too messy. I was going to have to get Esteban up to scratch before the clock ran out on whatever Alonso and his boss were planning. Before I had a chance to make any more exceptionally stupid decisions, for that matter.

But of course Albert Alonso wasn't going to let me squirm away so fast.

I woke up on the first day of dark of the moon to the busboy ringing in a delivery of expensive hothouse flowers from Esteban, enough to practically overwhelm my hotel room. He wasn't the only one: by midday, a round two dozen of my new highbrow acquaintances had sent me fancy paper cards expressing how sorry they were for my ordeal. I set most of them aside to shoot off polite responses later, but kept one from Louanne Hachi, who in addition to the usual pleasantries wanted to know if I could meet her the next day for a drink at my hotel. It was rare enough for a deb to propose a visit during dark of the moon that I got curious about what she'd have to say.

I sat a little longer over the last message that had come in through the hotel. I didn't feel in the least ready to meet with Albert Alonso yet, but I knew putting him off would only make things worse—and I couldn't deny that dark of the moon was a good time to have a meeting you didn't want other folks to know about. In the end, I wrote back that I'd see him the next day, at the bar at the salon round the corner from the hotel. After all that sand and salt, my hair needed more attention than I could give it on my own. I didn't like the expense, but I'd always known maintaining this position would have a price tag, so I might as well make a virtue of necessity. And if Alonso felt out of place in a fancy beauty parlor, that was his lookout.

I was sipping a martini through a straw when Alonso strode into the salon bar, and immediately tripped over his own feet in the suddenly low grav. I hid a smile behind the cocktail-box. The bar constantly fluctuated through various different gravity settings, so you could check out how your new hairstyle looked in any sort of an atmosphere. Then if you didn't like what you saw, you could storm back into the beauty parlor in a rage and start over again. They had one just like this on every luxe-liner, though of course the drinks on the New Monte version were twice as expensive.

I pretended to be absorbed in my martini while Alonso picked himself up, with some dignity, and bounced over to my table. He skimmed the menu, then eyed my cocktail-box with disfavor. "I suppose it's too much to ask for a plain old glass in this joint?"

"Purely hands-free, Mr. Alonso," I said, and showed off my brand-new nails, still drying.

He raised an eyebrow, but didn't say anything about my choice of patterns—ocean-blue with little white holograph waves rippling down from the tip. If anybody asked, I planned to say that I didn't intend for my misadventures on Lorelei to poison me against the ocean, and this was my way of proving it. It might even have been true.

"Well," said Alonso, pushing the menu aside without ordering, "I'll keep it brief. I'll admit, you gave me a start, there on Lorelei." His voice was neutral. He was giving me plenty of room to drive myself right into a dead end.

I'd given some thought, by now, as to how I should play this. "I guess we had a little bit of a miscommunication," I said, and gave him a smile with a little Evelyn Ojukwu in it—sweet and apologetic, and wanting so *very* much to be helpful. "I know you didn't give me any particular instructions, but I'd kind of got it in my head that you wanted me to keep an eye on her—and then I couldn't even manage it. I lost her in the crowd *that* fast." I snapped my fingers.

"And then you found her again," Alonso remarked.

"Yeah, knocked out on the floor of a bar. I didn't work out that was part of the plan until after that shuttle took off without us." I let just a little indignation seep into my tone. "I know it's my fault for jumping the gun, but you could've warned me that I had a time limit."

"Funny. I thought *you'd* made it pretty clear that you weren't on payroll yet," said Alonso. I waited, frozen; then he gave me one of those kindly smiles, and the tension dissipated. "Well, no harm in taking a little initiative. Seems like you've got to be in pretty good with a certain dame right now, at least, after that heroic rescue."

This was the other thing I'd been worried about. "I couldn't say I'm in good," I said. "Not above half." I felt my hair flatten down as the grav shifted back to full. "All I did was find her after the damage was done, but *she* doesn't know that. All she knows is someone coshed her on the head, and there I was."

"Well, she can't think you're the one that coshed her," said Alonso, mildly enough. "Not unless you're a lot worse at this than I'd have figured."

"I don't think she suspects me of that, exactly," I hedged, "but she's got the wind up, and she's suspicious of all comers at the moment, yours truly included. She's playing it sweet for the press, that's all." I gave him a regretful, I'd-love-to-help-if-I-only-could sort of look. "I hate to say it, Mr. Alonso—the opportunity was a fine one, and I'm sorry to have blown it so fast, but I truly don't think I'll be of much use to you when it comes to Miss Mendez-Yuki."

I thought that was a relatively graceful exit, and was a little dismayed when Albert Alonso only smiled. "Now, don't you sell yourself short," he told me, with a paternal sort of air. He sounded like a schoolteacher telling a bright kid they should pick a more challenging assignment—or my old boss, when I said that I couldn't pick a pocket without someone else helping as distraction. "Nobody said she has to trust you with her security codes. She's only got to take enough of an interest in you that her attention's not elsewhere. From what you say, it certainly sounds like she's done that."

I backtracked hastily. "Sol Mendez-Yuki's no flat, Mr. Alonso. If I try too hard to catch her eye, she'll just ignore—"

I'd forgotten to pay attention to the grav, and found myself nearly slipping off my stool as it dropped again to three-quarters. Albert Alonso, who'd got the rhythm of the changes by now, hooked his feet down in time and anchored his hangdog bulk firmly to the spot. "Now, you're not that naive, Miss Ojukwu," he said, kindly. "A little bit of mystery never made a pretty girl less compelling, nor a little bit of mistrust, neither. You never seen a noir flick? She won't ignore you. You're not the ignorable type."

This was not going entirely as I had planned. "Maybe I don't like the notion of what might happen if she takes too close an interest, either. Or," I added, deciding to play another angle, "if you folks do either, come to that." I looked at him appealingly. If he was going to be paternal, I might as well try my best to remind him of the kind of daughter you wanted to keep out of trouble. "To be honest, Mr. Alonso, this is getting a little too hot for me. I've always been strictly small-time, you know that. Cozying up to socialites is one thing, but sabotaging satellites—that's the kind of thing that scares a girl. It scared me! I might've played this whole thing smarter, if I wasn't so on edge. But it didn't rattle Sol Mendez-Yuki, and that's how I know she's out of my league. Esteban, I can handle."

Alonso looked a study as he was listening to all this, but after I finished up, he shrugged. "Well, I can't say it's what I hoped to hear, but I guess that's how it goes sometimes."

"I'm sorry," I said. "I really am." Maybe I'd played the right card after all—and then again, maybe I hadn't. But I was almost sure, after all those card games in Biraldi, that I was better at reading him than he was at reading me. "I'll stay out of your hair, I promise."

"That would be wisest," agreed Alonso, mildly. "If you foul anything up for us—"

"I won't!" I said hastily, and put my hand to my chest. "Swear on my mother's grave. If I have my druthers, I'll be out of here well before you get to the denouement. Though—speaking of, it'd help if I knew when that was to be."

"Two months and three days," said Alonso, "and if you think you can land the Mendez-Yuki boy in that time, I certainly wish you luck."

"Well, I'd better, hadn't I?" I said glumly. "I'm kind of getting a sort of a sense that if I take too long, there won't be any point to the venture in any case." The trouble with planning to take half a fortune in a broken engagement settlement was that you needed the fortune to still exist by the time you broke the engagement.

"I won't tell you you're wrong," agreed Alonso. From how strong he'd been coming on at the beginning of the interview, I'd expected him to be more vexed about being turned down. I wasn't entirely sure I liked the sudden easy-breezy attitude, but there wasn't much I could say about it. "Well, don't forget to check your PD, Miss Ojukwu. It may happen we'll ask one or two more little favors from you. Don't make that face, girl—it's no bad thing to have my colleagues owing you a favor. That's something you can put in the bank."

"Sure," I said, feeling glummer than before, as he got up to go. I slurped up the dregs from my cocktail-box, hearing the raspberry sound of an empty straw echo loudly in the near-empty bar, and then, before I could stop myself, found myself asking, "Hey, wait a second."

Alonso turned halfway back around and cocked an eyebrow at me.

"The layover on Lorelei—what was that all about, anyway? Why was it so important to stick Sol Mendez-Yuki in a sandcastle for a few hours?"

"What's that matter to you, if you're not working the Sol angle?"

"It matters an awful lot if I want to stay out of it," I said. "I'm no fool. I don't want to get on anybody's bad side by accidentally putting a wrench in a place it doesn't belong."

Alonso shrugged. "The dame was making a deal to offload some stock. She was supposed to seal the business later that day, after your pleasure jaunt. We just made sure she didn't get back before the person she was dealing with left town."

Well, no wonder she'd wanted to reschedule the trip. Still—"Couldn't she just make another deal?"

Alonso managed to give off the general impression of a shit-eating grin without actually moving any muscles in the vicinity of his mouth. "Before her debt comes due? Let's just say the merchandise would be a challenge to offload and leave it at that. See you around, Miss Ojukwu."

He was right; I really should've left it at that. I had plenty of other homework to focus on, like a plan of action for getting Esteban to pop the question without making it seem like I was in any way desperate for a diamond.

But instead, I went home and spent the next few hours tapping into the passenger lists for all the transports that had left New Monte during that crucial period of time when Sol Mendez-Yuki and I had been stuck on the satellite on Lorelei.

I'd had a lot of practice in this kind of research. It's the kind of prep work you always want to do when you're getting ready to hit up a luxe-liner—a little digging to get a list of names, followed up by a lot of cross-referencing into public records and glossy articles. A luxe-liner carries a lot of passengers. It's always good to have an idea in advance about which marks are the ones you want to get to know, and which ones are too hot to handle.

The information I wanted this time ran pretty much along the same lines. It was time-consuming, but by the end of the next day I had a solid shortlist of people that Sol Mendez-Yuki might've been aiming to cut a deal with—and as far as I could see, 'shortlist' was sure the right term. New Monte hadn't done much business in physical goods for at least a generation now, with the exception of a few special cases. There was Jango Salusti, a wholesale entertainment importer who ran the Freenet circuit, and Dov Lieberman, a kosher wine and liquor transporter making the Shabbat stopover, but when I factored in the fact that whatever goods Sol had been hoping to ship had an expiration date on them, there was only one candidate who really stood out as a possibility.

Dr. Wilhelmina Lake was an info smuggler, hauling encrypted corporate data and black-market memory-scans through the ERB transits on solid-state media to sell to the highest bidder while the news was still hot, before it could leak through normal channels. Then again, word on the street was that not all her sources had the opportunity to leak after the data dump took place. Everyone knows memory-tech is still in the R&D stage. There's not a lot of legislation around it yet. Accidents happen.

Still, smuggling secrets certainly rakes in the rocket fuel, so long as you're not particularly squeamish. If Sol Mendez-Yuki was between an airlock and a spacewalk with Alonso's boss, and happened to have seen an opportunity—well, I didn't want to know, and it wasn't my business, and I shouldn't have looked it up to speculate to begin with; and anyway, it wasn't like I was in a position to go holier-than-thou on anybody. I told myself all of that, and it did just about as much good as all the other things I'd been telling myself lately, which was to say not very much at all.

So there went pretty much all that time I'd been planning

to relish to myself during dark of the moon, shot to all hell. I'd meant to write another letter to Jules, a real one to replace the one I hadn't sent, but I didn't do that either. I missed her more than I had words to say, but I didn't feel up to wrapping a bundle of lies and half-truths up in a peppy package.

WHEN IT CAME time to meet Miss Louanne Hachi in the lobby that evening, I welcomed the distraction. She was plenty happy to see me, too. "Miss Ojukwu," she said, and grabbed my hands. "I am here to buy you a drink. I'm here to buy you five drinks. As many drinks as you want, it's on me."

Well, that sounded good to me, but to Evelyn Ojukwu— "Gracious! Five drinks seems an awful lot."

Miss Hachi laughed and let go my hands. "I forgot you were from Kepler. Well, space it out then. But you're a heroine in my PD, and you ought to be treated as one."

I prepared my standard disclaimer. "You mean finding Miss Mendez-Yuki on Lorelei? It wasn't anything, honestly, only I thought Mr. Mendez-Yuki—"

"Oh, of course," said Louanne, "you're dizzy for Stevie. That's what they're all saying." Her tone was maybe a little too studiously neutral. Maybe she was just judging my taste. "Well, when I dropped in, both Mendez-Yuki were singing your praises to the heavens, so it seems like the love gods are smiling on you."

"You saw them?" Miss Hachi was paying a lot of calls this dark of the moon. It seemed like some levels of drama were enough to shake up the routine of even a New Monte deb. "How is Miss Mendez-Yuki recovering?"

Louanne made a face. "The docs want her to rest up and

not use her brain much. *She* says the best way for her not to use her brain is to go to as many parties as possible and quote-unquote network—her words, not mine—instead of doing real work. She'll be all right, thanks to you." A beat. "No thanks at all to Lorelei management. That's the other thing I wanted to talk to you about, above and beyond the praise-singing."

I blinked at her, and she glanced towards the bar. I followed her over to where a human lounged behind a counter cleaning glasses: another way you could tell this was a fancy hotel. She ordered a Vacuum Pressure, and I got a rainbow spritzer, and we took them both over to a booth in the corner.

I waited patiently for Louanne to nibble all the way through her garnish pickle. Finally she said, "It was criminal, you know, how the shuttle took off without you two. You should never have been left there in the first place. There ought to be a suit brought, but for some reason Sol won't bring it."

"I guess she must have her reasons."

"I guess she does," said Louanne, "but if so, she's not telling me."

She took a sip of her drink, and I looked down at mine. I could guess why Sol had decided not to bring the suit. What did it matter exactly which Lorelei employees had been bribed, bullied or blackmailed into trapping us on that satellite? If anyone started digging dirt, she'd get smeared before anyone else. But I couldn't exactly say that to Louanne, and frankly, I didn't see why she thought it was her business anyway—though while I was here, I might as well try to find out. "Miss Hachi—please forgive me, I don't want to tread on a sore topic. Miss St. Clair... implied that you and Sol were once..."

"Oh, it's not delicate," said Louanne. She smiled easily, though it wasn't in her eyes, "I think you pretty much got the idea, didn't you? We thought at one point an arrangement might've been beneficial for both of us, and then, unfortunately, the circumstances changed. You know how it happens." She shrugged one shoulder. "But I told you we've always been friends and we are still. Times like this, I just wish she'd let me help her."

If I were Sol, I wouldn't be inclined to trust the girl who'd dropped me like a hot potato the minute I didn't have a dollar sign attached with too much of my private business either. "Well—it's up to her either way, isn't it? There's not much anyone else can do about it."

"There is something," said Louanne. She set her drink down again, and looked at me. "You got left there too, Miss Ojukwu. If *you* were to act as the plaintiff, then—"

"*Oh,* no. No. I couldn't possibly—" Ruthi Johnson couldn't go upsetting Albert Alonso's affairs, that was for damn sure, but what about Evelyn Ojukwu? "Put myself in the spotlight like that! Certainly not without consulting my parents or our financial advisers—"

"I'd front the money," said Louanne, which did get my attention. I stared at her, and she amended, with barely a hitch, "I mean, not actual money, but I'd front the legal team. My family's got lawyers from here to Hyperion, they'd be thrilled to take on a case like this. Your family wouldn't have to risk a thing."

I raised my eyebrows at that, drawing my shoulders up a little higher. "Pro bono, Miss Hachi? I appreciate the thought, but I assure you, my family's financials are not such that we need to accept charity—"

She raised hers right back. "Miss Ojukwu, I wouldn't dream of insulting you that way!" She smiled at me, and I saw that we were finally coming to the meat of the conversation. "Certainly we'd have to take a reasonable percentage of any settlement, to cover those legal costs. And I can't have any doubts that there will be a significant settlement, can you?"

I had doubts, and plenty of them. The Hachi lawyers might be good, but whether they could stand against the T.O.U.'s was another question altogether—especially when one potential plaintiff was in hock to them up to her ears, and the other one was more or less on their payroll. But of course I couldn't tell her that. "You're a bit of a shark, aren't you, Miss Hachi?" I said, instead, letting a little admiration slip into my tone. Being a shark wasn't a bad thing, among the moneybags of New Monte; this was exactly the kind of polish Evelyn Ojukwu was here to acquire. "Tell me honestly, what is it that's really getting your goat—the fact that Sol suffered out there, or that she's sitting on such a potential pile of cash and not doing anything about it?"

Louanne laughed, as I'd hoped she would. "Both, of course. I don't know what Sol's playing at, but it wouldn't be the first time she's cut off her nose to spite her face." Her voice had old, deep fondness in it, with equally old resentment marbled through it like fudge in ice cream. "If she chooses not to reap the full benefits of her situation, there's no reason you and I shouldn't come to an arrangement instead. It won't hurt her, and might help. Maybe if she sees that we're getting somewhere, she'll realize what she's missing and jump in to get her cut after all."

Unfortunately, all that sounded perfectly sensible—which meant I was going to have to find a reason, and quick. In the meantime, I temporized. "It really sounds like a wonderful opportunity, Miss Hachi. Only, you know how difficult it is when you're so far from your family, it's over a month to Kepler and back, and—" And in three months, I meant to be well out of here, with Esteban's breach-of-contract settlement in hand.

On the other hand, it occurred to me, in three months, I meant to be well out of here—and I was going to need someone to help me draw up a contract for Esteban to breach. Traditionally the template was supplied by the less influential partner, as a charming way to balance inequity among the kind of people who all had standard contract templates ready to go. I'd set aside a small chunk of my luxe-liner cash to spend on legal advice, but if Louanne Hachi was going to go out of her way to offer me a lawyer for free, it really would be spitting in zero-G to turn her down.

"And," I said, looking down demurely, "I should have my family's support if I'm going to launch a lawsuit like this. But of course you're right. It's wildly negligent, what happened to us, and they *ought* to pay." I let indignation fill my voice, and saw Louanne smiling a little. She thought she was the one who'd fired me up—me being too naive to get properly angry on my own behalf—and she liked to see it. "Once dark of the moon's over I'll send them a message letting them know about the situation, and I'll let you know as soon as I hear back. I'm sure that if I explain what happened, they'll be a hundred percent behind us on this."

"That's reasonable," said Louanne. "Though I'll admit, I was hoping we could start the process sooner than three months from now."

"I'd like that too, but—" I drummed my fingers on the table. "Well, how about this? Why don't I start meeting with your lawyer in the meantime, so that when we hear back from my family, the case is all ready to launch? I don't mind putting in the extra prep work." I chewed my bottom lip, then leaned forward, the little provincial confiding in her worldy wise mentor. "To be honest, Miss Hachi, I'd appreciate having the contact information for a lawyer of your recommendation anyway. I don't know anyone close, and—well, it's not that I think I'll have a need of one, but you never know what might happen or when you might need advice on that sort of thing on short notice. *You* understand."

"Sure," said Louanne, as if she did—which was good for me, since I'd pulled the hypothetical need for a traveling deb from Kepler to have all-hours access to an attorney straight out of my rear end. "All right, I'll put you in touch with—hmm, let's make it Galaxy Khan, and you can start figuring out the plan of attack—and if you need any advice, please do ask." She smiled at me again, warmly. "I promise you, Miss Ojukwu, you've made a friend today. Most folks on this satellite wouldn't go a step out of their way for anyone else. It means a lot to see someone disprove the rule like you did on Lorelei."

"Oh," I said, "I'm just as selfish as anybody. I just don't like to see anyone disappointed in me." Which was true enough, in its way. A successful con relies on not disappointing anyone while you're around to see them. By the time the disappointment rolled in, I always made sure to be on my way somewhere else.

CHAPTER 9

ANOTHER INVITATION FROM Esteban arrived at my door practically as soon as the sun reappeared from behind Pluto. Since the invite was for a costumed event just a few hours later that evening, that gave me precious little time to get myself in gear. Under other circumstances, I might have turned him down and leaned a little harder on being hard to get—but the clock was ticking now, and I couldn't afford to turn down opportunities anymore.

"Mr. Mendez-Yuki wishes to express that you look lovely tonight," said Esteban's car, when I slid breathlessly into the backseat.

"And how would he know?" I said.

"That information is unfortunately unavailable."

The bot's tone was as crisp as a piece of toast. I could see how these machines got their reputation for sass. I leaned back against the seat. "So whose car are you when you're at home, huh?"

"This car is the preferred vehicle of Mr. Mendez-Yuki," said the car. "However, he is taking another car tonight so that this vehicle may be free for your usage. Miss Mendez-Yuki is arriving by hovercycle."

Well, of course she was. "I bet her doctor was just thrilled about that," I murmured.

"I have permission to provide appropriate conversational updates on Miss Mendez-Yuki's health," said the bot, "if—"

"No thanks," I said, quickly. The programmed conversational update on Miss Mendez-Yuki's health was likely to be about as informative as a propaganda newsfeed from Vatican. "Why don't you cut the conversation module and get me caught up on the latest from La Ciella, OK?" The famous soprano's arrival on New Monte was providing the excuse for this particular event, so I might as well at least pretend to know what I was talking about when I met her.

"You're looking lovely tonight," Esteban told me, as he came up to meet me in the anteroom. I wondered if he'd forgotten he'd already told his car to tell me the exact same thing. "You like the opera so much, I thought you wouldn't want to miss this." Less romantically, he added, "My father was very insistent I come. It's terribly inconvenient, as my soil-cycle experiments are at a crucial juncture. I regret very much having to leave them unobserved. But since it was unavoidable, I thought the evening would at least be bearable if you were here."

"It was kind of you to think of me," I said, blandly. It was a bad sign that I was starting to get bored with my own lines so soon in the evening.

"I worried that perhaps a party would be too much for you so soon after your ordeal—but honestly, no one would think, to look at you, that you'd undergone such a traumatic event so recently." His look was genuinely admiring. "You look as if you'd never seen a day's trouble in your life."

I gave him a bashful smile, ingenue all over. It *was* a compliment, though not the way he thought it was. I'd put a lot of effort into looking like I'd never seen a day of trouble, and a person deserves to be proud of anything they've worked at. "I often think it's harder to be the person waiting, when someone you care about is in danger. I know what happened on Lorelei was an ordeal for you too, and I think you've held up wonderfully."

"Well, it's not the first time," said Esteban. "My sister can be awfully reckless at times. It's a wonder my hair isn't gray." He touched his sleeked-down black locks, rather self-consciously.

Esteban was vain over his hair, I remembered. Jules used to razz him endlessly about it. "What a pity that would be!" I chirped, and then laughed. "No, I think you would look distinguished with gray hair. Though of course I like it very much as it is—" I broke off, looked away, then glanced up at Esteban shyly through my curled lashes. Evelyn Ojukwu had briefly forgotten that playing hard-to-get was part of the party line, and needed a quick change of subject before she got sappy, so it was perfectly natural for her to ask: "But how *is* your sister? Recovering still?"

"To hear her tell it, she's never felt better," said Esteban, dryly, "and from how *often* she says she's never felt better, I would guess that she's rarely felt worse. Usually during dark of the moon she at least tries to pretend an interest in my work, but I caught her dozing off in the middle of an explanation about micro-climates—"

I made every effort to show off how extremely interested I was in hearing about micro-climates and soil cycles as we approached the Nipawattanapong ballroom. Once we came to the door, Esteban absently offered me his arm.

I took it, anything but absently. Arranging to go to a party together was one thing; people among the New Monte set did that all the time. A public entrance arm-in-arm like this was something else again, and generally tended to mean that the persons involved were going some kind of steady—often down a road that had a canopy and a bouquet at the end of it. I didn't know if Esteban had been thinking about that, or whether he'd just offered me the arm out of gentlemanly instinct while his head was off with the *Eisenia fetida* in his soil samples. Still, even if Esteban didn't notice what he'd just done, there were plenty who would. More than a few eyebrows lifted as the Nipawattanapong's butler-bot ushered us onto the ballroom floor, and I saw several debs leaning over balconies to whisper to their neighbors.

There seemed more balconies on the whole than a person would expect from your standard ballroom— after a month on New Monte, I was starting to consider myself something of an expert on your standard ballroom—and it took me a moment to work out why. There was a central dance floor, sure enough, but instead of your usual circle of folks holding up the walls round the edges while they indulged in nosh and libations, the outer rim of this party was made up of a bunch of independent hovering bits of ballroom floor, like opera boxes. Where an opera box normally had just one gate-and-dock mechanism, though, each of these party-boxes had four—one to each side. The effect was something like one of those geometry puzzle-games they give to kids to teach them how to make shapes: some of the boxes above us were locked into long chains with each other, some set into blocks or wedges, and some floated all by their lonesome, blithe and independent.

Just as I was putting the picture together, the butler-bot toggled a switch, and the piece of floor we'd made our entrance on sailed up to join the others. Instinct told me to grab the railing in front of me for steadiness, but I managed to put the kibosh on instinct in time to give a little gasp and sway back against Esteban instead.

I should've gone with instinct. When it came to steadying a person, Esteban Mendez-Yuki was about as much use as a piece of taffy. Both of us went stumbling into the railing. "Oh! Oh, I'm so sorry, Mr. Mendez-Yuki," I exclaimed, giving him ample time to get back on his own feet while I pointedly failed to recover my balance. I wasn't going to let him miss this cue.

"Are you all right, Miss Ojukwu?" Esteban finally managed to pick up on the hint, and turned to straighten me up. As his hand settled onto the chiffon over my hip, I saw a blush creeping under the color of his face.

"I should've been paying more attention. Though I'm afraid it's your fault really. You were being so interesting—" I glanced up quickly to see if by any chance this was laying it on too thick.

But, as I'd noted before, it seemed hardly possible to lay it on too thick for Esteban Mendez-Yuki. He smiled down at me. "In that case, I'll have to accept the blame. Are you steady now?"

"Yes, I think so. Thank you, sir." I dipped a little curtsy, smiling back at him. He withdrew his hand politely, but I noticed he let his fingers trail over my side before pulling away. It was the kind of contact that in the usual way of things I'd barely notice, but in a ballroom in the closed hothouse atmosphere of New Monte, where every public gesture mattered...

Well, it was one more thing checked off my list, that was all.

"Well," said Esteban. He was still a little flushed. "Would you like a glass of wine, Miss Ojukwu?"

"I would love one," I said. "It looks like the bar's over there. How do you steer this thing, anyway?"

"Obviously, it should be the same way as an opera box," Esteban said. "There must be a control panel somewhere."

He turned to run his hands under the balcony to look for one, just as the platform emitted a beep and announced, "Direction confirmed: Bar." It began chugging slowly around the room, setting a wide course around all the other platforms.

Esteban coughed, and turned back around. "Well," he informed me, unnecessarily, "it seems like it's an AI control system."

I grinned. "You haven't been to a party here before, either?"

Esteban sighed. "Would that were true! I've spent more dull nights here than I can count—since the Nipawattanapong are in business with Father, we're more or less required to put in an appearance at everything they host. But of course they didn't have the place set up this way before. This is all in honor of La Ciella. Designed with the anti-grav opera theme, you know." I leaned back and tried not to look in the least flabbergasted by the notion of anybody having so much wealth that they could add a hundred whirling platforms to their ballroom just for a single night, for the sake of a party theme. "And," he added, as we passed a particularly large and bustling arrangement of platforms, "there's the Nipawattanapong themselves. I suppose we might as well get the obligatory greetings out of the way." He looked significantly less than thrilled by the prospect. "Platform, bring us in over there, if you would."

Personally, I could've stood to grab that drink before

we dove straight into the meet-and-greet, but why bother asking me? I was just the arm candy.

Our platform docked itself onto the end of the line of seven or eight that had gathered around the Nipawattanapong. Where the two platforms locked, the balcony rails swung open, allowing us to mingle with the rest of the little group.

There were nearly twenty people crammed together on the collection of platforms, so it took me a minute to realize that one of them was Sol. She was leaning on the balcony behind the Nipawattanapong, wearing what had to be an approximation of some famous opera costume. It was a tuxedo kind of thing, close-fitting and embroidered in a hundred different colors of shimmering silk thread, with a shirt cut deep down the front to show golden-brown skin that practically glowed.

Nobody could deny that she was looking about a million standard bucks, and I had no doubt she'd worked just as hard at it as I had, too. Part of me wanted to think she'd done it for me, but then, I was sure her Monday through Friday flirts were thinking the same thing. Besides, she hadn't even turned my way yet. She was busy chatting up some woman in a near backless dress. I couldn't much hear what they were saying, but it was obvious from the way Sol did the casual lean-in over that balcony that she was aiming to impress, and from the way the other woman raised her breather to her face that being impressed was plenty fine by her.

Not that it was any of my business, and Esteban was introducing me to the Nipawattanapong now, anyway. I tuned in just in time to hear him say, "Miss Evelyn Ojukwu, who kindly agreed to accompany me tonight."

I dipped as deep a curtsy as I could in my tight trousers

and corseted vest. In the limited time I had, I'd done some very hasty research on anti-grav opera costumes to see what I could assemble out of my existing Evelyn Ojukwu wardrobe that would be on-theme. The result hopefully hinted at the opera breeches role: flowing chiffon neckline, absurdly billowing sleeves, but not a centimeter of give in the embroidered silk emphasizing the curves of my waist and hips and thighs. I had to be a little careful how I moved in the thing. As always, fashion had its price.

One of the Nipawattanapong—there were three of them, two middle-aged women and a slightly younger man, and I'd no idea who was related or married to whom and how—laughed and said, "Esteban, we'd nearly given up hope of you showing up. When we saw Sol arrive without you, An said to me, 'He certainly wouldn't have come by himself, so if his sister didn't drag him here it seems unlikely we'll have the pleasure—'"

"And Su told me," a second Nipawattanapong added, "that you weren't a sulky little boy anymore, and you certainly could make it to a simple reception on your own without being dragged by an adult."

"I'm glad to see I was right. And grateful to the lovely Miss Ojukwu, who surely must be a bigger draw than any of us!"

"Though La Ciella must come a near second. It's such an honor to meet her up close, it's so difficult to get a sense of a person on a stage when you're in a box. Have you met La Ciella yet? Oh, of course you must. My dear!" She reached out and touched the woman that Sol had been flirting with on the shoulder. On cue, the singer turned around and gave us a bright smile.

Personally, if I'd been La Ciella, and I'd just had my

meet-cute with Sol Mendez-Yuki interrupted to make nice with a bowl of oatmeal like Esteban, I wouldn't have exactly been doing cartwheels—on the inside, at least. On the outside, I'd probably have looked a lot like La Ciella did now, assuming the price was right. She and I weren't so different, if it came to it. I spent a lot of time singing for my supper, too.

"This is Esteban Mendez-Yuki, my dear," the eldest Nipawattanapong was saying. "He's due to take over MYCorp in a few years. Of course you know that MYCorp is one of the opera house's most generous friends—"

"Not that our Esteban ever took much of an interest," drawled Sol, from behind La Ciella, "until the lovely Miss Ojukwu started frequenting our box."

La Ciella aimed her brilliant smile in my direction. "It's always a pleasure to meet another connoisseur."

"Oh, I'm no connoisseur," I demurred. "We don't have the anti-grav opera out on Kepler, you know, but now that I'm here, I just can't get enough. Mr. and Miss Mendez-Yuki have been terribly patient with me."

"Oh, well!" said the middle Nipawattanapong, "if you'd like to learn more, Miss Ojukwu, we'd be happy to have you accompany us sometime. We *are* connoisseurs, as you've probably guessed."

"I'd love to visit the opera with you," I said. "I'm very much looking forward to seeing La Ciella perform, as well. I'm sure I'm not the only one, either." I smiled sweetly over at Sol, though as jabs went, it wasn't much of one.

I expected Sol to stay behind and go on flirting with the opera singer, but somehow she ended up on our platform with us when we set off again for drinks. "A cold beer for Sugunya-khun, plum wine for Anyama-khun, and a limonata-ferma for La Ciella," she said conversationally to Esteban. "Help me remember, all right?"

"Does that mean we're expected to ferry you all the way back there as well?" sniffed Esteban. He'd been getting huffier by the minute, all through our little chat with the Nipawattanapong. "As if we hadn't better things to do!"

"Well, not if you don't want to," said Sol. "Though you know your father would probably be happier if it was you plying the Nipawattanapong with drinks, not me. You know how important he thinks—"

"I *know*," snapped Esteban, "but I don't care."

"Suit yourself," said Sol, easily.

This was starting to look like the kind of family affair that I normally try to stay out of. I pressed myself back against the balcony of the platform and tried not to draw attention. Unfortunately for me, Esteban chose that moment to remember I existed. "Miss *Ojukwu*," he said, grabbing onto my arm, "shouldn't have to spend the whole party attending to our *father's*—"

"Your father's."

"*Our* father's whims!" Personally, I thought this was a little rich, given that he'd already told me the only reason he'd asked me to this little affair to begin with was because his father expected him to go. Still, I tried to look supportive. "Perhaps you're happy to arrange your whole life to suit him, perhaps he expects *me* to arrange my whole life to suit him, but it hardly seems fair—"

Sol blew out a long breath. "My life's easier when you and your father are on good terms, is all." She glanced at me, eyebrow raised. "Certainly the last thing I want is to put a wrench in poor Miss Ojukwu's plans for the evening."

"Oh, you couldn't possibly," I said, meek as a mail-bot. Our platform locked in at the bar, and the argument paused briefly while we climbed out onto the broader platform. "Don't worry about me," Sol said to Esteban, once we'd all secured our opera-themed drinks. "You two lovebirds go on and dance. I'll hitch a ride back over on someone else's platform."

"I'll *do* it then, if it means you'll stop nagging me!" said Esteban, switching positions for no reason that I could see, except pure sib contrariness. "Fine. I'll play errand boy. Miss Ojukwu—"

"I don't mind coming—"

"There's no need for you to waste your time on all this," Esteban went on, steamrolling right on over me. "You may as well stay here with Sol and make sure she doesn't—I don't know, hang glide off the railings, or do anything else idiotic."

He stormed off towards the bar, leaving me in exactly the last place I wanted to be: alone in a crowd with Sol Mendez-Yuki. "It's sweet of you to look out for your brother," I said, demure behind my breather. "But that lovely lady's going to be disappointed if you don't turn back up. I'd hate to hold you back."

Sol didn't turn a hair. "La Ciella? Of course it's always an honor to meet an artist, but I'm quite content with the company I'm keeping over here." The once-over she gave me would've set half the girls in the room to blushing. "You're certainly dressed to impress tonight, Miss Ojukwu."

"I could say the same for you," I said—but I kept my tone light, doing my best to pretend I hadn't seen that up-and-down look and didn't understand what it meant. "Well, I'm sure you know how it is. Just a little bit of peril, and everyone's convinced you're nearly at death's door." Then I lowered the breather and gave her a big, bright smile. "But now I'm being a hypocrite. After what you went through on Lorelei, I'd been worrying over you something awful. I'm terribly glad to see how well you look."

"Oh?" Sol's mouth slanted upwards. She leaned in, stretching her arm along the balcony behind me. "I'm glad I'm giving off a good impression so far, Miss Ojukwu, but don't you want to look a little more closely before you give a final assessment?"

Honestly, what I wanted to do was give Sol back as good as she was giving. I kept thinking about how self-satisfied she'd been, going through the motions with me on Lorelei. She deserved a good shake-up. I was sure I could've been the one to make her flush first.

But of course Evelyn Ojukwu couldn't do anything like that, so the only half-satisfying option, I figured, was to stonewall Sol out by just being Evelyn Ojukwu as hard as I possibly could. Evelyn Ojukwu, sweetly concerned for the well-being of her sweetheart's sister Sol, who would never in a million years dream of shoving her back against a wall and pushing all her buttons 'til she forgot her half of the playbook.

Well, if Sol was hoping to trip me up by tempting Ruthi Johnson out to play in public, I was going to have to disappoint her. On the other hand, if I got to see her getting frustrated with the game before I did, that would be a kind of a win, too.

So I laughed gently, and took a step away from her outstretched arm, and further into the crowd, incidentally jostling one or two of the other debs who'd clustered around the bar as I did so. I was putting on a pretty good performance, I thought, and New Monte might as well reap the benefits of it. "What a terrible flirt you are, Miss

Mendez-Yuki! But you needn't joke with me. You must know I asked Mr. Mendez-Yuki all about your health already."

"I'm sure you did," said Sol, eyeing me.

I smiled at her vaguely, took a sip of my plum fizz, and scanned the crowd around us for anyone I knew well enough to draw into the conversation. Just as I spotted Louanne Hachi, Sol said, "To be honest, this crowd is starting to get to me. Would you like to break away a little?" She nodded towards the air over the ballroom, dotted with floating platforms.

I did not want to break away a little, not with her. "Mr. Mendez-Yuki took our platform," I protested. "Anyway, he'll be looking for us here, when he gets back."

"Do you think our hosts would let their guests get stuck that way? There's plenty of platforms on call." Sol snapped her fingers, and, sure enough, I saw an empty bit of floor start making its way over from the edge of the room where it had been parked. "We'll stay close enough to the bar that he'll see us. I'd like a little room to breathe, is all."

"All right," I said, "but I just saw Miss Hachi over there, and maybe she'd like—"

"Oh, I'll catch up with Louanne later. She's got a date tonight." Sol took my arm and steered me around—all very courteously, of course.

"Does she! I'd love to meet the person in question, if—"

"I'll tell you all about them," promised Sol. She stepped out onto the platform, and there wasn't much I could do except step with her. As our little piece of ballroom pulled away from its fellows, she grinned at me and added, in a lower voice, "If you're really all that interested, though it's not like we don't have plenty to talk about already."

I pursed my lips, and then un-pursed them. Now that we were a few feet away from the bar, it wasn't likely that anybody else was going to hear our conversation over the amplified sound of the orchestra below playing Opera's Greatest Hits. However, the people around could still see us, and I didn't intend for anyone to witness anything that would leave them wondering where my interests lay. "If you wanted to talk, you could have called me on my pad. You didn't have to kidnap me in the middle of a party."

"I don't trust my messages not to be bugged," said Sol. "Anyway, you might not have answered." She leaned back against the railing. "Generally I do reasonably well with rejection, but your case is somewhat special."

"You had plenty of time to say anything you wanted to me the other day," I said.

"I don't know what much else you could have to talk to me about now. It's not like anything's changed."

"No?" said Sol. "No new insights from your little chat with Albert Alonso?" Her voice was light, but her gray eyes were dark as the spades on a card.

I should have known. "Speaking of bugged lines," I murmured. I raised up my breather-mask, its chiffon streamers trailing over my arm. "What's a girl got to do to get a little privacy around here?"

"I didn't bug anything," said Sol, "but I did get a little mechanical surveillance to follow you if you went anywhere. Somehow it seemed like it would be worth the investment."

"Fair enough." I suddenly remembered her frank grip, when we'd shaken hands on the beach. I wasn't being sarcastic; it did feel fair to me. She had her weapons, and I had mine, and if she wanted to talk about my chat with Alonso, well, I guessed I could talk about it. "I've got to admit," I said, "I'm a little impressed by how fast you got rid of your brother. How'd you manage it?"

"His father's business is a bit of a sore subject for him. He's not," she added, pointedly, "a particularly materialistic kid. But I'm sure you've picked that up."

"A sore subject for him, but not for you?" I said, widening my eyes a little. "Now, from what I've heard, that surprises me."

"Why's that?"

"Once you've put a lot of work into a thing, you kind of figure on reaping the benefits of it, that's all. From what I hear, that's not in the cards for you. It must sting a little, to watch it all go to someone incompetent—"

"Esteban's not incompetent."

"Well, uninterested, at the very least."

Sol raised her eyebrows, cool once again as any hothouse cucumber. "Miss Ojukwu, this is starting to get dull. You're not the first person to try to set me up against my brother, and I'm sure you will not be the last."

"Oh, I know that. I'd have no more luck trying to pry you Mendez-Yuki apart than I would convincing a high-roller to drop his money into a charity instead of a poker pot." My voice came out a little sharper than I meant. "I guess I just can't help but wonder what sort of frustration would have to be enough to get a nice girl like you to start playing Albert Alonso's kind of hardball. You *are* a nice girl at heart, aren't you, Sol? A chivalrous type? Soft touch with widows and orphans?"

Sol took a sip of her whiskey—she drank it straight—and rolled it around on her tongue for a moment before answering me. "It's been some time since anyone called me a nice girl," she said, after a moment. "But I don't play Alonso's kind of hardball, either. If this is because I had someone follow you around when you'd already admitted you're trying to con us, I don't exactly think that's in the same league as—"

"I'm not crying foul about that," I said. "I've got no complaints about the way you've handled me." I heard the innuendo the moment after I said it, and tried not to grimace as Sol's mouth twitched. Let her think I'd meant it that way. "It's the other deals I'm a little curious about—the ones that were going to raise so much money that Albert Alonso sabotaged a whole space station just to keep you out of them. Your business is your business, of course. It's not my job to pry. I'm just saying, it's an awful lot of fuss over legitimate cargo."

Sol propped one elbow on the balcony and looked at me with some interest. "For a self-proclaimed crook and con artist, Miss Ojukwu, you *are* rather judgmental," she remarked. "What exactly are you accusing me of, here? You might as well come out and say it. It's not as if I've been shy with you."

When she put it like that, there didn't seem much point in being coy. I shrugged and said, "Dr. Wilhelmina Lake left the station while we were on Lorelei. Alonso mentioned your cargo was time-sensitive. The kind of prices she pays for certain sensitive information, you could—"

"Dr. Lake," said Sol, slowly. "Dr. Lake the data smuggler? The brain trafficker?"

"Oh, sure," I said, "if you want to sound like a cheap glossy."

Sol's fingers tightened round her whiskey glass. "You think I'd be working *with* her?"

I'd wanted to shake that cool of hers, and I was starting to get a sense that I'd done it—but now that I had, I wasn't sure I liked it so much. I rested one hand on the balcony and turned to glance out at the dance floor. The girls and boys hopping around down there in their shimmering costumes were heirs to fortunes, every one. Nobody ever made a fortune without stomping on somebody or other, and nobody ever held onto one, either. "I don't know you all that well, Miss Mendez-Yuki," I said, without looking at her, "any more than you know me. Our mutual friends aren't to either of our credit, but you started out with a whole lot of cards that I didn't, and you got yourself in with Alonso anyway. How do I know where you draw your lines? Like I said, it's your business."

Sol was quiet for a long time. "I really cannot fathom," she said, eventually, "why I should want to justify myself to you."

"Then don't. Let it alone. You think what you want of me, and I'll think what I want of you. Isn't it best that way?"

"Maybe it is," said Sol. "And maybe that's how it'll be." She put a hand on my shoulder, right where the ruffle of my shirt settled on my collarbone. I could see she was still mad as anything, but the pressure she put on me to turn back around was gentle all the same.

And maybe that's the reason I did turn, or maybe I turned in spite of that; either way, I met her eyes, and she met mine.

"I'm going out tomorrow around noon, Miss Johnson," she said, softly, "to inspect my useless cargo. Warehouse 319. You're welcome to meet me there, and see for yourself."

"Aren't you worried I'll bring Alonso and his boys?" I inquired. An attempt at a sally, for all the good it did me; she just laughed in my face.

"Why should I care if you do? You must know they

know all about it already."

And of course I did know that—and while it might've been safer for me to stay ignorant, it still burned me to know that all the other players in the game had pieces I didn't, and *she* knew that. For all she knew barely a thing about me, she'd picked that much up right off the bat.

And she knew, too, what her dark eyes and her low voice and her closeness and the touch of her hand on my arm were doing to me. She'd gotten that one pretty much off the bat, too.

We stood like that for a moment, looking at each other, and then she glanced away from me and said, "Well, there's Esteban coming back. I suppose we'd better go back on in to the bar to meet him."

The platform started to shudder in again, back the way we'd come. Sol turned to scan the docking area and left me still standing there, reminding myself over and over that those gray eyes of hers had hooked in a dozen stupider girls, and I didn't have to be one of them just because she gave me a heated look.

But I knew I was going to be stupid. There wasn't anyone there to stop me but myself. And when it came to saving myself from myself, it had already been proven that I just was not reliable.

CHAPTER 10

I SPENT ALL the rest of that night trying to convince myself I wasn't going to go meet Sol the next day. I stayed out as late as I could manage, dancing dull two-steps with Esteban and drinking probably one or two more plum fizzes than was prudent. It was an accidental-on-purpose kind of thing. I told myself I wasn't going anywhere at noon tomorrow, except maybe down to the hotel spa for a prairie oyster and a head massage.

And instead, I found myself—head throbbing, temper foul, but wide awake—heading down at eleven-thirty to catch the shuttle down into New Monte's innards, where they hid the warehouse district.

I hadn't spent a lot of time on the undersides of artificial living environments since we got out from under the South Twenty-five. It took me back some, and not in a way that I liked.

It wasn't that the warehouse district looked seedy or run-down. In fact, in some ways it was cleaner than topside. Like all satellites, New Monte kept up round-the-clock maintenance to make sure nothing slipped out of place that could cause any problems for life-support, and down here the bots didn't have to worry about who they inconvenienced when they went in for a cleanup. Waste got recycled as soon as it was dropped, and the climate was controlled to a fraction of a degree—

centrally controlled, not like in a fancy mansion topside, where the owner could make it snow on a whim so long as the systems made sure it got hot somewhere else to make up for it. The warehouses down here weren't set up for those kind of special effects. There wasn't any point; nobody who owned them wanted to be seen visiting if they could help it. That would look a little too much like an admission that money sometimes involved work.

Still, the more commercial satellites at least had plenty of bot-bustle on the warehouse level. Some of the places I've been, there was so much traffic you could wait half an hour just to cross a hallway. On New Monte, the identical cargo doors were all shut, and the featureless corridors were empty all the way down to their foreshortened horizons. If I wandered down the smaller walkways in between the warehouses, I'd find the stairways that led down to living quarters for the undersiders; if I went down far enough, I might even see some of those people coming and going. Up here, though, in these big wide corridors meant for pallet-trays of goods to parade easily up and down them, the only thing I heard most of the way down was the sound of my own footsteps.

Sol was waiting in front of her warehouse, as she'd said she would be. She saw me coming, but it took her a moment to clock me. I'd left Evelyn Ojukwu's fancy wardrobe up in her fancy hotel room, and I looked a far cry from a deb.

The corner of her mouth tilted up as she took in my baggy tan coveralls, plain rubber breather, and oversized beanie. "Is it Ruthi Johnson today, then?"

I shoved my breather down to hang around my neck. "You got me. All that glamor was an elaborate disguise, but this—" I gestured up and down, "—is for sure the genuine article."

Those coveralls were the kind of thing a janitor or a tech would wear out on a call, with plenty of pockets for stashing away cards and tools. I kept them on hand for whenever I didn't want anyone taking too much note of me. The slouchy hat wasn't a standard part of the outfit, but thanks to all those plum fizzes, I hadn't had time to do anything presentable with my hair except hide it and hope for the best. It's not usually the look I go for on a meet-cute, so it was a good thing this couldn't be one.

"I didn't mean it as an insult," Sol said. She, of course, looked like the cat's usual quality of pajamas—no cape, small mercies, but her fine-tailored professional outfit still screamed that she was someone to be reckoned with.

"Oh, was it a compliment? Because that doesn't say as many nice things about you as you'd probably like to think either." I jerked my head towards the door. "Well? We going in?"

Sol tapped a code into the wall and one of the sections of the large cargo door slid aside, with a weary rumble. She swept her arm out dramatically. "After you."

I stomped straight in, but the only thing behind the first door was an empty holding room with about as much personality as a solitary confinement cell. A bot glimmered to life as we passed through the doorway. "All visitors to Warehouse 319 must be logged—"

"As the owner, I'm waiving the requirement," said Sol, and the bot folded itself obediently up into the wall again.

I lifted an eyebrow. "You don't want to have me logged? What if I conk you on the head and do a cut-and-run with your cargo?"

"Run with this stuff for long and it wouldn't be worth much," said Sol. "If you manage to offload it where I haven't, you'd have earned whatever you can get. We're not going in anyway—it's freezing in there." She reached up and tapped another code into the second wall.

The blank gray surface shimmered into translucence. I stared for a few long moments through the window at the warehouse beyond. Finally, I said, conversationally, "Is this the part where you tell me you brought me here to rub me out?"

Sol's warehouse was a meat locker. There was no more gracious way of putting it. No matter how far back I looked—and there was a fair ways to look back; it was a sizable warehouse—all I could see was thousands of dead birds, wrapped up neatly and stored on hundreds of clean stainless-steel shelves.

I didn't know what I'd been expecting of Sol's self-justification, but it wasn't this. If she was storing data in there, it was a hell of a way to disguise it.

"Kosher duck," said Sol, with a kind of bitter pride.

I said, "Kosher... duck."

"Millions of dollars worth of frozen kosher duck," said Sol, and leaned her head forward to thunk against the now-clear wall between us and the fowl in question. "And it's all stuck here on New Monte where it's not a damn bit of use to anyone."

I looked out again at the sea of dead ducks that was causing Sol Mendez-Yuki such despair. The whole thing was bizarre enough that I'd almost forgotten that my head was throbbing and my eyes were baggy and my hair was pretty much unspeakable. "You want to unpack this for me a little?" I asked, eventually.

"A business venture," said Sol, "gone slightly sour. You must be familiar with those." She lifted her head back up from the glass wall. "There's a shortage back on Earth right now of kosher poultry products. Do you know what kosher is? The trade route through Brukhim-Haboim—"

"Yeah," I said, "I know what kosher is."

"Well, last year, Earth's Western Hemisphere got hit with a bad case of avian cholera. It was obvious there was going to be a shortage for the next two years while the population rebounded—of all kinds of poultry, and I certainly haven't been the only one to jump on that—but transporting products with specialty restrictions between planets is complex, and most major shipping corporations aren't willing to put in the work. They don't see why they should care about the needs of such a small segment of the population, and don't want to put in the effort to do it right." She gave me a sidelong look and a smile, with a flash of her usual insouciance. "I'm not afraid to put in a little effort."

This was a side of Sol I hadn't seen before, and by rights it should've bored me stiff. I've never had any interest in quote-unquote legitimate business—why should I? It's never done me one bit of good, and at least the illegitimate kind's a little more honest about how it works and who it screws over. Still, I found myself imagining her in a boardroom—not that I'd ever been in a boardroom myself, but in the flick version of a boardroom, anyway—swaying a roomful of jaded investors into belief on charisma alone, and for a couple moments I could see the appeal. I could imagine her around a gambling table, too, measuring the odds and weighing her chances, every eye around the table mesmerized by her long fingers as she dared a roll of the dice.

Then she gave a short laugh, and broke the spell. "That's what I thought, anyway. Start my own business, establish a reputation, pay off the last bit of my edu-debt to MYCorps, and leave the company to my brother—a clean cut, no apron strings. But it's all about timing, and it seems that I missed mine."

"Dov Lieberman," I said, remembering suddenly back to the exit manifests I'd looked over for that crucial period when Sol had been trapped with me on Lorelei. "That Earth trader who was docked here the other night. He's got a kosher-certified transport vehicle."

"Insured through MYCorp," said Sol. "Like most transports that pass through this system. He usually works for a fellow called Gavriel Herschel, but they had a falling-out, so he was looking for another company to back him—well, I won't bore you with the details. We worked out a partnership, but he had to get out before dark of the moon, and he won't be coming back through until after my debt's due. And without a sure way to get it off-satellite, no one will even give me back the money I put in for them. Even frozen meat won't last more than a few months after passing through an ERB."

She leaned back against the clear wall, tipping her head upwards to stare at the ceiling. "Every day these carcasses sit here, they're worth less. Soon enough they won't be worth anything at all."

I'd wondered why whoever it was that Sol had been dealing with hadn't simply waited for her to get off Lorelei; now that piece of the puzzle fell into place. Plotting a course through space when you had to park planetside for twenty-four hours out of every seven days to wait out a religious holiday based around old Earth calendars—well, there was a reason the kosher trade routes were limited. If Dov Lieberman had other deliveries to make, waiting out dark of the moon on New Monte might have ended up in setting him back weeks. And he hadn't sunk his own capital into buying up stock.

I looked at her, and I looked at the dead ducks behind her, sitting forlornly on their shelves. There was enough meat in that warehouse, I knew, to feed thousands of people, and I knew nobody on New Monte needed it a bit.

"Why'd you bring me here, Sol?" I said.

Her eyes focused on me again. "What do you mean? I told you why."

"So you're not smuggling memory-scans," I said. "Good for you, but you could've just told me that to start with. I thought for sure you were going to show me a shipload of stranded orphans you were rescuing or something. Maybe the meat-locker tour really pulls in the dames when you're on your A game, but I'm having a hard time figuring out your angle here."

"My angle," Sol echoed. "You want the honest truth?"

"Another day I might take a flattering lie," I said, "but I don't think I'm feeling it today."

"Fair enough." Sol drew in a breath, and then let it out again, slow. "The truth is that I'm close to reaching my frustration point with all this—this *nonsense*."

Somehow, in her mouth, it sounded more like profanity than any of the words I'd have used. For the first time, I really could see in her face just how angry she was under all that cool—angry and scared, too, though she wasn't admitting to that.

"I suppose it's not exactly fair to you," she went on, "to take advantage of the, ah, leverage we hold over each other to use you as a kind of venting board—but it's a stupid situation, and I wanted to complain about it to somebody. That's all." The last thing I was expecting from her was a smile; it caught me all off guard. "Whatever you came to New Monte for, I owe you one for that."

Of all the low blows I'd ever been dealt, that genuine smile of Sol Mendez-Yuki's had to be one of the worst.

"You don't owe me a damn thing," I said. I could hear the roughness in my own voice. I hoped she'd just take it for anger. And I *was* angry, if it came to it. The trouble was that it mostly wasn't Sol I was angry at. "You know I don't mean any good to you and yours."

"You didn't have to come and be talked at, either," said Sol, "and yet here you are."

"Here I am," I echoed, and cursed myself again for it, while she looked at me with that smile like she could see straight through me. For a girl whose life was falling apart all around her, she had a hell of a lot of chutzpah.

I took a breath and pulled myself together. "Well, is that it? Anything else planned on the grand tour for today?"

Sol straightened up from the wall. It clouded up behind her, hiding all those useless little dead ducks from view. "I guess that depends on you, Miss Johnson. I've got another errand to run down here, but you don't have to stick around for it."

"You know anything I do stick around for will most likely get back to Alonso," I said.

I was hoping she'd wise up and kick me back up topside, but she only laughed. "He knows all about it already, just like he knew about this. There's not a lot I've got going on that he *doesn't* know, Miss Johnson. That's what makes you such a relaxing companion, at this time in my life." She was completely back to herself again; the smile she gave me this time was much more the kind I was used to from her, all charm and challenge. "But that's a selfish angle, of course. I'll understand if it turns out you're not enjoying my company as much as I'm enjoying yours."

"And here I thought I was keeping you on your toes," I

muttered, and blew air out from my cheeks. "Well, in for a pace, in for a parsec, I guess. I'm already down here, might as well take the detour if it'll save the fare back." I glanced over at her. "You are gonna pay my fare back up, aren't you?"

"I'll do better than that," said Sol. "I'll give you a lift."

She let us out of the warehouse, and then pressed the button that called her car—or what I figured was going to be her car. I should've known it would be a hovercycle, and not a fancy one, either. I didn't know much from bikes, but I could make a guess it had been expensive to start with. Now it was more beat up than practically any vehicle I'd ever seen.

There was an equally battered leather jacket hung round the handlebars, which she swung round her shoulders over the top of her well-cut shirt. It changed the look of her more than I'd have expected. She still looked too classy for the underlayer, but she didn't scream upper crust anymore, either.

She swung up into the seat and tossed me the helmet that hung over the handlebars. I caught it, and then spun it by the strap. "Aw, Sol, you should've known better than this."

"Hmm?" said Sol, engaged in starting the engine.

"Look alive," I said, and when she looked up, startled, I threw the helmet back at her. "Should've brought two. Didn't you learn from Lorelei?"

I had the satisfaction of seeing her look exasperated. "Miss Johnson, for—"

"I'm not getting on that thing unless you wear your damn helmet," I said. "I'm all right paying the fare back up if it comes to it."

Sol sighed, and got off the hovercycle again. She hung the helmet back up over the handlebars, with exaggerated care, and then turned back to me as the hovercycle slid discreetly back into the parking slot where she'd stowed it. "I don't have two helmets," she said, "so it seems we're walking."

That was all right by me. This day had already been bad enough for my sense of detachment. Hopping up behind Sol on that hovercycle would have brought us entirely too close for comfort—well, comfort was maybe the wrong word; I'm sure I would've been more than comfortable. Too close for safety, that was it, helmet or not.

She led me down one of the main corridors, then opened a side door onto a set of concrete stairs that zigzagged up and down between the levels. I expected her to head towards the surface for whatever stop she had in mind, but she turned the other way; after a moment, I shrugged and followed her. The heels of her well-made boots clacked on the empty concrete steps as we headed down.

"So where are we going, anyway?" I asked, after a little while. The air temperature was getting colder as we went down; it was always either too warm or too cold in the underlayers. It was more important to keep the machines happy down here than the people. "You got a shipload of stranded orphans to show me after all?"

"You seem a bit stuck on those orphans. Do you have parents, Miss Johnson?"

"You got me dead to rights," I said. "I'm just a poor girl all alone in the world. If only I'd had folks to bring me up proper, maybe I wouldn't have come to the straits I'm in."

"All right," said Sol, amiably enough, "you don't have to tell me."

I kept my eyes on the stairs ahead. "I am telling you. We don't have 'em."

Sol said, "Well, there's a difference between us, Miss Johnson. I do."

I thought it was pretty rich of her to talk like there was only *one* difference between us, but I didn't say anything about that.

There weren't all that many humans doing low-level grunt work on New Monte either—no major drone industries, just the basic IT support and emergency techs you needed to service the bots who kept things running smooth on the surface. It was about another twenty minutes' walk down past the warehouse levels before we hit the call centers and housing blocks. We stopped at a door that looked exactly like all the others, with a housing number printed across it in large black letters. Sol tapped in the entry code, and the noise-blocking door slid open to let us in.

It was like stepping from full-grav to zero-G, all at once. The other side was still doors in corridors—everything in an underlayer is always doors in corridors; no such thing as even a dome-sky—but all of these doors practically vibrated with personality, and half of them were wide open while their inhabitants shouted at the folks in the room across the way. The noise of shouting was everywhere. There were too many people crammed together in every housing block for anyone to ever have quiet. It didn't matter how many warehouses were standing empty up above; there were always more chances to make more money on storage space than you could get from letting plebes live in it.

Sol strode through all the chaos like she was used to it. Her haircut was still too expensive for this place, and the trousers under the leather jacket a little too well-tailored, but it wasn't anything obvious and nobody stopped what they were doing to stare at her too hard.

I followed in her wake, feeling cramped-in and stifled, like a chicken shoved back in an egg. I'd been born in a place like this, left, come back, left and come back again. I'd shared a room with a dozen other children and been grateful for it at the time, because at least one of the other kids was Jules. Later I'd shared a room twice as big with only six other kids, Jules included—plus the old man who ran the scam-gang—and spent nights upon nights lying awake trying to figure out how we'd get ourselves out of there. When we started up with the luxe-liner racket, I really thought this time that we'd left the underlayers behind us for good.

But there wasn't a 'we' down here now. Just me, and just for a visit. I hadn't let Jules down yet.

Sol came to a stop in front of a door with a big, gaudy sunflower painted onto it. Unless things were real different here than in the blocks I was used to, that probably meant it was a family apartment, rather than a communal resource, call center, or gang ward. "My little brother painted that," Sol said, and then knocked on the door.

I was still trying to figure out what she meant by that—there was no way in hell she could be talking about Esteban—when the door opened. The teenage girl inside gave her a glance, rolled her eyes, then turned around and yelled, "It's *Sol*!"

Sol headed straight into the room, where two younger boys immediately converged on her. I sidled behind her, and leaned back against the wall next to the door, arms folded across my chest.

The girl was the first to notice me. She looked like she was about fifteen, with sleek black hair like Sol's, wearing the kind of short bright jumper Jules had gravitated towards at that age. It was a few years out of style now, which probably meant secondhand, but she'd accessorized it back to chic. "Hey, Sol! Who's this?"

"That's Miss Johnson," Sol called out. She was laying out envelopes on the table. Each of them looked fat enough that I had to guess they contained a certain amount of cash. "Miss Johnson, say hello."

"Hello," I said obligingly.

"Sol never brought anyone here before," the girl said to me. Her hand was on her hip, and her head cocked, bright and challenging. "Why'd she bring you?"

"Beats me," I said. "I'm just along for the ride."

The girl stared at me hard. I could see her assessing my cheap bland coveralls, my disastrous hair and my lack of makeup—the same as I would have done, in her shoes. Then she rolled her eyes again and turned away, dismissing me as irrelevant.

"Hey, Rosa," Sol said to her, as the boys flopped back down onto the couch where they'd been sitting, "where's your ma?" Her accent had slid over to something that almost sounded right down here—almost, but not quite, the way the leather jacket almost fixed her look.

"Not *my* ma," said Rosa, loudly, as another woman came out of the back room. Unlike the kids, this woman didn't look a thing like Sol. She was pale as my own mother had been, with graying dark hair and greenish eyes. If you squinted, you might say the two younger boys looked something like her around the chin. She was holding an empty freeze-dry packet, and had clearly just been in the middle of making dinner.

If I'd met her up at a deb party, I might have guessed she was fifty. Down here, I'd place my bet a decade younger. "Miss Mendez-Yuki," she said to Sol. "It's good to see you."

"I wish you'd call me Sol, like the kids do," Sol said, with a smile.

It was her usual charming smile, but it was all the wrong kind of charm for this place; I could tell she knew it, and didn't know how to fix it. The woman smiled back, politely.

It was obvious that she'd no intention of doing any such thing. "Sorry to say, your father's under the weather—"

"Or the table," said Rosa, not bothering to mutter.

"It's fine," said Sol. "This is just a quick visit anyway." She hesitated a moment, then asked, "Have you heard from Felix at all?"

The woman's face clouded, and she shook her head, twisting the empty freeze-dry packet in her hands. I recognized the logo on the label. We used to eat the same brand of dirt-cheap soya jerky, manufactured on Mars Ten and shipped all through the galaxy since the earliest days of the Expansion.

"It's fine," Sol said again.

She took a breath, and then pulled out another easy smile. "Well, that's about it, I think. That should set you up for the next semester, but you let me know if you need anything else, all right?"

"Bye, Sol," said the middle boy from the couch, without looking up, but the youngest boy jumped back up from the sofa.

"You're leaving? Didn't you want to see my rocket? Georgi's got it, but—"

"I'll see it next time," Sol said.

"I can run over and get it, just a couple minutes—"

"Next time. I'll call ahead, so you can make sure you have the rocket here. And anything else you want to show me."

"Will you bring your *friend* next time, too?" asked Rosa.

I was pretty sure she was just saying it to see if she could get under Sol's skin. I could sympathize. Sol, of course, only laughed. "Could be. Why, do you want me to?"

182

"Sure," said Rosa. "She'll be impressed by how nice to us all you are, I bet." She turned to me, one eyebrow raised in the kind of over-the-top sneer only a teenager can pull off. "You're impressed, yeah? We're all *so* impressed by Sol."

"Rosa!" said the older woman, sharply, but Rosa wasn't the kind to be so easily shut up.

"It's not so hard to get in on this action. Sol loves her private charity case—"

Honestly, she was adorable. "You're saying that like it should be news to me," I said, kindly. "You better *hope* I don't take her for all she's got. I'm not so much of a philanthropist."

Rosa's mouth snapped shut. While she tried to phrase her comeback, I turned to the boys on the couch and said, "Hey, which one of you painted the sunflower on the door?"

"That wasn't either of us," said the middle kid, and the youngest one said, "That was Felix."

"I wondered. Well, it's not bad." I looked at Sol. "You ready to jet?"

Sol looked back from me to Rosa, then sighed and said, "Sure thing."

Rosa glared daggers at me as we walked out. I just grinned at her. I'd given her plenty of time to put me back in my place; she'd be faster on the draw next time around. It's a bad habit to let yourself get caught tongue-tied. Life's too short for should-have-saids.

We navigated our way back through the housing block in silence. I was thinking about that soya jerky, and the kosher duck shipment over our heads, and the way everyone around that glitzy Mendez-Yuki dinner table had looked at me when I popped that anti-rad pill at the dinner table two weeks ago.

It had been weeks since I'd seen any food that told you clearly where it came from, or how it got there. On the parts of New Monte that people thought of as New Monte, nobody worried about that—or rather, they had people to worry about that for them, so they could pretend they didn't have to. All that money, all that shine, acted like a curtain to block out the plain fact that this living environment couldn't sustain itself without a complex network of trade routes to ferry in the things they needed from settled planets that came by them naturally or could produce them for cheap. Under all the glitz and glamour, New Monte was a real place, a genuine artificial place, just like all the other ships and satellites that I'd grown up on. I'd almost forgotten that, too, til Sol brought me down here.

It wasn't until we got out to the empty main hallway that Sol remarked, "If only you did want to take me for all I had, we'd have an easier time of it."

"If only you had anything left to take," I said. "Those kids are your sob story, right? That's what got you into trouble." When she was silent, I added, "Hey now, you're the one who wanted to get all this stuff off your chest. You said it yourself, you can't hardly care about being embarrassed in front of me."

"That is absolutely not what I said," said Sol, "and I certainly *can* be embarrassed in front of you." She said it with such sincerity that I had to laugh; then she glanced at me, the corners of her mouth turning up. "After all, who doesn't want their mysterious and beautiful nemesis to think well of them?"

"Laying it on thick!" I said. "Come on, you can't distract me that easy. Spit it out, it'll do you good." And then, when she didn't say anything, I went on, "All right, I'll take a guess. Little brother Felix plied you with a song and dance about money he needed for an emergency, then disappeared with the cash?"

Sol's mouth did the same kind of thing it did when I bad-mouthed Esteban. "I'd already been helping Elly— that's my biological father's current spouse, the one we met—with some supplies for the younger kids. Felix didn't want to tell me about the loan he'd taken out at first. He wanted to go to art school, and you know how it is trying to get an education when you're satellite-born. The cost of tuition, plus transport—all right, what's with the face?"

"Sorry," I said. "Just, *art* school?" Talk about your bad returns on investment!

Sol, for once, didn't look like she saw the funny side. "Well, what were his choices down here? New Monte's a playground for the wealthy, there's no opportunities here for anybody else. You can't even get a ship job to work your way planetside, since nobody stops here long enough to hire crew. If you're born down here, it's a call center or a cube farm, or—"

"I'm not saying I don't understand why you wanted to help the kid get planetside," I said. Look at Sol Mendez-Yuki, lecturing me about class privilege! It was cute, in a condescending kind of way. "And art school sounds like fun if you got the starting capital for it. But putting an arm and a leg in hock for something like that, it's the quickest way to end up owned by someone who means you no good. He should've known that."

"You'd think." Sol's grin was mirthless, this time. "I didn't have the cash on hand to pay his way outright. Everything I had was already sunk into that brilliant business venture I just told you about. So I agreed he could sign the loan over to me. I assumed that once I saw the profit, I'd clear him out of it, and he'd pay me back as time went on. And I do pull down a MYCorps salary—it goes more quickly than you'd think, in New Monte, but it's livable. Bailing him out would set me back a few years, but I could manage it."

"Only then little brother disappeared, and you realized that he'd just been a way to get at you." I tilted my head to consider her, as we started up the stairs to the warehouse level. "It's an old trick, only usually the lure is a fabulous return on investment down the line, when the original lender pays you back. Most folks get snared on greed, not guilt."

"Thanks," said Sol, dryly.

"And after all that, you're still dropping off cash presents for the rest of the family, too. Boy, don't you put yourself on a pedestal!"

"For all I know, he really is at art school," Sol said. "You know how hard it can be to keep up with people once they travel. Anyway, the rest of the family's worried over him, too, and they all still need the help." She hesitated, then gave a one-shoulder shrug and turned her face forward towards the stairs. Without looking back at me, she said, "And my sister's right, you know. I do want to impress them."

I wasn't exactly sure what to say to that admission, so I didn't say anything.

The stairs felt longer going up than they did down. I'm fit enough for a couple good dance sets, but I've never been a gym bunny. Sol, of course, didn't show a sign of strain. I wondered what she did for exercise. Fenced, probably, or boxed, or something else equally dramatic. Finally, once the silence had stretched for a while, I huffed, "Well, if you're going to be a mark, at least you're a classy one."

Sol exhaled something that wasn't quite a laugh. "Up on a pedestal, all right." We'd gotten all the way up the stairs before she suddenly added, "The part I really find myself not wanting to tell you is that I never even thought to look for my biological father and his other children until last year."

"So? I've got plenty of blood I never looked up, either." I still had the address of my mother's people back in Brooklyn—a text file I'd transferred over from PD to PD, ever since I was six years old. If worse came to worst, she'd told me once, Jules and I could make our way back to Earth, and if her community was still on dry ground, they might lend the prodigal daughters a hand. Well, worse had near come to worst, plenty of times; all the same, I'd never been tempted to take Jules back there. Why should I undo all that running it had taken Mame so much trouble to do in the first place?

"All right," said Sol, "but you weren't, I'd think, in a position to do much for them anyways. Whereas I was, or had been, and I hadn't. It never occurred to me to do so. And then my mother died, and suddenly it was made clear to me that the place I thought I'd made for myself in my stepfather's world wasn't so much of a place as I'd thought." She'd been walking a half-step in front of me; now she slowed, came to a stop, and turned to face me again. "I didn't go looking until I needed something. That's the part I'm ashamed of, Miss Johnson."

It felt oddly like she was asking my forgiveness for it—or my absolution, or something. "What makes you think I would have done any different in your shoes?" I snapped.

Sol shrugged. "In my shoes? I don't suppose either of us knows what you would've done in them. Those kids, though—I have a feeling that you'd understand what it feels like in their shoes much better than I do."

I snorted. "Seems to *me* you're getting an awful lot from three seconds of conversation." Of course I'd been a bratty kid with a chip on my shoulder at one point, but I sure wasn't the only one. "I don't know a thing about your sibs, except to guess from context that they're most likely hard up. Well, this may come as news to you, but more people in the universe are hard up than not. Just because I've had a few hard times myself doesn't mean I've lived the same life they have. You're pretty hard-up too, come to that. You just don't think of yourself like that because you're not used to it."

Most folks raised in the high life who find themselves suddenly short of the shine don't think of themselves like that—and I'm usually not the one to tell them. It's much more to my advantage if they keep throwing the dough around like they always have done, before they start remembering that they don't really have it to throw. Of course there's a difference between rich-poor and poor-poor; it takes a good while to slide from one to the other, and even then there's plenty of things you get from having grown up in the glittering set that you don't lose with your money. Still, sooner or later, an empty bank account means an empty bank account. Having once had a full one doesn't make you any better than people who never did.

Sol hadn't really gotten to the point of thinking of herself as officially hard-up either, I could tell. She blinked, and then suddenly flashed me a grin, all the confidence that had slipped away in the underlayer suddenly came back in force. "Do you like me better as an honest pauper?"

"Of course not," I said. "We've already established, I'd like you a lot better if you were rolling in simoleons. If you had anything to take—"

I broke off. Sol raised an eyebrow, her voice teasing. "Well? Don't stop there."

I stepped up to her, until we were practically nose-to-nose—or would've been if I'd been wearing heels. I didn't care about that. I didn't care about my messy hair, either, or my dry skin, or the bags under my eyes. Sure, things like that mattered, but you could make anyone forget about them if you sold it hard enough.

"If you had anything to take," I told her, "I'd have you wrapped all the way round my little finger before you knew what hit you, is what."

Sol said, quietly, "The rich have it good."

Her eyes held mine. Her hand drifted up towards my face.

I shoved away, checking her shoulder as I pushed past her. "Yeah," I said, without looking back, "they sure do."

CHAPTER 11

OF COURSE SHE chivalrously paid my fare back up before she got on her hovercycle and rode away. That's the kind of thing I mean about people who can't figure out they're not rich. But Sol grew up on the surface of New Monte, and folks up there throw their dough around as easy as breathing.

The place Esteban took me for dinner a few nights later was about as prime an example of New Monte waste-taste as you could find. It was called the First Star, and a meal there cost about as much as a personal spaceship would run you in some of the further systems.

The place was put together like some kind of carnival ride. You settled yourself into a tiny glass-windowed pod, velvet-cushioned seats all round the edges and a fancy table in the middle, and then made a stately circuit on a track that took you out the First Star's own private airlock into space for the scenic view of Pluto. Booking a reservation at the First Star was committing yourself to a three-hour dining experience, minimum—and you couldn't even take advantage of the setup to get romantic, because every twenty minutes your pod completed a round and rolled back through the kitchen so the chef could slide another bowl of expensive foam onto your plate.

Esteban told me that Sol had recommended it to him.

Let nobody say Sol Mendez-Yuki didn't know how to have her revenge. Esteban himself, he confessed with great candor, wouldn't have the faintest idea where to take somebody for a fancy dinner; generally he thought eating out was a huge waste of time, but of course it was different where I was concerned, and so much more pleasant than spending time with all those awful people at all those shallow parties! I nodded seriously and told him I couldn't agree more.

I can't say a three-hour dinner with Esteban is the slowest time I've ever spent, but it sure was up there as a contender. By the time we were halfway through the seventh course, I was starting to wish that Esteban would start putting up a little resistance to being conned, just so my brain would have something to do with itself. At this point I could do a sympathetic murmur in my sleep.

How *had* Jules borne it all that time? I knew that she hadn't been playing the same doe-eyed debutante I was now. I'd been around for enough of their conversations to hear her hitting him with her usual combination of bubbles and brine, and he'd looked...

Well, if I had to admit it, he'd looked a significant few degrees more starry-eyed than he did now, talking himself up to sweet little Evelyn Ojukwu.

That didn't mean I wasn't doing my job. Esteban liked me plenty. If I'd tried to pull Jules on him, he'd have backed away, and fast. The rebound factor was exactly what made him so easy to reel in. As far as he was concerned, a siren had been just about to crash him hard on the rocks, and he was desperately looking for a nice safe harbor to land in.

I could masquerade as a safe harbor for a few weeks longer, but lord, it was dull work! I'd gotten tetchy with

Sol for assuming that she was meeting the 'real' Ruth Johnson just because I'd gone down there to meet her without my face on. Still, for all that I hated to admit it, she hadn't been entirely wrong. I'd been too much of a mess to watch my mouth down there, and I'd said what I'd thought without worrying two bits about it.

The sad thing was that I'd almost have taken that hangover headache again, as long as it came with the chance to talk straight-up to someone like a human being.

I wasn't cut out for the solitary life, that was the whole trouble. Playing Evelyn Ojukwu all day, every day, with no Jules to talk to at the end of it—well, honesty is a dangerous drug, and I'd never realized how addicted I was until suddenly I had to go cold turkey. Still, no matter how much I was jonesing for a real conversation with somebody, I couldn't make the same mistake Sol had and start thinking about her as a fix. If I did...

"So is tomorrow all right, then?" said Esteban. There was a tense note in his voice, and I pulled myself back to the here and now in a hurry. I couldn't afford to keep my head out in the asteroid belt and miss more context than I already had.

"I suppose I can't think of anything else I'm doing tomorrow," I said cautiously.

"Then it's settled," Esteban said. He nodded, once or twice, very firmly. "My father is—I'm sure he's—well, of course, he'll certainly be delighted to meet you. And I'm sure you'll make—that is to say, I can't imagine he'd think anything other than—"

Easy enough to get the gist of what I'd missed. "I'll try not to be too nervous," I murmured, "and to make a good impression, of course. Of course I wouldn't want your father to think poorly of your choice of—of friends." I made sure to stumble over the word a little.

"My father isn't particularly interested in my friends," said Esteban, with a twist of petulance. "But of course, you're more—I very much *hope* you're more than a friend, Miss Ojukwu. You must know that's why my father's interested in meeting you."

He turned my hand over and kissed my palm. This is a move that can be smooth, if pulled off with panache. Esteban tried it like an over-eager puppy. I dutifully opened my eyes wide and drew in a breath. "I hope," he continued, "I'm making my intentions clear, Miss Ojukwu, and I hope they aren't obnoxious to you." The small smile he wore was a little nervous—but not, really, all *that* nervous. Not anywhere near as nervous as he deserved to be.

Part of me rebelled at making things this easy for him. He shouldn't feel optimistic, not given how far away Jules had been, last time I saw her, from feeling optimistic about anything at all. Still, I reminded myself, the more puffed-up he got with himself now, the harder the fall would be on the flip side. "I suppose I didn't expect things to pick up so fast," I said, slowly, and then dropped my eyes in embarrassment. "But—my goodness, I suppose I didn't expect anything about you, Mr. Mendez-Yuki." A lovebird would have gagged, so sweet and shy was I. "All I wanted from my trip to the Sol system was to see the anti-grav opera, and pick up a little polish, and then go home again without getting myself into trouble, or getting my heart broken. I expected I'd meet a lot of high-flyers out here, and I'd have to keep myself on guard, but you—"

I lifted my eyes back up to Esteban's, and took a moment to silently thank all the people in my life who'd taught me how to talk to a mark without letting any irony sneak into my voice. "You're not going to break my heart, are you? You seem like a—like a very genuine person, and if you did think you were likely to break my heart, I'd appreciate a little warning first, is all."

"I never would, Miss Ojukwu," Esteban assured me. "I think honesty is the *most* important thing." He liked being described as genuine, I could tell. Self-aggrandizing virtue shone out of every inch of his face—and I didn't feel an iota of guilt, not one little bit, because I knew that his honesty was as much of a con as mine was. He didn't know it himself, but I did. "I would never present myself under false pretenses to... well, to anyone, I hope, but especially not to you. I would never, ever want you to be hurt that way."

"Oh!" I said.

Even Esteban couldn't miss the fact that the scene and the moment were clearly right at this point for him to lay one on me. Unfortunately, the layout of the dining pod was all wrong. I don't know what the interior designers of the First Star were doing with themselves; if you're planning a romantic dining experience, this is the kind of thing you ought to think about. It took everything I had to pretend that it was perfectly natural for me to sit limpidly gazing at him while he slid himself awkwardly round the velvet seat cushions, knocked a set of cocktail spears off the table, paused for an agonizing moment to decide he didn't need to retrieve them, and continued his slow advance. Then, after all that, I had to let out a little startled gasp when he took me in his arms, when anybody with two brain cells in her head to rub together would either have been halfway to him already, or—more likely —halfway round the other side and ready to take the first exit. But of course I'd committed to the clueless naïf from Kepler, and now I had to keep selling it.

Anyway, he finally managed to plant his mouth on mine. I was in the process of going tactically limp when we were interrupted by a bright light and a small but polite cough. The pod had just slid back into the kitchen, and the insulated glass shell was peeling back so the chef could bring us the eighth course of this interminable meal.

Esteban sprang away from me. I lifted my hand to cover my face in simulated profound embarrassment, which gave me a chance to cover my laughter. The chef maintained an admirable poker face as she whisked away the tiny half-eaten wasabi soufflé and replaced it with an equally minuscule cantaloupe savory.

We settled back into our places on the opposite sides of the pod, though Esteban anxiously took my hand across the table after the shell closed. I let him keep it, as a sign that his attentions had not been unwelcome, though it made it real difficult to eat the cantaloupe savory—he'd used his left hand, and hadn't noticed that he had hold of my right. Bitter melon isn't my favorite, but I could've used it to get the taste of Esteban out of my mouth.

I was braced for him to try for another go on the way home, but although he sent me a couple of sidelong glances, he stayed politely on his side of the car. I think he felt my delicate sensibilities had been strained enough for one day. I didn't love the role of Evelyn Ojukwu, but I couldn't deny she had her upsides.

He did give me another palm-kiss before he let me out, and I gave his hand a gentle squeeze in return. "Just be yourself tomorrow, Miss Ojukwu," he told me. He'd managed to plaster a veneer of condescending macho confidence over his usual filial petulance. People become insufferable when they think they're irresistible, men especially. "Nobody could ask for anything more of you."

"Oh, I hope so," I cried earnestly, and tripped flittingly on into the hotel.

I managed to hold onto the flittiness just until I got up to my hotel room, and then fell into the closest chair, feeling about a million years old.

I WANTED TO get Evelyn Ojukwu off my skin that night. I took a long steam bath, and found my hands lingering over all my own scars as I washed them: the splatter-burn, that gunshot graze, the tattoo I couldn't see on myself but never could forget was there. Even Esteban probably wouldn't be oblivious enough to miss that one. He wouldn't have recognized the specific gang insignia any more than his sister had, but no deb would get herself low-quality ink like that. I could have gotten it removed, but I didn't want to forget the time we'd spent in the South Twenty-five any more than I wanted to be back there—and anyway, having that sign on me had come in useful more than once, when I needed to have an in with the kind of people who would recognize it. Still, it made for another good reason to be grateful that demure was the name of the game.

I'd been prepared to let Esteban get a certain degree of handsy, if it seemed like it was necessary for the overall success of the plan. Now it seemed like I'd be able to manage with a couple of semi-passionate clinches— though I couldn't say I was much looking forward to those either. I'd certainly kissed worse, but I'd had a lot more fun doing it. I sank down lower in the tub, and wished it wasn't too soon to wash my hair again.

I would've liked to curl up in a pair of old flannel

pajamas, but all I had in my closet was Evelyn Ojukwu's little baby-doll nighties. I took the hotel bathrobe instead, and wrapped myself up in it while I checked my PD. Most of it was the usual kind of junk messages—coupons, special offers, and weeks-old political updates from planets halfway across the galaxy. An invitation to a party at Louanne Hachi's, which I made a note to accept, and an invitation from the Nipawattanapong to go see the opera with them, which, remembering Esteban's irritability around them, I made a note to turn down. Midway through the list of nonsense, there was a message from Sol. It looked like she'd forwarded it through the hotel, at the time when Esteban and I would've been at dinner.

The message read, *Hope you enjoyed your evening out. Rumor indicates you'll be dropping by tomorrow. I thought I'd let you know that I don't plan to make myself scarce.*

I bit back a grin—then remembered that I was alone, and let myself laugh aloud. Trust Sol to politely warn me that she was planning an attack!

I was trying to figure out how to respond when my PD beeped another notification. All the messages from off-planet that had gotten held up during the last dark of the moon had finally trickled their way through the data filters—and as soon as I looked at the header, all thoughts of Sol dropped straight out of my head.

Ruthi,

I was figuring I'd wait to write you until I heard from you and had something to write answers to, but I forgot how stupid long data takes to send through the ERBs. And I know you'll be stressing, so then I figured I'd write after all. I just wish I had more to say.

I guess I can just go ahead and answer the questions I can imagine you've asked in whatever letter you sent me. I've been going in for my regular checkups. I've been eating. I've been leaving the house once a day. STOP NAGGING. They say the kid's healthy. Just six weeks until they slice her out of me and pop her into the incubation tank, and then another five months before they uncork her for real.

I'm healthy too, I guess. Bellavu's a bore, but I'm keeping myself busy. I've been helping Vin Messina and his pals out with a wheat cleanse—

I put down the PD for a moment to swear. I'd told and *told* Jules to keep out of obviously illegal scams while I was gone.

—and have made a few extra simoleons that way, so you're not the only one who's working on feathering the nest. Don't get your hackles up. What did you expect me to do, sit on my hands for months? You're a hell of a hypocrite, you know. I may not be at my best right now, but I'm not dead. *And you know I'm being careful. Probably more careful than you.*

I don't know what else to say. I'm not mad at you. At least not most of the time. Sometimes, a little, when I think how your face went when I told you I wanted to keep her. Which isn't fair. You can't help your face (HAH). Anyway I'll be over it by the time you get back. I'm just not much fun to be around right now. And I don't know how to stop you worrying. I'M FINE.

So you'd better be all right too. Don't pull any of your stunts. I mean it. Maybe ask yourself once or

twice what I would do. You ever done that before?
I guess I'll see you when I see you.
Love,
Julia

I didn't know what I'd expected from Jules' letter. Given how flat she'd been when I left, I guess I hadn't really thought it was guaranteed to be a mood-booster. Still, at bare minimum, I guess I'd figured that I'd get something out of hearing her voice in my head. I guess I'd thought it would make me feel more like myself.

I could hear Jules' voice when I read the letter, sure—but even in my head, it didn't sound the same as it had when I left.

I hadn't seen her in more than two months. She was farther away from me than she'd ever been. The plain text of the letter, bare of all her usual effects and emotes, just underscored the fact that back there on Bellavu she was going through something I wasn't part of. She'd be a different person when I came back. I'd be a different person when I got back to her, too, and I didn't know who that person was.

Kiddo,
When my hair starts going gray, my rinses are coming out of your half of the take. If I come back and find you and the sprog in a detention cell or deported, we are having some words. Can't you sit tight for a few months? When I told you to keep your head down, I guess all that nodding you gave me was just for show?

You can guess what letter I just read. God damn it, Jules, I am having a hard enough time here without going into a panic that you're gonna get yourself in

bad trouble back there.
 Love,
 Ruthi

I sent the message on before I could think better of it, and then stared at the empty screen, feeling rotten. I'd forgotten to sign it world's best sister, too. Then again, so had she.

Maybe I shouldn't have come, after all. Maybe it had all been a mistake from the start. Sitting on my hands was the one thing in the world I was just about worst at—Jules had been right about that—and it had driven me wild to sit there on Bellavu, after all the work I'd put in to get us there in the first place, and watch her brood on the failure of her great romance. If I tried to cheer her up, I got snapped at. If I said anything about Esteban, all she'd say was, 'I know you never liked him anyway.' It wasn't even true; until he broke her heart, I hadn't had much of an opinion on him one way or the other. What I didn't like was this idea she'd had that she was going to run off with this fellow she barely knew and somehow expect a happy-ever-after to materialize. But of course I couldn't say *that* either, or she'd think I was I-told-you-so-ing. So I tiptoed around her, watching my mouth even more carefully than I did now that I was Evelyn Ojukwu, and hating every minute of it. It didn't even help; the more I bit my tongue, the more she decided I was judging her with my eyes, and took that as a reason to sulk off anyway.

And then, two months in—settled in on Bellavu, lining up doctor's appointments and balancing budgets, trying to save enough money to sink back into the next luxe-liner trip while wondering how the hell we were even going to pull that off with an infant in tow—I'd gotten that fuck-off letter from Esteban's lawyers.

I'd been about ready to explode. But I couldn't explode at Jules; she hadn't even known I'd written the Mendez-Yuki to begin with. So instead I let my anger simmer, and after a while all that simmering anger had boiled down into a plan, the first real plan I'd had in months. A plan that would let me do *something*. At that point, doing anything felt better than doing nothing.

And I'd thought, after all, it would be worth it, to bring Jules back the kind of future she'd been imagining. To prove to her that I could grab a happily-ever-after for her, with or without a chump like Esteban Mendez-Yuki.

The risks hadn't been real to me, then. They sure felt real to me now. Bellavu's benefits came with costs, same as anywhere else; all that free resort healthcare was reserved for respectable tourists, and they weren't shy about deciding when someone wasn't respectable enough anymore. If anything happened to Jules, how long would it be before I even knew anything about it? If she got kicked off-moon, how long would it be before I could find her again? And if we forgot how to be who we were together—the Johnson girls, Jules and Ruthi, world's best sisters for any given world—how long would it be, even after I got back, before we learned it again?

But the time to worry about all that would've been before I came. I'd gone too far to turn back without anything to show for it. I was committed now, just as much as I had been when I stepped into that bar, back on Lorelei.

That had been a hell of a stupid move, too—but I guess I hadn't really regretted that so much in the end, when all was said and done.

For the first time, it made me feel a little better to admit to myself that I really didn't feel too bad about what had gone down on Lorelei. I didn't regret that Sol Mendez-Yuki knew my real name. At least somebody here did. I didn't regret showing her all my cards. She'd turned around and showed me hers right back, and it seemed like she didn't regret that either. She had a smooth veneer, but I was more or less sure the rough edges she'd shown me down in the underside had been genuine. It seemed like we had one thing in common, after all: the relief of knowing there wasn't anything more worth bothering to hide. Who would have thought a person could get such a kick out of mutually assured destruction?

I didn't even regret rolling around with her on a beach. I'd almost certainly never touch her again, but at least I didn't think she was going to forget me in a hurry.

I looked back down at my blank *message sent* screen, and then I thumbed back to Sol's message about seeing me the next day, the one I'd just been reading before Jules' letter came through.

I sent Sol a message back that said, *Looking forward to it,* and added a flirty little wink image, just to see if I could get her head in a twist.

Then I rolled over and fell asleep. It certainly was easier than it would've been, if I'd tried right after reading the letter from Jules. Of course, what I dreamed—but I didn't have time, when I woke flushed the next morning, to linger on what I'd dreamed. I had a meet-and-greet to get ready for.

CHAPTER 12

I'D READ PLENTY of articles in the glossies on what to wear when first meeting your significant other's financial head of household. It was more or less along the lines of dressing for a job interview: sleeves and hemlines at least two inches longer than the minimum standard, buttons all buttoned and ties all tied, and select a slim but functional breather to show that you were serious-minded.

The one I picked out had a dignified pinstripe pattern that matched my tailored pantsuit. It was a softer, flirtier pantsuit than the clean-cut ones I generally saw Sol wearing around—more girlish than elegant, with short bell sleeves, flared jacket waist, and puffs round the cuffs of the trousers—but I could've worn it to the boardroom and not raised any eyebrows. A crisply expensive mulberry-silk belt, evening gloves and a matching hair bandeau completed the wealthy-professional look. I might as well have worn a sign announcing *Miss Evelyn Ojukwu Has Been Trained From Childhood To Be An Asset To Any Enterprise*. Both Sol and Esteban were waiting for me in the lobby of the Mendez-Yuki mansion. Esteban, for once, looked like he might have put actual effort into his consciously respectable cardigan. Sol looked like she'd just gotten out of a meeting, and, as usual, could've worn the same exact suit to a party that night and still turned heads. Esteban opened his mouth, but

Sol got in first. "I was so glad to hear Esteban had invited you," she said, and took my hand warmly between two of hers. She grinned at me. Next to her, Esteban started to frown. "Honestly, given what you did for me on Lorelei, I'm a little ashamed he beat me to it."

"Well," I said, smiling, "it isn't a competition." I slipped my fingers out of hers, and turned to Esteban.

His ruffled feathers smoothed right down, and he smiled back at me. "We have lunch laid out in the other room," he informed me. "My father is waiting there. He prefers not to stand, these days."

"We shouldn't keep him waiting, then," I said, and took his arm as we progressed down the hall.

I'd been expecting we'd eat somewhere grandiose enough for a formal banquet, but the room we ended up in was exactly the right size for four people to talk comfortably without feeling cramped. Ten Esteban Mateo Mendez-Yuki Senior sat at the far side of the table. He started to stand when we got in, but all three of us immediately shouted, "Please, don't!" You couldn't have said anything else; he looked practically as old as God.

I hadn't been expecting it, to be honest. In my head, from the way Esteban Junior talked, I'd built up a sort of picture of the Mendez-Yuki patriarch as a square-jawed, stern fellow in a broad-shouldered suit—an executive type straight out of central casting, trailed everywhere by a cabal of yes-men on strings. Maybe that was how he'd been once upon a time, but it was hard to believe this man had dominated anything more recently than a decade ago. I could easily see why all of New Monte had been expecting him to kick the bucket well before his wife. To be honest, I was a little afraid he might keel over in the middle of lunch.

He gave me a perfectly sweet smile, and croaked,

"Welcome, Miss Ojukwu."

"It's an honor, sir," I said, and pulled my arm out of Esteban's to sweep a curtsy.

"It's *my* honor to present her, Father," said Esteban, hastily, and ushered me to my seat on his father's left side before taking the chair opposite. That left Sol at the foot of the table. She crossed one leg over the other and lounged back so far that the chair was balanced on its back two legs.

"My son—" Mateo Mendez-Yuki coughed, and then went on coughing for a bit, while the human butler materialized next to him with a handkerchief, and I sat frozen to my seat in case something I did set him off worse. Finally he cleared his throat of whatever had been stuck in it, and started again. "My son speaks very highly of you. And of course we all owe you a debt of gratitude, for your service to Sol."

"Your children have both been tremendously kind to a stranger," I murmured, and then had a moment of second-guessing whether I'd offended anybody by calling them both his children. But nobody reacted and so I added the rest of my planned little speech: "I feel I'm the one who owes your family a debt, for welcoming me so warmly to New Monte."

He made a small dismissive gesture with large bony hands. "I feel sure you would have fallen on your feet, Miss Ojukwu."

I wasn't sure if that was a compliment or not. "I'm glad I didn't have to," I said.

"Oh, it's been our pleasure," said Sol, sparkling, and Esteban, once again lagging behind, hastily jumped in to agree.

Then came all the questions about my family, while the

waiter-bots came round and delicately sprinkled meteor salt into our lobster soup. Esteban had half-warned me a grilling might be in the offing, and I was glad to have answers ready when he started asking about which wave of colonization my family had arrived in, and whether our investors still had any Earth-based portfolios. Still, while he clearly had a solid sense of the diamond business and the Kepler economy, I had a kind of a sense he was playing softball with me—or at least, I did until I realized that there were one or two questions he asked me twice. The second time he did it, I saw Sol grimace. Esteban looked down at his soup.

Neither Sol nor Esteban contributed much in the way of conversation. I'd been expecting a barrage of barbs from Sol, but most of her attention was focused on her stepfather. She let him steer the conversation, but every time a pause threatened to go on a little too long or a wheezing session halted him in his tracks, she'd glide in with something to take the pressure off. I guess that's the kind of skill that comes in handy in a business setting, but I wasn't used to seeing her so self-effacing, and I wasn't at all sure I liked it. I'd almost rather have had the barbs.

As for Esteban, I don't know that I'd ever heard him so quiet. Contrarily, I was inclined to think worse of him for it; there was Sol doing all the heavy lifting of keeping the conversation afloat, and Esteban not lifting a finger to help, despite the fact that he'd set the whole thing up. He knew he wasn't coming off well, either. Every time Sol jumped in with the assist, he'd scowl down into his teacup and take another sulky sip.

Well, if it was anyone's job to buck up Esteban's ego, it was Evelyn Ojukwu's. When Mateo Mendez-Yuki asked me yet another leading question about underwater diamond mines, I dredged my memory for as much as I could remember about Esteban's dirt research and tried to kick off a rousing conversation about the possibilities of implementing Earth-style farming on Kepler's limited artificial landmasses. It was a no-go; as soon as I mentioned the word 'soil,' he cut me off. "It's kind of you to show an interest in my son's little hobby, Miss Ojukwu, but let's not get off track here. Several of my clients invest in the Kepler mines, but I'm starting to hear concerns that some of the richest veins may be played out—"

Another coughing fit interrupted him. Sol glanced at Esteban, and stepped in. "To my mind, Miss Ojukwu, it's an interesting question. The first wave of planetary settlers did always intend to be self-sustaining, and never foresaw the complex galactic trade routes that we maintain today— in fact, one could argue that the K2 diamond trade played a significant role in making those trade routes what they are. Could your Kepler rebuild itself around Earth-style farming after all, if the diamond mines do play out? Esteban, do you think—"

"They'll never see a *profit* from that," his father interrupted testily.

Esteban hadn't said anything, and from the sourness in his face, it didn't look like he'd appreciated the assist, either—though from all I could tell, Sol had meant it kindly. After that, I guessed it didn't surprise me so much that Esteban stayed quiet. If he couldn't talk about anything he wanted to talk about, he was the sort who wouldn't think there was much point to talking at all.

If it were me in his shoes, I thought I would have taken the opening Sol gave me, and to hell with the old man. Age might earn you some right to rudeness, but the fellow was practically a mummy and in no shape to win a battle of wills. But then, I guess it's easy to say what I would do. I don't have too many memories of getting my ego trampled on by either one of my folks. Both of them had cashed in their chips before they had much of a chance.

I hoped Jules had never felt that dampened by me.

Anyway, I let myself cool a little towards Mendez-Yuki Senior after that. The real Evelyn Ojukwu would've probably been dying for family approval, but for my purposes, it was more or less incidental. Building an ongoing relationship with the in-laws wasn't exactly a going concern here. The important thing was that Esteban believed I was on his side.

On the other hand, being out-and-out rude to a respected senior citizen wasn't on the agenda either. It was possible that a little resistance might stiffen Esteban's spine, but I didn't honestly trust him to have enough of a spine to stiffen, and anyway, Esteban wasn't much good to me disowned. So I gave my short, polite answers, and every so often cast an anxious glance at Esteban, but made a point of not doing any more to roll the conversation along than I absolutely had to.

That left Sol to pick up the slack, and it didn't seem like she had too much trouble with it. She was easy with the old man—easier than I'd expected, given how hard she'd been struggling to get away from him and MYCorps. Of course if you listened hard, you could see how she was managing him; it was a professional face she was wearing. A secretary might have looked the same.

I wondered how many people had ever seen the raw frustration she'd shown to me, down there in the kosher duck warehouse. I'd be willing to bet you could count the number on one hand, and none of them were in this house.

We were about down to dessert when the butler appeared by the doorway, and coughed politely. "Excuse me, sir, but

M. Villereal is on the line."

The old man scowled. "I thought I told those fools no disturbances," he snapped—or would have snapped, if he'd had enough wind in his lungs for it.

"I'm told it's extremely urgent, sir. May I bring the phone in?"

"Villereal—"

"The Aifa merger that Villereal's working on is in a critical state right now," said Sol smoothly. She'd gotten in there almost before there was a pause, but I'd seen the lines of confusion starting to draw down on the old man's face before Sol saved him the embarrassment of asking. "If the issues with Hoight-Chulanot aren't resolved, it could set us back months."

"That idiot Villereal," wheezed Mendez-Yuki Mateo, "never did have any initiative." He sounded pleased to have dredged up an opinion on the matter. "Well, you know what we're willing to offer, Sol—you may as well go handle it. Send me the report later. Oh," he added, as an afterthought, "send a copy to your brother, too."

Sol shot a glance at me, and then at Esteban. I could see she didn't want to go, but there also wasn't a lot she could do about it. She rose and gave me a bow. "Miss Ojukwu, I apologize—"

"Oh, please," I said, "I understand perfectly. You have responsibilities."

"Formally," muttered Esteban, "she doesn't. Not over mergers and acquisitions."

"Well, she knows what to do," said his father, testily, "unlike some I could mention, so she may as well do it."

"Esteban," said Sol, "if you'll trust us to entertain Miss Ojukwu while you're gone, you can go meet with M. Villereal—I'm sure it won't take more than half an hour."

But Esteban had already ruffled his feathers up in the opposite direction. "That would be unconscionably rude," he snapped. "In fact, I think you're both being impossibly rude to our guest. It's simply not possible that it could wait until later this evening, I suppose!"

I saw from Sol's face that it could not. She looked at Esteban, bit back a sigh, and then gave me another bow before striding off after the butler, the tails of her suit jacket flying behind her.

"I don't mind," I said to Esteban. "Really, I don't." In fact, I should've been thrilled. Whatever plans Sol had been brewing up to interfere with my meet-and-greet, she hardly could do it from deep in the middle of a business crisis.

Still, with Sol gone and Esteban even sulkier than before, I was awfully glad that all we had left of that interminable meal was dessert.

The butler's reappearance a half hour later finally released us. "Ah," said Mateo Mendez-Yuki. "That's my signal, I'm afraid. Miss Ojukwu, you'll forgive me not standing to say goodbye."

I rose from my chair and sidestepped away from the table so I could dip as much of a curtsy as was possible in my suit trousers. "Thank you very much for receiving me, sir."

"It's been a pleasure." The Mendez-Yuki held out his hand; I extended mine, and he gave it a perfunctory kiss. "I always try to encourage Esteban in his good decisions, on the occasions when he makes them." He was wheezing heavily now, forcing himself to get the last of the words through. "Esteban, I suppose you may consider yourself encouraged."

So I guess he hadn't even noticed me being frosty, after all.

Then the butler wheeled him away, which left me and Esteban, looking at each other across the table.

"He has a medicine regime to take at certain times of the day," Esteban said, after a moment. "It's very strict."

"I hope his health is not so poor as all that," I answered, insipidly.

"He does well for his age, but…" Esteban shrugged, and pushed back his chair. "Since you're here, will you take a tour of the house, Miss Ojukwu?"

I said that I would be delighted.

"I try not to get angry with him," Esteban said, as we picked our way around the rim of the indoor heated waterfall. "It seems fruitless now, when there's no chance of him changing. He's never seen the importance of anything outside his own sphere, but who could expect him to?"

"Mm," I said.

"It's stifling," he complained, while we wandered under a hanging rose garden that could've been romantic, at the right time and with the right person. "Everything I value, genuine intellectual achievement, the increase of scientific knowledge for the benefit of society—it's all childish foolishness to him. A waste of time that could be better spent elsewhere, on such petty things as profit, or social standing. Those are the only things that really matter to *him*. The accounts, and the family name. I find it hard to think of anything less important."

As someone who'd never had much of the one or the other, I found it hard to dismiss their importance altogether. But Esteban certainly wasn't asking for my opinion. "Hm," I said.

"He wishes I were my sister, and he resents us both for it," he told me, as we ambled through the ballroom where I'd made my grand entrance, my first night on New Monte. "He takes it for granted that I've got no choice but to grow up and become him, eventually—or become her, I suppose.

The weight of his expectations is stifling beyond words. I suppose he just can't imagine any other outcome."

"Can *you*?" I said.

"What?"

The question had slipped out before I could stop it; I was just so tired of this endless conversation! "I was just wondering," I said, "because—well, you're so obviously unhappy, and I hate to see it. Couldn't you just leave?"

Esteban stared out across the empty ballroom. We weren't just where he'd been when he first spotted me and mistook me for Jules, but I suppose it was close enough for sentimentality. "I might have. I meant to. I'd thought I might apply for a research position. There was—a person," he said, with a sidelong glance at me, "who encouraged me to such a course. I was ready to throw everything away, to live as an ordinary scholar, away from all this decadence." He waved his hand vaguely at the mirrors and the shine and the floating chandelier, dimly reflecting the half-lights from the floor that had switched on to illuminate our path when we walked in.

I had to wonder what exactly qualified as 'ordinary' and 'away from decadence,' if you were Esteban Mendez-Yuki. I couldn't even remember now what names and reputations Jules and I had been traveling under, but we certainly hadn't been presenting as impoverished by any means. The honest poor didn't ride luxe-liners, nor get dealt into card games with the glittering set.

"But then," Esteban went on, "I discovered that— that the person I'm speaking of—had been deceiving me, all the time I'd known her." 'Discovered,' like he'd Sherlock Holmesed it all on his own. "Mercenary qualities, I regret to say, aren't restricted to people like my father. I suppose there's no way to know what a person's really like, no matter how they may seem."

"That's true," I murmured, and I thought back to Jules, her eyes shining, swinging round my lintel on the liner to tell me that Esteban had proposed to her.

"Poor kid!" I'd said, or something to that effect. I couldn't remember what language we'd been talking in. Probably at least half Yiddish; it made conversations a little more private, and avoided the risk of accidentally calling a bot's attention with particular words or phrases in English or Espero Trade. "You'll be waiting to let him down until we get to Bellavu, right?"

"Nope."

"Really? Well, I guess that a clean break's the kindest, but it'll make the rest of the trip kind of—"

"Wrong kind of nope." My sister's face had been as bright as I'd ever seen it. "Ruthi—listen, he's not just one of those billionaire bubbleniks, he's *smart*. We're gonna go to Earth, we're gonna go to one of those big old schools there—he'll do research, and I'll—"

"School?" It was practically the first time I'd ever heard her say the word. School was for people with money, or people who grew up planetside, where governments had resources to spare. On the satellites and smaller moons, you could sometimes land an apprenticeship in the dominant industry for decent money—if the place still had its industry, and didn't have charter restrictions locking in membership to descendants of the original population. Otherwise, education generally meant just enough tech training to get a job in the support centers, remoting into malfunctioning AI and turning them off and on again. I'd worked like hell to make sure Jules had better options than that. "Since when is that on the agenda?"

"Since now, I guess!" Jules had laughed, the way you do

when your eyes suddenly focus the right way on a magic-eye puzzle. "You know what Esteban studies, right? Dirt! He spent six years on Earth studying *dirt,* and he loves it. Could talk for hours about it. Could get paid to talk about it. That's the actual plan, he'll get paid to talk about dirt! What a con, right? How do you even figure out that you care about dirt enough to spend your whole life looking at it?"

"So... Stevie convinced you that you want to study dirt."

"You don't have to know beforehand what you want. I always figured you did, but Esteban says you don't. You go and they tell you about—poetry, and fashion, and fish—anything you want, just for fun, and then you figure it out. A whole year, two or three years, just to figure it out! And the money people pay for that—but I wouldn't have to worry about that with him." She'd laughed again. The more she did, the more it was clear she was serious. "He'll help me with my homework! Can you even imagine?"

"Jules," I'd said, "if you want to go to Earth and take classes, we could—" I didn't know what we could do. We were making money on the luxe-liners, but I didn't think it was enough for the kind of education she was talking about. I didn't know for sure. I'd never looked into it. I'd never even thought about it. It wasn't the kind of thing people like us did.

But I'd make it work for her, if that's what she wanted. "We could—"

"Stop that," Jules had said. Her voice had gone sharp, suddenly. "I see you running numbers and starting to fret—just stop it." Then, just as sudden, she'd beamed at me. "It's not your problem! It's mine and Esteban's now. We're cute and we've got brains—not to mention all that money. You don't have to worry about me anymore."

"*Don't* I? Jules, what the hell's gonna happen when he finds out you're not who you say you are?"

"Guess we'll see tonight when I tell him, won't we?" I must've looked a picture; she'd tapped me on the nose and then bounced backwards. "Don't make that face. This is love, baby! If I'm getting married, I've got to do it under my real name, don't I?"

I could have said something then, but all the normal ways I had of talking to her about anything had been kind of blown sideways in the blast of the bomb she'd dropped on me. Whatever I said would have come out all tangled up in hurt and confusion. I'd been worrying about her for twenty-four years, and I wasn't going to stop just because she told me not to.

I could pretend, though, if that's what she wanted. I'd been proud of myself, even, for the way I held my tongue.

That feeling had lasted all of a hot second, of course. Well, hindsight's twenty-twenty. If I'd raised more red flags, would things have been different? Maybe Esteban never would have noticed all the things about her that didn't add up. He hadn't noticed anything about me, and he should've been at least twice shy by now. It was hypothetically possible that if she'd kept her mouth shut, they could've had their happy ending—so long as Jules didn't mind living her life as somebody else. And maybe she wouldn't have.

She hadn't mentioned the notion of school again since Esteban dumped her. The one time I tried to bring it up, she'd just shrugged and said, "It was a stupid idea to begin with."

"It was a naive idea to begin with," said Esteban, back in the Mendez-Yuki ballroom, and I looked down so he wouldn't see my eyes. "Anywhere I go, I'll always be a target for people who want to take advantage of my wealth and my name, the same way my father was. Perhaps, if he'd married someone who had real feelings for him, he wouldn't be so—well, and there's his health to consider, too. A disappointment would be dangerous. As difficult as it is for me, I do have a responsibility to him that I can't escape." He looked into the middle distance. His tone invited me to find him tragic. "I was tempted to forget that, but I see that now."

Personally, I didn't think that Mateo Mendez-Yuki was the sort to die of a broken heart. I didn't think it would be all that hard for Esteban to go by a different name, either, if he'd had a mind to. He certainly had enough of them to pick and choose from. He wouldn't be the only poor little rich kid in history to shake off his baggage and do something else with his life.

Naive little Esteban: he was scared, that's all. One girl had pulled off her breather to show a face he didn't expect, and suddenly he'd realized just how disorienting the unknown could be. There wasn't anything keeping him in New Monte now but a bad case of cold feet. Still, that was the kind of disease that could be fatal—to ambition, at least, if not to life.

But I wasn't here to diagnose Esteban's problems; I was here to add to them. "Did you love her?" I said.

"What? How did you—"

"It was a little obvious," I said, tugging at my evening gloves. It worked for a nervous gesture, and I thought I might want my hands free in the near future.

Esteban gave a small, pained laugh. "I suppose," he said, "I'm doing this all wrong. I shouldn't be talking to you about the last person I—I felt something for, I know. My sister would advise me that it's not a successful romantic strategy. But I'm not very good at strategy, and I want you to understand."

He stopped, then swung around abruptly to face me. "I thought I did love her, but she wasn't real. This idea of running away from my father and what he wants me to be—I suppose that wasn't real either. I can try to step into the role that everyone wants of me, but I don't think I can bear it without at least someone who can accept me the way I am. Someone who can *listen*."

"What about your sister?" I said. I shouldn't have derailed the conversation right then, not when it was going right where I wanted it to go, but I was real curious what he'd say.

"Sol?" Esteban blew out a huff of air. "She tries, of course. She helps me as much as she's able, but it all comes naturally to her. The business, the image—the strategy, if you please." In his mouth, they sounded like dirty words. "She's practically my father's right hand. She can't understand what it's like for me."

He grabbed my hands in his, suddenly, and pressed them tight. I was glad I'd thought to take off the gloves. "I need someone alongside me who does understand. Who can give me room to be myself, when I'm away from him and all his friends. Someone kind, and sweet, and—and lovely—and—and willing to believe in me—and on my side. Miss Ojukwu—*Evelyn*…"

So I guess I hadn't derailed things that much, after all.

I could've said something, but given this whole love scene seemed to revolve around the fact that I was good at keeping my mouth shut and letting him talk, I figured it might be best to keep my reaction to a limpid gaze.

The atmosphere was almost perfect: the low-lit ballroom; the high emotions; the empty silence. The place smelled of cleaning fluid, but you couldn't have everything.

"Evelyn," Esteban repeated, and tugged me a step closer to him. "I think I *could* be happy, if I had someone like you." He looked down at me, almost desperately. "Do you think you could be happy with me? If I were to ask you to stay with me—to marry me…"

I like to think, for poor old Evelyn Ojukwu's sake, that if she'd been a real person she would have asked him straight-up whether he thought he'd be happy with her specifically, or with anybody generally like her.

But since my Evelyn Ojukwu wasn't a real person, all that could really be said about her was that she was a girl generally sort of like herself. And when Esteban pulled her in for a clinch, Evelyn Ojukwu responded in exactly the yielding, passive way that a girl generally sort of like herself would.

I have to admit it: while Esteban kissed me, I kept peeking out through my eyelashes to check that Sol hadn't stormed in through the ballroom door to forbid the banns. It would've been exactly the kind of dramatic moment she lived for. She could've worn her cape and everything. But she must have been real tied up with whatever business had pulled her away from our dinner, because from then to the time when I left the Mendez-Yuki house with an heirloom ring under my evening gloves, I didn't catch a single glimpse of her.

At least, I thought so until I went to look for the car that Esteban had arranged, and found, instead, Sol Mendez-Yuki on her hovercycle.

CHAPTER 13

SHE WAS WEARING her helmet. The round shape didn't suit her long face at all. She looked like a carrot dressed up as a potato. That didn't stop her from giving me as wicked a smirk as I'd ever seen, as she lifted up her right hand to show the other helmet dangling off it. I couldn't help it: I grinned back at her. After that polite performance at dinner, it felt awfully good to see the Sol I was used to.

"If you're offering me a lift home," I said, "I think I'll wait for the car."

"I'm not," she said. "I'm offering you a lift to the anti-grav opera. Didn't you get the invitation from the Nipawattanapong?"

It took me a second to realize that it was only a little past nine. It felt I'd been in the Mendez-Yuki house forever. "I told them I couldn't make it," I said. "Anyway, the show's already started."

"Are you telling me that you can't pick up a plot in the middle?" said Sol, and went on before I could answer. "It's La Ciella's last performance. I promised her I'd try to make it."

I raised my eyebrows. "Then it doesn't exactly seem tactful to bring another girl along, does it?"

"The relationship between myself and La Ciella," Sol said, "is purely that of artist and admirer. Like most of the girls I seem to know, she doesn't have time for anybody who can't offer her significantly more beneficial patronage than I can. Besides," Now it was her turn to lift an eyebrow at me from under the rim of her helmet. "Escorting my little brother's light-of-love to the opera house? To meet with our business partners, no less? What could be more innocent than that?"

Looking at Sol, I could think of a whole lot of things more innocent than that.

But I hadn't been to the anti-grav opera in weeks, and after I left New Monte, I wasn't likely to get a chance again. When she tossed me the helmet, I caught it. It was going to do horrors to my hair, but after the performance I'd put on last time, I couldn't very well refuse.

The streets on the surface of New Monte are always bustling with people, especially at night—day and night being relative terms, of course, artificially imposed to allow for optimal human circadian rhythms, and occasionally altered for special events or public holidays. During the day, they light up the solar lamps so all the people looking in the fancy shop windows get their daily dose of Vitamin D. At night, the outer wall of the satellite goes clear, and you can see all the way through to the edge of the solar system.

Outdoor lights on buildings might mess up the pretty effect, so they don't let too many people have them. People on foot navigate by starlight, with a bit of help from the satellite's systems to subtly boost visibility. The AI driving the cars do the rest. I would've thought hovercycles usually had built-in AI navigation too, but either Sol's didn't have it, or she'd turned it off.

I'd never been on a vehicle that a person was driving themselves before. With my arms wrapped round her waist and my thighs glued to her hips, every move she made to steer left or right sent a jolt through my whole body. I felt the wildness of the turns in my gut as she zoomed in and out of traffic, and the rumble of the engine surged through me in sharp unpredictable jags. I could hear the generalized background noise from all the well-heeled revelers as we sped by, but most of what I could see was the back of her head, and the stars going out and out and out.

Sol Mendez-Yuki and her goddamn dramatics. I spent half that ride convinced we were going to die and the other half cursing Jules for having been right all along about me and that thrill-seeking rush. When she pulled us up to a stop in front of the anti-grav opera house, I felt it like a wrench—not because the stop was sudden, but because I'd wanted it to go on forever.

She swung off and unbuckled her helmet. I followed her more slowly, ignoring her outstretched hand, and trying not to let her see that I was breathing so hard I might as well have just run a marathon—but she knew, of course she knew. I could tell by her crooked smile as she looked at me.

"So that's why they call you a lady-killer," I said. "How many people have you done in on that death trap?"

"Be nice about my baby," said Sol, "or I won't give you a ride back."

I thought about getting off Sol's hovercycle in front of my hotel at the end of the night, weak-kneed, with the sound of my own blood pounding in my ears. I curled my fist so Esteban's ring bit into the inside of my palm. "Your friend really will think you've skipped out on her, Miss Chivalry," I said, and headed for the door—but there I was balked by an exceedingly polite bot, chrome face and velvet bow tie, who informed me that in order to preserve the artistic integrity of the show, it was absolutely forbidden for anybody to enter until intermission in forty-five minutes.

"Never mind," said Sol, coming up behind me after having dispatched the hovercycle away to wherever vehicles around the opera lived when they weren't in use. "That's just how they get us to pay too much money for cocktails in the opera bar while killing time." She grinned at me. "Shall we support their capitalist agenda?"

"For an insurance corp bloodsucker," I said, "you sure do crack wise." Right now, I didn't think she was supporting any agenda but her own. There wasn't any way she hadn't known about the entrance policy when she brought me here. Still, there didn't seem much else to do, so I followed her to a set of dark steps that led towards a recessed entryway below the opera house. A silent bot met us at the door and led us past rows of dark booths full of murmuring moneybags, their silks and jewels dimly glimpsed in the low light, to a table tucked away from everyone in the back. A good place for private conversation, or a rendezvous; I wondered if it was Sol's regular table, and how many people she'd brought there before.

It looked like everything was made from wood—about as luxurious as you could get, on a satellite town billions of kilometers away from any natural forests. Velvet cushions lined the seats and backs. The menu that they handed us didn't have any price tags on it. Sol saw me looking. "Don't worry," she said, "I'm buying."

"You can't afford it."

"Neither can you," Sol pointed out. She wasn't wrong there. I'd been hoarding my reserves as much as I could, but after five weeks on New Monte I was definitely having to watch my professional expenditures. "Besides, my family gets the opera subscriber discount."

I lowered the menu and frowned at her over the top of it. "Look—"

The waiter-bot chose this moment to appear at our table. Sol ordered herself a Rising Overture, then looked at me. I sighed, and pointed to something called a Floating Masquerade. If Sol wanted to throw her nonexistent cash away on me, who was I to say no?

But I found myself saying it all the same. "Sol, if you've been working on a grand plan to get rid of me, I'm not sure taking me out on a fancy date's gonna do the trick. Don't you have better things to spend your money on?"

"Who says I want to get rid of you?"

"Well," I said, "sure, I guess I might be jumping to conclusions there. Maybe you've come round to my way of thinking and decided a chunk of the family fortune's no great loss after all. That'd make my life easier."

Sol leaned forward. "Listen," she said. "I'll be straightforward with you, because I've come to value that about our conversations." There were real candles on the table, sending flickering shadows over the golden skin of her collarbones. Looking there was a mistake. I lifted my gaze to her dark eyes, intent on mine, sparking in the light from the fire; that was worse. "I'm working up a new plan, Ruthi Evelyn Ojukwu Johnson. I'm trying to get you to like me enough that you'll come around to my side."

The way she looked at me knocked me all the way back. "You have got to find a confidante who's not a con artist," I said, when I got my breath back. "I'm saying this for your own good here. What about that Louanne

Hachi? She seems nice."

I thought that might get a rise out of her, but she didn't blink. "My goal has generally been not to drag anybody into this who might be placed in danger from the crossfire," said Miss New Monte Chivalry of '32, just as if the only risk was Louanne throwing herself in front of bullets. Personally, I thought it was even odds that when push came to any sort of shove, helpful Miss Hachi would throw Sol straight under a bus instead. That was how New Monte worked—for everyone except the flower of chivalry over here, who wouldn't even give me the satisfaction of showing enough human pettiness to trash-talk her ex. "You, on the other hand," she went on, "placed yourself in the middle of this mess. Of course, if you're not enjoying the conversation, you're welcome to leave."

"I'm just saying, as a professional, it's hard for me to watch. You can hardly expect to play someone if you tell them where to look and see it coming!"

"Who says I'm trying to play you?" said Sol. "Playing myself, more like, by giving myself an excuse to spend time in your company. Self-indulgence at its finest, and telling myself it's strategy."

While I processed *that* neat little bit of flattery—let nobody ever say Sol Mendez-Yuki wasn't a smooth talker—she reached out her hand so the wait-bot could pass her the drink she'd ordered. Rising Overture or whatever they called it on the menu, it pretty much just looked like a whiskey neat. She took a sip and went on. "In any case, I think we could both use a good time after tonight. My stepfather, for all his virtues, is not the world's greatest host."

"Well, if we're being on the level." I couldn't just keep

letting her pay me compliments in candlelight; that was nearly as dangerous as hopping up behind her on a hovercycle. "You won't blame me for being rude if I tell you I've had more fun scrubbing station smocks than I did at that dinner. I could almost feel sorry for your brother, if he wasn't such a—"

I broke off and frowned down at my own drink, which was served in the middle of a featureless levitating ball. A straw protruded out of it. Only on New Monte would they expect you to drink something sight unseen, and assume it'd all work out fine. "Well, we won't see eye to eye on that one, I'm sure, so if you want a nice time then I'll spare you."

"No, by all means," said Sol. "I'm willing to talk about my brother if you are."

"It won't help with your plan much," I said. "You're a charmer, Sol, but you'd have to pretty much pull a miracle out of your ass to earn points with me while singing Esteban's virtues. And it's not exactly like he's been singing yours to me." I stopped again. It was a cheap shot to let Sol infer that Esteban had been poor-mouthing her, and whatever else was going on here; it felt like we'd moved beyond the realm of cheap shots. "I don't mean he's been running you down. But he sure hasn't been talking you up either."

"Yes," said Sol, "I'm sure that's true. I don't seem to do anything right these days where he's concerned." Her smile was wry. "Do you think my brother and your sister used to sit around complaining about their interfering older siblings?"

"Who says I'm interfering?"

Sol gave me a look.

"Well, sometimes a kid needs a little interference."

All the things I hadn't said to Jules were still bouncing around in the back of my head, crashing into that crack about faces she'd made in her letter. I shoved it all back, and focused on Sol again. "Seems to me *you* could use a little interference, come to that. Why isn't your brother helping you out of your fix? He's got the cash to burn. He could probably pay off Alonso for you tomorrow, if you asked him. And if he did, and you weren't in hock—"

I broke off for the third time. I looked at my drink again—I didn't trust it, but I was starting to feel like I could use it—and then took a gulp. It didn't taste like much but fizzle-water at first, until the kick started in.

Sol took a sip of her whiskey or whatever it was, then set it down carefully on the table in front of her. "Esteban receives a regular allowance from a trust. He's sunk most of it into his research, and it's never occurred to him there'd be a need to save it up. The kind of sum he'd need, to bail me out—no. He couldn't lay his hands on that easily. Since he can't help, I'd rather not worry him with it."

I thought about pointing out once more to Sol that pouring out her problems to someone besides her nemesis might do her some good. On the other hand, I wouldn't have picked out Esteban for a bosom confidante either, if I had real troubles on my tail. "All right, so Esteban doesn't have the dough. What about your stepfather?"

Sol hesitated, then admitted, "My stepfather could do it. But of course people pay much closer attention to his financial transactions than they do to mine. If word were to get out that he was transferring large sums of money to an organization like Alonso's, questions would be asked. He might not wish to take the risk."

"Well, he'd have to, wouldn't he? If—look, I don't

know exactly what Alonso wants from you—"

Sol looked mildly surprised. "Don't you?"

"He wouldn't have told me. I don't work for him." I kept my voice level. It felt like about the hundredth time I'd said it and not been believed. I don't know why it mattered so much; it had certainly been close enough to being true. "So no, I don't know."

"In that case," Sol said, slowly, "I don't know that I should tell you, after all. It's rather in Mr. Alonso's interest to keep the transaction secret."

"You said it yourself, I'm already in it up to my neck." When she didn't answer that, I pressed on. "It's to do with the work you do for your stepfather, isn't it? Corporate sabotage or something. They're going to make you give them some kind of insider information, and then sell it off. Am I on the money?"

"Not too far off." Sol considered her whiskey glass, thoughtfully. "An advocate has determined that a detailed scan of the contents of my skull would be worth exactly the same amount of money on the open market as the sum that I happen to owe. Remarkable coincidence, really."

I stared at her. "How does that equation balance?"

"Scientific value only, you understand. R&D, towards the continuing analysis of the potential benefits of memory-tech. The fact that my memory holds an enormous amount of secret and potentially very damaging information entrusted to me by our clients and partners is completely incidental. Memory-scan technology hasn't been cleared for commercial use, so that can't be factored into the cost, and our corporate NDAs don't yet cover it." She took a sip of the whiskey. "It's all amazingly legal. Months to set up the valuation paperwork, of course, but they left themselves plenty of time. I believe they'd started the process before my younger brother Felix ever left the planet."

I looked at my own drink. I wished I thought I could blame it for the queasy feeling in my stomach.

I'd known whatever Alonso wanted from her wasn't good. Honestly, this wasn't the worst thing it could've been. Memory-tech is getting better by the day. Nine and a half times out of ten, the subject comes out of the procedure none the worse for wear—at least so long as it's not in anybody's interest that they don't. Still, any experimental tech has its dangers, especially the kind that requires someone to mess around in someone else's brain. Somehow I didn't think Albert Alonso had lined up an appointment for Sol at the best hospital in town, either. What did he care if she came out of it the same as she'd gone in?

I thought about some yes-man flipping through Sol's memories, pulling out those three hours we'd spent on Lorelei, and pinning them up to go through in more detail later. Then I stopped thinking about that quick. I had a couple hours to go before I could take a shower, and if I dwelled on that too much, I was going to start to feel like I needed one.

But it didn't matter, because it wasn't going to come to that. "All right. So if your stepfather doesn't want a major corporate catastrophe on his hands, he'll *have* to bail you out."

"Even if there were to be a leak of the kind that Mr. Alonso's superiors propose—" She said it so dispassionately you'd never think the leak we were talking about would come straight from a raid on her brain. "—it's easily possible that MYCorps could escape with its reputation intact. The value of the information to any purchaser will be significantly greater if nobody ever knows the breach has occurred."

"You're saying it would be better for your company bottom line to *actually* give away everything private you know about your customers to the mob, so long as everyone kept it quiet, than to maybe look a little bit like you were doing it even if you weren't actually doing squat."

"You grasp the situation." Sol paused a moment, then added, "Obviously, releasing our client's confidential data is unacceptable, regardless of the bottom line. I'd like to think that my stepfather would agree with me on that, but I admit I'm a little reluctant to put it to the test—especially without knowing what might be asked of me in return. MYCorps prefers not to take a risk without a clear return. Unfortunately, if I don't have a solution six weeks from now, I may not have a choice."

Her voice was calm enough, but I thought about that flash of anger down at the warehouse district, and knew she had to be feeling more than she was letting on. I exhaled. "No strings attached, huh?"

"Strings are how my stepfather operates." Sol lifted up her glass of whiskey and studied it thoughtfully. "He has his priorities. Those haven't shifted, but he's somewhat less flexible in thinking about them than he used to be."

"It looked to me like he leans on you pretty heavy," I said.

"He's been kind to me, by his lights. Taken responsibility for me. Given me an education, opportunities. If I stayed on New Monte forever, I'd never starve."

Remembering her offhand mention of edu-debt back down by the warehouse. I wasn't sure 'given' was the right word. "Not even when the old man's gone?"

"Not so long as I kept working for MYCorps." Sol considered the remains of her drink, then tossed it down her gullet. "If I manage to extricate myself from the organization while my stepfather's still capable of holding the reins, Esteban can have the chance to grow into the hole I've left—if that's what he wants. If not, they'll have to find some other solution. But if I'm still working through a long-term contract when Esteban takes over, I'm afraid it will be a good long while before I get another chance to get out, even if I balance the ledger completely. He'll need me too much."

"And you won't be able to say no to his helpless little face."

Sol smiled, a little ruefully. "I don't know that he'd ask me to stay—but that doesn't mean I could leave."

"Yeah," I said. "I guess I get that."

"I guess you do." Sol leaned back against the booth. "You said it was always just you and your sister, is that right? No parents?"

"Well, we didn't just pop in out of thin air, if that's what you're asking. We're not homeless clones or de-funded gene experiments or anything glamorous like that. Just your standard—"

"Don't say space trash," said Sol.

I lifted my eyebrows at her. "Unaccompanied minors, is what I was going to say. We had Mame for a while, but she kicked the bucket when I was eight."

"No aunts or uncles to take you in? Grandparents?"

I shrugged. "Both parents were drifters. Mame ran away when she was practically a kid still—her family was strict religious, and she got sick of it. She wanted to see the stars, but stalled out on Earth's moon until

Ba found her there and started teaching her card tricks. He'd been in the diamond mines on Kepler—took up sharking as a side gig during a stalemate strike, and got kicked off-planet after getting on the wrong side of some high muckety-muck. Mame always told it like he was a Robin Hood or a revolutionary who swooped in to her rescue, but I've told enough glamorous lies myself to take that with a grain of salt. Anyway, he didn't leave behind any kind of paperwork that might get us a planetary citizenship, so it doesn't matter much either way."

I broke off, hearing the hint of bitterness in my own voice. Sol must have been able to hear it too, but she didn't say anything, just kept looking at me out of those dark straight-set eyes of hers. There was a kind of reticence in her face, but no matter how hard I looked, I couldn't see any judgment—and thinking about poor old Mame, I started feeling contrarily like maybe a little bit of judgment was what I deserved. I had no call to go talking my folks down just because I was feeling like a heel myself. "Whatever his deal was," I said, reluctantly, "he stuck with her—they stuck with each other. I remember him a little. I'm pretty sure I remember when he died. I guess that's something."

"It's a good story," said Sol, "no matter how much is true."

"My ma got pretty good at her cons, in the end," I said. "I'm sure your ma must have told you one just as romantic, when you were little. Cinderella and the prince, right? How Mateo Mendez-Yuki swept a beautiful poor girl off her feet and brought her to a palace?"

"Unfortunately," Sol said, "I don't think my mother was as talented a storyteller as yours." She tilted her head, studying me. "She could have stood to learn a few tricks from you, to be honest. You've got the knack of making friends, of making people feel like you belong."

I laughed. "Belong? Among all you gold-plated gimcracks?"

I'd meant it to be a jab; instead, it got me a smile. "Well, I didn't mean to insult you. I'm sure it's not *only* us gold-plated gimcracks who find you very likable."

"Thanks," I said, and found myself sliding a grin back at her, like we were sharing a joke. "You're right, though—your crowd falls for it the easiest. But it's nice to have the effort appreciated."

"Believe me," said Sol, "I admire the skill tremendously." She lifted her empty glass, as if to toast me; I batted my lashes at her outrageously over the Evelyn Ojukwu smile. As I'd hoped, she laughed, before adding, "There was a time, you know, when I was not exactly a New Monte hit either. My accent was wrong, my opinions were wrong, certainly my parentage was wrong—"

"And then you hit puberty," I suggested, "got a makeover montage and a hovercycle, and suddenly—!"

The smile I got this time was fainter. I tried not to be disappointed about it. "I did eventually learn how to exert some control over the kind of attention I received," she said, and I remembered Gaea St. Clair talking about how Sol's lack of prospects let her be as outrageous now as she wanted. I was more sure than ever that Gaea St. Clair didn't have the faintest idea just how deliberately Sol played at being Sol Mendez-Yuki. She carefully put down the glass she'd toasted me with. "Before then, there was only really one person who never thought there was something wrong with me."

My own smile slipped off my face. It wasn't hard to see where this was going. "It doesn't surprise me," I said, "that he never noticed anybody was treating you different. Your brother's not the noticing kind. At least not for other people's problems."

I took another gulp of my drink. The sippy-straw was probably a good idea, all in all—it kept me pacing myself, rather than tossing it back the way Sol had done. "You know, I'm not even saying that your brother's the world's worst. I expect I could pick and choose any random handful of folks on New Monte and a good half of them would turn my stomach worse than he does, if not more. It's just his bad luck that the person he hurt is the one who matters to me. You can't expect me to forgive that."

"I'm not expecting you to forgive it," said Sol. "Nor am I asking you to. But I think the part you're playing now isn't good for either of you."

"Nice of you to be concerned for my well-being."

"Scoff all you want," said Sol, softly, "but I mean it." She leaned forward. "I like you, Miss Johnson. I'd like to see more of you. I'd like to hear more of your stories, and even out the score a little for all the time you've graciously spent listening to me." The candlelight flickered over her face, her mouth. She didn't say anything as coarse as 'I'd like to take you to bed'; she didn't have to. All she had to do was lower her voice, and she had me thinking it with every perfectly innocent sentence in that almost-perfect aristocratic accent. "I don't know if you're working with Alonso. If you say you're not, I'm willing to believe you. But this pointlessly vindictive revenge plot—"

"*Really?*" I stared at her handsome firelit face, shimmering with sincerity like something out of an old screen romance. "Really, it matters more to you that I'm gonna play a mean trick on your feckless brother than if I was helping out in a plot to steal bits of you out of your *brain*?"

Sol blinked. "Well—"

"Which I'm not, but if I were—come on, you've got to know you're worth more than that! Or are you just so used to talking that way that you can't turn it off even for someone like me?" That Floating Masquerade was making itself felt now, all right. "My girl, if I could just get you for a *week*, I'd shove a good dose of selfishness up—"

"So do it," said Sol. Her eyes locked back on mine. "Have me for a week. A month. However long you want me for. I wouldn't complain."

A shiver ran through me. "Hell," I said, hoarsely, "I'd make sure you wouldn't."

"So why not put your money where your mouth is?" Sol's low voice slid straight down my ears to a place below my stomach. She lifted her hand across the table and brushed a stray bit of hair away from my forehead. "Stop playing around with my brother, and bet on me instead."

My mouth was dry. "Yeah? And what would I get for my stake, if I did?"

"Why don't you tell me?" Her fingers slid down to caress my cheek; her thumb brushed my lips. "Whatever you want, Ruthi Johnson—if I can make it happen, I'll do it. Let me help you and your sister. There's still plenty of time—"

Half-mesmerized as I was, that jarred me out of it. "There's *not*." I reached up and grabbed her hand in both of mine. I couldn't stay here and let her talk me out of the plans I'd worked so hard for. Not now, when I was so close. Not even though all she'd said, characteristically, was that she'd find a way to help me and my sister out of our troubles, without a mention of me reciprocally helping her out of hers. Maybe especially because of that.

"There's *no* time," I snapped, and pressed her palm down hard over my right hand so she'd feel the sharp pressure of the Mendez-Yuki family engagement ring underneath my glove. "It's already happened. I'm engaged to your brother, and the contract-signing's in five weeks. After that, I'm out. That's all there is to say."

My heart was thudding. The way Sol looked at me, there was a moment when I thought she could hear every beat of it.

Then she jerked her hand back out of mine, sat back in her booth, looked away across the speakeasy, and exhaled, her long face suddenly remote. "I guess it is."

She checked her watch, then turned back to me, formal and full of propriety. "We'd best be off, Miss Ojukwu, if we don't want to miss the second act of the opera. Unless you're tired out? You've had quite a day, and I'd understand if you preferred to be on your way home."

She'd promised me at least half an anti-grav opera. I was damned if I was going to miss out on it just because she couldn't leave well enough alone. "And be so rude as to leave you without an escort?" I slipped out of the booth and took the hand she offered to help me leverage myself to my feet, though I didn't need it. Two could play at the politeness game. "Let's at least finish out the show."

CHAPTER 14

THE NEXT COUPLE of weeks passed in a whirlwind. Nobody loves an engagement more than the network-happy nouveau riche of New Monte. People I'd spoken to once or twice before thronged around me at parties to deliver their heartfelt congratulations, as if we'd been meeting at the same minibars for years. I had wondered whether anyone was going to ask me whether we'd hold off signing the formal contract until the elder Ojukwu or their C-suite representatives could make it out to supervise the proceedings, and had a score of excuses prepared as to why that wasn't going to be necessary. In point of fact, nobody ever asked. Everyone seemed to take it for granted that a girl from a boutique outfit with an eligible on the line would race as fast as she could to get his corporate assets on lockdown before he changed his mind.

And a race is more or less what it felt like. As a Mendez-Yuki in the making, my social calendar was filling up faster than flights back to Earth for the Expansion Centennial. I went to lunches with the Hachi, dinners with the Nipawattanapong, and every party thrown all up and down New Monte's main drag. I told a hundred different people in strict confidence how much the Kepler gem trade could benefit from having an in with the MYCorps insurance empire, and got so I didn't even register the standard response about little Esteban stumbling over a diamond in the rough.

Esteban himself probably wouldn't have appreciated that little bon mot any more than I did, but for the most part he stayed home and worked on his experiments. He'd done his part in wooing me, and now he could kick back—after all, he had me to cover his social obligations. I had no doubt that this was how the rest of our married life would have played out, if I had any intention of sticking it out through the wedding. It didn't bear much resemblance to the picture Jules had painted for me, that was for sure. We took a meal together every other day, and had the same conversation each time: he'd tell me what he'd done in the lab, then he'd tell me how much he was looking forward to our marriage, then he'd wrap up by kissing me and head on back over to his soil samples. Whether the kiss fell on the hand or the mouth depended on the day and on his mood, but I managed to keep the heavy petting to a minimum.

Honestly, the person I saw the most of during that period was the Mendez-Yuki butler, who also turned out to be the Mendez-Yuki party planner—or rather, the liaison with the party planner, since the folks who get married on New Monte are far too important to have the time to talk to party planners themselves. It turned out all you really had to do to get him to unbend a little was sit him down and listen to him ramble for five hours about different kinds of booze. His name was Joe Morgan, and he had two wives and five kids on four different satellites, all working in some arm or another of the Mendez-Yuki business and not one of them buttling.

Every job has its collateral damage, but I did have an occasional twinge about poor old Joe Morgan. He put his heart and soul into pulling that engagement party together, and did his damnedest to create the illusion that I was having a say, even though I knew that if push ever got down to shove I didn't even have a veto on the color scheme. (MYCorps logo colors, of course—black, gold and cream—with a dash of Ojukwu green for the sake of politeness.) Of course I was determined to be about the most accommodating bride New Monte had ever seen, but Joe Morgan didn't have any reason to expect that. I was almost touched by the careful effort he put into managing me in advance.

And then, of course, I spent a fair bit of time with Sol— with Sol, and not with Sol. It was a peculiar situation. We weren't hardly speaking to each other, at least not so much as we could avoid it. Whenever she looked at me, I got a kind of sense of coiled tension. Sooner or later, that spring was going to go off, and I didn't know what would happen when it did. All the same, she kept taking me out on all those dinners to meet the Mendez-Yuki business partners. It had to be done, and clearly Esteban wasn't going to do it. If there was a dry note in her voice as she explained to all the MYCorps partners and clients what an asset I was going to be to the company, she kept it well-hidden enough that it seemed I was the only one hearing it.

What a pain in my ass that girl was, anyway! There she'd lounge at every meal, class and competence from her long nose to her short nails, and smoothly efface herself from the conversation. All the other executives and insurance agents and assorted muckety-mucks babbling on carelessly about money and markets—I spent hours upon hours sitting there knowing that if I paid attention and had the right kind of brain for it I could probably use these dinners to make myself another fortune. And instead, I couldn't convince myself to pay attention to anything but Sol, constantly in the edges of my peripheral vision, playing the good employee and the good daughter with what was clearly a bare quarter of *her* brain cells, if that.

I should have been spending those dinners thinking about what to do for Jules after I got my hands on our portion of Esteban's millions. Instead, I kept thinking about those million-dollar kosher ducks, rotting away beneath our feet.

It was a damned shame. Sol ought to have been running her own show, dazzling everyone around her like she did out in the ballroom when the stakes were low. If she hadn't been brought under that golden umbrella when she was a kid, she could have been a confidence artist bar none, and maybe she'd be better off for it now. But her good fortune had brought her to bad debt, and worse luck had brought her to me, to distract her with all this Esteban nonsense right when she should have been thinking up how to get out of her own troubles— because I had distracted her, and I knew it. She wouldn't even have come on that Lorelei trip if it weren't for me. Alonso had been right when he said it didn't matter if I officially worked for him or not. I'd ended up doing him just as much of a good turn either way. All I'd done was save him the trouble of paying me for it.

I liked Sol. There was no denying that by now. I didn't much fancy being a part of what brought her down. But as much as her smile and her low voice had turned my head, those weren't the only things that had me feeling rotten about the whole setup.

I've never been wild about the way the wealthy waste

their money. Relieving them of a certain portion of it never bothered my conscience one way or another; there was plenty more where that came from, and I always knew I could make better use of it than they could. This felt different.

It's not that I was building up any kind of romantic dreams about Sol being cut from a different sort of cloth than the other people I'd conned over the years. A sob story was just a sob story, and I'd sold enough of them myself that I wasn't about to swallow hers wholesale. Sure, she'd help her sibs if she could, but I didn't think she was jumping to give up her opera seats or her fancy capes or any of the rest of the conspicuous consumption she'd grown up with. I could imagine a version of her who lived the way I did, but that was just fantasy, no more real than my Evelyn Ojukwu. No matter how things went down, Esteban wasn't ever going let his sister lack for much.

Still, redistributing money from one person to another was one thing, and redistributing it right into a black hole was another thing altogether. Sol's shipment would have been useful, not just to her, but to more than a few people down on Earth when she got it there—maybe even some of them my own long-lost relatives, not that that mattered. Now it wasn't going to be of any use to anybody, just because it wasn't convenient to Alonso that it should be.

I'd spent all my life in artificial environments. In a place like that—even a place like New Monte—you didn't waste food, and you didn't waste water, and you knew that if a shipment was late or lost, it meant that someone would go hungry. I'd always figured myself to be more or less on the side of the people who put things where real people who needed them (like me and Jules) could make use of them. This time, though, I'd gotten myself on the side of the people who threw things away. I was finding that I didn't like it much.

If I'd ever expected myself to find a moral line in the sand, I wouldn't have guessed it would come over a bunch of kosher ducks, but there you go.

Anyway, I decided I might as well do Sol one last good turn before we left each other's lives for good. It would be a good way to spring that tension between us, I thought; a good way to get ahead of the part of myself that was a little too tempted by her unprofitable propositions. I didn't want to weigh down the cash I was bringing home to Jules with the pile of doubts I'd been accumulating along with it. It was worth going a little out of my way to leave New Monte on an upswing. Of course, if Alonso found out, I'd be well and truly in the soup, but if I played my timing right I'd be heading back to Bellavu with my well-gotten gains before Alonso knew anything about it.

Sol had a problem: a cash deficit around product that she couldn't sell.

If I dug a little bit into some memories I hadn't looked at for a while, I thought I might be able to come up with a solution.

Mame always told us she'd never once regretted ditching her inward-looking little community on Earth for a life among the stars. Maybe that was true, though thinking back on the way we'd lived, I found it hard to believe. Still, there'd been more than one night when we'd all been crammed into some below-surface compartment, walls too hot from the satellite engines and air too stale from over-recycling, when Mame would soothe Jules' whimpering by telling us about the place she'd grown up. A real planet, the home planet, with a real surface and real weather and cities that reached up into a real blue sky.

I've never seen Borough Park, Brooklyn, but Mame's old snaps filled out some of it for me, and her words did the rest: blue Earth sky over the tall gray front steps of Temple Beth-El, the men all in black with their round hats and front curls, the women in long skirts and flat shoes. Mame always thought it would still be just that way, if she ever went back. Maybe that's why we never have. It's good to have the address of her parents, and the name of her favorite sister. I like knowing she passed those things on to me. No matter how much I try, though, I can't put myself or Jules in the pictures she showed us: all those law-abiding women, with their skirts over their knees and their sleeves over their elbows and their hair wrapped up in scarves over faces pale as Mame's.

I kept on telling some of Mame's stories for a little while after she died. Jules was still small enough then that she wanted to hear them. But she got older, as kids always do, and by then I'd picked up other stories to tell her anyway—stories I got from the people we were hanging around with, about riots and righteous paybacks and jobs gone gloriously right. Those kinds of stories had a lot more to do with our here and now than anything we heard from Mame about her home back on Earth.

Jules and I still talked together in the Yiddish that Mame had spoken to us when we wanted something that reasonably approximated a private language. Otherwise, I packed what I picked up from her away on a back shelf in my brain, and didn't think much about it—just one of those odd bits and pieces of self that doesn't quite fit into the life you're living, or the person you figure yourself to be.

Whoever thought that all that would've come in handy on New Monte, of all places?

I hadn't brought the right kind of clothes with me, so it took me a few days to put the outfit together, and another few days to track down Gavriel Herschel, the Brukhim-Haboim business factor that Dov Lieberman had had the falling-out with. He wasn't a part of the glittering set himself. Brukhim-Haboim was newer than New Monte—one of the little second-generation satellites that fundraised their struggling way into space with sub-subculture dollars, well after all the governments, corporations, and eccentric billionaires that rode out on the first Expansion wave. Mame, who thought it was a meshugeneh project, had followed the updates on faulty infrastructure and founders' infighting as avidly as the makeups and breakups in an earial. She hadn't lived long enough to see the big plot twist, when the chance discovery of water on a nearby moon kicked off an ongoing transition from failing diasporic experiment to conventionally profitable transit hub.

Gavriel Herschel was only the second person to have his position on New Monte, and by all accounts was not particularly inclined towards schmoozing. He managed a warehouse for passing cargo along the kosher transit routes and otherwise kept himself to himself. Sol had tried to get a meeting with him three times, and each time he'd turned her down. I got that information from Joe Morgan, who knew just about everything about Sol's schedule that it was possible to know. I didn't think he'd take a meeting with me either, if I tried to set one up in advance. That's why I didn't try.

Gavriel Herschel lived out towards the edge of the

New Monte business district, about a half-hour walk from my hotel. I didn't mind the exercise. The headscarf meant none of my new friends were likely to recognize me, and while my long skirt and flat shoes might not have been glamorous, they were much more comfortable than anything in Evelyn Ojukwu's wardrobe. When I rang the doorbell on the Herschel building, I scoped out the mezuzah on the door lintel. Mame had lost ours when I was five, and we'd had to clear off a ship in a hurry. This one was a whole lot nicer than that.

A functionary of some sort came to answer the door. I had to stifle a grin when I saw her. We were practically mirrors, even down to skin tone—which did surprise me a little, given all those pale faces in Mame's pictures. The only difference was that her over-the-knee skirt had pinstripes, and a suit jacket to go with it. "Sorry," she said, "but we don't take—"

"Sholem aleichem," I interrupted her.

The functionary blinked at me. "Aleichem sholem."

"I'm hoping to see Mr. Herschel," I said, in Yiddish.

She shook her head, and answered in a language I almost recognized. Then she said it again in English. "I'm sorry, I don't speak Yiddish. Do you—"

"English is fine." Of all the accents I've ever done, Mame's is still one of the easiest to imitate. I put on my big eyes and my distraught expression: just a good girl far from home, and looking for a landsman to trust in. "Do you think Mr. Herschel has got time to see me? I think maybe he's the only person on this satellite who can help me."

"I'll—" She looked me up and down, her face softening. "I'll see," she said, and ducked away again behind the door.

For Gavriel Herschel, I became a widow from Borough Park, stranded on New Monte and trapped in a bad business deal by a shady customer while trying to keep up my husband's business. Dov Lieberman's reputation was slandered to high heaven that day. Herschel gleefully drank up the news that his old partner had been out there doing poor girls wrong. I couldn't leave Sol out of it entirely—Herschel didn't have his head in the sand, and I couldn't guarantee that he didn't know they'd been dealing together—so she turned into the cruel warehouse owner who was charging me an arm and a leg for the storage of my cargo. Until and unless some kind soul with a kosher-certified transport vehicle helped me get it back to Earth, for a reasonable cut of the profits.

The role demanded more lies, and bolder ones, than the part of Evelyn Ojukwu ever did, and I walked out of that room feeling more like myself than I had in an age. After all this time, there was something awfully satisfying in finding a use for the baggage Mame had left me with.

I'd had Ba in the back of my mind, too, come to think of it, when I picked out this deb-from-Kepler drag. He hadn't left me much, but I had his trustworthy face and his card-sharp skills, and—if Mame was to be believed—his idea that the owner of a diamond mine was kind of a ridiculous thing to be. I'd been using all that plenty. Maybe there would be a point to all the other useless odd-shaped pieces of myself as well, if I just lived long enough to figure them out.

As I strolled back from Gavriel Herschel's office, my mind strayed back to the notion of how different everything was likely to be when I finally got back to Jules. The thought didn't scare me like it usually did. We were going to have to be different people to each other, but maybe that wasn't all bad. There were all kinds of parts of me buried under big-sister Ruthi that hadn't seen the light of day in years.

Take, for example, the part of me that had wanted to chuck everything and run off after Sol when she made me that pitch in the opera speakeasy. For the first time, I thought I could understand how Jules had felt way back on that luxe-liner. If you got high enough on chemistry, it made you kind of lose your grip on basic mathematics—and it sure was a kick, it *sure* was a kick, sitting across from somebody you *knew* was too good to be true, and hearing them sell you on the kind of future you never thought you could have.

Of course I knew that when something seemed too good to be true, that's when you were at the most risk of losing your shirt. Of course I couldn't afford to let the part of me that wanted to go all in on Sol in any way get into the pilot's seat. Still, in a way it was good to know that part of me was there. I was even kind of looking forward to telling Jules about it, when all this was done. I wanted to tell her, hey—I get it now.

But before that, I'd have to have at least one more real conversation with Sol, to explain the deal I'd made with Gavriel Herschel on her behalf, and how she could take advantage of it.

It was never a hardship looking at that girl, but I'd never gotten a view from even halfway up the moral high ground before, and the idea of it held a certain extra appeal. If she was watching the surveillance footage right now, she must be wondering what I was up to. Maybe she even thought I was pulling a little more sabotage on Alonso's account. I tried to figure how her face would look, when she learned how I'd set things up for her instead. You couldn't base it on the way she'd looked after I'd scooped her up on Lorelei. She hadn't known a thing about me then, and had been suspicious of me—with reason—and half-concussed on top of it.

I hadn't done her much good since, but at the very least we had been honest with each other. This time, if I told her I'd just wanted to do her a solid, no strings attached, there was even a chance she might believe I was on the up and up.

Well, maybe a few strings. String one: she'd have to think about me at least a little, when all this was done, and it couldn't just be to curse my name, either. I might stay on as public enemy number one until Esteban's tender feelings got a little less sore, but sooner or later he'd forget about me. Personally, I'd bet on it being sooner. The effects of the bad turn would fade away, while the lasting impact of the good one stuck around. She couldn't hate me forever, if I gave her the chance to build her own business and get the hell out of New Monte.

String two: she was going to have to build her own business and get the hell out of New Monte. When I thought of her, after all this was done—and I was going to give myself a little more leeway to do that once there was no chance I'd ever see her again; nothing wrong with a little romantic nostalgia about the never-was that might have been—I didn't want to be picturing the buttoned-up dutiful version of Sol who'd been chaperoning me through all those Mendez-Yuki dinners. I wanted to be able to see her the way she looked out on the dance floor, or up on that hovercycle: totally confident, a little bit wild, and absolutely free.

The memory of Sol on a hovercycle should have reminded me to look both ways before they crossed the street—that girl was a heart attack on wheels—but I still had a good few blocks to walk before I hit anything you might reasonably call hustle or bustle, and my mind was drifting. It was the late afternoon, and the stars were starting to shine through the dome overhead as the light-cycle faded out.

The scenery was demure for New Monte, square buildings with the names of firms written in elegant script over the doors and just a little bit of tasteful ritz around the windows. MYCorps' main office was somewhere around here, though from what I'd seen, most of the real decision-making happened over personal calls to the Mendez-Yuki mansion, or around overpriced dinners in the restaurant district. Still, New Monte held onto some faint vestiges of its business drag. People who spent nine-tenths of their lives going from playground to playground needed somewhere to show off their professional togs during the other ten percent, and even on New Monte it would be a little tacky to sign a contract at an open bar.

In any case, it was getting late enough that everyone was already off dressing for dinner. No one on the satellite's surface did business at the unholy hour of five o'clock in the afternoon. That was why I'd picked that time to begin with, though I was going to have to rush if I wanted to make it back in time to make my own toilette. The streets were dead quiet, and the scenery around me pleasant but uninteresting. There wasn't much to interrupt my daydreaming.

Excuses, excuses: the plain fact is that I was too busy building fairy tales to notice the car that came gunning for me until it was almost too late.

If I'd been paying attention, I would've noticed something was wrong as soon as I heard the engines from around the bend. No properly functioning AI would've let any car run that fast. In the moment I didn't have much time to do anything but smell the exhaust, feel the sudden blast of hot air, and fling myself frantically sideways. I didn't know why the car was coming for me, and I didn't much care right then, but I was in no way ready to be rubbed out. I personally considered that I had a hell of a lot to live for.

But whoever had hijacked that car's AI didn't see it that way. I managed to dive out of the way just in time to avoid the first pass. My knee hit pavement with a blooming burst of pain, and I went sprawling.

I scrambled to get back up, my heart rabbiting in my ears over the screeching sound of a U-turn. It was coming for a second try, and I was still barely on my feet, let alone ready to run. I thought for a second about plastering myself up against one of those bare office-fronts, but rejected the idea pretty quick. I didn't get a sense that the fellow running the remote knew or cared much for other people's property damage.

There was one other car parked on the street, half a block up. If I could get flat under it, that might shield me some from the damage. I started scrambling towards it as fast as my banged-up knee would let me, knowing that I wasn't going to reach it in time—

When all of a sudden there was a different, even louder engine roaring up next to me, and Sol's voice shouted, "Get on!"

The hovercycle took off when I'd barely gotten one leg over it, flying along at a wildly unbalanced forty-five degrees to the ground. My elbow came within a hair's breadth of banging against the concrete road. The only thing keeping us upright was the speed that Sol had us going at. We were so off-kilter that I didn't even feel the rush of air as the other car careened past us in the other direction, but I could see it passing out of the corner of my eye. We'd missed a collision by a millimeter.

Bit by bit, Sol hauled the hovercycle up into a vertical position, but she didn't ease up on the speed until we were halfway into the town center. Me, I just focused on keeping my hold on her waist. I was feeling awful shaky, in a boneless, zero-grav sort of way. It would've been a real case of dramatic irony if after all that I'd killed myself in falling off the ride.

Finally, Sol pulled up to a stop. It took me a moment to realize she'd brought me to my own hotel. "Will you be all right, Miss Ojukwu?" she said, without looking over her shoulder at me.

"I will be," I answered, honestly. "I'm not yet." I took a deep breath, trying to calm the shakes down, and then let my head thunk against the solidity of her shoulder blades. Any other guest might have walked out and seen us and started up the gossip mill, but right then I couldn't find it in my heart to care. "God damn it," I whispered into her back. "God fucking *damn*."

I'd faced plenty of trouble in my life. It wasn't that I'd never taken a good hard look at the chance that I might not make it through the day ahead of me. But danger was one thing, and straight-up assassination another again. Nobody had ever tried to kill me before—at least not me *personally*.

Sol's back stayed straight for another minute, while I did nothing but breathe. Then she said, "Do you want me to walk you up to your room?"

I should've said that I didn't want to put her out. I should've said that I'd be fine. But I could feel the wobbliness even in my good knee, not to mention the one I'd banged up while trying to get away from the murder car. The honest truth was I probably could use an arm, and the more honest truth was that the last thing I wanted was to be alone. I lifted my head up from her back. "Yes," I said. "Please."

It wasn't until we were both standing that she noticed the blood that had soaked through my long skirt. "You sure I shouldn't be taking you to a doctor instead?"

"It's just a bruise and a scrape. Needs washing out, that's all."

I started to limp up the stairs towards the entrance. Sol put out a hand lightly on my arm to stop me. "Hey—why don't you take some weight off that? Lean on me."

I hadn't known if she would offer, but I was dead glad that she had. I half-turned, but before I could take her up on it, the front doors of the hotel opened to let out an empty hoverchair. As it sailed down the steps towards me, I caught sight of the cameras pointed down the front of the hotel that let the AI registrars monitor incoming attendees. Not every guest could take all those steps up into the lobby. When those cameras saw me limping, it must have triggered some kind of protocol.

Honestly, the last thing I wanted right then was to trust myself on yet another AI-piloted vehicle. I didn't realize until just then how reassuring it had been to feel all Sol's twists and turns on the hoverbike, and know I was riding something with a human in control—a human who didn't want me dead. But those cameras were watching, and if I disdained the perfectly practical chair in order to drape myself all over Sol, there was no guarantee the video wouldn't get out. I sank into the chair, gave my room number, and waited for Sol to take the excuse to jet.

She didn't jet. She followed me all the way up to my suite on the seventh floor. I stood up to open the door with my passcode. "Beat it," I told the chair, and it sailed away.

Then I turned to Sol. Now, having gotten me all the way here, she'd skedaddle for sure. If I hadn't been so beat, I could've figured out something to say—some way to thank her gracefully for saving my ass, something that wasn't just a wail demanding not to be left alone right then—but as it was, I couldn't string two respectable words together. I just stared up at her, silent as a screen set to mute.

I must've looked some sad baby animal levels of woebegone, from the way Sol's face changed as she looked at me. Under any other circumstances, I'd be embarrassed to be that pathetic. "Come on," she said, and slipped her arm over my shoulders. "Let's get that knee cleaned up."

She got me to my armchair, then went back to close the door behind us while I sank gratefully into it. Sitting down was a mixed blessing. Now that there wasn't any motion to distract me, my bruised knee was throbbing up more than ever. Still, hurting was better than scared. With four walls around me, I was just about starting to feel like I might be safe again.

With four walls around me, and Sol right there—but I didn't dare start making the presence of another person a prerequisite for feeling safe, and especially not Sol Mendez-Yuki.

Even as I thought that, she came to kneel down in front of me, and started rolling my skirt up my legs. She carefully unstuck the bloody fabric from my scraped-up skin. It stung.

The silence was starting to get thick. I said the first thing that came into my head, which turned out to be, "You know, this is not the reason I would've picked to get you on your knees for me." Sol looked up, and I felt my face go hot. "Sorry. I'm sorry. That's a hell of a way to thank you for—"

"It's all right."

"I don't have much of a filter right now," I said, weakly.

"I bet." I caught a glimmer of amusement in her eyes, before she looked down to frown again at my knee. "I don't suppose you have any disinfectant or anything lying around here, do you?"

I blinked at her. "Why wouldn't I?" Who travels without basic first-aid supplies?

"Right." The amusement reached her voice, this time. "Why wouldn't you?"

"Top drawer in the table by the bed." She got up and went over, while I frowned at her back. There was a dark stain on her trousers where my bleeding leg had been pressed up against hers on the hovercycle. "Thanks," I said, awkwardly. "Truly. You didn't have to help me." Now that I had a moment to think, it was dawning on me how very much she hadn't had to help me. She didn't know the deal I'd just made on her behalf. It would've been easy enough for her to sit back and let someone else pull the wild card out of the pack.

Sol just shook her head. "It's lucky for you I was working late at the office." Of course she was the only person in New Monte who worked late at the office. She came back over with a disinfectant wipe and a cold compression wrap, and knelt down again. She started swiping methodically at the blood, then added, eyes fixed on my leg, "Which meant I was close enough to get there in time when the spy-cam I've got following you sent out the alert. It's not exactly polite, regardless of the outcome. I can't apologize for the action—there's no point in apologizing for something that you intend to keep on doing—but I do apologize for the fact that it's necessary."

Irrelevantly, I was noticing her accent again—not quite the cut-glass New Monte classic, but not the deliberately slangy drawl she sometimes affected, either. Maybe this was just what she sounded like when she wasn't thinking too much about what she sounded like. "What alert? I mean, I figured you'd still have surveillance set up, but—" Another thought struck me. "So you know where I was coming from too, don't you?"

"I know you were coming from an office in the area. I hadn't had a chance to look up whose, yet, or figure out why." I hissed as the wipe took the crusted blood off a particularly sore spot, and she grimaced. "Sorry."

"It's fine." She wasn't doing any worse than I would have done myself. "I wouldn't have figured you debs got much in the way of first-aid training."

"It takes a couple of spills before you can really get comfortable putting a hovercycle in manual." She carefully set the wipe aside, then reached for the compression wrap. "But it's been a while."

As she started to unroll the wrap, I said, "I was at Gavriel Herschel's office this afternoon."

Her hands went still for a minute before she went back to what she was doing, her dark head bent over my leg. I couldn't see her face. So much for that fantasy. "Oh?"

"I had a nice long chat with him. I did fudge a few of the facts about your cargo's ownership. Should I apologize for not asking permission?" I watched Sol's hands, long and capable, winding the cold wrap round and round my knee. The pressure was comforting; the feather-light brush of her fingers along the inside of my thigh was distracting. She didn't answer, so I went on. "He's got another freighter coming in the week before your debt's due. If you're willing to work through me, he can take your damn kosher ducks to sell on Earth."

Sol was quiet. She carefully fastened the edge of the cold compress to itself, then took my leg and placed it straight, with equal care, on the ottoman that went with the armchair. Then, finally, she looked back up at me. "So that explains why they acted today."

"What?" I said.

"The T.O.U. Now they don't have a use for you anymore."

"They do have a use for me," I said, and couldn't keep all the bitterness out of my voice. "Distracting you. Whether or not I mean to do it—look, I know the fix you're in, and I know all this stuff with you and me and your useless brother is just making things worse. That's why I thought I ought to—"

And I stopped, because I saw what she meant then. It was a funny thing: I'd been so busy grappling with the fact that somebody *had* tried to kill me, I hadn't even thought yet about the who or the why of it. "But once I start helping you, instead of hindering, I scoot myself right on out of the assets column and into liabilities."

Sol wasn't the only one who'd been distracted by this whole business. I'd been so busy putting on a show for her that I forgot she might not be the only one who had me under surveillance. Alonso might look genial, but he wasn't dumb—and if the T.O.U. were watching my movements, they'd have figured out the implications of my visit to Mr. Herschel real quick.

I knew Alonso was dangerous. I knew the fact that we went back a ways and I'd always played nice with him didn't put me on any kind of a safe list. I knew all that, but I sure hadn't been acting like it. A little forethought was all it would've taken to make sure I didn't get caught out like a damn amateur.

Jules had been right. I'd always been careful enough when it was the both of us on the line. Now I was here, I'd been so busy worrying about her that I'd forgotten to look out for myself.

"Well!" I said, brightly. "Have I ever been a fool!" Another thought struck me. "That's the alert you set up, isn't it? You told your surveillance bot to tell you if it looked like trouble was coming for me, so you could show up in some shining armor. You're really acing that rescue romance playbook, aren't you?"

"I didn't think the likelihood was very high," said Sol, low. "It was just a precaution."

"A pretty prophetic one, as it turns out, so pat yourself on the back."

Sol let out a breath, and bowed her head. Her hand was still resting lightly on my thigh, just above my bandaged knee. I wondered if she'd forgotten to remove it. Then she raised her eyes to mine again. There was a tired look in them. "I'm sorry, Ruthi."

"You saved my life," I pointed out, a little waspishly. "Like I said—you aced it."

"If it weren't for me, you wouldn't have needed the rescue. That's got to lose me a few points at least." Her lips curved in a smile without humor, and she quoted herself, mocking: "'My goal has been not to drag anyone into this who might be placed in danger'—I won't forget that pretentious little statement in a hurry, and I imagine you won't either. Telling myself it was perfectly safe to tell you all sorts of things, so long as you weren't on my side, and then doing my damnedest to get you on my side anyway. It's rather despicable, isn't it? Or at least poorly thought out. When I saw that car coming for you—"

I'll say this for her technique: seeing Sol wallow pulled me out of my own head real fast. "You're flattering yourself real good if you think you're puppeteering me," I told her. Only a fool would think they had any real chance of luring someone away from the Sol system's hardest gang with charm alone, and Sol wasn't a fool—just a person trying a desperate bluff with a real bad hand. I reached out and flicked her chin, not gently. "You should've been an opera singer yourself, the way you make dramatics out of things."

"I think I object," said Sol, "to characterizing a concern for your life as melodramatic."

"Not the first time I've gotten myself in a tight spot, and it won't be the last either." It was easier to believe when I was trying to convince her, rather than myself. "Anyway, if it weren't for me swapping gossip with Alonso about Lorelei, *you* wouldn't have needed the help. I think if we're counting all in all, you're still pulling ahead."

Sol's brows knit together, but she didn't answer.

I looked down at her, her soft black hair and her furrowed brow and her hand still absently settled on my leg. I didn't know how many of those worry lines were really for me. Putting a damsel into distress couldn't fit her self-image. If I did take damage in the fallout from all this, I had to figure it would wound her pride more than her heart.

Still, for a long, long time there had been only one other person in the world to fret about whether Ruth Johnson lived or died. I liked it that she was worrying. I liked the way she'd wrapped that compress around my leg like I was something worth taking care over. I liked that she hadn't remembered to let go.

"I know you're all in a lather," I said, "because someone else had the chutzpah to think she could maybe do you a good turn, rather than reverse-wise. Still, I did just set up a pretty plum business deal for you, so you might at the very least say something like 'thank you, Ruthi.'"

Sol blinked up at me. Then her face softened, the faint smile that curved her thin lips slipping from sardonic to something that looked like it might've been genuine. "Thank you, Ruthi," she echoed, and I put both hands to her face and pulled it up towards me.

Her hand pressed down hard where she'd left it on my thigh. I could feel the throbbing in my knee picking up the pace with my heartbeat. I slid one hand round the back of her head to tug her closer to me, fingers tangling in her fine dark hair, and kissed her even harder, relishing the eager way her mouth opened under mine and the burn of her fingers on my skin.

Then she suddenly jerked her hand away from my leg, and sat back hard on the ground. It was almost the most graceless thing I'd ever seen her do. She grabbed for the hand that I had behind her head and pulled it down, fingers tangling tightly with mine. "No," she said. Her breathing was ragged. "This isn't happening. Not now."

I stared at her. I could see the indents of my teeth on her lips. "If you tell me you don't want me," I said, levelly as I could, "you're a liar after all, Sol Mendez-Yuki."

"Of course I do." From the way her hand tightened, I could tell she was just as frustrated as I was. "But damn it, Ruthi, you're engaged to my brother—"

"You know that's not real!"

"It's real to *him*," said Sol, "and there's some lines I won't cross." She took a breath, trying to get herself under composure. It didn't work all the way. I could still see the wildness and the wanting in her eyes as she looked at me, but that didn't do me a whole lot of good, the way things were. "If you're thinking you've got to pay me back for that rescue after all—"

"Oh, *fuck* that!"

She let out a short cough of a laugh. "All right. I didn't think so. But still."

"Still," I echoed, and yanked my hand out of her grip, wishing hell on her and her scruples, and the whole damn Mendez-Yuki clan.

"Oh, hell," I said again, in a different tone, as memory poured back in on me. "There's a family banquet tonight, isn't there?"

Sol's eyes widened. "Oh," she said. "Hell."

"How much time we got? Not much, it can't be." I looked at her, in her elegant work suit, her hair all mussed and her lips swollen and smeared with the lip gloss I'd put on for my meeting with Herschel—near-nude on me, but darkly visible against her lighter skin. Suddenly I had to bite back the urge to laugh. "Given givens, this is gonna sound like a bad come-on," I said, "but if you don't mind shimmying out of those nice pants of yours, I might be able to get that bloodstain off."

Sol looked back at me with an answering glint of amusement in her eyes. In spite of everything, I found myself glad to see it. I was having to face the fact that making that girl laugh was its own reward. "It's not the worst pickup I've ever heard," she said, "but there's no need to put yourself out. Our bot can do the laundry at home."

"Bots never do the tricky stains right, I find," I said, "but suit yourself. No pun intended." I pushed myself up out of the seat, testing the weight on my bad knee. The compression wrap was bringing down the swelling a little. I thought I'd just about be able to walk on it without showing my hand, so long as I found the right thing to wear. This morning I'd earmarked a clingy little sequined number with fringe that swung from mid-thigh to the knee. That certainly wouldn't be in the cards now.

Sol followed my thoughts. "Maybe you'd better not go, Ruthi. You won't be able to hide that leg."

"That's what you think." I slid myself carefully out of my much-abused skirt, then hobbled bare-legged over to the bathroom to put it to soak in the sink. Modesty has never been one of my vices.

When I came back out, Sol had gotten to her feet. I'd hoped to catch her ogling my ass, and maybe she had been, but by the time I turned around she was frowning at my knee.

I took a breath, squared my shoulders, and then nodded towards the door. "You'd better get a move on, if you want to have time to change out of that suit."

"I suppose I'd better." But she went to the door with a certain reluctance, not like her usual swagger, and when she reached it she turned back again. "You know—if you wanted to leave this hotel, and get a room at our place—"

"The better to keep tabs on me?" I said, sweetly.

"Yes," said Sol, soberly. "And make sure someone's around, if the T.O.U. make another play."

I laughed at her. "I know you're just dying to rack up another rescue, but if you're going to call cut before we get to the good parts then I don't see much point in replaying the hits. The T.O.U. won't risk a mess anywhere it can't look like an accident. I'll be fine, so long as I stay in public places." And then, when I saw her still hesitating:

"Alonso's my pal, not yours, remember? You should get going now."

She didn't look thrilled about it, but she went.

It didn't matter whether I wished she hadn't. I believed everything I'd said to Sol—believed it with my head, anyway, if not with my shaky knees. I didn't need to rely on glamor girls swooping down to rescue me out of the blue, and I didn't want to, either. I could take reasonable precautions my own damn self.

And what was the other option, ask Sol to stay here with me just because of a few jittery nerves? Absolutely not. I'd picked this solo expedition myself. If Jules had married Esteban the way she planned, it would've been solo expeditions forever. Maybe it still would be; who knew how things would shake out, or what Jules would want. I had to be able to hack it in the face of little setbacks like this. My knees might be weak now, but they'd be rock-steady by the time I got to that banquet, even if I had to prop them up with thigh-high boots to get them that way.

Nothing of note happened at the banquet anyway, not any more than it had at any of the other half-dozen fancy dinners I'd sat through. I swayed through three slow dances with Esteban, leaning on his shoulders like a woman in love, and pretended I didn't see Sol watching me. If she was looking for pain, uncertainty, or second thoughts, she was going to be disappointed.

CHAPTER 15

I DID TAKE more precautions after that. I asked Esteban to come pick me up in his car if we were going somewhere together, and I asked Joe Morgan the butler if he could come to me rather than reverse-wise. When I went somewhere with Sol rather than Esteban, she came to pick me up herself, too. She didn't need to be asked. We didn't talk any more than we had in the weeks before my little misadventure. It almost might not have happened, except that I kept my skirts and trousers long, and when we were alone in the car she didn't bother to pretend she wasn't looking at me.

Otherwise I spent the three weeks until my contract-signing as much in public as anyone could who wasn't on the celeb-circuit. I left cameras in my hotel room when I was out and fast-forwarded through the footage before going in, making sure nobody and nothing had left me any surprises. I sent my polite regrets to parties hosted by people I didn't know, or anywhere I might have to travel solo, and when dark of the moon came around again I stocked up on soya and locked the door behind me. Let the rest of New Monte assume I was already absorbing myself into the Mendez-Yuki bloc. Evelyn Ojukwu was busy with her engagement party, and it wasn't like she was going to stick around long enough to need more New Monte friends anyway.

Unfortunately, some gigs couldn't be fobbed off so easy. Jay and Sumitra Yuki-Chattiar informed me a week before the contract-signing that they were taking me out to dinner at the Old New Monte Inn. I'd been expecting this sooner or later from someone or other, but with everything else that had happened it had gone clean out of my head. The Old New Monte Inn was an unshakable tradition for the pre-engaged—an infamous little spot that did a roaring trade in good-natured public hazing of New Monte's matrimonial successes; where hoi polloi paid good prices to enjoy the mild embarrassment of the moderately famous. Officially the victims weren't supposed to know anything about it before they got there, but of course the whole thing was about as much of a surprise as a CEO giving themself a raise.

I'd been all ready to play along, but now I was supposed to be playing it safe, and I wasn't entirely sure the two things were compatible. Still, canceling wasn't in the cards, not unless I wanted to brand myself the worst kind of bad sport. I couldn't even tag-team a ride with Esteban or Sol, since the Mendez-Yuki would be making their own trip to the Old New Monte Inn at some point before our ceremony. It did give me a certain degree of joy to think about how much Esteban would hate the entire operation. That didn't make me any more comfortable about the notion of trusting myself to a strange car to get there. Sol might still have me on surveillance, but a lot of things could happen to you in an empty vehicle before anyone had time to show up and stop them.

But I shouldn't have worried, not with Miss New Monte Chivalry on the case. Just as I was trying to make up my mind whether I'd be safer walking to the Old New Monte Inn than driving, Louanne Hachi came to the lobby looking for me.

"All right, let's see what you're wearing," she said, by way of greeting, and looked me up and down. "Bubble-hem? Smart choice. You must have heard about the zero-G. But are you going to be able to manage those heels?"

I blinked at her. "I thought we were meeting at the inn."

"Oh, Sol said you might appreciate the company before the ordeal. Not that we think you're a delicate flower or anything, but—"

"No—no, she's right. I'm grateful." Taking my cue, I put on my delicate-flower face, little bitten lips and big anxious eyes. "I know it's silly, but I've been all nerves over this. On Kepler, the point is generally for representatives of major business ventures *not* to make public spectacles of themselves, but the rules on New Monte seem all upside down from that."

Louanne arched her eyebrows, in exaggerated alarm. "Oh, no, don't you dare start thinking *that*. We're not so uptight as you lot out there, of course, but there's limits."

"Miss Mendez-Yuki," I said, innocently, "seems to be able to get away with anything."

"She doesn't get away with it, really," said Louanne. "She could if she wanted to. I learned a lot from her, myself, about how to walk the lines. Now she's… a self-parody." She was smiling, but I didn't get the sense she really found it all that funny. Louanne Hachi had liked the old version of Sol Mendez-Yuki—the girl who was just different enough to be interesting, who'd figured out how to make herself fit the place she'd been put in, and never thought what she might owe to the place she came from. It couldn't make her feel too good that Sol didn't seem to like that girl too much herself anymore.

Then she put on another comical grimace, the witty

mentor once again. "But of course we're all self-parodies at the Old New Monte Inn, anyway. You've got to allow the tourists their fun. You won't bruise anything but your sense of good taste, though I expect that will be painful enough."

"How painful exactly?" I said, plaintively.

"Well… I'm not supposed to give it away, but I guess I could give you a few hints." She grinned at me. "Though not for free, of course. How's that lawsuit coming along, anyway? Galaxy says you never got in touch with her."

"Galaxy?" I said, blankly, and then remembered—that was the name of the Hachi lawyer who was, in theory, going to help me sue Lorelei, so long as Louanne got a cut of the damages. I'd been waffling about getting in touch with her, wondering whether it might not be better to hire someone independent to help me with my engagement contract after all. Louanne's lawyer seemed likely to be the pushy type, and picking up any more attention from the T.O.U. right now felt awfully like poking a wasp's next.

On the other hand, I'd spent more money than I was planning on security cams lately. It wasn't like I meant the lawsuit to go anywhere in the long run—and what was the worst they could do, after all? Take out a second hit on me?

I put my hands together in a pleading gesture, and said, "Miss Hachi, if you let me know what to look out for at the Old New Monte Inn, I promise I'll message Ms. Khan *tomorrow*."

WHEN SUMITRA SAW us getting out of the car together in front of the Old New Monte Inn, she heaved a dramatic sigh. "Spoilsport! Now she knows all about it, and she won't be any fun at all."

"We can make our own fun," said Jay, and handed over a gaudy tiara bedecked with plastic crystals. It looked cheaper than anything I'd worn since I arrived on New Monte, including the battered jumpsuit I'd put on to meet Sol at her meat locker. "Here's for you, Miss Ojukwu."

I made a face, but put it on. As soon as it touched my head, a line of iridescent sparkles popped into the edges of my field of vision on either side. Sumitra held up her PD so I could see myself in the mirror function. With the glowing holographic veil that the tiara projected around my head, I looked like a disco ball had gotten dressed up for a Halloween party.

I twisted my mouth up in as comical an expression as I thought non-comedian Evelyn Ojukwu could get away with. "It's... well, it's—I don't think I'd imagined it would be so, ah..."

"Majestic?" suggested Jay.

"It's possible that's the word I meant," I said, politely.

"All right," Sumitra conceded, "I suppose there is still a *degree* of fun to be had here."

Jay held out an arm to me; I took it, projecting resignation, and then turned around to mouth *thank you* at Louanne Hachi, who grinned and threw me a wink.

As I crossed the threshold, I felt the tingle of a grav-barrier, and then my feet abruptly slid out sideways from under me. I tightened my grip on Jay, who had already grabbed for one of the handles set around the inside of the door. Louanne, following us in, let herself bob upwards and nabbed a handle near the ceiling with the ease of long practice. She'd done her best to cram as many basic principles of zero-G etiquette into my head as she could in the ten-minute car ride, and I'd done my best to act like someone who needed them.

Most people raised planetside don't run into complete zero-G much, outside of the occasional artistic experience. Even steerage-class spaceships generally keep a partial gravity field up; it's cheaper than paying for the damage caused by inexperienced travelers. But the Old New Monte Inn's entire vibe was early Expansion, and that included the weightless dining experience. The place claimed to be the first restaurant established on New Monte, and while technology marched on around it, the Old New Monte kept a death grip on its floating furniture and 'gourmet' astro-food.

Gaea St. Clair and a few of the other luminaries of New Monte's social scene were already tethered into their seats at the highest of the tables, locked into position a few feet below the ceiling. They waved cheerfully to us. I gave them my best nervous grimace back.

"I'll give you a boost towards the table," said Jay. "If you miss first time round, don't worry, they're used to that. We'll just try again."

"Oh," I said weakly, "lovely."

The next moment, I was soaring through the air towards the high table. The shimmering holographic veil streamed behind me, and diners at the lower tables clapped and cheered as the sparkling light passed through them. Instinct attempted to kick in; I shoved it back. It would have been easy enough to grab the chair and swing myself gracefully up into it, but the people watching were here for a different kind of show. Instead of sticking the landing, I let myself bounce off the table and flail a foot sideways before Gaea grabbed me by the arm and hauled me into position.

I heard more laughter and applause from the crowd as I

sheepishly tethered myself in. "Thank you," I murmured to Gaea.

"It was painful to watch," said Gaea, and took a sip from her cocktail-box.

Jay, Louanne, and Sumitra all kicked themselves up after me. They were followed by a waiter in a vivid teal bridesmaid's dress, who handed me a flask boiling over with something that looked awfully like dry ice, but probably wasn't.

"But I didn't order anything yet," I protested.

"Oh," said Sumitra, smirking, "you aren't ordering for yourself tonight."

"Drinks for the bride-to-be," said Jay, "are always on the house at the Old New Monte Inn."

"So long as you drink plenty of them."

"After all, you *are* the entertainment."

I didn't have to feign Evelyn Ojukwu's reluctance as I held out my hand. Mystery drinks weren't much my speed at the best of times, and after my near miss the other day, I wasn't feeling particularly trusting.

I didn't really think Alonso would try and slip anything really poisonous into the potables at a popular tourist joint. Even an ordinary case of food poisoning at the Old New Monte Inn would make the news, and I couldn't figure that I was a big enough nuisance to be worth the headline. I might've pissed the T.O.U. off, but there weren't any fortunes riding around in *my* head. Then again, a few rounds of the Old New Monte's standard Bachelorette Surprise might do some of Alonso's work for him, even without any illegal additions.

Still, even though the sober-patch I'd slipped under the collar of my dress would limit the effects of ordinary booze, as well as the most common hypnos and downers—and even though logic told me the drink probably wouldn't afflict me with anything worse than heartburn—I still had to give myself a moment before I raised it to my lips and took a gulp.

It exploded in my mouth like comet candy, which was a little unfortunate given that it tasted like someone had tried to put out a chemical fire with cough syrup. I coughed loudly, put a hand to my throat, stared at the drink, made a face of visible determination, and then took a second cautious sip, accompanied by the sounds of applause from all the tables below.

"I'll drink it," I promised, waited a moment, and then added, in Evelyn Ojukwu's most scandalized tones, "But I'm certainly not going to chug it!"

Everyone laughed. Sumitra took my arm in hers, in that affectionate way debs sometimes will do. It generally doesn't mean much beyond the fact that you happen to be showing the right age, gender, and class markers to get the friend hat for the day, but if those are the markers you want to be showing, then the friend hat is a pretty good look. "Let no one say," she told me kindly, "that we peer-pressured you, a fairly short person, into chugging this, a very large alcoholic drink. Peer-pressured you into drinking it, yes, we've undeniably done that, but only as quickly as you feel is appropriate for your health."

"We only throw very *safe* engagement parties here on New Monte," drawled Gaea. "Now, on the Jupiter belt—"

Louanne grinned behind her hand, and Jay and Sumitra exchanged tolerant looks. I sipped my drink as quickly as I felt was appropriate for my health, which was not very, and plastered an attentive look on my face. Gaea St. Clair was rapidly becoming one of my favorite things about New Monte. As a person I couldn't say she did much for me, but as a conversational placeholder she was better than a bad scandal. Every minute she spent talking was a minute that I didn't have to do anything besides look decorative.

But of course it was too much to hope that Gaea could monologue the whole night. As the waiter arrived with the first course—rice balls stuffed with caviar and wrapped in edible plastic for easy zero-G consumption—a clanging sounded from one of the tables below us. One of the guests below had started hitting their cup with their spoon. (You didn't even need utensils to eat most of the food served at the Old New Monte, but for some reason everybody had a spoon anyway.) "Contract speech!" she hollered. "Contract speech!"

It didn't take long for the rest of the tourists in the restaurant to pick up the chorus. Gaea, effectively drowned out, leaned back and projected an air of indifference. Jay and Sumitra smirked. Louanne patted me on the shoulder. I heaved a sigh, and pushed myself around to face the other guests.

"Good evening, everyone," I said, and then flinched as the words reverberated around the room—the veil must have been miked, and somebody had flipped the switch. I tried to follow that up with a small curtsy, which went about as well as you'd expect in zero-G. Laughter all round. I coughed, and started over. "My name is Evelyn Ojukwu, of the Kepler Ojukwus, and next week it will be my great good fortune to sign an engagement contract with Esteban Mendez-Yuki of MYCorps."

Everybody cheered and banged away on their glasses harder than ever. Next to me, the waiter in the bridesmaid's dress said the ritual words that Louanne had warned me about, with an air of infinite boredom: "Why don't you tell us about him, honey?"

The guests took up the chant with glee. "Talk him up! Talk him up!"

I couldn't blame the tourists. Given a one-night chance to make a megabillionaire dance for my entertainment, I'd use it too. Under other circumstances, I'd have looked forward to giving them a show.

Under ideal circumstances, I'd have been talking up anybody in the whole world besides Esteban Mendez-Yuki.

Still, I'd spent plenty of time in the past two months singing Esteban's praises, and after enough practice even the biggest whoppers slide out easy. With a simper and a stammer, I reeled off the standard list. Esteban was kind, he was intelligent, he was considerate, he cared; he never hesitated to share his thoughts, his feelings, his knowledge—

"His money!" someone shouted from below, and was promptly shouted down by all their companions. "Let her talk! Look at the poor kid—she's in love!"

Well, even at the Old New Monte Inn, some social fictions prevailed.

I clapped my hands over an imaginary blush. "I'm—" I turned back to the waiter, and said, plaintively, "Can't I have another one of those drinks?"

The waiter, of course, had one ready. I drained it halfway, then turned back to the crowd. "I'm the luckiest girl in the world!" I blurted out, whirled around, and propelled myself back into my seat with a thud, ignoring the laughter and applause that roared up from behind me.

"And if you enjoyed that very special preview," the waiter announced, in a monotone, "don't forget to buy a raffle ticket. Three lucky winners tonight will receive an invitation to see the lovebirds sign their contract in person, all proceeds from raffle sales go to Esteban Mendez-Yuki's favorite charity."

While the waiter told the crowd all about how much Esteban cared about the faint remnants of Earth's rainforests, the rest of my table showered me with sympathetic smirks. "So," Jay said, leaning back. "Now that you've shouted Esteban's virtues to the skies, it's time for us to go ahead and do our best to make you regret it. Who's got an embarrassing Stevie story to tell?" Then, promptly raising a hand: "I do! Pick me!"

I laughed, as I was supposed to, and noticed that the mike had been turned off again. "Is this part of the tradition too?"

"Well, it's not for the audience," said Sumitra, with a wave of her hand down at the plebes below, "but a person ought to know what they're getting into, don't you think?"

"Not," said Jay, "that those swim trunks on Lorelei wouldn't have given you a clue. But if you thought those were a trip, you should hear about the month that Esteban got into a panic about atmospheric failure and tried to convince us all to start carrying oxygenized fanny packs—"

Sumitra followed up with a story about Esteban getting lost on a boating expedition and refusing to ask for directions; Jay jumped back in with an anecdote about Esteban throwing a fit when Gaea beat him on some kind of exam; then Sumitra told us all about Esteban's first time trying to lead a business meeting, in excruciating comic detail. I was starting to get a kind of feeling like my fiancé's favorite cousins were trying to scare me off.

Twice more during this portion of the evening, the

tourists started banging on their drinks again. Apparently bachelorettes were expected to deliver at least one lecture per drink. The first time, I politely repeated my first speech nearly word-for-word. The second time, I got up and explained to the room how adorably unique Esteban was, and then re-told Jay's story about the fanny packs.

That was probably about when Sumitra decided to up her game. After the next round of drinks was delivered, she said cheerfully, as if it was part of an ongoing conversation, "*And,* of course, there's the mystery woman from a few months ago. The gold digger from the luxe-liner, with the paternity scam."

A freeze-dried shrimp fell off my skewer kebab. It bobbed past me in the zero-G, and I focused on grabbing it. Once I'd caught it, I looked up again at Sumitra, eyes wide. "He told you about that?"

"Ah," said Sumitra, "he told *you* about that! And here he swore I was his only confidante!"

"Well," said Gaea, leaning forward avidly—she was a few drinks in by now herself, and showing it—"*I* haven't heard a thing about it, so—"

"Whoops," said Jay. "Sumitra, sounds like you spilled some beans you shouldn't have spilled."

"Oh, well." Sumitra had the grace to look a little embarrassed. "If he gets mad at me, I'm blaming the hooch. He was *so* broken up about it, though, it really was silly—as if he's the first person who ever let a little parasite like that talk his pants off! Never mind the paternity scam, I told him, he's just lucky he didn't catch any diseases."

"Miss Ojukwu's lucky, you mean," said Gaea, and laughed, and Jay and Sumitra did, too; so did nearly everyone at the table, except Louanne Hachi. She looked a little disdainful, but didn't say anything as all her friends hyukked it up around her—and I looked down, my fingernails biting into my palm, because they didn't know, they couldn't know, who it was they were really laughing at.

A memory flashed: Sol, and the way she'd covered for me at the Mendez-Yuki banquet right when I was about to make myself the butt of the joke. I suddenly felt sure that if she'd been there, she would have said something to stop them from laughing like that. Even if I hadn't been there myself to watch her do it. Even if she hadn't known anything at all about the poor lying kid who'd knocked boots with her brother—the gold digger, the parasite, the girl who wasn't good enough for any of them, and was worth more than all of them put together.

She was a smooth customer, Sol Mendez-Yuki, but I was pretty sure that was real. Against all the instincts I had, everything I knew about people like her, I trusted that to be real, and the awareness of how badly I wanted her there right then hit me like the sock in the stomach I wanted to give Sumitra.

Score one for chivalry, after all.

But Sol wasn't here to challenge her cousin to a duel for me, so I was going to have to turn the conversation myself, before I did something I'd regret. I coughed, and raised my breather delicately. "I really don't think we should be talking about this. I know it was, um, very personal, for Esteban."

"Oh, you're so *sweet*," cried Sumitra. "I expect Stevie will be glad to have your shoulder to cry on."

"Hear, hear," said Louanne, seizing the moment, and tapped her fork on her cup.

It felt like I'd just given my last speech ten minutes ago, but the audience took it up with the same level of gusto they'd been showing all night. Swallowing down my anger, I unbuckled myself from the chair, pushed myself around, and cleared my throat for the fourth time.

"Hold on, honey," said the waiter in the bridesmaid's dress, appearing suddenly at my elbow, and turned on the voice projector. "Hello, everyone, we have some raffle winners, will lucky number tickets 25248, 29089, and 35772 please stand up to receive their invitations."

The lucky number ticket holders obligingly stood, and I focused in on them. I was glad for the chance to look at someone I didn't want to murder right then. One of them was a middle-aged lady clutching a comically oversized breather who had Earth tourist written all over her. The second was an elderly person without any clear gender markers who immediately handed their invitation over to an enthusiastic teenager.

The third had salt-and-pepper hair, a broken nose, and a goatee. It took me a second to figure out why his features set alarms to screaming in my brain. After all, it had been weeks since I saw his face, on a tiny security-cam under a bar—and after I saw it, I'd done my best to forget it.

Maybe Alfred Alonso's favorite henchman was just a big fan of the olives at the Old New Monte Inn, but I really didn't think I could count on that. Especially not when he'd just picked up Alonso a free pass to the biggest Mendez-Yuki event of the season.

I had to leave as soon as possible, that was clear. Whoever this man was, I was pretty sure that neither he nor Alonso knew I'd seen his face on Lorelei, and I wanted it to stay that way. If I played my cards right, I could skedaddle before he knew I'd got the wind up, and hopefully forestall whatever plan Alonso had in place. Unless they *did* know I'd seen him on Lorelei, and the whole point of him popping up here was to spook me enough that I'd panic and bolt without taking proper precautions, which I'd been damn near close to doing.

"Miss Ojukwu," said Sumitra, nudging me with her elbow,

"They're waiting for you."

I'd almost forgotten that I was supposed to make another speech.

I looked at the girl who, a few minutes ago, had called my sister a parasite, and then turned back to the crowd. I was grateful to her, in a way. The surge of anger I felt when I saw her friendly face had clicked my brain back on. I lifted my glass, smiled brightly at the crowd, and began wandering my way through a paean to all the bits of Esteban's anatomy that were even vaguely socially acceptable to discuss. I dwelt lovingly on long chins and high cheekbones, well-muscled shoulders and perfect backs. I'm pretty sure it was funny; at least, the people below seemed to be laughing. Even Alonso's henchman looked like he was enjoying himself. I guess it was nice in a way that he enjoyed his work. Me, I barely knew what I was even saying. I was too busy working myself out an escape route.

When I ran out of ways to praise the Mendez-Yuki physique, I drained the end of my drink, chucked my cup into the air with wild abandon, and dipped the crowd a significantly more extravagant curtsy than the one I'd attempted at the beginning of the night. On the rebound, I let myself go bouncing into Jay, who bobbed backwards into Louanne, who crashed into Sumitra, who knocked her half-empty drink right onto the tourists sitting below her. One of them shrieked and batted it back upwards, after which it spun slowly through the air on a long arc across the table, liquid sloshing out of its narrow opening in all directions as it rotated. The design of the zero-G cups meant I couldn't quite get the satisfaction of a full-on drenching, but every drop that fell on a designer dress soothed a little bit of my spirit.

The crowd below screamed with delight, and Gaea—just about the only person at the table who'd remained unscathed throughout the entire disaster—laughed out loud for the first time tonight. "Miss Ojukwu," she said, "it seems first impressions never *do* lie."

"Help," I said faintly, "I can't get back in my chair."

Jay, resigned and rum-speckled, reached out to help me back to my seat, then caught a good look at me and stopped. "Uh-oh. Uh, Miss Ojukwu—"

"Oh, *no*," cried Louanne, and dove over to hover in front of me. It didn't do a lot of practical good—zero-G was a thoroughly three-dimensional environment—but I suppose she had to try. "Oh, Miss Ojukwu, I'm so sorry! Your beautiful dress!"

During all this engineered slapstick, I'd taken the opportunity to rip my beautiful dress right down the back seam of its demure bubbled skirt. Now it was exposing my beautiful ass (in extremely expensive silk underwear) to the Old New Monte Inn's entire clientele.

I looked down and let out a horrified shriek, as if I'd noticed this for the very first time. Then I grabbed at the two halves of the skirt and tried pathetically to clutch them against my knees. Louanne reached out to steady me so all my flailing didn't send me somersaulting off into the zero-G again. Sumitra winced and looked away, overcome with contact embarrassment.

"I'm so sorry," I said, weakly, "but I don't think I can stay out any longer."

I fully expected Louanne to offer me a lift home at this point, but before she could, Gaea St. Clair piped up, "I'll give you a lift back, if you'd like."

"Miss St. Clair!" I had no idea what had prompted her to offer me this particular gift horse, but I wasn't about to say no. "It would give me all the pleasure in the world to accept." Relief made a good stand-in for tipsiness, as I wobbled around to her side of the table, still clutching my skirts. "Everybody, I'm so sorry to cut the evening short—"

"Oh, don't worry," said Jay, wryly. "We got our money's worth."

"And Miss Hachi, I want to thank you in *particular!*" I turned around and threw my arms around Louanne Hachi, who was still doing her heroic best to stabilize me. As we teetered together, I hissed in her ear, "The man who won the raffle—ticket number 35-something— I'm sure he was working on Lorelei, when Sol and I got stranded. I don't know what he's doing here, but if we're going to work on that lawsuit, your people ought to look into him." I felt her go stiff in my arms, and immediately released her to grab for my floating skirts again. "Oh *no*, I can't keep any kind of hold of these things! Miss St. Clair, please, let's go quick!"

I didn't look anywhere near the direction of Alonso's henchman when I left the scene. Hopefully he didn't know I was wise to him, and I wanted to keep it that way. In the meantime, I'd let Louanne Hachi do the research for me. She was the one who'd seen profit in the situation; maybe she'd turn up something I could use to tip the hand in my favor.

"Miss St. Clair," I said a few minutes later, as we spun out onto the road, "I want to thank you again for—"

"Listen." Gaea put a hand on each of my cheeks and turned my face to her so she could stare at me solemnly. She'd taken one last chug of her drink before leaving, and it seemed like it was hitting her hard. "Miss *Ojukwu*." She emphasized each syllable of my fake name, sing-song, and getting the middle one wrong. "You must promise me that you will not allow yourself to be discouraged by the Yuki-Chattiar."

"Discouraged?" She had to be tipsier than I thought, if she was just blowing that subtext open. I wasn't sure whether to be amused or irritated. I'd put in almost as much work pretending I didn't notice Jay and Sumitra's hints about Esteban's unsuitability as a partner as they had on dropping them. "Why would I be—"

"They're not sure about you," Gaea went on, ignoring my interruption completely, "and I suppose I don't blame them. I've never particularly liked you." She punctuated her words by jogging my face back and forth between her hands. "You were very! Clumsy!"

"I apologized," I said, resisting the urge to inch backwards.

"You did," agreed Gaea, and, thankfully, let go of my face and sat backwards against her seat. "I accepted your apology. You may be clumsy, but you seem responsible, on the whole. Your conduct is terribly provincial, but you understand what we *owe* to our *economic infrastructure*." I had to work hard to keep my face under control. Who knew people really talked like this? "MYCorps is a very important company. It needs a responsible guiding hand. We thought that would be Sol, but nobody's counting on *that* anymore. I suppose I would have preferred somebody I knew to step into those shoes, but, well!" She laughed, dismissing that idea. "*I* wouldn't marry into that family, but it's a wonderful opportunity for *you*. You'll do as well as anyone, and far better than no one."

"Thank you," I said, seriously.

"Thank *you*," answered Gaea, equally seriously, and patted me on the head.

I had to bite my lip.

"You're wondering," Gaea went on, after a moment, "what business it is of mine. *I'm* not a Mendez-Yuki. I've never even imagined I might become one, like poor Louanne." She clicked her tongue, and then fixed her eyes very intently on me again. "But I am something more important, Miss Ojukwu. I am a *business partner*. I am a St. *Clair*. We supply *all* MYCorps' data and encryption services. Who has more business worrying about the Mendez-Yuki marriage than that?"

"I can't think who would," I agreed, and couldn't resist patting her on the head in return. I half-expected her to swat at me, but she just gave me a gracious nod and a smile, apparently content that we were in accord.

"Miss St. Clair," I said, after a moment, "what *would* happen if MYCorps destabilized?"

"Oh, chaos," said Gaea, waving a hand, and flopping back once again on the seat. "Imagine all those shipments going through the Pluto-Centauri ERB without sureties! Imagine all the lost clients! The impact on the markets! Imagine all that business going to *other corporations*!" She groaned, stared despairingly at the roof of the car, and proclaimed, "The notion haunts me."

I couldn't say that thinking about Gaea St. Clair's hypothetical financial losses gave me any particular heebie-jeebies. Dropping a few millions might be just what the doctor ordered for her. "That's terrible," I said, brightly. "And what if—" I hesitated a moment, but she *was* awfully drunk; I didn't think she'd remember much of this conversation. "What if there was a data breach at MYCorps? What would happen then?"

"Oh, *that* couldn't happen," said Gaea St. Clair. "Not with *our* technology. Could you imagine? MYCorps is the official insurance vendor for the Pluto-Centauri ERB. They store valuation data for everything that leaves the solar system. *Everything.* Developing technologies, Earth-sourced food and biologicals, personal records— the implications of a leak could go far beyond the financial, for every company that ships product through the ERB, every satellite that relies on imports from the Sol system, and every individual who participates in the intergalactic economy. *That,* Miss Ojukwu, is why you should be very glad that *my* company handles the data security, and *you* and little Esteban are only responsible for the accounting. Or rather, will only be responsible for the accounting. Once you are married. Which I sincerely hope you will be, and best wishes to you both." She gave me a sweet, bright smile. "I hope I've removed a weight from your shoulders."

"Oh," I said, weakly, "they're breezy."

"Good," said Gaea, who promptly put her head down on one of said shoulders, and started snoring.

I'd never have guessed her for such a handsy drunk; still, I had to admit, it was pretty typical Gaea St. Clair. Just when I could have really used some self-centered babble to distract me, she did the most self-centered thing she could possibly have done, and left me to brood.

Still, she had her uses. Human shield, for one. Nobody tried to kill me the whole way home. You've got to count your wins where you find them.

* * *

I CAN'T SAY that sleep came easy to me that night, but I didn't waste my time. First, I sewed the split seam of my dress back together. I'd never wear it again in New Monte, but I could always sell it secondhand later. Once that was done, I kept my promise to Louanne Hachi, and emailed her lawyer. Galaxy Khan was a consummate professional with unfashionably cropped silver hair, who didn't bat an eyelash when I asked to meet her in a karaoke cafe rather than back at her office. "Miss Hachi tells me," said she, perched with legs neatly crossed on the karaoke bench, "that you're looking into legal action you may be able to bring against Lorelei Satellite Syndicate for their potentially criminal negligence in failing to evacuate yourself and Miss Mendez-Yuki. I have some time available around my other duties, and I'm happy to assist. I understand you think this man may be involved?"

She passed me a picture: silver-shot hair, broken nose, Lorelei Libations shirt. "Gosh," I said, impressed, "Miss Hachi works fast."

"His name is Bartimeo Iapetus Flecks," said my new lawyer-slash-private-investigator.

"That's a mouthful! Do you think he goes by all of it?"

"That," said Galaxy Khan, dryly, "has yet to be determined. In any case, we're investigating his credentials and his connection with the Satellite Syndicate."

I eyed her. "I'm sure you and Miss Hachi both understand—I'm still waiting to hear back from my family about the lawsuit, so in the meantime, it's important to proceed with the utmost—"

"Discretion," said Galaxy Khan, patiently. "Of course. It would be unwise in the extreme to let the Satellite Syndicate know that we're contemplating legal action at this time. Miss Hachi and I simply wanted to let you know that matters were underway."

"I appreciate it," I told her, sincerely. Miss Hachi and her legal team had a lot more resources to bear than I did—and call me prejudiced, but I didn't really want any of Alonso's minions lurking around underfoot at my contract-signing ceremony if I could figure out a way to keep them out of it, lucky raffle winner or not. "Speaking of matters that are underway—" I coughed. "Miss Hachi also may have mentioned, this potential lawsuit isn't the only legal issue I've got on the table right now."

Galaxy Khan flashed me a smile like a shark's. "Miss Ojukwu," she said, "We've had contract documents drafted up for Miss Hachi's eventual alliance for the past ten years. It would be no trouble at all to amend them to your particular circumstances."

Poor Louanne! Maybe there was a version of her who could've hung onto her girl when the going got tough; maybe a part of her even knew what she was missing. But she'd been raised on New Monte rules, and their bank books just didn't account for all the things you wasted while chasing that fat bottom line. And I couldn't feel too sorry about that, either, when I looked at the number of standard simoleons written into the engagement contract that Galaxy Khan had helped me to draw up. It was a perfectly reasonable agreement. In fact, it was significantly more reasonable than the Hachi template that we used as the baseline. Theirs had provisions that spanned everything from dowry transactions to trademark rights to inherited citizenships from ancient nation-states back on Earth.

I didn't need any dowry payment, and I couldn't care less about trademark rights. Moreover, I told Louanne's lawyer, if I was ever the one to call quits on the union, I'd be happy to slink off with my engines in stealth mode and make no further claims on the Mendez-Yuki estate. That was a concession sweet enough that it had the Mendez-Yuki lawyers ready to swallow just about any pill that went with it.

If, on the other hand, Esteban was the one to decide he wanted out after the contract was signed—well, that was the big pot of gold, the jubilee, the jackpot. Anyone who married aspirationally knew that it was even odds they'd someday get ditched for a younger model. A person had to provide for their old age. Galaxy Khan and I were in perfect agreement that if the Mendez-Yuki turfed me out, I had the right to make sure the landing was soft.

If Jules had signed a contract like this before breaking the news to Esteban, she wouldn't have had to worry about anything for the rest of her days. As for the sprog, that kid would've inherited a massive stake in MYCorps, not to mention citizenship in six different Earth nations and twelve satellites. No Mendez-Yuki lawyers could have kept us away from getting what was owing to her.

Then again, if Jules had really been the kind of girl who came with a lawyer to help her write up an engagement contract, Esteban wouldn't have ditched her to begin with.

Bless the Mendez-Yuki, anyway, and their multiple assets and multiple citizenships and multi-lingual business ventures. None of the legal team would blink an eye to see that among the long list of Evelyn Ojukwu's legal names and corporate aliases was a small company registered to Ruth Idefayo Johnson.

CHAPTER 16

I SPENT THE evening before my engagement party in front of the mirror in my hotel bathroom, practicing my speech. Not the one I was going to give when we formally signed a piece of paper in front of all the who's who of New Monte—I didn't give two hoots about that—but the one I meant to give after, when Esteban and I were alone.

I'm no stranger to prep work, but I'm not normally big on line readings. They can't help but sound stilted in conversation, and I'd rather let the dialogue come natural. This time had to be different. Every other job I'd ever pulled had rested on my ability to play someone else. For *this* job to succeed, I had to finally introduce Esteban to Ruthi Johnson, and I'd been surprising myself enough lately that I didn't feel comfortable seat-of-my-pantsing it.

"You almost got it on the first day," I told the mirror. I was wearing one of Evelyn Ojukwu's baby-doll nighties and my bathrobe over it. The bathrobe wasn't the only thing throwing off the Evelyn Ojukwu look.

Today, for the first time in months, I'd gone to get my hair professionally relaxed. Now it was wrapped up in the Bantu knots I'd wear to bed. Tomorrow, I'd have loose, springy waves flowing over my shoulders, just like the ones Jules wore on the regular. When I read this speech out to Esteban, I'd look as much like her as I ever did.

I didn't look like her tonight, any more than I looked like Evelyn Ojukwu. "What did Jules tell you that scared you so bad, Esteban?" I asked my familiar-unfamiliar face in the mirror. "It can't just be all that money we earned playing potshot poker on the luxe-liners, can it? Because, you know, eight out of ten times we were playing fair—you folks are really all just pretty bad. Did she tell you about how we tricked our way out of the South Twenty-five gang, how she pretended to sell me off to an organ-trader so we'd have the cash to catch our first cruiser? That was my idea, pal. I was the one who planned it, and I was the one who drugged the sleazebag to get out on the other end. Did she tell you the names of everyone we ever scammed? Did she tell you about all the nights the cons didn't come off, about all the times we didn't get a bed, didn't get a doctor, didn't have anything that cost anything? Is that what scared you, more than all the crime?"

I broke off and frowned at my face in my mirror, which had taken on a grim, angry look I didn't like. I wasn't here to throw myself a pity party. I just needed Esteban to be off-balance enough that he'd take the first exit off the road to the altar without ever looking back.

I pulled a face, snorted air out from my nostrils, and watched my cheeks and jawbone settle themselves back into their regular smooth lines. Then I looked down again at my notes, and tried again. Maybe a faint smug smile would help the delivery. "Did she tell you all the fake names we ever had? Probably not. She was too little to remember half of them anyway. Me, though…"

I broke off again, but this time, it wasn't because I'd

gone off-script.

Someone was knocking at the door of my hotel room.

I sat very still for a minute, staring down at the pad that had all my careful notes for tomorrow—for the one day I had to get through, before I could leave this satellite behind for good—and then I pulled up the video feed from the camera I'd set up over the door.

When the image came up, it was Sol Mendez-Yuki.

In some ways, opening the door to her was an even worse idea than it would have been to let in Alonso or one of his goons. But I did it; of course I did.

We looked at each other for a moment in silence. She was still wearing the same outfit I'd seen her in that night at the pre-engagement dinner, as Joe Morgan led us through the final plans for the engagement party—a silky cream jumpsuit that buttoned all the way up with gold studs, and a tailored black jacket over it, with a gold-edged breather to match. MYCorps logo colors. No capes for Sol this time, not for an event where she was representing the family, but she didn't need them to draw the eye. Even the cookie-cutter glitz of the hotel hallway took on personality with Sol Mendez-Yuki using it as a backdrop.

"Can I come in?" she said.

"Sure," I said, and smiled at her as I stepped backwards and gestured her inside. "You here to throw me a bachelorette bash?"

She didn't rise to the bait—just looked back at me gravely, with an intensity that gave me a kind of shiver. "Ruthi," she said. "I'm sorry to disturb you tonight—"

"If you were all that sorry, you wouldn't be here." I pulled the door shut behind her, then went across the room and flopped down in the armchair. "All right, spill it. What's the angle this time? I don't know how you think it'll make any difference to Esteban at this point if I break his heart now or twenty-four hours later—"

"I'm not here to talk about Esteban," said Sol. She set her breather down carefully on the small table by the door. "I'm here to talk about me."

My heartbeat picked up a little. I told it not to get excited. "Well! That's a nice change."

"You'll perhaps be glad to know," said Sol, "I've figured out a solution to my problem with the T.O.U." She leaned against the closed door, arms crossed over her chest. "Unfortunately, since nobody else knows I *have* a problem with the T.O.U., you're going to have to be my emergency contact on this one."

I looked at her blankly. "*I* figured out a solution to your problem with the T.O.U."

Sol's mouth quirked. "Ruthi," she said; the tenderness in the syllables made my name sound like an endearment. "They shorted out a whole satellite just to stop me from making my last deal. You really think they're not going to come claim what they're owed before I see any profits from this one?"

"If you think we can't outsmart Alonso and his band of thugs—"

"I think he's got a lot of thugs." Sol tilted her head back and let it rest against the plastic of the door, her eyes lifted to the ceiling. "And I think I don't have enough time. The debt's due in two weeks, Ruthi."

"And the freighter's leaving in one!"

"The cargo still has to get to Earth, and the sales data has to get back. And in the meantime, Alonso's men are going to come take what they want. Unless it becomes absolutely impossible for them to do so."

"... I don't follow." My heart wasn't bumping anymore; it was sinking.

"It's data they're after, that's all. What's in here." Sol tapped her forehead with her forefinger. "Passwords, access, insider knowledge. If none of that data's in there, then what have I got that's of value? They might as well just cut their losses and let me pay off my debt myself. Your business deal should go perfectly smoothly."

"Sol," I said, slowly. "Tell me you're not talking about what I think you're talking about."

"Memory extractions," said Sol, to the ceiling, "are also getting very good these days."

"The hell they are!"

She lifted her head off the door to meet my eyes, and smiled at me. "Targeting to within ninety-five percent accuracy really isn't bad. They'll only need to take everything related to the work I do for MYCorp—it's not like I won't have plenty left."

"Oh, you think?" I surged up out of my chair, furious. "What the hell is wrong with you? *All* memory-tech's still unlicensed! You know how many things can go wrong once someone starts playing around in your head? Letting Alonso do the scan is bad enough, but at least that's supposed to leave your head pretty much the same as it found it. A wipe—"

"Means I can't betray anything," said Sol, "or anyone. No reason to hurt anybody I care about. Nothing to hold over my head."

"Nothing *in* your head, maybe! I haven't spent a month following you around to all those damn dinners not to know how much of your life you've spent on your father's company. If you can't remember any of that, you think you're going to be the same person you were? You're just going to throw away the person you are now like a piece of trash?"

Sol shrugged her shoulders back against the door.

My fists clenched at my sides. There were hero complexes and there were martyr complexes, and this was going a fair ways over the line, it seemed to me. Suddenly I could understand how exasperated Louanne Hachi had sounded, when she talked about Sol cutting off her nose to spite her face. "And all this over what—your company rep? There's no business worth that!"

"My integrity is worth that," said Sol. "My family's worth that."

"The hell *they* are!"

"Well, I think they are," Sol said levelly. "Your opinion may vary, of course, but I don't think that's your call to make, is it?"

I made myself stay still, made my hands drop, made myself breathe in and out. "Of course," I said. "What right have I got to an opinion? I only practically got myself killed trying to help you, is all—and you do know some of us don't do that every damn day of the week, don't you? I know it probably looks a little different to a high roller like yourself, you'd put yourself on the line for anything that moves, but for some of us that means something real—"

Her eyes were locked on my face, like I was telling her something she hadn't known before—and maybe I was, more than I'd meant to. I cut myself off before I could embarrass myself any further. "Anyway, you're right. It's not my call and you don't owe me anything and if I stuck my neck out for nothing that's on me. I'm just saying, if you don't want my opinion, then why the *fuck* are you here?"

"Well," said Sol, softly. "A few reasons."

I twirled a finger savagely in the air.

"Emergency contact, like I said. I've made an appointment at a place on Second and Salle, and I don't expect anything to go wrong, but on the infinitesimal-chance—"

"You come out blank or brain-dead?" I snarled.

"—that there's an unexpected result, someone will need to alert my family and explain what's happened." She hesitated a moment, then added, "Both my families. Elly will need to know too, especially with Felix still missing."

"Right," I said, "those kids in the underside. It'll be great for *them*, when you don't remember why you cared about keeping their family afloat. No more simoleons from big sister Sol."

Well, I never said I was above emotional blackmail, but I like it better when it works. Sol just gave me a long look to show me that she knew exactly what I was doing, and went on as if I hadn't said anything. "I could leave a message, but that kind of thing is practically begging to be hacked and printed in the next daily news. If it comes to it, I'd rather that there was somebody who could explain in person."

"Fine," I said. "Dandy. Sounds like a fun job. Except I won't be here anymore." Now, more than ever, I was determined to get the shuttle off New Monte as soon as I possibly could after the contract was signed. If Sol wanted to spend the next two weeks throwing herself on her own sword, the very last thing I wanted was to be around to see it.

"I think you will," said Sol. She uncrossed her arms from in front of her, folded them up behind her head, and looked up towards the ceiling again. "I made the appointment for tomorrow morning."

For a moment all I could do was stare. Finally, my breath came back to me. "*You what?*"

"Hell, Ruthi," Sol murmured, "you think it's going to be so much fun for me watching you get engaged to my brother that I was going to clear my schedule for it?"

It took me three, maybe four steps, and then I was up in her face. I grabbed her by the front of her fancy jacket, feeling the fine silk crush under my hands.

She was looking at me again now, which was most of what I had wanted. I let go. I took a step back and shoved my hands into my pockets.

"Two reasons, you said."

"A few," Sol agreed.

She unfolded her arms from behind her head. Then she reached out to take my hand in one of hers. I didn't help nor hinder, letting her handle it like a piece of wood. She looked down at my wrist and arm, tense with anger and other things, and made a rueful face. Then she lifted my hand up to her mouth and brushed her lips across the back of it.

It was a typical Sol gesture, courtly, dramatic; I'd seen her do it before, but the way she held my eyes as she did it made this something different.

A shiver went through me. I didn't say a word. She put my hand carefully down again, and bent her head to kiss me.

I pulled away almost immediately. She let me go. "Some lines," I said, mocking her inflection, "you won't cross, huh?"

"I guess it looks a little different to me," said Sol, "now that—well, you said it yourself. I don't know who exactly I'll be after tomorrow, given the givens. If this is all that I—" She broke off, absently smoothing her hand over her lapel, the same place I had crushed it. Then she met my gaze square on again. "Whatever I may want, I don't have the right to ask anything from you. If you don't say you want me to stay, then I'll go."

I didn't say anything, and she gave a one-shoulder shrug before turning to put her hand on the doorknob.

She'd got the door open maybe three inches when I stepped up into her space and shoved her back flat against it, slamming it shut again. For good measure, I reached up behind her to click the deadbolt with my left hand. The right stayed where I'd shoved her, on her breast.

Her breath came out sharply. Then she grabbed me with both hands, hoisting me up as high as my toes would take me, and was kissing me like she'd been waiting to do it for years, like she'd rather burn the building down than wait one minute longer.

Or maybe that was just me projecting.

I let my heels thump back on the floor and pulled her down with me. We'd kissed before, had our hands on each other before, but it hadn't been like this. There was nothing thoughtful or calculated in the way we were moving now—no caution, no playbook, neither of us holding back. I was still kissing her as we staggered backwards towards the bed, pushing her jacket off her shoulders as we went. Her hands slid under my terrycloth bathrobe, then found the top edge of my barely there nightgown and dove underneath that too, caressing every part of me she could reach. I hit the bed with the back of my calves, and sat down with a thump as she dropped to her knees in front of me.

I had a moment to admire the handsome picture she made, all gold buttons and romantically disarrayed hair, before she shoved my robe off one shoulder with a hunger that wasn't chivalrous at all.

The strap of the nightgown followed, and her mouth locked onto my bared breast, sucking on a nipple that was painfully taut. I had to grab my other breast myself; both her hands were already busy sliding up my legs, rucking the hem all the way up, her thumbs stroking further and further up the inside of my thighs.

I'd had a plan. Of course I'd had a plan. I had no trouble remembering the plan. All I had to do was spend the night knocking every other thought out of her head. There wouldn't be any interruptions; I'd stolen her PD out of her jacket when I grabbed her a few moments ago. I knew what I was about. I was sure I could make her forget all about tomorrow's appointment. Then, after she fell asleep, I could lock her in the bathroom until she saw sense.

This now—this was a little reverse-wise from what I'd been thinking. But as her fingers started working between my legs, and I heard my gasping breaths becoming moans in my own ears, it became intimately clear to me that this was actually a much better plan. I could focus on her better, after. After she finished what she was doing. Oh, lord, she had better not stop what she was doing!

My breast suddenly went chill, as her mouth came away from it. Then a second later, more heat, lower— her head was between my thighs now, and I was helpless to do anything but fist my hands in her hair and roll into the rhythm she was setting. She was playing me like an instrument—or no, not like an instrument, not like anything that didn't have a say in how it got played—and it was more instinct than art, anyway, the way she knew that this kind of desperate wordless noise meant *yes, here,* and that one meant *harder,* and that one meant *oh, God, do whatever the hell you want* until with one last long shuddering yell I let my hands fall from her head and collapsed flat backwards onto the bed.

I'd had a plan. I had a plan. I gave myself a few counts, just breathing in and out. Then I felt the bed sink with the weight of another person, and pushed myself up again.

She was propped up on her elbow, gazing down at me. I was half-naked and utterly debauched; she wasn't even down a single button. I'd expected her to look a little like the cat who got the cream, which she did, but mixed with the smugness was something else.

"I didn't mean to go so fast," she murmured, and caressed my lips with her finger, light and almost tentative. "You all right there?"

Oh. Back to chivalry. Of course.

In one quick motion, I rolled over on top of her. She was taller than me, but I was heavier. I shook my bathrobe all the way off my shoulders, then leaned down, pushing her flat into the bed. "Sol," I breathed in her ear, "if you want slow, we can do slow."

I bit the lobe of her ear lightly, then moved my mouth to her neck, relishing the way I felt her shiver. I pressed my pelvis against her and slid my hands along her collarbone, tracing a line to the first gold button of her jumpsuit. Then, very carefully, I undid it.

Underneath the jumpsuit, she wore a stiff piece of shapewear that pressed her chest into the flat-fronted silhouette required for the line of the jacket. Lucky for me, it hooked down the front. More lucky for her, maybe; I didn't mind taking my time. My mouth was still moving on her neck. Before I left, I meant to leave a mark.

Four slow buttons and three hooks later, I'd bared her breasts to just above the nipple, my fingers and mouth moving deliberately over every inch of bared skin. Her heart was going at a rocket-engine rate. She hadn't yet made a noise other than quickening breaths, but when I fumbled over the fifth button, her hands came up over mine; with a gasp of impatience, she jerked the rest of her jumpsuit open, gold buttons flying around the room.

I grinned at her, feeling the flush rising in my own face. It was a hell of a thing to do to a good garment, and I'd likely be annoyed when I stepped on those buttons later, but right now triumph was turning me on almost as much as her hands had done earlier. "Slow enough for you?"

Sol's breath came out hard in a laugh. "I yield!"

"I know," I said, kindly. I unhooked the last fastener on her shapewear and the whole thing slid open like a jeweler's case, her slim breasts revealed for me like a treasure. I tweaked both of them between my fingers and thumbs. She arched helplessly up against me, breath coming out in a hiss, and I took advantage of her distraction to kick the bathrobe with her PD in it further under the bed. Then I set myself to the serious business of getting her out of the rest of her clothes.

I had to roll off her to pull the coveralls all the way off—typically, she'd dressed to seduce, not be seduced—and then, out of habit, sat up to put them away neatly, because you treat nice things nice if you want them to keep on being nice. Before I could hang them over the edge of the bedstead like I'd planned, she grabbed my wrists and tugged me back on top of her, leaning up to capture my mouth again. The coveralls fell in a crumpled heap on the floor. I let them go, and returned my attention to her mouth, her breasts, all the new-bared expanse of her hips and belly. I could afford to be generous. Now that she'd ruined the only thing she had to wear out the door tomorrow, it would be that much easier to keep her here.

I trailed my mouth down the line of her sternum, taking my time over the muscles in her stomach and pelvis, learning how each one tensed and shook as I keyed her further up. She strained up under me. I could feel her breathing hard enough to know she was turned on good, but not much else that was useful. I heard a noise start in her throat, but she locked it back. Maybe it was habit or maybe it was pride, but she seemed determined not to make a sound.

She'd had a genius for reading my body, but I wanted a little more to go on than guesswork. I lifted my head up. "Well? Talk to me, my girl, I'm no mind reader."

"No complaints," murmured Sol.

I raised my eyebrows, waiting, and her golden complexion went bright red. "What, you want me to yield *again*?"

I laughed out loud, and slid back down. After a moment, to my delight, I heard her low voice, hesitant at first, then gaining in confidence: "A little bit—little bit to the left, Ruthi. A little bit more there—no, not so hard, you don't need—don't need hands up there, what you're doing is—no, that's—that's good, Ruthi, just like that…"

I listened, adjusted, found the right rhythm for her hips. The instructions tailed off, but the words kept coming; by the end she was just calling my name over and over again, "Ruthi, *Ruthi*—"

I practically came apart all over again, hearing her say my real name like that, in a way I'd never heard anyone say it before. Right then she wasn't thinking about anyone but me, didn't belong to anyone but me—not her brother or her stepfather or MYCorps or Albert Alonso and the T.O.U., me, just me—and I knew then I was going to do whatever it took to steal her away from all of them. They couldn't have her. She was mine now.

I HADN'T MEANT to fall asleep. When I woke up, we were all entangled on the bed, arms wound around each other and legs criss-crossed. I tried to slide myself quietly free, but as soon as I shifted, she stirred.

"It's early yet," I said, though in fact I had no idea what time it was—but it couldn't be all that late, since the artificial sunlight was just starting to glow in through the window. Eyes closed and face slack, Sol looked very plain and vastly worth protecting. I pushed her fine, tangled hair out of her face, then bent to kiss her forehead. "Go back to sleep."

Sol's eyelids slid halfway open. Suddenly all the force of her personality was back: not a drowsy kitten but one of the larger cats, the wild ones. "What if I have better things to do?" she murmured.

I stiffened, wondering if she meant her appointment—but instead she rolled over until she had me pinned on the bed, and smiled down at me.

I smiled back, relaxing. I could wait a little bit to lock her in the bathroom.

I reached up for her, and then I heard a loud knocking

coming at my door.

Sol's eyes flew wide open, and so did mine. We stared at each other. I couldn't think who else would possibly be banging on my door unless it was something related to the engagement party—or something related to Albert Alonso. I couldn't even decide which option sounded worse.

"You'd better get somewhere out of sight," I hissed. The steady pounding was getting louder. How long could I stall for? It was early, and plenty of people slept in the nude. If I shouted and said I was getting dressed, that might be enough time for her to get over to the bathroom, for me to wrap myself back in my robe and find all the clothes she'd left lying about last night, and oh, lord, those damn *buttons*—

But before I could even call out a word, the knocking stopped. Sol froze in the process of climbing off me. We did some more staring at each other, and then I heard it: a series of telltale clicks, followed by a set of beeps.

Someone out there had picked the padlock. *And* they knew my standard passcode.

The door swung open.

"For fuck's sake," said my sister Jules. "You have got to be *kidding* me."

CHAPTER 17

I COULDN'T HAVE said just what I felt, seeing her. Relief and irritation and guilt were all sloshing around somewhere in the mix, but that wasn't the half of it. She wasn't supposed to be here, wasn't even supposed to know that *I* was here, and the fact that she was here couldn't mean anything but trouble—but she was here. She was here, and she was safe.

Sol recovered fast, under the circumstances. In the blink of an eye she was standing up, wrapped up in a sheet like it was the latest Earth fashion. "You must be Ruth's sister," she said. Well, nobody looking from one to the other of us could have taken us for anything other than sisters. She gave as elegant a half-bow as a person draped in nothing but a sheet could manage. Given this was Sol Mendez-Yuki, that was still a deal more elegant than I personally felt she had a right to pull off. "Jules, isn't it?"

Jules ignored her. Aside from the fact that she was furious, she looked all right. Better than when I'd left her—for weeks after Esteban dumped her, I hadn't even seen her muster the energy to get mad, so the anger was definitely a step up so long as you discounted the fact that it was all aimed at me. Her hair was shorter, and her face a little rounder, and her stomach...

I sat straight up. "Jules Johnson, you took a month-long space trip still *pregnant*? What's wrong with you?"

"What's wrong with *me*?" Jules echoed, incredulous. "You think I was gonna leave a half-baked fetus in a uterine tank on Bellavu while I bounced off to—" She broke off, glanced sideways at Sol, and switched over to Yiddish. "You told her our real *names*?"

"I *told* you to stay put," I snapped back, in English. Yiddish would've been smarter, but I was feeling perverse. "What if I hadn't been where you thought? Or what if I'd already started back by the time you got here, and I got back to find *you* gone? Lord! Jules, what's the first rule? You always make sure I know where you are!" I yanked on my nightgown to pull it straight, and launched myself out of the bed so I could stand to face her. (Out of the corner of my eye, I saw Sol slide into the bathroom.) "When I think what might have happened—"

"Oh, don't you even start," Jules slung back at me, still in Yiddish. "Don't you go turning this around, Ruthi, not this time. I *knew* you'd be here. Did you think I wouldn't read the glossies? I knew you'd gone off to do something stupid, I just didn't know *how* stupid you got!"

To be honest, I really hadn't figured she'd read the glossies—at least not the ones in which Esteban might feature. When I left, it had seemed like it could be months before she'd be ready to even glance at anything that might show his name. "Well, I'm glad you did find me," I said more calmly, "but—"

"*Are* you glad?"

"I like it better than the notion that you might've come here by yourself and never found me, sure!"

"Well, I bet you'd have liked it better if I'd come tomorrow," said Jules, "after your whole little Lady

Eve game was wrapped up, and no spokes to be thrown in your wheel. Were you ever going to tell me—" She broke off, taking a harder look at Sol, who'd just re-emerged from the bathroom. "Is that Stevie's *sister*?"

"It's a pleasure to meet you," said Sol, courteously.

"First I heard that a con like this involved knocking boots with the target's nearest and dearest," Jules said, to me. "This takes the cake, it really does!"

She'd switched back to English for that, which had to be deliberate. "Are you going to talk like that about someone who's right there?" I demanded. "Who taught you manners?"

"You're gonna pick right *now* to lecture me?"

"Sure, if you're going to act like a child—skipping your surgical and ditching your doctors—" I was getting madder just thinking about it. The paperwork we'd had to forge to get her set up with that fancy OB-GYN on Bellavu, not to mention the bribes I'd laid down to make sure she had all the best care, and now— "Was there even a gyn on the ship you took? Did you check the rad shielding to make sure it was rated for prenatal?"

"Yes, there was, actually! You think I can't plan a thing for myself, don't you? But I'm not the one who went haring off without telling me anything."

"Sure, be mad if you want, but I'm already here, this is already near done—couldn't you have been mad at me for leaving when I got back?"

"It's not the leaving I'm mad about, it's the lying!" Jules shouted, and I winced. "I wanted to figure myself out, not for you to try and figure it all for me!"

Sol pressed a hand lightly to my shoulder from behind me. "This seems like a private conversation," she murmured, "so I'll say goodbye now."

I whirled to her. "You hold on just a minute! I'm not through with—"

"*You* hold on a minute!" said Jules, and grabbed my shoulder to turn me back to face her. She'd had an inch or two on me since she was fifteen, and when she was this close I had to lift my eyes to meet hers. "You listen to me, Ruthi. You never let me get the last word, but you're going to have to swallow it this time, all right? You don't get to be mad at me for not sticking to the plans you made for me when *you're* the one who lied! You can't just decide to fix my life without telling me anything about it! And I don't want to hear another word out of your mouth unless it's that you're sorry!"

I took a deep breath in, and let it out. Words rose in my throat, but I looked at her staring furiously back at me, and swallowed them all back down again. "OK," I said, instead. "OK, I'm sorry. I *am*. But—"

The door to my room clicked shut.

I jerked my eyes away from Jules, back towards the door, and then turned in a circle to do a frantic scan of the rest of the room. There wasn't much there to see. Jules, dull hotel décor, armchair, dresser, closet door (open), bathroom door (open). Abandoned bathrobe and abandoned suit jacket and scattering of gold buttons on the floor, but no coveralls. No gold-edged breather. No Sol.

How could she have left when she couldn't fasten up her clothes decent? The coveralls had been open all the way, and underneath…

I spun back to the open closet door.

"Ruthi," said Jules, an edge in her voice, "what are you—"

"Isn't that just typical!" I stared at the empty hanger.

"It takes some brass balls to steal a girl's shirt right out from under her when you don't know if you're going to remember her well enough to return it!"

No use in chasing her down the hallway to drag her back. Even if I had a chance of overtaking her, the hotel staff wouldn't exactly smile on me kidnapping a Mendez-Yuki out in the open where anyone could see. The whole plan had been to keep her here. Since I hadn't been able to do that, the only real option I could think of was—

"Ruthi!" snapped Jules.

My eyes focused again on my sister, four months older than when I left her and standing right in front of me, already so different and still so very much the same. She had every right to expect my full attention, but today—for maybe the first time—I couldn't give it to her.

I reached forward and grabbed her hands, gripping them tight. "Look," I said, a little desperately, "you're right. Okay? Last word yours, all yours. You're right, and I was wrong."

Jules' mouth opened and then shut again.

"I know I should've talked to you," I went on, "and I know you've got every right to be mad, and pretty soon we're gonna hash it all out. But I don't have time to do it all right now."

"Why? Because you got your *engagement* to get to? Because I don't think—"

"Because I'm falling hard for that girl who just left, and she's heading out to get her brains scrambled if I don't do something to stop it!"

There was a pause. Then: "Falling hard," said Jules, slowly.

"Sure!"

"For that girl."

"You saw her!"

"Sol Mendez-Yuki."

"Right."

"Who just stole your shirt and hot-footed it out of the room."

I glared at her.

"I'm just trying to get this straight, is all."

"Well, she's got her reasons," I muttered. "They're damn fool ones, but she's got 'em."

Jules extracted her hands from my grip, sat down in the armchair, and flopped backwards. "Ruthi," she said, to the ceiling. *"Ruthi."* I couldn't see her face, so for a moment I thought she was crying; a second later, I realized my sister was trying to hold back a serious fit of the giggles.

It had been a long time since I heard her laugh like that, and in spite of everything, my heart lifted up.

"Thank you," she said to the ceiling, "for this. Thank you, God. I've not always been much of a fan, but this might just have me believing in miracles. Do you know how long I've been waiting to catch this girl being the bigger mess?"

I took a breath. "Jules—"

She shoved herself back upright, then looked at me and burst into helpless laughter again. "You got conned, sis! This Mendez-Yuki dame straight-up Ruthi'd you!"

She was expecting me to snap back at her, like she'd always done when I slanged her sweethearts, like anyone does when they're feeling a whole lot of things and their sibling's not taking them seriously. I only wished I had time to do it. She could laugh at me as much as she wanted, later, and I'd be as offended as she wanted, but right now...

Right now, I didn't have time to fall all the way back into being one half of the Johnson sisters just yet.

I sat down on the edge of the bed, facing my sister. "You're right," I said. "I got played. It's embarrassing as hell and I promise I'll tell you all about it. But I meant it when I said I don't have time just yet. It's—what time is it, anyway?"

"Just past—" Jules took a deep breath, trying to get her giggles under control. "Just past eight in the morning."

Later than I'd thought, but not so late as I feared. If I knew Sol's sense of drama, she'd scheduled her operation for the same time as the engagement party was due to begin; that gave me a little bit of time. "Okay," I said. "Here's the situation, kid. I'm due to sign a contract at noon—" Jules opened her mouth; I held up a hand to stop her. "Let me get through it. My girl's in bad trouble, and all I've done is make things worse. It's all going down today, and I've got to stop it."

"Ruthi Johnson," Jules taunted me, "riding to the rescue." She paused, then said, in a different tone, "So you're ditching the con on Esteban? Just like that?"

I looked at her. "Do you want me to go through with it?"

"I—no! I—" She stopped, staring down at her hands. The laughter was all gone out of her again. "If we con him for his money, that just makes everything he said about me true."

That hit me like a punch in the face. I opened my mouth, then shut it again. She was still talking, and I wasn't going to interrupt, not this time. "I don't want a dime of his. If I want any kind of revenge, it's the chance to make sure he knows it." She jerked her chin up again, her eyes fierce as she glared at me. "And if you did it for me, it wouldn't mean *anything*."

I let out a long breath. "Okay," I said, and was glad to hear my voice relatively steady. The mistake I'd almost made was so much bigger than I'd thought. "Well, then, there you go. I'm ditching it."

Jules was still giving me the gimlet eye. "What?" I said. "That's what you want, isn't it? Turns out it's what I want too. So what's the problem?"

"You're not conning *me* again, are you? Playing like you're dizzy for this deb and then planning to give me the slip? I *know* you, Ruthi. You never walk away this easy. The way you hang onto things, it's like you sweat glue."

Well, it's not how I would have put it, but she wasn't exactly wrong—the idea of walking away from all that money, all that *work* I'd put in, itched at me like a bad case of steerage rash. But I knew how to live with an itch. "I'm not playing you, Jules," I said, and pitched my voice as sincere as I could. Her doubts were another itch I'd have to live with—no, not an itch, an ache. Something that hurt all through me, deeper than skin. "I swear that won't happen again. If there are any truths you want from me, go ahead and ask for them."

"Sure," said Jules. "Okay. Tell me why you lied to me."

I looked at her, and she glared back at me. This was more, I realized, in the nature of a test than anything else. She thought she knew perfectly well why; she just wanted to make me say it so she could get mad again. But you shouldn't ask a question if you don't want a real answer. "Hell," I said, "why do you think? You're the one who said it, about me hanging on. You'd said you wanted to go get married, and I wasn't ready for it."

Her eyes widened—then narrowed. "So it's *my* fault that—"

"No," I said, tired. "No, it's not your fault. There wasn't anything wrong you did. Only I didn't expect it, and it shook me. I don't know you so well as I thought. So it was easier not to tell you, and make like I still did know, and the things I knew to do for you were still things that you wanted. I messed up, Jules. I already said it, but I'll say it again if you really want to grind my nose in it."

I wanted to add the rest of it: that she was all I had. That I'd trusted us to be rock-solid, and the thought of losing that had felt like the dome over my head springing an oxygen leak. But it wasn't worth saying, not if it might end up like a chain stopping her from going and doing what she wanted. I'd seen too much of that here with the Mendez-Yuki.

Across from me, Jules was biting her lip. I thought—I hoped—that she'd heard what I said, what I meant to say, instead of turning it around for another thing to snap about. But I also thought that probably she did want to grind my nose into it a little. So I said it again for her, without her asking: "I messed up. I messed up with you, and now I've messed up again here. If I've got any chance of putting it right—"

I heaved in another breath, and let it out. This was the hardest part. "I'm going to need help," I said, and met my sister's eyes. "Jules, will you help me?"

Jules was silent for long enough to make me squirm. Then: "You want *my* help," she said, slowly.

I nodded.

"To save *your* ass."

Technically, it was to save Sol's—but if she agreed to help out, I knew it wouldn't be for Sol. I nodded again.

"Do you know," said Jules, "far as I can make out, this is the first time you've ever asked me?" Suddenly, she grinned at me, and it was like we'd never been apart and nothing had changed, and like everything had changed at the same time.

It turned out she was a grown person, my sister Jules. "As I remember it, I've asked you for help plenty," I said. "What about all those times when the laundry piled up—"

"It's not the same," said Jules, "and you know it." She sighed and pulled herself upright. There was an angry glint in her eye, still, and I knew she hadn't forgiven me yet, but she said, "Now tell me what the game is."

CHAPTER 18

So THERE I was a few hours later, skulking outside an illegal memory lab facility on Second and Salle in a plain black breather and my old coveralls.

Right on cue, Sol's hovercycle rounded the corner.

And right on cue, the tough who'd been leaning on the car that was blocking the rest of the street straightened.

I knew that car. It had almost been the last thing I'd ever seen.

I knew the face, too, though this was the closest I'd ever seen it. He'd shrunk the goatee to a chin strip, but there was no disguising that broken nose. I really try not to make snap judgments about men with unfortunate facial hair, but I can't help it if people insist on living down to my expectations.

"Miss Mendez-Yuki?" said Bartimeo Iapetus Flecks—and as Sol pulled to a halt, he slid a gun out of his pocket. I swallowed down the dryness in my throat. He'd probably had that every time I ran into him before. He was only just about as dangerous as he'd ever been, not more. "I hate to interrupt your day," he went on, "but Mr. Alonso wants to have a word."

Sol's finger hovered over the ignition. Her cool gray eyes swept over Flecks. I could see the moment when she assessed the odds: one tall, wiry dame with some fancy hovercycle tricks versus an armed professional who didn't seem too bothered about the damage that gunfire might do to satellite environmental systems. I wondered if she remembered his face from Lorelei. Probably not; he'd taken care not to be seen. Regardless, she slid her grip to the handlebars and swung her leg down from the hovercycle. "I don't often see people without an appointment," she drawled, "but I guess in this case I'll have to make an exception."

He opened the front door on the passenger side with exaggerated courtesy, keeping his gun trained on Sol with the other hand. I took a deep breath, shook my shoulders loose—and then, just as he closed the door again, sauntered out from behind the column.

So Sol maybe wasn't the only one with a sense of drama.

"How about a lift?" I said.

Flecks raised his well-groomed eyebrows at me. "You always try and hitchhike with strangers, Miss?"

"Oh, no," I said. I tipped up my breather, and smiled. "Friends only—and only when we're going to the same place."

His eyes narrowed. The gun he'd been pointing at Sol swung towards me. "What are you trying to pull? Last I heard, you weren't exactly in Mr. Alonso's good books."

"You haven't heard the latest," I said, and nodded towards Sol's profile in the front seat of the car. "Who do you think it was gave him the tip-off she was here?"

Flecks stared at me a moment longer, then gestured towards the car.

On a different day, I might've taken a moment or two to reassess before getting into the backseat of the thing that had tried to kill me. There was a version of Ruth Johnson who got weak legs and a rabbity heart when the prospect of mortality came up to meet her; I'd met that girl a few times by now. She was right in here with me, and she didn't like the prospect of climbing into a murder car driven by Alonso's favorite hitman at all.

I didn't have time for that Ruthi today. I couldn't show weakness here, any more than I could sitting round a poker table with a hand full of twos and threes, and all my chips on the table.

It didn't matter how bad my hand was. Today, I was playing to win.

Sol stared straight ahead as I slid in behind her. Her slightly disdainful expression didn't shift an inch. I leaned forward and patted her arm. "Cheer up," I murmured. "Wouldn't you rather I be here than anywhere else?"

She didn't answer. Even when the car began navigating towards the center of town, and our destination must have been increasingly clear to her, she never said a word to me. After a few minutes, I pulled out my PD—or rather, Sol's PD, in my cover-case—and ignored her right back. The clock was ticking, and had been ticking, from the moment Sol showed up at my door last night. And there were a few people in her contacts who needed to know that the missing Mendez-Yuki was on her way to the party at last.

When we turned down the street that held the Mendez-Yuki mansion, Flecks caught my eye in the rearview mirror and smirked. "Hey, Miss Ojukwu," he said. "You want me to drop you somewhere a little more discreet? Those folks out there are gonna wonder why you're not inside already."

"You let me worry about me," I said, and pulled my breather back down over my face.

Flecks shrugged, and continued on into the line of cars waiting their turn for the parking elevator. A staffer in MYCorps gold came and knocked on our window.

"Invitations?" he said, and Flecks promptly pulled a gold-edged bit of paper out of his pocket and handed it over. It was, of course, the one he'd won at my bachelorette party.

The staffer checked it, scanned the code in front, and then handed it back. His brows were furrowed down. "Sir," he said, "the invitation allows for you and a plus-one, but I see three people—"

"Oh, leave it alone!" said Louanne Hachi, shouldering her way down the receiving line to greet us. "Don't you know who's in that car?"

Through the window, I could see that Galaxy Khan, Gaea St. Clair, and Esteban Mendez-Yuki himself were all right on her heels. They clustered by the front passenger door as Sol climbed, stiff-shouldered, out of the car. "Sol!" Louanne cried, and grabbed her by the hands. "We've been waiting ages for you!"

"What's *kept* you?" demanded Esteban. He was wearing a classy white suit with tasteful gold trim around all the collars and cuffs, far more Sol's style than his own, and someone had clearly sat him down and spent a solid hour on his hair to get it to do a kind of high-rise on top of his head. He kept patting at it, with a nervous motion, and seemed surprised by the volume every time. "We've been waiting all morning! Where have you been?"

"And who," said Gaea, disdainfully, "is *this*?"

'This' was, of course, Bartimeo Iapetus Flecks, who'd just come round from the other side of the car. He looked like he was going to push right past Esteban, but Galaxy Khan was in his way. If she recognized him, she didn't show it—but she didn't look at all inclined to let him by, either.

Everyone's attention was on one or the other of them, which meant it was probably a good time for me to slip out of the car.

"Why, Sol," said Louanne, eyes wide, "this must be your *date*!" Sol opened her mouth, but Louanne didn't let her get a word in. "Is that why you were so late? You had to pick this handsome fellow up?"

Esteban looked at Flecks. He looked at Sol. His brow wrinkled. He looked back at Louanne. "Louanne, I don't think—"

"Oh, Esteban," said Louanne, "you can't really expect to know everything about your sister, you know. She's allowed to surprise you from time to time." She grinned at Sol, who looked as if she was struggling to hold onto her blank expression. Esteban followed her gaze suspiciously, with the air of someone beginning to suspect his leg was being pulled. "Now, you've got to tell us *all* about yourself," Louanne went on, and latched onto Flecks' arm. "What's your name? How did you and Sol first meet? What *barber* do you go to—Esteban, come over here, look at his beard, I'm *sure* you'll want to get the name of his barber."

As Louanne babbled on, I slipped into the crowd, anonymous in my coveralls and full-face breather. Behind me, the car that had almost killed me rolled peacefully into the parking slot and vanished underground. I cast one last glance at Galaxy Khan, standing by Louanne's side—nobody seemed concerned that Louanne had brought her lawyer as *her* date—and left them behind, pushing my way through the crowd of people at the entrance around to the side of the house.

My pal Joe Morgan had given me very strict instructions about my arrival at the engagement ceremony. I wasn't supposed to arrive by the front entrance where anybody could see me before it was time. I had to get my driver to drop me right by the delivery door, where I could sneak straight into the dressing room (of course the Mendez-Yuki mansion had a designated dressing room) and wait there in peace until it was my time to saunter out for the signing.

Before turning the corner round to the kitchen wing, I took my breather off and stashed it in my handbag, then shucked off my coveralls and shoved them in after it. Underneath, I had on a black pantsuit: one of the blander outfits in Evelyn Ojukwu's wardrobe, but it was certainly respectable enough to get me in the door.

I had to wait a few long moments after ringing the bell. It was hard not to tap my feet in impatience. Finally one of Joe Morgan's underlings answered the door, with a cute little MYCorps-branded apron tied round her waist and a matching cap on her head. When she saw me checking the time on my PD, the expression on her own changed from irritation to confusion. "Miss Ojukwu?"

"There's no need to apologize," I said, all graciousness. "I don't mind waiting, truly."

I waltzed in past her and let the door swing closed, while she fluttered her hands behind me. "I'm so sorry, I can't think how this happened! We had someone on the door, but Mr. Morgan said that you'd already—"

"Oh, it's always chaos at these events," I told her airily. The background bore me up; as we entered into the kitchen area, another one of Morgan's minions narrowly avoided nailing me with a tray of canapes, while a steel-tech server hauled a wagon of flowers in the opposite direction. "It's so easy to get confused." The canape tray disappeared round a corner to reveal Joe Morgan himself on the other side, berating a bot with some kind of frosting dripping all down its side. I slid my arm round the waist of the woman who'd let me in and turned her hastily down the same hall as the canapes. "Which is why I'd hate to hold you up any longer. I know I must have interrupted your whole schedule, turning up at the wrong time like this. Thank you *so* much again for coming to my rescue out there, you really did save the day!"

I disentangled my arm from her waist, gave her a friendly pat on the back to push her forward in that direction, and then dodged back into the kitchen. I was hoping to move quick enough to avoid Joe Morgan's eye, but he was on high alert mode that day. He spun away from the bot, looking appalled. "Miss Ojukwu! What are you doing back here again? Where's your *dress*?"

"Don't worry!" I shouted back. "Everything will be right on schedule, I promise!" I dodged his outstretched arm and zoomed out the door on the other side, then turned left, in the opposite direction of the dressing room. Poor old Joe Morgan; he deserved better than he was getting from me today. Especially since it was thanks to him that I'd finally memorized all the back routes in the maze of the Mendez-Yuki manor.

Another turn brought me to a bathroom. I ducked inside and tied the apron I'd stolen from the girl who let me in around my waist, then took a minute to put my hair in a tight bun on top of my head and shove her cap down over it. I pulled out my face kit and thickened my brows, then did a little reverse contouring to change the planes of my chin and cheeks. Finally, I gave myself bright red lips and orange eyeshadow in a palette unlike anything ever seen on Evelyn Ojukwu's refined face.

The makeup tricks wouldn't fool anyone who looked at me too hard, but then, that was the point of the uniform: to convince everyone I passed that they didn't have to. Anyway, it wasn't like any of the guests would expect to find the girl of the hour gawking in the stalls next to them. As far as most everyone at this particular event was concerned, Evelyn Ojukwu was sitting pretty right back in her dressing room, waiting patiently for her moment in the sun.

I'd have been happier with some kind of food-related prop—nobody looks twice at the person carrying the canapes or the cocktail-boxes—but I didn't want to go back to the kitchen and risk another encounter with Joe Morgan. It had been bad enough to bump into him there once; if he saw me like this, it would mean more questions than I could answer. I set my body language to radiate insignificance and made my way at a purposeful pace towards the ballroom, just another one of a dozen servers hired at special expense to show everyone that the Mendez-Yuki could afford to tell other humans what to do.

I came in behind the banquet tables, and took a second to get my bearings. The place was wall-to-wall well-wishers. Joe Morgan had walked me through all the décor plans, most of them designed to pack more people in—floating risers and tacked-on balconies, velvet ropes for folks to lean on that kept the doors and aisles clear—but the reality of it still took me by surprise. All the Mendez-Yuki events I'd been to previously had been tastefully exclusive, a careful selection of New Monte's brightest stars with a comfortable amount of firmament between them. Here it looked like half the satellite had turned up to see Esteban Mendez-Yuki sign himself a bride.

The scope of the crowd did the impossible, and made the room itself seem small. I hadn't seen a place this packed since double-drinks night at the Biraldi casinos. Screens overhead showed the feed from the cam-bots circling the center of the room, focused on the empty dais in the center. An antique wood table stood there, laid with a pair of gilded paper contracts. A timer counting down in the corner of the screen told me it was ten minutes to showtime.

This—the ballroom, the contract, all of it—was the culmination of everything I'd been working for. Three months of sewing myself into someone else's skin every day, just for the chance to sign that contract in front of the biggest audience I'd ever played for. I took a moment to look out over the crowd and feel the twinge of it.

I could have done it. I could have done it still: put Evelyn Ojukwu's face back on and walked down the aisle, feeling all those eyes on me and knowing I'd pulled the wool over every single one of them.

Then I turned and started eeling my way through the edges of the crowd, up to the balcony over the banquet table, where I'd told Alfred Alonso to meet me.

CHAPTER 19

ALFRED ALONSO HAD brought along a pair of opera glasses and was leaning on the balcony edge, squinting down over the crowd, when I came up behind him.

"Mr. Alonso," I said. "Glad you could make it."

I saw in the way his shoulders stiffened that I'd surprised him. Still, he wasn't the type to jump. He swiveled slowly around, propped an elbow on the balcony, and inspected me through his opera glasses before lowering them. "I was jazzed to get the invite. But since you're up here, and not down there, I'm starting to worry there might not be much of a show." His eyes were hard in his hangdog face. "Which makes me wonder exactly what your game is, here."

It will certainly raise some eyebrows, I'd said, in the note I sent Alonso that morning, *if the groom's own sister isn't at my engagement signing. Miss Mendez-Yuki's about to make an extremely unwise decision, and I think both of us would prefer she didn't. If I give you the address, do you think you could convince her to stick around for my special day? There's an invitation waiting for you at the desk of my hotel.*

It wasn't a genuine invitation, of course. Those were strictly rationed, and I couldn't officially requisition any extras without inviting some questions (especially from Joe Morgan, who did not welcome last-minute changes to the guest list). But I'd saved that first invitation Esteban sent me all those weeks ago, on real Mendez-Yuki stationery with a real access microchip embedded in the MYCorps logo; all it took was a little judicious tampering to get something that would work to let Alfred Alonso into the inner circle.

For all I knew, he'd already been planning on using the invitation Flecks had won before he got my note. Or maybe he would've just sent Flecks as a proxy to remind us all that the noose was still around our necks rather than wasting his own precious time. Either way, I'd known he wouldn't be able to resist this bait when I dangled it. His prey had almost slipped the net this morning; as soon as he saw the address, he'd have known exactly what she was up to. He wouldn't want to lose any time in reminding her personally of everything she and her family had to lose, if she went off-script. And he had to do it here—because if Sol didn't show to her little brother's engagement signing, then people might start to think something was up in the Mendez-Yuki inner circles, and if something was up, the stocks went down, and the value of what he was selling out of Sol's head went right down with it.

Which was, of course, why he was so antsy right now. "I told you what I wanted," I said. "Hasn't Mr. Flecks checked in with you? But I've got to tell you—"

"About that," said Alonso. He grabbed my arm, hard, and pulled me closer to the balcony. He gestured down with his opera glasses. "You see that?"

I looked where he was pointing, and saw Flecks standing by the double doors of the entrance, with Galaxy Khan standing next to him. It was hard to see his face from this distance, but he looked like he was holding forth on some topic or other. Louanne, on the other side, had her arm looped through Sol's and a smirk wreathed over her face. If she was nervous about standing so close to a character she had to know was shady, she didn't show it in the least—but then, a New Monte deb never thought anything could hurt them, besides another New Monte deb.

"Sure," I said, impatiently, and turned away. "I see he did what you sent him to do, and brought Sol back here where you two can keep an eye on her and make sure she doesn't try another runner. But we've got bigger fish—"

"He was supposed to bring her up here as soon as he got here. Instead, he's down there hobnobbing with Hachi family lawyers."

"It's not so easy to get away from Sol's friends sometimes," I said. "They like to shove their noses in."

"Like you, Miss Johnson?" said Alonso, gently.

His hand was still locked round my arm. This was the man who'd called in a hit on me, and he had the nerve to sound more disappointed than proper mad.

I drew in a breath, and let it out again. When I spoke again, it was conciliatory. I'd played it cool for Flecks, but defiance was never the right tack to take with Alfred Alonso of the T.O.U. "Look—I called you this morning to square things up between us. I didn't like us being on the outs."

"That's the first bit of sense you've said in a while." Alonso's fingers on my arm relaxed a little. He leaned back on the balcony again. "You've let me down a time or two. I can't deny it. But you did me a good turn today, and I don't deny that either. So why don't you take a breath, and tell me what this is all about, and why you're not where you're supposed to be?"

I swallowed. "Mr. Alonso," I said, "you're not going to like this."

Just at that moment, a fanfare swelled from the ceiling. The doors on either side of the ballroom opened. On one side, Esteban walked in, and took up his position at the start of the aisle. But nobody was looking at him; everyone's attention was focused on the woman who'd entered opposite.

Her perfect springy waves flowed over her shoulders and down the back of a spider-silk gown in gossamer gold. Thousands of seed-pearl fringes swung together as she walked, hiding her curves and transforming her into a shimmering, insubstantial cloud. Her breather was covered in matching silk, and the fringe floating from her pearl coronet covered every bit of her face that the breather didn't already obscure. She looked like every deb's dream come to life.

Alonso looked from me, in my MYCorps apron and hat, to the person drifting across the ballroom floor below. His mouth worked for a moment before he said, in a low measured tone, "Who the fuck is that?"

"That's what I've been trying to tell you," I said. "It's my sister, Mr. Alonso. It's Jules."

Jules and I look alike, but not all that alike. She's taller than me, and her hair's different—and normally I'm a little rounder than she is, but right then her whole silhouette was curvier than I ever got.

But my whole look for today had been designed with Jules in mind. This was the event that she should have had; she'd been there in every detail, hovering at the back of my head, long before I ever knew she'd actually be here to see it. If there ever was a time she could pull me off, this was the one.

In spite of everything, I felt my heart go a little wibbly, seeing her sweeping down the aisle in her full glory. My baby sister, and there she was, all eyes on her, head held high like a queen's. It was a little appalling. I've never been sentimental about weddings—not that I've had the chance to attend many, except the ones I was scamming—and here I was practically about to burst into the chorus of 'Sunrise, Sunset'. It was a good thing none of this was real; Jules had better watch out when it was, because clearly whenever it happened I was going to be a genuine embarrassment.

If I survived long enough to be around whenever it happened, which certainly wasn't a given right now. Alonso's hand had tightened around my arm again. "Was this the plan all along?" he demanded, in a low voice. "Pull the Rachel and Leah, and hope nobody will notice the fuss when the breather comes off? Because that's the most *fool* thing I ever—"

"It was absolutely not the plan," I hissed back.

Down below, Jules and Esteban each sat down at the table. Esteban's lawyer picked up a copy of the contract, and began to read it aloud, in a rapid mutter. The document was a good forty pages long, so this was going to take a while. I still had some time.

I swung my attention over to the people around us. Everyone had started up their conversations again; they all knew nothing exciting would happen for the next ten minutes at least. It gave me some audio cover, but I kept my voice to a whisper anyway. "She showed up this morning in a fury. While I was trying to sort out this whole Sol situation for you, she snuck off with my dress—when I got here she'd already sailed in pretending to be me. What could I do? I can't exactly expose my own sister as an impostor!"

"She's going to have to expose herself sooner or later," said Alonso. "Can't keep that breather on forever." He'd relaxed a little again. The corner of his mouth twitched. He was starting to find the situation funny.

He wouldn't for long. I stuck my chin up, and tried to look like a person who was trying to look brave. If he saw how scared I was right now, that was all right. "If that was just it, I could swallow it—but it might not be just my scheme she's out to ruin." Alonso's attention swung back towards me, fast, as I went on. "My sister's a wild card right now, Mr. Alonso. She's mad, and hurt, and not thinking straight—you think she wants to marry that man down there? After all this? She's not in it for a ring. She's in it for revenge. And she was there when I found out Sol was headed to the memory parlor—I don't know what she'll do, but she might blow the whole thing wide open. Tell everyone about the debt Sol owes you, and the data risk. Sink MYCorps. Sink Esteban. And blow your profits right out of the water."

For the first time, I saw real shock play itself out unchecked on Alonso's melancholy face—shock, followed by anger. I was going to have bruises on my arm tomorrow. "Miss Johnson," he said, quietly, "that's extremely unfortunate."

"So is the way you're holding onto that woman," said Galaxy Khan, stepping up behind us. I turned, and saw her eyes widen a moment as she recognized me, but only for a moment. Galaxy Khan was a cool customer, and my engagement party wasn't her job right now. She flicked her attention right back over to the task at hand. "Mr. Alfred Alonso, I presume? I apologize for intruding when we're not formally acquainted, but might I have a word with you outside?"

She hadn't kept her voice low, and people around us in the crowd were turning to look. Alfred Alonso, eyes narrowed, dropped my arm like it was an overheated battery. "Wasn't easy to get these seats," he rumbled, and then turned a venomous look at me. "And I'd rather not miss the show."

"There's a screen out in the hallway," said Galaxy Khan. "Unless you'd prefer to have this discussion right here?"

We followed her down the stairs, shoving past laughing people with canape stains on their shirt-fronts and champagne glasses in their hands. They didn't notice Alonso's grim face casting shadows as he passed by, and if they noticed, they didn't care. Why should they? They were here to have a good time, and it didn't matter, as it never mattered on New Monte, who else around them might not be.

Back in the hallway, Galaxy Khan took a left turn and pulled us into an alcove stacked with spare cleaning bots. On the screen above, Esteban's lawyer was reading out a listing of New Monte's conditions governing hospital visitation rights.

"So," Alonso said, as soon as we were safely tucked away behind the stack of bots, "Miss Mendez-Yuki got herself another lawyer, did she? Won't do any good. She knows she's got no case. She signed those papers, fair and square."

"I don't know what you're referring to," answered Galaxy Khan, "but what I've heard about their experiences on Lorelei last month, I would say that Miss Ojukwu and Miss Mendez-Yuki have an extremely good case against you for reckless endangerment, as well as conspiracy to commit assault."

Alonso said, "I don't know what you're talking about."

"No?" Galaxy Khan pulled up her PD and showed a mugshot of Bartimeo Iapetus Flecks. "Do you recognize this man, Mr. Alonso?"

"Nope," said Alonso.

"I just had a very interesting conversation with him. He understands that we won't press charges against him—so long as he testifies for our inquiries. Lorelei Enterprises, of course, will be facing extensive charges for their negligence, but I understand his official employers weren't the only ones paying him that day." When Alonso was silent, she added, "Of course we expect you'll bring considerable resources to bear in defending yourself. But the publicity alone, I'm sure, could be very damaging for your operations in this area."

Alonso was quiet a long moment. I could make a guess at what he was thinking. An accusation from a small-time turncoat like Flecks wasn't much, in and of itself. It would be easy for the T.O.U.'s legal eagles to make all that disappear. Couple that with a public accusation from one Jules Johnson about blackmail on the Mendez-Yuki family, though, and the addition of a motive might make things look a little more dicey. Once you added in Sol herself—Sol with all her secrets already blown open, and nothing left to lose—well, even if the T.O.U. managed to wriggle out of the situation unscathed, Alfred Alonso might not be so lucky. The Funeral Director was even less precious than he was about cutting assets loose when they weren't any use anymore. He couldn't have any illusions about that.

"Well," he said, finally. That more-in-sorrow-than-in-anger note was back in his voice, but something about it sounded off. "It seems like everyone's caught a real bad case of the stupids today." His fingers tapped against the side of his trousers in an erratic beat. I'd seen him make that gesture before, in games with high stakes—though not with me, never with me. When we'd played, back on Biraldi, he'd never really thought that he might lose.

"Excuse me," said a voice from behind us.

We all jumped, except the unflappable Galaxy Khan. "*Extremely* sorry to interrupt," Joe Morgan went on, stepping into our bot-enclosed alcove, "but one of the chocolate bombs has exploded early and we're going to need all the bots stored in this area." There followed a short, speaking pause, as he assessed us as a group: one Hachi family lawyer, one middle-aged man in a suit just a little too loud for the situation, and one girl in a catering apron who was keeping her face turned firmly away.

Galaxy Khan stepped smoothly in front of me, PD in hand. "Forgive me for stealing one of your staff, Joe, but there's an issue we need her to consult on. The Mendez-Yuki can bill the Hachi for her lost time, if you like."

I'd never heard a vaguer excuse in my life, but the mention of billing seemed to have done the trick, because Joe Morgan said, apologetically, "For any—ah, business discussions—might I recommend the boardroom on the second floor? But please do remember that all spaces at this event ought to be considered public." Then he wheeled the stack of bots back off towards the kitchen, leaving us all staring at each other in the alcove again.

Galaxy Khan coughed and straightened her impeccable cuffs. "Well. The second floor boardroom, then?"

"No need," said Alonso. The interruption had given him time to compose himself again, and his voice was back to bland. "I think we're about done here. I expect your client will think better of this before long." He glanced up at the screen and added, "And I'm real afraid, Miss Johnson, that so will your little sister. Sooner rather than later, maybe."

I'd known I was likely to receive a threat like that at some point tonight. Now that Jules was here, it was the obvious way for him to come at me. Even so, hearing him say it, my heart thudded right down to my knees.

"Now I'm going to have to leave this event a little early," he went on, without looking at me, "to make some arrangements. You understand."

He turned and started back towards the door into the ballroom. Where Jules was.

"Wait," I said.

"No," said Alonso, without turning.

"*Wait!*"

This was it for both of us: time to bet, or fold. I'd played plenty of games of poker with Alfred Alonso back in Biraldi City; I knew how he expected it to go. You didn't challenge a man like Alfred Alonso too far. In the end, you always folded. You always took the fall, and let him win.

"Mr. Alonso," I said, "what if I did it?"

Alonso slowed, at last. "Did what?"

"What if I—" I looked at Galaxy Khan, standing in the back of the alcove listening to us, and then back to Alonso. "—told her the truth? What if I told her about how I hired Flecks to sabotage the Lorelei Beach?"

Alonso stopped in the doorway.

"I had all kinds of reasons," I pushed on. "Even if he fingers you, it'd just be his word against mine. I wanted to get the Mendez-Yuki family's trust. I wanted to play the heroine for them." I glanced at Galaxy again; her face was impassive, but I could see her fingers moving on her PD, reporting back everything she heard. "What if I signed a confession, right now, and you—"

He swung round to stare at me.

"And I what, Miss Johnson?"

"And you went about your business," I said, "whatever your business happened to be. You kept your nose perfectly clean, and went on making all your extremely legitimate deals, and didn't worry your head about me or Mr. Flecks a bit. And whatever happens today, out there—you didn't take it out on Jules."

It felt familiar, saying it. It took me back. I half-expected to hear the call that the boss was ready for me to come in and count out that week's take; all the money we'd made fleecing tourists who didn't know how young the card sharks came in Biraldi. Sometimes Jules came with me to the casino, when I didn't feel all right leaving her alone, but I was always the one to bring the take in to the accountants, and always the one to take the punishment if we hadn't hit our goalposts.

Sometimes Jules had played cards with Alonso, too, while I was in there with the boss. She'd been little, then, and proud of her skill, always. She hadn't always been smart enough to let him win—but whatever he lost, I'd always made sure he recouped it off me the next day. And then he'd smile, and let me keep half, for being such a good girl. He liked to think of himself as kind, really, did Alfred Alonso.

He'd remember how it used to be, too.

"If you didn't take it out on Jules," I repeated. "If you promised in writing you wouldn't. And you gave her what I should've made—ten percent, you said it might be? Ten percent of Sol's debt. I know you already cleared that number with your boss, and I've earned it. I earned it this morning alone."

"If it weren't for you, your sister wouldn't be putting our profits at risk to begin with. And Yappy Flecks wouldn't be here to run his mouth off to lawyers and make trouble for both of us—"

"You can't blame me for that!" I protested. "I've done my best for you today, you know I have. If she does blow the whistle, ten percent won't mean anything either way—and if she doesn't, it'll be peanuts from your total payout. Mr. Alonso, *please*—" My voice cracked. I thought about Jules in her dress, and Jules shouting at me this morning, and Jules huddled in our hotel room in Bellavu, all those months ago; I let it all out to show on my face. "You've got a family, don't you? You always liked the way I looked after Jules. Let me make sure she's looked after."

There was a long silence.

And then Alonso let out a sigh, like the rumble of a vacuum-bay door closing, and said, "Ruthi Johnson, you're not so bright as I thought you were, but I guess I can't say your heart's not in the right place." His fingers were still, now. He'd faced the prospect of a real big loss, and come out the other side, the way he always did. "Ten percent's too much, but I could do two. Yes—two percent ought to set her up just fine."

I'd been hoping he'd let me keep half, like he used to, but I guess I couldn't blame him for being in a bad mood. Anyway, he was right; two percent was all I needed. I closed my eyes, briefly, and then gave a quick nod.

He looked over at Galaxy Khan, and so did I. Galaxy Khan looked down once more at her PD, then smiled pleasantly, and slipped it away. "We'll be happy to support Miss Mendez-Yuki in pressing charges against whoever put Flecks on payroll. As long as we can establish that Lorelei Enterprises was negligent in their hiring practices and allowed a known criminal to suborn their safety and security measures, the Hachi will be satisfied with the outcome of this matter."

It made perfect sense. The Hachi had loaned their lawyers so they could get their cut. They didn't care who got criminal punishment; they were after corporate damages. In a lot of ways, Louanne Hachi wasn't all that different from Alonso. She thought of herself as kind, too—but on New Monte, you followed the profit.

And Alonso smiled back, and gave a small, satisfied nod, before turning to me. "You should tell that woman the truth about what you hired that boy Flecks to do," he said, loud and clear. "It's the right thing to do."

"Miss—Johnson?" said Galaxy Khan, and at that moment the door from the ballroom flew open, and Sol came running out.

"Galaxy, what are you—"

She broke off; her gaze passed over me, took in Alonso, and then jolted back to me, disbelieving. She looked up at the screen, where Jules sat reading attentively from what looked like the last page of the contract document, and then back down, and then up, and down again, and for a heart-stopping moment I thought she was about to say my name—my real name—which would have been about the worst thing she could do.

Galaxy Khan's eyes flicked to me, and then back to Sol. "Miss Johnson," she said, with just a bit of an edge, "was, I believe, just about to confess to being a fortune-hunter who hired a man to attack you on Lorelei." I could have kissed her.

Sol's eyes on me sharpened. I could hear the rustling of paper from the screen overhead, but I couldn't look away to check what was happening. *Please*, I thought, stupidly, like she'd hear me if I just stared at her hard enough. After this morning, she had every reason not to trust me. She wasn't my sister, who'd seen me be a dozen different people, and rolled with a hundred lies that I'd never had time to brief her on. She wasn't my partner. We weren't a team.

I was so close—and if she acted like any reasonable person, and called me out on all my bluffs, it would ruin everything for both of us.

Sol rubbed her finger absently over a mark on her neck that I recognized, and glanced away, her face disdainful. "Miss—Johnson, was it?" she said, coolly. "Well, I suppose that tracks."

My knees went practically weak with relief.

I stiffened them up. "All right," I said, and turned around. "Mr. Alonso, you and I have some things to write up, and we'd better do it fast. Miss Khan, would you be so kind as to witness these docs?"

Behind me, Sol said, "Now I don't want to interrupt what's clearly very important business, but if Miss Oju—Miss Johnson's down here, would *someone* kindly tell me who's up there marrying my brother?"

The name-catch was laying it on a little thick, I thought—still dizzy with disbelief that she'd really trusted me—but bless her, she'd learn. Alonso didn't notice, anyway. He had already propped up his PD and was starting to scribble. Without looking up, he said, "You want to take this one, Ruthi?"

"Not really," I said. I was fighting back an awful urge

to laugh. Now that I'd signed up for the big house on his behalf, my old pal Alonso and I were apparently back on a first-name basis. "Miss Mendez-Yuki, you're going to have to wait a minute, all right? Here you go, Mr. Alonso. You want to read this over?"

I passed Alonso my PD, with my signed confession on it. I could tell how rattled he'd been by the whole business, because he gave me his whole PD back to read in turn, with the document he'd written glowing on the screen.

A document officially signing over to Ruth and Julia Johnson a two percent stake in the debt owed by Solada Mendez-Yuki Alvaria to the Terran Original Undertakers, effective immediately.

I mailed myself a copy; I mailed Jules a copy; I mailed Sol a copy, and then I held out my hand, with Alonso's PD in it. "Miss Khan," I said. My arm wanted to shake. I let it. It was allowable, I thought, under the circumstances. Even Alfred Alonso couldn't think it was strange, given what I'd signed away.

As Galaxy Khan pulled up her electronic signature to witness the document, the music coming from the screen swelled up again. I hadn't noticed while the lawyer was muttering his way through the reading, but we must have been getting the public feed in here, because a brisk announcer's voice said, "Now the reading of the engagement contract has been completed, the parties will exchange documents for the signature. Traditionally, the engaged couple removes each other's breathers after the signing."

"Mr. Alonso," I said, my voice only wobbling a little, "Can I have my PD back? Whatever Jules is going to do out there, I figure she'd want me to see it."

I cast a glance at Sol, and added, "It's no business of mine anymore, Miss Mendez-Yuki, but you might want to see this too."

Then I marched back towards the ballroom without looking behind me to see if she was following.

She caught up to me right at the door. She opened her mouth; before she could say anything, I leaned up and whispered in her ear, "In a minute, we're going out the other exit. *Fast*."

She let out a breath, then nodded. Suddenly, we heard a commotion from inside. I swung the door open just in time to catch the tail end of the collective gasp.

It was a spectacular reveal. Jules had painted her face all in day-glo reflective colors, so that she wouldn't spend years afterwards being recognized as The Dame Who Jilted New Monte's Most Eligible. The side benefit of this was that when Esteban pulled off her breather, the lights of the cameras reflected on her face and lit it up like a neon avenging angel.

The makeup was enough to fool the facial recognition software, but even Esteban Mendez-Yuki couldn't fail to recognize the profile of the woman he'd dumped when it was literally right in front of him. "*Julia*!" he gasped, and reached out for her.

I couldn't tell you whether he planned to declare his undying love, or hold her there for the lawyers; either way, she wasn't having it. She pulled her hands regally back. "Unfortunately," she said, clearly, "it will not be possible for me to sign this contract."

She leaned in close to his ear, and said something the microphones didn't catch.

The look on Esteban's face changed—to what, I couldn't say; something between shock and shame—and he whispered something back.

Jules shook her head and stepped backwards. While every single camera in the place was still trained on Esteban's dumbfounded expression, she turned and walked regally back the way she had come.

If I'd gone a little wobbly watching her entrance, it was nothing to the way I felt seeing her exit. I almost burst into tears, I was so proud. I wanted to watch her all the way out, and then run up and give her the world's biggest hug, but there wasn't time. We were still on the clock here—and while the cameras and the attention of the audience were all trained on her, I had just enough of a time window to drag the groom's sister unnoticed out the front door.

Once we got out, I let out a breath and turned to Sol. "And now," I said, "we really better book it, before—"

"Before *what*?" said Sol. "No, wait—don't answer that yet." She pulled me down to the bottom of the staircase, near where we'd gotten out of the car, and whistled.

Her death trap of a hovercycle spun up out of the car park.

Given that the last time I'd seen that hovercycle it was parked in front of the memory parlor, it seemed like a dang miracle to me. "Where'd this come from?" I demanded, as I clambered on behind her.

"It *can* go automatic," she called back. "I had it on remote following us the whole time." The engine kicked into gear, and her voice got louder to carry over it as we gunned off onto the streets of New Monte. "I expected it would come in handy after you did whatever you were going to do to get me out of this!"

I chewed on the implications of that as I took a firmer grip on her waist. Sol had her hovercycle's directional system on; over the roar of the engine, I could just barely hear the clear automatic voice rattling off intersections at a rate that seemed almost too fast for any human being to follow them.

"Now," shouted Sol—who really had been exhibiting remarkable patience—"would you like to tell me what the before is that we're trying to beat?"

I almost choked, as the laugh I'd been holding inside me ever since Alonso signed that contract bubbled over.

"Before Mr. Bartimeo Iapetus Flecks escapes from Louanne Hachi, and Alonso finds out that he never rolled over on him to begin with—and you're not planning to press charges against anybody—and he signed over two percent of your debt in exchange for exactly nothing!"

It was the greatest bluff I'd ever pulled. I let my head drop against her back and practically howled.

From the stiffness in Sol's back, she didn't think it was so funny. "Ruthi, this seems like a lot of trouble to go to for two percent!"

"That's what he thinks," I crowed. "Baby, two percent's everything! If all you owe him is ninety-eight percent of the stake—then that valuation letter he rigged up says your brain-scan's two percent more valuable than anything you owe him, and even on New Monte, he can't take more than he's owed! He'd need me to sign that two percent back over if he wants to make his claim before your duck deal goes through—so you better make sure he can't get me, while he hasn't yet figured it out!"

Sol's back stayed frozen a moment longer.

And then she started laughing too. Her shoulders shook with it, the air rang with it. I should've been scared, probably—the speed we were going was a far cry from legal, and on top of that the driver was having a fit of hysterics—but I don't think anything in the world could have scared me right then. Maybe I'd just pissed off one of the most powerful syndicates in the galaxy. So what? I could beat them again, if I had to. Right then, it seemed like I could do anything.

I'd saved Sol Mendez-Yuki.

And she—Sol Mendez-Yuki, dazzler of debutantes and rescuer of damsels, Miss New Monte Chivalry herself—had *wanted* me to save her.

And wasn't that a hell of a thing!

CHAPTER 20

WE PULLED UP to a stop in front of a building I didn't recognize. From the sign out front, it seemed like another hotel, but not a glitzy type like the one I'd been staying in. This was the kind of layover spot where the staff didn't have cameras out front and didn't ask questions.

"Come on," said Sol, and grabbed for my hand. Adrenaline was sparking through me—I wanted to jump, to shout, to shove her down on the nearest couch—but I held my tongue all the way through the lobby, up into the elevator, down the sixth-floor hallway, and into a small room that she already had the keys for.

Only once the door was safely closed behind us did I turn to her. In as cool a voice as I could manage, I drawled, "So tell me, Sol Mendez-Yuki, how much of that went down like you thought it would?"

Sol looked down at me—and then she gave a kind of a laugh and sat straight down on the nearer of the two beds, like her knees wouldn't hold her anymore. "I don't know what I thought was going to happen," she said, "but it wasn't that. You—how did you get *Galaxy Khan* to lie for you like that?"

I raised my eyebrows, and handed her PD back to her. "You think she thought she was lying for me?"

Sol looked at it, and said, "Ah."

"I sent your pal Louanne a message for you—told

her that you'd traced Flecks back to Alonso, and were ready to be plaintiff for her team on a lawsuit against Lorelei. She jumped at the chance. She'll likely be a little disappointed when she finds out you've changed your mind again, but—" I gave my best one-shoulder shrug, Louanne Hachi-style. "Circumstances change. She knows how it happens."

Sol's mouth twitched. "Don't look like that," I told her. "You leave things in my hands, you got to let me do it my way. It won't hurt Louanne Hachi to front the legal costs; she was taking a gamble anyway. And I needed Galaxy Khan in the picture for Alonso to buy it. If you're so worried what she'll think, you can blame it on me later."

"Leaving Louanne aside for the moment," said Sol, "what would you have done if Alonso *hadn't* bought it?"

"He was always going to buy it," I said—more confidently than I'd felt at the time, if truth be told, but events had proved it true, so what did it matter? "I've played enough poker with Alfred Alonso to be sure of that. What would *you* have done if I hadn't turned up to save your bacon?"

"Gone through with what I said I would do," said Sol. "I did mean every word of it. But you always were going to come." She said it matter-of-factly, as if she hadn't just gambled her entire future on a con artist and a criminal. Nobody besides Jules had ever put that kind of trust in me, and I almost didn't know how to cope with it.

Then, of course she almost ruined it all by adding, "Well, you were always going to try, anyway. You've got something of a hero complex, you know that, Ruthi?"

"*I've* got—!"

"Let me get through the monologue," said Sol, with a shadow of a smile. "Then you can fight with me. I expect you'll want to. I used—"

"I know." I kicked a heel up against the door and leaned backwards, arms behind my head. "It was all part of your brilliant plan to break up my engagement with Esteban, so you hung yourself out as bait. You think I haven't worked that out yet? You even told me yourself what you meant to do, the night Esteban and I got engaged. You can't say I didn't have fair warning."

"It was all honest enough," Sol said, "as manipulations went—fair enough, under the rules we'd set. But beating you at a game that you'd started was one thing, and asking you to put yourself in real danger for me was another thing altogether. It was brought home to me in a rather spectacular fashion that pulling you in at all had been reckless, selfish—"

"Yeah," I said, "I seem to remember some chatter along those lines."

"After the attempt on your life, I told myself I was going to leave you alone from now on. The memory wipe was the best idea I'd had. I thought I might as well go ahead with it."

I hauled myself up straight again and wandered over to the chiller on the other side of the room. Lucky me—there was a small bottle of wine in there. I cracked the top and took a sip from the bottle without bothering to look for a glass, before turning back. "So what changed your mind?"

"Pass me that," said Sol, and held out a hand.

"Monologue first."

"It's on my room tab."

"I own two percent of your brain now, remember?" I lifted the bottle and pointed it in her direction. "Talk."

Sol let out a breath, her eyes fixed on me. "My noble

resolution to stay away from you," she said, "lasted perhaps two hours. Then we went to that banquet—" Her voice changed, shifting lower. "—and you danced on that leg like you'd never heard of a bruised knee in your life. It had to hurt like hell. I was certain I'd catch you wincing, at least once. But no matter how long I looked, I never did."

"Sure," I said, a little surprised. I'd practically forgotten all about the banquet. Nothing important had happened then that I could remember. "Well, you know, what do you think a con artist does?"

The corner of Sol's mouth twitched. "No offense, but I guess I was a little surprised to find you were as good a con artist as all that."

My professional pride should have been hurt by that—but the thing was, I knew she was right. If I'd been putting in a hundred percent on the Evelyn Ojukwu game, she'd have passed me over as just another deb, and from the beginning, I never had wanted that. "I guess I wasn't trying that hard," I said.

"I guess you weren't." Sol paused. "I really can't have any of that wine?"

"Don't you have a rep as a smooth talker?"

"Not when the stakes are high," said Sol. "I begin to stumble then." She frowned down at her hands. "Don't misunderstand me. I'd seen you be charming, and clever, and brave, but—apologies for how arrogant this is going to sound—I don't know that I'd ever before seen you do something I was certain that I couldn't do. I couldn't see a way out, that night, but maybe you could. All of a sudden, I thought that maybe you could."

She reached out her hand again for the wine, and this time, I gave it to her. She took a gulp, closed her eyes and then opened them again. "When I came to you last night, you looked like hope to me, Ruthi, that's all. I've—"

"You've been having some pretty filthy ideas about an abstract ideal, then," I murmured, and Sol nearly choked on her wine.

"I'm trying to express my sentiments to you, if you hadn't noticed!"

"Sorry," I said, aware that I didn't sound it particularly. "It was a good line."

Sol set down the wine bottle on the end table, with some force. As I blinked at her, she said, calmly, "If you think this is a line at this point, then there isn't a hope for me after all."

Her eyes locked on mine. "You said, last night, that all this meant something real to you—that's true for me, too. It's been true for a while now. I know that I've gotten you into more trouble than I've gotten you out of. I'll pay you back your two percent as soon as I can, but that doesn't cover the half of it. I'll follow you around until you get sick of me, if you want me. But I wouldn't blame you if you didn't."

"Follow me around?" I said, taunting. "Where—pulling two-bit cons? Changing diapers? You think you're gonna give up the whole Mendez-Yuki of the New Monte Mendez-Yuki gig for that?"

"As for changing diapers," said Sol, "I'm about to be as much of an aunt as you are, aren't I?" She pushed herself to her feet. "As for the two-bit cons—well, if you wanted to go in with me on the legal kind of gambling, you know, whatever profit's left on those kosher ducks could be the least of it. I'm not saying you have to. But I think you might get a kick out of it." She flashed me a quick grin, with a glimpse of the old breathtaking confidence.

I knew, by now, how much of an act that was, and I liked her the more for it.

She took a step towards me. "And as for the New Monte Mendez-Yuki—you know I was ready to get out long before this." She looked at my face, searching. "I was all set to set off on my own, but I'd much rather do it with you. If you'll have me."

I couldn't hold it back any longer; I started laughing all over again. "If I'll *have* you? What do you think I am, a philanthropist?"

Once I'd begun, it was hard to stop. I had to grab onto her shoulder for balance. She brought one arm up under me, supporting me, and I could see the smile beginning to spread on her face.

"If I'll have you," I repeated, when I'd got my breath back. "Boy! For a registered lady-killer, things sure go over your head. You sold me a line and a half to get me to gamble on you—you think I'm not going to collect? No one around New Monte does anything for free, except you. I'm expecting to get paid back for this every way you can dream up—"

She leaned down to cut me off with a kiss, and at that exact point, we heard a furious pounding on the door.

"Hey!" shouted my sister Jules, "Ruthi! Open up in there!"

Sol stared at me, a question in her eyes. I tapped my PD. "GPS," I said. "We always link them up when we're on-planet together. But you can't say her timing today has not been *spot* on."

Then I turned around to open the door, and let my sister in.

She'd told me that we shouldn't wait for her, that she'd be fine getting out of the Mendez-Yuki mansion on her own; she had the whole map of the place from me, and didn't need my help to duck and cover. I'd wanted to argue, and hadn't. I was a little proud of myself for that. (Jules wasn't, so someone had to be.) Still, new habits take time to build, and a part of me hadn't been easy until I saw her standing there in the doorway, safe and well and triumphant.

She waltzed past me, ignoring Sol, and flopped down on the bed. She sat up just long enough to pull off her breather, then tossed it across the room and collapsed flat again. At some point between the contract-signing and the hotel—presumably while dodging the glossy-cams—she'd shucked the dress and now wore only a plain black jumpsuit, but her face was still painted in neon colors.

She closed her eyelids, zagged in green and orange, and demanded, "Well? Did Alonso buy it?"

I grinned, though she couldn't see it. "He bought it."

"Good for you," said Jules, eyes still closed. "I mean, I don't really care *that* much. No offense to your new girlfriend there." Sol's face, on hearing this, stayed politely bland. "But I'm glad you didn't get yourself knifed or something. Anyway, I was pretty killer, wasn't I?"

I had to close my eyes for a second myself, against the sudden sting in them. I hadn't heard her sound this much like herself in months—since before that ill-fated journey on the *Simoleon*, half a year ago.

"Yeah, kiddo," I said, through the lump in my throat. What a leaky pipe I was today! "You were the absolute tops."

Sol cleared her throat. For a moment, I'd almost forgotten she was there. "Excuse me, but if I can ask—

what did you say to my brother? After your—public announcement?"

Jules' eyes flipped open. She pushed herself up to a sitting position, and gave Sol an unreadable look. "Oh," she said. "Well. Nothing all that rude, actually. I just told him that if he ever got his head out of his ass long enough to want to know his kid's name, he should send me a line through my lawyer. If I'm feeling nice, I'll send him a report card."

Sol hesitated a moment. When she spoke, her tone was very careful. "And what did he say, after? I saw you shake your head. What did he say to you?"

I tensed, wondering what awful thing Esteban *had* said, and how Sol would react—I could just see her pulling the same old big-sister act, trying to excuse and apologize it away, which would start us all off on exactly the wrong foot—but Jules just smirked, not particularly nicely. "Oh," she said, "he asked me to marry him again, obviously."

Sol stared at me, wrong-footed; I shrugged in response; and Jules, radiating smugness at having confounded the both of us, stretched up her arms behind her and lay back down on the bed.

It sure wasn't a joke Jules would have made four months ago. That didn't mean she wasn't joking now—and it didn't mean she was, either. I'd never really understood most of the story between Jules and Esteban, beginning or ending. I'd only pretended to myself I did, that was all.

Either way, just this once, I could let Jules have the last word.

CHAPTER 21

IN SOME WAYS, Solada Alvaria and I already knew a good chunk of what there was to know about each other.

In other ways, we didn't know a whole lot about each other at all. For example, it turned out that Sol was, of all things, a morning person. Worse: she was a morning jogger.

"Six AM," I told Jules, over the sound of the shower, "she woke up today."

"I *know*," said Jules, but I didn't think she did; she'd still been snoring in the other bed when Sol slipped out of my arms to go pull on her sneakers. Jules could sleep through near anything, a fact of which Sol and I had tried not to take too much advantage. For sure we'd be booking two separate rooms on whichever cruiser took us off-satellite, once we'd gotten all our ducks in a row.

"Six AM!" I repeated. "And I swear she stays up until three most nights, too. I don't know when she sleeps." I popped my anti-rad and made a face before washing it down with a sip of coffee. "At least she's got the decency to get the brew ready."

"Yeah," said Jules, sourly, "rub it in." She looked at her orange-ish juice and sighed. With a heroic effort, I stopped myself from pointing out that if she'd just kept her appointment on Bellavu, she could be sipping espresso-laced absinthe right now for all anyone cared.

I was still working on breaking old habits. And she'd be right to say that the whole thing was my fault as much as hers, anyway.

"I'm not saying it's *great* brew," I offered, instead. "Could be worse, though, for someone who probably didn't know what instant coffee was three days ago."

On cue, the noise of the shower switched off. A second later, Sol came out of the bathroom, wrapped in a robe. She raised her eyebrows when she saw me. "Sleeping Beauty awakes!"

"It's *eight*," I said, plaintively.

"Yes, you're a martyr." She dropped a kiss on the top of my head, then turned to Jules, with a friendly smile. "Morning, Julia."

"Ugh," said Jules, glowering down at her cup. "I need another croissant." She looked at me. "You want anything?"

"Sure," I said. The pastries from the continental buffet were dry as dust; still, they were free, and you couldn't beat free. As Jules swung herself to her feet, I added, "Sol?"

"Oh, I got something on the way back from running—"

I pointed to the empty plate that used to hold a croissant, and Sol laughed. "That one was for whichever of you wanted it. I ate mine already."

"You remember to take your anti-rad before you did?"

"I certainly did," said Sol. She gave me a sidelong look, and added, "Protecting your investment?"

Jules gave an audible snort and left the room.

I smirked at Sol. "Haven't got my money's worth out of it yet."

"Mm," said Sol. "Better fix that." She put one hand on either side of my chair; I wrapped my arms up around the terrycloth of her bathrobe, and she leaned down to kiss me.

I pulled back after a minute. "You're dripping on me."

"Yep," agreed Sol, and kissed me again, bringing all her considerable technique to bear.

Certain aspects of this morning person thing, I could get used to.

After a minute, she straightened; I made an involuntary noise of protest and she grinned that cat-canary grin of hers. "Well, I'd like that too, but unfortunately, I've got an appointment."

I pressed my hand to my heart. "Good heavens, an appointment! Who with, the St. Clairs? The Nipawattanapong?"

Sol looked at me, the laughter fading out of her eyes. "With Esteban," she said. "You know I've got to, Ruthi. I can't just disappear on him without a word."

I let my hand fall off my heart. "Yeah," I said. "I know." I picked up the cooling coffee she'd made me, and took another gulp of it. "What are you gonna tell him? All of it? About me, too?"

Sol nodded, slowly. "After all this, I think I have to, don't I? He's got a right to know."

I had a half-dozen suggestions for half-truths she could tell that might go down better, and make her leaving easier. But no matter what I thought about Esteban, I wasn't exactly in a place to tell her that lying to her sib was the right way to go. Still: "It doesn't exactly seem like a fair cop. All of this—" I waved a hand, a gesture intended to encompass me, Jules, and everything that had happened over the last three months. "Most of that isn't on you, but I don't know if he'll see it that way. I could come with you, if you wanted—"

"In the normal way of things I'd never turn down your company, but in this particular case, I'm extremely sure that having you there wouldn't help." Sol picked up my cup of coffee, stole a sip herself, and made a face. "You've been drinking this? Why didn't you tell me I made it—"

"You made it fine," I said. "That's how it's supposed to taste. You're sure?"

"I'm sure." She exhaled. "It's better this way, I think. I'll tell him the truth, and I'll give him some time to think about it. And then I'll write him from Earth, and we'll go from there."

She smiled at me then, and no matter how hard I looked, I couldn't see that it was anything but genuine. "It's selfish, but honestly, I'm glad he's likely to be angry at first. It would be harder if he asked me not to leave." She must have seen something in my face, because she added, "It would be harder, but it wouldn't stop me. Believe me, Ruthi, I've never looked forward to anything in my life so much as I'm looking forward to getting on that ship off New Monte with you."

When you'd sat at as many gambling tables as I had, you knew that a big show usually meant some kind of bluff. But I looked at her—hair wet, face plain, drinking bad instant coffee out of a cheap hotel mug, no glitz or glamour about her but what she carried inside her—and realized that I did believe her, one hundred percent. I didn't even have to think about it.

"Easy for you to say," remarked a sardonic voice behind us, "when you've never seen her get ship-sick. Wait 'til we're a week out. It's not a pretty sight."

I swung around to see that Jules had come into the room again, and was watching us with a gimlet eye. "Thanks," I told her. "A real rock of support, you are."

"Well," said Sol, "I suppose that's my cue." She disappeared into the bedroom, then came out a moment later wearing a pair of bland coveralls. My own favorite boring brown breather was slung around her neck. She struck a pose. "Well?"

I grinned at her. "If it's not the *real* Sol Mendez-Yuki."

"You know it. All right, I'm off—" But instead of suiting actions to words, she leaned down and stole another quick kiss.

I shoved her back, laughing. "Get going! You're embarrassing the youth."

"True," said Jules, dourly, and Sol shot her a half-apologetic look before heading for the door.

I watched Sol's slim back and straight shoulders until the door swung closed behind them, then took another sip of my coffee. "She seems all right, doesn't she?"

Happy, I meant—happier than she had been, before I pulled her out of her setting and down into mine. That's what I wanted to think, anyway. But of course Jules hadn't known her before then, and couldn't answer me.

"Look at you fretting over her!" Jules surveyed me with an ironical eye. "You've gone and landed yourself the daughter of one the richest men in the system. Anyone else would get themselves set up with an apartment and a pension. Shouldn't she be taking care of *you*?"

"Oh, she'll get her turn," I said, and smirked. Jules made a gagging noise. I meant it too, though. I didn't think Sol was likely to give up on the chivalry act any time soon. "Anyway, I guess I've gone and gotten in the habit of taking care of someone or other. And now that it doesn't seem like you want it to be you—"

Jules sat up straight, at that, and the rest of what I knew I ought to say slipped out easier than I thought it would:

"You don't have to stay with me, you know, if you don't want."

"With *you*, you mean," said Jules, her voice mocking and a little bitter as she emphasized the Yiddish plural you.

"Maybe." I shrugged. "Who knows? I like her a hell of a lot, but she's not used to living like we live. If it turns out we don't suit, I guess I'll cry about it, but I'm not making any bets yet."

"You won't cry about her," said Jules. "I never saw you cry."

"*You* never saw me cry. Doesn't mean I never did it." I grinned at her, and Jules looked down. "That's something that'll change. I'll make you bring me hankies, now, if Sol Mendez-Yuki breaks my heart." A beat. "If we're still traveling around together. But I mean it—you don't have to stick with me. You could do something else with your life. Whatever you want."

"I don't *know* what I want." Jules picked up a croissant and glowered at it. "Except I sure *don't* want to be changing every diaper all by myself, so it's not like I'm taking off tomorrow. I thought—oh, hell, Ruthi, we're talking about this now?"

It wasn't exactly a conversation I felt ready to have, either. Still, I was more ready than I had been, six months ago, on the *Simoleon,* when Jules said she was leaving with Esteban. "Gotta talk about it sometime," I said. "Might as well be now."

"I—all right." She fidgeted with the croissant. "You screwed up, sure, but I guess I owe you a sorry of some sort, too. I know I was cold-shouldering you for a while back on Bellavu. It's just that—all my life you've been doing everything hard for me, deciding where we go, what we do. I can't be little sister forever, you know?" The croissant was rapidly disintegrating. Little flakes of pastry settled down onto the sheets. "And then it all fell apart and I just needed to be took care of *again,* and—I guess that part's not your fault. You've done your best for me time and again, I *know* that. I just—needed things to be different."

Four months ago, I wouldn't have known what she meant. "Yeah," I said. "I guess I get that."

We sat. I took another sip of coffee. "I missed you," Jules said, finally. "I missed you a whole lot."

My throat closed right up. I had to swallow and take a breath before I could tell her, with some semblance of composure, "I missed you more than I got words for."

I could tell that seeing me that soppy had gotten her off-balance. She crossed her arms, looking down. "Every time I had to eat my own cooking, I missed you."

"You hate my cooking," I said, startled.

"Sure," said Jules. "It's terrible. But also, turns out, cooking for yourself is kind of hard."

"Funny thing about that, huh."

I wanted to get up and hug her, but she didn't look like she wanted hugging, so I sat where I was. "You know," I said, "we've been thinking that the next stop'll be Earth."

"That'll be risky, with the T.O.U. mad at you. Can't your partner take care of selling off Sol's cargo?"

"Sure, but Sol wants to see if she can track down where her little brother disappeared to—the one who was supposed to be going to art school. She's been worried for him anyway, and moreso now that we've gone and pissed off the T.O.U. even more than—well, anyway, the point is, I guess we'll be looking at a lot of schools and school-type things."

Jules' eyes narrowed. "Ruthi—"

I held up my hands. "I'm not planning your life out for you, all right? If there's anything you want to do about that, that's all on you until you ask for help with it. I just wanted to mention, in case it was worth mentioning."

Jules let out a breath. "Okay." Her face didn't have much expression to it. I couldn't tell quite what she was thinking—whether she'd filed the idea away to consider later, or whether she'd put it in the bin marked trash. Either way, it wasn't up to me. "And after Earth, where to? Another luxe-liner?"

"I don't know," I said. "I guess we'll have to figure that out." I didn't know exactly what 'we' would mean at that point—me and Jules and the sprog, or me and Sol, or all four of us together, or some other combination I hadn't even pictured.

It scared me a little, the not knowing. Still—there was something to be said for the notion that the future might be something more than a long road with room for just two people on it.

I was pretty sure Jules felt the same, because she nodded, with the ghost of a smile on her face. "Yeah. I guess we'll figure it out."

My little sister. My grown-up sister. I smiled back at her, then shoved myself to my feet. "Well—I better get moving too. I gotta go see a man about some ducks."

ACKNOWLEDGMENTS

WITH TREMENDOUS THANKS to all the people who collectively turned this pile of nonsense into a book:

Sarah Emily, who has been cheering Ruthi on since 2016.

Sophia Kalman, Freya Marske and Kelsey, who have been cheering Ruthi on since 2017.

Meredith Rose Schorr, for the publishing wisdom.

Alex Schaffner, Ari Brezina, A. A. McNamara, and Shoshana Flax, whose collective brilliance improved every draft at every level.

Michael Lin, Heather Tucker, Sophie Herron, Ren Hutchings, Shannon Kao, Naomi Kanakia, and Iona Datt Sharma, who brought fresh eyes to various 'final' versions.

My incredible agent, Bridget Smith, who ensured it had an ending, and then ensured it had a beginning by continuing to believe in it long past when anyone else (including me) would have given up.

My wonderful editor, Amy Borsuk, who gave it a new lease on life, and then made it far better than it had ever been.

The rest of the amazing team who turned it into a book, including sensitivity editor Bri Gavel (any missteps are in spite of Bri's wise words); copyeditor Laurel Sills (any textual errors ditto); publicity team Jess Gofton and Natalie Charlesworth (thank you for making sure that anyone would look at it); and cover artist Martin Stiff (thank you for ensuring that it will be beautiful when they do).

All of my brilliant and talented friends, both the ones who were there when I started this book seven years ago, and the ones who've come into my life since I finished it.

My amazing family, who have never tired of dedicating time on zoom calls to exclaim over cover art and space on their bookshelves for increasingly large volumes of text.

And my wife (!) Beth, who has made everything in my life better, including every single word of this book.

ABOUT THE AUTHOR

Rebecca Fraimow is an author and archivist living in Boston. Her short fiction has recently appeared in *PodCastle*, *The Fantasist*, and *Consolation Songs: Optimistic Speculative Fiction for a Time of Pandemic*, among other venues. Her short story in *Consolation Songs*, "This Is New Gehesran Calling", appeared on the longlist for the 2021 Hugo Award.

FIND US ONLINE!

www.rebellionpublishing.com

/solarisbooks   /solarisbks   /solarisbooks

SIGN UP TO OUR NEWSLETTER!

rebellionpublishing.com/newsletter

YOUR REVIEWS MATTER!

Enjoy this book? Got something to say?

Leave a review on Amazon, GoodReads or with your
favourite bookseller and let the world know!